2/11

"Fans of Lackey's epic Valdemar series will devour this superb anthology. Of the thirteen stories included, there is no weak link— an attribute exceedingly rare in collections of this sort. Highly recommended."

—The Barnes and Noble Review

"This high-quality anthology mixes pieces by experienced authors and enthusiastic fans of editor Lackey's Valdemar. Valdemar fandom, especially, will revel in this sterling example of what such a mixture of fans' and pros' work can be. Engrossing even for newcomers to Valdemar." —Booklist

"Josepha Sherman, Tanya Huff, Mickey Zucker Reichert, and Michelle West have quite good stories, and there's another by Lackey herself. Familiarity with the series helps but is not a prerequisite to enjoying this book." —Science Fiction Chronicle

"Each tale adheres to the Lackey laws of the realm yet provides each author's personal stamp on the story. Well written and fun, Valdemarites will especially appreciate the magic of this book." —The Midwest Book Review

Finding
the Way

Finding the Way

And Other Tales of Valdemar

Edited by
Mercedes Lackey

DAW BOOKS, INC.
DONALD A. WOLLHEIM, FOUNDER
375 Hudson Street, New York, NY 10014

ELIZABETH R. WOLLHEIM
SHEILA E. GILBERT
PUBLISHERS
http://www.dawbooks.com

First Printing, December 2010

1 2 3 4 5 6 7 8 9

DAW TRADEMARK REGISTERED
U.S. PAT. AND TM. OFF. AND FOREIGN COUNTRIES
—MARCA REGISTRADA
HECHO EN U.S.A.

PRINTED IN THE U.S.A

Acknowledgments

"Finding the Way," copyright © 2010 by Mercedes Lackey and Larry Dixon

"In Burning Zones We Build Against the Sun," copyright © 2010 by Rosemary Edghill and Denise McCune.

"Unintended Consequences," copyright © 2010 by Elizabeth A. Vaughan

"The Education of Evita," copyright © 2010 by Mickey Zucker Reichert

"A Charm of Finches," copyright © 2010 by Elisabeth Waters

"Healing in White," copyright © 2010 by Kristen Schwengel

"Songs of a Certain Sort," copyright © 2010 by Brenda Cooper

"Otherwise Engaged," copyright © 2010 by Stephanie Shaver

"Heart's Choice," copyright © 2010 by Kate Paulk

"Heart's Own," copyright © 2010 by Sarah A. Hoyt

"The Time We Have," copyright © 2010 by Tanya Huff

"A Bard by Any Other Name," copyright © 2010 by Fiona Patton

"Change of Life," copyright © 2010 by Judith Tarr

"Lack of Vision," copyright © 2010 by Nancy Asire

"The Groom's Price," copyright © 2010 by Michael Z. Williamson and Gail Sanders

Contents

Finding the Way

Mercedes Lackey and
Larry Dixon

The air was so still that not even the thinnest reeds were moving. A steady chorus of frogs was interrupted now and again by the splash of one of them jumping into the swamp-water or the dull plop of a fish rising to take a bug. All in all, it was deceptively peaceful. Sherra watched the float on the end of her fishing line and let her nictating membranes rise slowly over her eyes to wash away the pollen. It was spring, so of course the air was thick with pollen here on the edge of the swamp. It hung in the air and left a golden haze on everything. Sherra rather liked the pollen, actually, because with the sun shining on it, the air itself seemed gilded, but it was giving some of the humans over in Singing Stones Vale fits; they were going about with red, watering eyes and running noses, poor things.

If Sherra were to open her mouth, she would even taste the pollen: soft and a little sweet (which was why bees loved it so), with a faint undertaste that would tell her where it came from. Resinous from the yellow pines, tangy from the swamp oak, perfumed from the mallow. Poor humans, who couldn't detect any of that. It seemed grossly unfair. If you were going to have to suffer from it, it was too bad you couldn't at least enjoy the taste of it. This was as unjust as getting a hangover without drinking.

She sat with her back to the sun, basking as much as fishing. *Hertasi* were technically cold-blooded, and as a consequence, they loved heat as much as their distant swamp-lizard cousins did. The sun was making her feel lazy; if she'd dared, she'd have settled in for a nap.

There were no humans waiting here at her little Guide Station now, neither Hawkbrother nor Traveler; Sherra was alone and had no one she needed to take across the swamp. That was all right, it meant she was left in peace as *hertasi* rarely were, and it was a state she cherished.

Most *hertasi* spent their whole lives within a Vale, sharing tunnels and caves with their extended families; they delighted in the close companionship of others and in their service to the Hawkbrothers. It was the way *hertasi* were; being idle drove them mad with boredom, and being alone generally made them feel uneasy. And they were scarcely overworked by the Tayledras. In a Vale, there were so very many *hertasi* that all of them had plenty of leisure time and time to socialize. They spent at least twice as much time on their own pursuits as in serving the Hawkbrothers, and because they were so social, a great deal of that was spent in groups of three or more.

But Sherra was . . . different. A throwback, perhaps, to when *hertasi* had been barely intelligent, if large, lizards, and certainly had not been self-aware; from a time when they each staked a claim to a bit of swamp and vigorously defended it against all comers except in mating season. Then they had been solitary; the only time *hertasi* were together would be a mother and her two or three offspring, until the young lizards were old enough to fend for themselves. Once they were old enough, if they didn't wander off on their own, the mother would drive them out of her territory.

That had been before Urtho, of course. The *hertasi* remembered Urtho with gratitude; he was in many ways, the father of the *hertasi* species. He had taken lizards with the intelligence of a dog, and made them what they were now—just as he had taken a now-extinct species of grasslands lupine and created *kyree,* a certain breed of giant songbirds and made *tervardi.* And, of course, the culmination of his work, the gryphons, which, so far as Sherra could tell, had been made up out of magic, and vanity, and air.

At any rate, Sherra was that rarity among *hertasi;* she preferred solitude and swampland to company and the *hertasi* tunnels and caves in a Vale. And with that preference had come what seemed to be a linked power: she was a Pathfinder.

No matter what wind and weather and changing seasons did to the swamp, she could find a path through it. In fact, she could find a path virtually anywhere, so long as she had a vague notion of where she should be going. However, it was here in the swamp where her talent was in the most demand; Gripping Mire was one of the most treacherous places in all of the very treacherous Pelagirs, and now, with the Mage Storms over and magic dispersed wildly instead of following neatly in the proper channels and ley lines, it was worse than ever before. There had been plenty of Change-Circles in that nasty expanse, and there was no telling what had been caught in them. Certainly she had encountered plenty of things that not even the Hawkbrothers recognized.

Sherra's talent, or Gift, or whatever it was, still served

her well. She could, and did, get everyone who hired her services safely to the other side. Yes, she charged a fee, for she was another rarity; since she lived outside a Vale, she had to supply all her own needs, which meant she needed to be paid. No one seemed to begrudge it, however, at least not once they had gotten well inside and had gotten glimpses of the sort of hazards Sherra could get them safely past.

Today there was no one wanting to be taken across, so today she could sit on the bank of the little fishing hole she had dug and waterscaped with an eye to making it very attractive to the fish she liked best, drop a line in, and sit drowsing in the sun while she waited for dinner to come take her bait. Back in her camouflaged hut there were cattail roots baking in coals in a clay pot, and a jar of sweet mallow tea cooling in the earthen pit dug in the corner for that purpose. If no one turned up in the next two or three days, she rather thought she would make her way across to the Tayledras side of the swamp and trade some of the swamp-herbs she'd gathered for pot-herbs, some of her coins for nice fabric. Not that she was a clothes horse the way the Hawkbrothers seemed to be, but her tunics were getting a bit on the shabby side, and making two or three new ones would be a way to pass the time between clients.

She yawned, stretching her jaws widely, and watched the float. Even the fish were feeling lazy, it seemed.

It was a good life out here, if a lean and lonely one.

The float bobbed a little, and she instantly became alert; and when the float suddenly plunged under the surface of the water, she was ready, and gave the smooth tug that set the hook. A few moments later, she hauled up a nice fat fish. More than enough for dinner. Enough for dinner and a tasty fish stew for tomorrow.

Perfectly happy with this, she tidied up her pole and line, slipped the fish on a green-twig stringer, and trotted back to her hut with both slung over her shoulder, humming under her breath.

This part of the swamp was "safe"—provided that you took simple precautions, watched out for snakes, and stayed on the obvious path. To either side of her, swamp plants grew, mostly rushes and cattails that waved high over her head. *Hertasi* were not exactly tall, and she was short even by *hertasi* standards. The swamp dwarfed her, but that was good, because it made it easier for her to hide.

Today was turning out to be a lovely day with nothing to hide from; the only thing that crossed her path on the way home was a little family of a mother coot and her flock of babies. Sherra emerged out of the rushes onto the bank of the sluggish river that fed the swamp, basking in the humidity and heat as she padded toward her hut.

It wasn't obviously a hut. In fact, unless you knew what you were looking for, you probably wouldn't even see it; instead, you would see a rock-studded hillock a little away from the riverbank, covered in grasses, weeds, and a couple of bushes.

The stone hut was under all that. Faux "rocks" made of pottery-clay fitted into the sockets where the windows were. The door was hidden behind a particularly lush fall of vines and a bush. She hadn't built the hut herself—her stonework wasn't that good—but she did keep the vegetation on it thriving. Some of her fellow *hertasi* had done the work, aided by two Hawkbrothers who used magic to fuse the stone, but it had been for another guide, almost a generation ago, and she had just inherited it.

She put down her burdens just long enough to take the hollow pottery "rocks" from their sockets, then slid behind the vine curtain to open her door.

The scent of slow-baking roots filled the single room. Inside, it was almost exactly like a smooth, stone-walled cave. It was oddly shaped—not a straight wall anywhere—with little nooks everywhere. One, right under a window, held her summer bed; her winter bed was actually beneath the floor level, in a stone-lined pit that was in turn lined first with insulating grasses, then sheepskins, then blankets. It had a wooden rim with a lid she could pull over herself and lock down from inside. Only once had anything ever gotten into the hut while she was hibernating, and this feature had saved her. She had woken in the spring to find the interior trashed, and deep gouges scratched into the tough ironwood lid. She never did find out what had come hunting food; what-ever it was hadn't found the dried vegetables and bags of grains in her stores at all to its liking, for it had left them alone. It had torn up her summer bed, thrown the furnishings about, and left the place a wreck. Some sort of big carnivore, bear-sized at least. The scent of her, sleeping just out of reach, must have nearly driven it mad. But if that creature—likely only barely able to squeeze through the door—had not gotten to her, it was unlikely anything else ever would.

There were two other window-nooks; one held her worktable, the other, a food-preparation area which even had primitive running water from a cistern above. The rest of the hut was full of shelves and chests that held her belongings. There was a fireplace with an oven built into the side, the multiple chimneys arranged cun-ningly to disperse the smoke so that it wouldn't be seen. When it came right down to it, she was one small *hertasi* who was not even particularly good at defending herself, living on the edge of a swamp full of nasty things. Stealth was her best friend.

She gutted the fish, then wrapped it in wet clay and put it in the oven to bake with the roots. Then she dropped down on her summer bed and picked up the book she had been reading last night.

It was only the third time she had read this particular book, so she was still enjoying it even though she knew how it would end. As always, human imagination was a wonder to her. How did they think of these things? Facts were one thing, but these made-up stories—where did they get their ideas?

This was a tragedy, as it seemed humans liked to read about sad things. In this case, it was a story about two humans from warring families who lifebonded and tried to run away together. It all ended badly, with the boy being murdered by the girl's cousin, and the girl taking her own life by leaping off a cliff. But what a story! So many twists and turns before the end, and how did the creator think of all these things?

She had a new book as well, but she wasn't going to touch it when she was also cooking dinner; it was too easy to get engrossed in a new story, lose track of time, and only realize that she had gotten lost in the tale when she smelled her dinner burning. And by that point, of course, it was rather too late.

Better to read an old, familiar friend so that she would remember to check her baking.

Even so, this was a particularly *good* story, and she had to wrench herself away to get her dinner out of the oven and ready to eat. But one thing about cooking in clay, it was very forgiving. A couple of taps with a little hammer, and there was her fish, flaky, moist, perfectly cooked and perfectly seasoned with the herbs she had stuffed inside.

She tipped the cattail roots out of the jar, took portions of fish and roots, sprinkled them with a bit of salt, and went back to her book, reading as she ate slowly. When she was finished, the remaining roots, the rest of the fish, more seasoning, and some vegetables and water went back into the pot and the pot went into the oven. By morning, it would be fish soup, which she dearly loved, and would last her the rest of the day.

As the light began to fade, she went outside and put the pottery "rocks" back in the windows, then closed and barred the door. Although she had, at great need, been known to go out at night—it wasn't a good idea. And it also wasn't a good idea to advertise her presence with any sort of light, nor with a source of scent. She couldn't do anything about what came out of the chimney, but she could at least keep the hut from being obvious.

Hertasi had very good night-vision, and besides, she knew the inside of her hut blindfolded. She didn't need a lamp or a candle to find her bed and get into it. She *could* have read some more, she did have a lantern, but there wasn't any good reason not to go to bed at sundown, since she'd definitely be awake at sunrise.

The very first morning sounds outside woke her immediately, as they always did, but there was another sound out there that was unfamiliar. It was the sound of hooves, but these hoofbeats had a peculiar, chiming ring to them.

Anything unfamiliar was automatically suspect; she stayed very quiet, listening to the sound of the hoofbeats pacing back and forth along the bank, as if the creature in question were trying to figure out a way into the swamp. There was an agitated quality to the sound;

the hoofbeats were definitely coming faster. It was like nothing she had ever heard before. Certainly not *dyheli,* and no horse she had ever heard had that chiming quality to its footfalls.

Finally, her curiosity overcame her caution, and she opened the door.

There on the bank, frantically pacing back and forth and yearning over the sluggish water was the most remarkable beast she had ever seen—shaped like a horse, it glowed in the early dawn light, whiter than lily blossoms, carrying a light, blue-dyed saddle and otherwise unencumbered.

A moment later, though, she knew what it had to be. Even she had heard of the Spirit Horses out of Valdemar, the Companions. The Vales were abuzz with tales of them and their riders, the Heralds.

She coughed politely to get the Companion's attention.

The Spirit Horse whirled to face her, ready to defend itself. Herself. So she wasn't so caught up in whatever was making her so frantic that she was oblivious to the dangers here.

Sherra bowed a little. She hesitated to speak—it wasn't likely that the Companion would know either the Hawkbrother tongue or that of the *hertasi.*

:Are you the guide?:

The words formed in her head, as some of the Tayledras spoke. She nodded, her snout moving quickly up and down. *Yes, Lady,* she thought hard.

:My Chosen is somewhere—in there, on the other side, I cannot tell. But I must find him!:

Oh, dear. This was one of those jobs for which you didn't get paid. Presumably the gods rewarded you . . .

Well, perhaps they will send more fish or fewer mon-

sters, Sherra thought to herself with resignation. "Can you understand me, Lady?" she asked aloud.

:Of course. We have the Gift of Tongues.: The Companion didn't have an eyebrow to raise, but Sherra certainly got that impression.

Of course you do. At least Sherra wouldn't be going cross-eyed and headachey with the effort of projecting her thoughts. "Wait just a moment while I gather my things."

The Companion pranced with agitation and impatience, but Sherra was not going into Gripping Mire without her kit. She gathered up her guide kit, which she always kept in readiness, shoved three packets of dried fish, her camp stove, compressed dung-and-grass fuel bricks, copper bowl and cup, and her special brews into the top of her rucksack, and slung it on her back. She strapped on her short, stout reed-knife and her longer hacking knife, hung her hand-crossbow from her belt on one side, the quiver on the other, and jammed on her hat. She poured what she could of her fish stew into a gourd and sealed it, tied the gourd to her belt, and with a sigh of regret, poured the rest down the drain into the midden, filling the pot with water and a pinch of soap flakes. She made sure the fire was out, and only then did she leave the hut, latching the door behind her, and putting the "rocks" back over the windows.

:Are you quite *ready?:*

Hmm. While Sherra could sympathize with the Companion's impatience . . . there could be only one person in charge in Gripping Mire, and that person was her. She picked up her quarterstaff and grounded the butt of it with a *thump.* "Lady, I know that your Chosen is somewhere out there, and you are concerned. But I know this swamp, and you do not. We either go *my* way at *my* pace, and you obey *my* orders, or you may go alone and I will go back to my fishing. I am sure you are a very important personage on your own ground and in your own land. But you are not there, you are here, and here your concerns are not nearly so important as our ability to survive Gripping Mire."

It was not the first time Sherra had been forced to make that speech, and she doubted it would be the last. And every time she did, the person she addressed was always taken aback, having assumed that the authority he (or she, though females rarely exhibited such arrogance, even if they felt it) had outside the swamp would carry within it.

Sherra dared not allow that. Not if the client was going to live to see the other bank.

This time was no exception. The Companion stepped back a pace or two, looking astonished that anyone would question her right to be the one in charge. Sherra stood firm. "The fish are waiting, Lady, and you just made me pour the stew that would have been my dinner down the drain. My terms, or not at all."

The Companion laid back her ears and narrowed her eyes, then grudgingly acquiesced. :*All right. Your way.*:

"Fine. Follow directly behind me and don't go more than an arm's length—my arm—off the trail that I set. There are mudholes in there that could swallow you up before you ever realized you were in trouble. And that is only the smallest of the dangers. Which direction is this Chosen of yours?"

The Companion pointed her nose in the direction that she wanted to go. Sherra oriented herself on that inbred compass that *hertasi* had, another remnant of their days as dull swamp lizards. When she was satisfied she would not lose the direction no matter what, she gestured to the Companion to follow, and headed up the path beside the swamp.

"You might as well tell me your name, lady," Sherra said, after a great deal of huffy silence. "Mine is Sherra."

She didn't look back over her shoulder; she was too busy studying the stretch of marsh ahead of her for a path that would take the much greater bulk of the Companion. But she could sense the rumbling of thoughts in the Companion's head.

:Vesily,: came the answer, finally.

"Well, Vesily, I hope that your human didn't decide for whatever reason he had to go into the Mire on his own. Even experienced hunters won't do that unless they have no choice."

Finally she spotted a path, marked by the presence of mat-grass, which needed actual soil, not mud, to grow. "Follow me. See this grass?" She pulled up a tuft. "Step only where this grows."

:You go into the Mire alone. What makes you different?:

"For one thing, I am a lizard, and we make notoriously poor eating." She chuckled. "For another, I have— well, I suppose it is a Gift of sorts. It's certainly more than just knowing the swamp very, very well. I can find paths to and through anything. I really don't know how, I just think about it, and I can see it."

This was the most talking she had done in a very long time, and she actually surprised herself with the amount she had said.

"Besides that, as you said, I know the swamp, and I know the danger signs in it. I suppose I have another Gift; I get a sense of when danger is near, even without signs of it." She shrugged, and leaped to the next grassy tussock.

:I do not know if my Chosen is in the Mire or on the other side,: Vesily said, as she picked her way daintily from tussock to tussock. *:I only know that it is time and he needs me. Until I actually Choose him, I cannot Mind-speak him, and I am not bound to him as I will be when he is truly Chosen.:*

"Depending on where he is, it might take us as long as three days before we can reach him." Sherra tested a dubious tussock with her staff, but it held firm. She envied the Companion's long legs.

She felt the Companion's dismay. *:Three days! But—:*

"You can't tell how far he is, and that's how long it takes to cross Gripping Mire. Unless you can summon a gryphon to go look for him—" That would certainly be preferable. Not for the first time, Sherra wished she lived on the Vale side of the Mire. It would be much easier to get one of the gryphons to scout. Or ask one of the Hawkbrothers to send out his bond bird; that would be almost as good.

The Companion's sigh was all that it took to tell Sherra that Vesily was no more likely to call a gryphon than she herself was. *:But doesn't that mean we will spend at least two nights in the Mire?:* she replied, clearly not happy with that prospect either.

"There are islands in there, and I know how to safeguard us," Sherra replied. "And I'll find things that are safe for you to eat. It won't be pleasurable, but it won't be a misery either, unless it rains. *Until* it rains."

She looked back to see Vesily shuddering at the thought. Well, Sherra couldn't really blame her. The Mire in the rain? Ugly proposition. Not as miserable for them as it would be for humans, poor naked things, but quite bad enough.

Already the insects had discovered them—the small

ones, at least, not the huge, hunting ones deeper in the Mire—and midges and mosquitoes rose from the surrounding area in clouds. But Sherra's tough hide sent them away, discouraged, and something about Vesily made them suddenly zoom off when they had gotten within a few inches of her white coat. Probably something to do with magic, and that was one thing more off Sherra's "worry" list. Without protection, it was quite possible for animals to be so drained of blood overnight by insects that they became too weak to move.

At which point, of course, they became something's dinner.

Since she had not had time for breakfast, she gulped the fish stew from her gourd while it was still warm, regretting the half pot she'd had to throw away. This had been a very good batch.

:What on earth are you drinking?: Vesily demanded after a while, her irritation plain.

"My breakfast, Lady, which you were too impatient to permit me to eat," Sherra replied, with equal irritation. "If you had not noticed by now, in order to set a pace that satisfies you, I must make three strides to your one, thus I am working three times harder. I am in great need of this breakfast."

Silence. Chagrined silence, at least.

Good. Sherra put her mind back on the path. The plants around them now were well over Vesily's head, never mind Sherra's—and more than once, Vesily had to balance awkwardly on two or three tussocks of safe ground, while Sherra searched for another to jump to.

Finally, there *was* nothing to jump to. "Well, Lady," she said, turning back to the Companion, "We have run out of dry. It is now time to get wet."

:. . . . blast.:

Sherra nodded her snout with sympathy. "The good news is that this part of the mire is relatively free of sucking mudholes. I'll only have to make sure we don't run into plain, ordinary *holes* that would break one of your ankles." She eased herself down into the dank, green water carefully. No matter what you did, swamp water was pretty nasty stuff, rank with rotting vegetation, and stagnant. Not even a lizard liked the smell of it.

At least it was only knee-deep here. Small blessing.

This was where her staff truly came into play, probing every bit of bottom before they ventured onto it. As long as it stayed this shallow, nothing really large and dangerous could hide under the water, and things like water vipers generally tended to slither away rather than attack. So all they had to worry about were underwater obstacles, and the occasional poisonous serpent that *wouldn't* slither away when disturbed.

Oh, and anything they might attract with the sound of splashing.

At midmorning, they came upon one of the islands that Sherra had told the Companion about, and at that point they were both ready for a rest. Slogging through water trying to make the best possible speed was not an easy task. They were both slimed, Sherra up to her waist, the Companion well above her knees. It showed more on Vesily; she had green legs now.

Sherra hauled herself up onto the firmer land with a sigh; Vesily groaned as she lurched up out of the water. Sherra had expected to have to fight for a rest, but it was Vesily who asked first *:Can we take a candlemark or so to recover?:*

Well! Sherra tried to keep from sounding gleeful. "Absolutely. Just let me dig a seep."

As Vesily folded up her slimed legs and dropped down onto the thatch of dried grasses that must have been accumulating here for a decade, Sherra cleared a patch of them away and dug a hole in the mat of roots until she was pretty sure she was below the waterline. This hole would quickly fill with water filtered through the roots of the plants and the earth itself, and once boiled, it would give them a clean source of water for a good drink before they moved on.

Then she flopped down on the grass next to Vesily.

Now that they were not moving, Sherra let her tired muscles relax, and let the warm sun soak into her. It felt wonderful. She had never pressed this far, this fast, into the swamp before. Vesily's urgency had infected her, but they were both paying the price of that urgency.

Her eyes started to close, and she let them. If Vesily was still feeling that driven, then Vesily could wake her up.

On the other hand . . . if Vesily was as tired as Sherra, they might not wake up until the sun set and evening's chill descended.

Bad idea.

So she left a little mental command to herself: *I will wake up when the sun is a little past noon.* That part of her that tended to such things noted the position of the sun on her closed lids, knew where it would be around about noon, and agreed. With that mental "watchdog" in charge, Sherra quickly reviewed their position.

It was good. They were in the middle of this island, there had been no indication that anything used it as a home other than marsh birds, they were below the level of the tops of the grass and, so, invisible. They were as secure as they could be without erecting walls.

All good, said the "watchdog." Sherra let herself

drowse. The watchful part of her kept an ear on the marsh sounds, the insects whining and buzzing, the frogs, the little marsh birds. There was some splashing that briefly disturbed her, but the sounds were small and irregular, so they were probably a fish or a frog jumping or striking at a bug.

Finally it was a little after noon, and she woke fully, feeling much better. The Companion was still dead asleep; interestingly, all the slime had flaked off her legs, leaving her lying in a shower of little green flakes, and her legs were pristine again. Well, that wouldn't last long.

Sherra set her tiny camp-stove to blaze, blowing on its vents until the fuel became an ember. She balanced a full cup of the seep-water on the stove's tines and revisited it after it had bubbled a few minutes. Sherra swapped that hot cup for a wide shallow copper bowl of seep water in its place, and left her bread in it to soak while a pinch of tea warmed up in the cup. She then got out one of the leatherbound vials from her pack and dripped four drops into the seep, swirled it with her tailtip, then had herself a drink of the tepid water there; it tasted green, but not bad, and now it was nice and clear. The drops made contaminants simply drop away to the bottom and clump there, leaving pure water behind. It took weeks to make a batch of the stuff, but even if it took years, it would still be worth it. Sherra slipped off long enough to gather some grasses and roots she knew the Companion could eat safely; for herself, she kept a few of the roots, augmented with the journey bread sticks she kept in her rucksack. The roots were unusual fare for her when guiding; normally she made do with the bread, while those she guided tended to their own needs. But normally she didn't have to set off in a tearing hurry with a client that hadn't made any preparations—and who, in any event, would have to eat so much that carrying provender was impractical.

When she had eaten—eating before Vesily did, because she was pretty certain Vesily would not give her much time once she bolted her own meal—she woke the Companion.

Vesily lurched to her feet in alarm, confused for a moment at finding herself in the swamp. Sherra just stepped calmly back for a moment while Vesily sorted herself out.

"I've gathered safe food for you, Lady, and the seep is full and clean," she said, gesturing to the pile of grasses and roots. "While you are eating I will scout ahead, and when you are finished, we can be off."

:How late is it?: Vesily asked, her eyes wide. *:How long did I sleep? I didn't mean to sleep!:*

"Lady, it does not matter, " Sherra replied with what she hoped was patience. "If you were tired enough to sleep, you were too tired to go on. Would you rather have stumbled into a sinkhole or a sucking mud-mire because you were too tired to stay to the path? Would you rather have attracted some predator? You slept; now we will make better time than if you had not."

Honestly, how experienced is this creature? she thought rather crossly, as she left Vesily to eat—or not—and struck out in the direction Vesily had given her. *How is it she doesn't know that exhausting yourself at the beginning of a journey only makes it longer?*

She didn't know all that much about Companions, really. All she could think was that they must be greatly pampered creatures . . . or else this one truly did not know her own limits. It was true, come to think of it, that she didn't particularly "feel" old in her Mindspeech.

Well, she would discover her limits quickly enough in here.

What Sherra was most concerned with, besides whatever roaming monster happened to prowl this part of Gripping Mire, was the presence of the sort of mudholes that Vesily could stumble into. Sherra knew how to free herself and a human from them, but a Companion? Four legs instead of two, no ability to grasp a rope or a branch, no way to get on top of the mud and slide on her belly——The only ending Sherra could see for that was death. A rather horrible death at that. This place was called Gripping Mire for a reason; the Hawkbrothers reckoned that it was at least half mudhole, and what the mud gripped, it seldom let loose.

So far they'd had decent luck—or rather, their luck hadn't been *bad,* and they had not encountered any of the mudholes so close to the path Sherra was picking that an unwary footstep or a slip would put either of them into the grip of the mud. Of course, that could change at any moment; one reason why she wanted to scout ahead.

She returned about the same time that Vesily was hastily choking down the last mouthful of food. :We should go,: the Companion said, imperiously. :Now.:

"Drink first, if you haven't, Lady," Sherra replied, just as imperiously. "The swamp water isn't safe to drink— and though I may not sweat, you do, and will. You'll need the water, and I can't carry enough to satisfy your big body."

Vesily made one of those little moves that telegraphed her astonishment—but she bent her head to the seep and drained it.

:It tastes like mud,: she said crossly.

"But it is safe mud." Sherra repressed a laugh. "Follow, then, and you'll see how much better time we make now that you are rested."

And now that you are not so inclined to waste your energy pushing against water. The only good way to get through the waist-deep water was to move with deliberation. Trying to rush only tired you out, and made you likely to step on something and fall, or slip and fall. Sherra's clawed feet were *made* for this sort of place, and even she had to move with care.

But she was right; they did make good progress, although Vesily looked increasingly frustrated as the sun began to sink toward the horizon and there was still no end to the swamp. Sherra ignored her frustration; she was too busy looking for a place to spend the night.

Just when she thought they might have to settle for balancing precariously on adjoining tussocks of grass, she spotted the sort of trees ahead that could only grow on what, in here, was nearly dry land. "Over there," she said, pointing. "There's another island. We can overnight on it."

By this point, the candlemarks of pushing through the swamp had worn Vesily down—or else, even she could see that it would be stupid to try to wade through this place in the dark. She only nodded, and obediently followed Sherra. Both of them clambered up onto the dry land, and the Companion uttered a sigh that sounded relieved.

:*I don't suppose there is anything I can do . . . :*

"Not without hands. Feed yourself, Lady," Sherra replied. "There should be plants on this island you can eat, and I'll point them out. Just stay within earshot and don't go too near the water's edge."

:*Why?:* the Companion asked.

Just then, a couple of ducks landed near where they had come ashore. And before Sherra could answer—

A massive pair of jaws containing far too many teeth erupted out of the water, snapping shut on both the birds.

The jaws vanished with a splash, leaving behind only a couple of feathers.

:... *Never mind.:*

Sherra did not bother to tell Vesily that what they had just seen wouldn't come into shallow water. It was basically a pair of jaws with a very weak body and stubby, almost useless legs. It relied entirely on stealth, and would never even consider going after something *her* size, much less Vesily's. If this persuaded the Companion that caution was in order, it was all to the good.

She left Vesily nosing about in the vegetation and looked for a good place to set up a secure "camp." Not a human sort of camp—humans always wanted a fire, and a fire was not a good idea for them except for making tea on the little campstove. Sherra had excellent night-sight, and a fire would leave her half blind, plus a fire in the middle of all this swampland would be an especially obvious beacon for anything looking for prey. Besides, most fuel she *could* gather here would be too wet to burn. On top of that, clouds had gathered, and while they weren't obviously stormy, the overcast didn't look as if it would clear out anytime soon. Good thing she didn't need to navigate by sun or stars.

The island proved to be even bigger than she had thought, and right in the center was exactly what she wanted: a stand of bushy weeds that were nearly as tall as young trees. She cut a careful path into the middle, cleared just enough room for both of them, then went out and brought back armfuls of dead grass and bracken to cushion the ground. When she had it padded to her satisfaction, she dug another seep just outside the "grove," and went to get Vesily.

The Companion seemed to have found enough vegetation to satisfy her, and looked up at Sherra with obvious weariness. *:I want to go on, but . . . I can't.:*

"No, you can't, and neither can I. Come, I have made a fairly secure place for us to spend the night." She beckoned, and Vesily followed.

She looked dubiously at the weeds. *:Those won't keep out anything,:* she pointed out.

"They don't have to. They only have to keep things from seeing and smelling us," Sherra replied. She walked to the seep, which was already full of water, added her purifying drops, and stirred. "Drink, then go on in. You'll see what I mean."

It was a measure of just how tired Vesily was that she just stuck her nose in the seep, sucked up the water, and plodded into the stand of weeds. Sherra took all of the weeds she had so carefully cut down, dragged them into the path, and methodically dug little holes to stick them in again. They'd be wilted by dawn, but in the dark it was unlikely anything would notice. And the sharp smell of the cut stems would help mask their own scent.

And Sherra had another trick up her sleeve as well.

When she made her way to the center of their cover, she found Vesily already curled up on the bed of bracken. Once again, the green slime of the marsh had dried and was flaking off, leaving her white coat looking just as immaculate. The Companion looked up in the dim light. Sherra took off her rucksack and rummaged through it, bringing out a little leather bottle. "If you had hands, I would tell you to put this on yourself, but since you don't, I'll take care of it." She poured a little of the pungent oil inside onto her hands, and briskly rubbed every hair of the Companion's hide with it, and then did the same for herself. It wasn't an unpleasant scent, rather like pine sap, in fact; Vesily sneezed once, but didn't object.

:That's to mask our scent?: she asked.

"And to keep away the big insects. There are mosquitoes in here that can carry off small human babies," she replied, only half joking, "But there are hunting bugs in the marsh that will take anyone apart if there's meat on them. Yellowbacks and bore-cutters, and sleep-spiders. They can't stand to be within yards of this, though." Sherra had rescued a tradesman on the Vale side of the mire whose legs were ultimately unsavable, despite Tayledras Healing, because of yellowbacks that had taken out coin-sized divots through his clothing.

:You . . . are full of surprises. And wisdom,: came the astonishing reply.

Sherra made a pillow of her rucksack, slowly chewed a piece of her journeybread as the dim light faded. "No one gets to an old age in the Pelagirs without surviving some hard lessons. So if wisdom means learning from your mistakes, then thank you. We *hertasi* are good at observing things from a careful distance, so we get wisdom from watching *others'* mistakes too."

Vesily made a sort of mind-laugh and said, *:One of my instructors in Haven warned me, "Experience is what you get immediately after you really needed it.":* And then Vesily's head sank down, and she was asleep, and as the stars came out overhead, Sherra closed her eyes and joined her in slumber.

They both woke at the sound of a roar.

If they hadn't been so paralyzed by sleep, they probably both would have leaped out of their own skins. As it was, Sherra could hear both their hearts racing, and she threw her arm involuntarily around Vesily's neck.

:What was that?: You couldn't stammer in Mind-speech, but Vesily certainly gave the impression of a stammer.

The roar came again, deep and primal, and extremely loud.

Not as loud as it could have been if the maker of the noise had been nearby. Sherra was very good at judging distances. It was somewhere out in the swamp, not on the island.

I have no idea, she thought very hard. *I've heard that thing three times as a guide, and I never wanted to get close enough to find out.*

Vesily was shaking so hard now that she was making both her own and Sherra's teeth chatter. *:Probably—a good idea—:*

The roar came a third time, and this time it was answered by one farther away. Sherra thanked all the gods she could think of that the answer was not on the island, nor was the island *between* the two creatures making that noise.

Sherra wondered if this was a challenge or a mating call. It could be either. It could be both. There were creatures that began with a fight and ended in mating ...

Or perhaps these two beasts were simply defining their territories. Or even ... talking. They exchanged bellows for a good long time without drawing any nearer to each other or to the island. Finally the nearest one ended with a series of heavy grunts, and both fell silent.

:Do we dare fall asleep?: Vesily wondered, as the quiet that had descended on this part of the swamp at

the beginning of the exchange now began to fill with frog chorus and insect noise.

Sherra thought about that for a moment, and wondered if she ought to tell Vesily the cold truth—that if something that was as large and dangerous as *that* thing sounded decided to come after them, there wouldn't be anything they could do about it.

She decided against it.

I am, she said, and yawned hugely on purpose. She loosened her arms from around the Companion's neck and yawned again. Vesily was warm and soft, and made a much better pillow than the rucksack. Sherra decided not to move. Vesily didn't make any objections, nor did she try to shove Sherra away. With the conscious decision that if something was going to eat her, Sherra wanted to be asleep when it did, she managed to drop back into slumber.

Waking, as always, came swiftly, and just as the first light of pre-dawn made it possible to see. Or rather, would have, if the usual morning fog hadn't accompanied the light. Sherra didn't need to see, however; she crept away from Vesily without disturbing the Companion, and got her fishing line out of the holder in her rucksack. On hands and knees, she felt her way to the water's edge, and cast the baited hook out as far as she could throw it. The fish were hungry; she was rewarded immediately with a bite. When she was sure the fish had taken the hook, rather than just the bait, she tugged sharply to set the hook, then slowly wound the line back in.

It didn't fight much, which told her it was a sluggish bottom-feeder. Somewhat to be expected out here. When she finally landed her prize, it was a barbelface. Not so bad; at least there were no scales to contend with.

With no rock to beat its head against, she killed it with a swift bite, having a care for the spines.

Then she used her short knife to remove its spines, and ate it. She preferred her fish cooked, especially bar-bel, but she could eat it raw. And raw, it was a safe source of moisture as well.

The light had strengthened, though the fog showed no signs of thinning, when she made her way back to Vesily. The Companion was still asleep. Sherra busied herself with deepening the seep and collecting the same sorts of plants she had seen Vesily eating yesterday. When the Companion finally woke with a start, Sherra was ready to leave as soon as the Companion had eaten and drunk.

:I shouldn't have slept so long!: Vesily exclaimed.

Sherra just shrugged. "You needed the rest, and the fog was too thick to travel in anyway. It is burning off now. By the time you are fed, we can go."

It was quite clear that Vesily's sense of urgency had not abated in the least. She practically bolted her food; prepared for that impatience now, Sherra had her ruck-sack on and belted to her waist and had her staff out and extended before the Companion was finished.

"Any change in direction, Lady?" Sherra asked.

The Companion gave her an odd look, then raised her head—and began to pivot. A moment later she stopped. Sherra nodded; it had occurred to her that since Vesily's goal was a person and not a place, things might have changed during the night. It looked as if her hunch was right.

"Your quarry has moved, Lady," she said, and took bearings of her own. "It is good that I asked. Let's go."

She had thought yesterday that Vesily was agitated, but the Companion's urgency was even greater now. Whatever mysterious forces drove her, they were stronger, which did not bode well for the Companion taking due care.

Well, that just meant Sherra would have to be doubly vigilant.

Easier said than done, of course.

Especially since the new track was taking them in the direction of whatever had been bellowing last night.

That was the bad news. The good news was that there was no path, and they were forced to wallow through water that came almost up to Sherra's chin. Now, normally *that* would have been the bad news, but anything that was going to slow Vesily down and keep her from dashing straight into trouble was a blessing. Sherra's broad feet and clawed toes were made for these swamps; Vesily's hooves sank into the mud and she had to pull them free to take a step.

But it was clear from the determination in every bit of her that she was not going to give up on this. So instead of recommending that they take a rest, Sherra just helped her to drink from Sherra's own water bottle, and they pushed on.

Then suddenly, in the late afternoon when there had still been no sign of an island, a path, or even a break in the reeds, Vesily stopped—froze in place, really. Sherra stopped as well.

:*Something is wrong.*:

Sherra referenced her internal place-sense. They were relatively near the Vale-side border of the Mire here, but far from free of it. Hells, the Mire could kill someone who was only a step *into* it.

:*Something is wrong,*: Vesily repeated. :*My Chosen— his thoughts are muddy, and—insane. I don't understand. This is not right. I am not supposed to have thoughts from a Chosen that are clear enough to understand like speech,*

*but I am getting impressions of need, and fear, and flee-
ing, and the thoughts—the thoughts echo. Somehow.:* The
Companion's tail flicked quickly and her muscles tensed
and bunched as if she was ready to bolt.

"Don't run. *Don't.* You'll kill yourself and never
reach your Chosen," Sherra said firmly. Vesily stood up
on her hind legs for a few moments, towering up above
the *hertasi,* and scanned the horizon with white-edged
eyes, her forehooves dangling at a human's eye-height
or more. Clearly, reaching this Chosen compelled the
Spirit Horses more than Sherra first thought. "I know
you want to run, but the Mire has to be traversed slowly
or not at all."

:But she's going the wrong way. He is,: Vesily Mindspoke plaintively. *:She is. He is. I don't understand this at
all! I was supposed to go find my Chosen, it wasn't supposed to be like this! Not all this swamp, this slowness. I
left Haven at a hundred times this speed. And you can go
faster! And you aren't!:* The Spirit Horse's Mind-voice
seethed with accusation, anger, hate, fear, worry, and no
small amount of guilt. Sherra came very close to swat-
ting Vesily with her staff. Hard.

Instead, Sherra glared and then replied, "Fine. You
want to go faster, try to keep up." She concentrated
anew on the Path, and found that it had changed. And
that it had a conflict. It told her to continue on—and
also, to go to their right, staying in the swamp. "This is . . .
odd," she told Vesily in a clipped tone, still a little angry.

:I know. I don't know what to do. I'm lost here.:

Sherra growled, "No one with me is *ever* lost. Temporarily disoriented maybe, but never lost. Come. We are
best off reaching the Vale, regardless, because they can
send out searchers and relieve our fatigue. We go with
the first Path I sensed." *Better to have a direction, even if*

it is a poor one, than to stand uncertain in this place, she thought.

:I heard that.:

"Try and keep up," Sherra said out loud, and her guide style altered considerably. Now, whenever there was a large tuft of watergrass, she leapt to it, and the Companion bounded along moments after. Her stick-probing became attack-like jabs rather than measured taps. Her thoughts, which Sherra hoped were kept to herself, was that this was largely guide theater. They were not moving that much faster, but the extra activity gave a sense of urgency that seemed to satisfy the Spirit Horse that they were making good time. Besides, the extra noise and splashing would keep the crocodiles, swampcats, and big hunting snakes away. Of course, it might attract something *else,* but life was full of gambles.

They paused, both panting and splattered with the slimy muck that now seemed to make its way into every crack and fold of their equipage, and Vesily got that far-off look again. *:We are going the wrong way. She . . . he . . . my Chosen is that way. You're taking us the wrong way.:*

"Trust your Guide," Sherra replied. "Oftentimes, only way to get somewhere is by passing it and going around something. You want to go in a straight line. That isn't how you get to *anything,*" Sherra said with a touch too much acid in the tone.

:So far you haven't gotten me to anything your way,: Vesily snapped back.

"You are welcome to leave me at any time, Spirit Horse, and it is not as if I am doing this life-risking for a great amount of pay! You Valdemarans are our allies now, so I owe it, but you haven't made me *like* it yet."

:You don't have to like it, you have to do your duty, same as me!:

"My duty isn't to argue with you, my duty is to guide you, and that might just end at any moment. The sooner I'm rid of you, the sooner I make way towards my own bed." Sherra stabbed her staff into the mud for emphasis, glaring up at the Companion. She could almost see the thoughts turning over like the gears and wheels of a mill, turning. The Spirit Horse was weighing the possibilities. Strike off on her own into the Mire, using the few techniques she had seen the *hertasi* do which she could duplicate, and make maybe a fifth of the time they were making now—even though her instincts told her the direction they made good time in was, in fact, the wrong direction? Risk lethal injury or outright death, never to see a Chosen at all, or stay with Sherra, to go get help?

Sherra turned so quickly she slapped her tail against Vesily's fetlock. "Daylight is burning."

The *hertasi* resumed her Path out of the swamp.

Vesily snorted and stamped in place, over a dozen times, but Sherra never looked back—or at least she did not look back in a way that the Companion would recognize as such. And when no one sees a tantrum, then *technically*, the tantrum never happened.

But Vesily did, indeed, follow Sherra.

Vesily was caught in a mud-bog twice before they made it to the edge of the Mire, once deep enough to reach the bottom of the saddle she bore; as a side benefit being stuck had the effect of making her too weak to argue with Sherra's advice. Sherra talked Vesily through how to escape the bog—how moving slowly and deliberately would allow mud to fill in to the vacuum that moving her limbs left behind—but it was exhausting, and most maddening, it was something that simply could not be paused. The effort had to be deliberate and continual, until freedom. And, in some kind of sick cosmic comedy, the mud hole butted against a rock shelf.

A circular one. And it, too, had mud tracked onto it by what appeared to be a human.

Vesily and Sherra looked at each other. *:Is that—?:*

"A Changecircle, yes," Sherra agreed. She bent to look at the tracks, and then peered into the Circle itself. "What is in here is not from this part of the world. That patch of reeds, it's dying. All those sedges are the wrong color, the wrong height." She followed the tracks to a stunted tree. "And now I see what must have happened. Your human could not take direction from the sun because of the clouds, but look, here is moss on the tree. The problem is, it is growing on the wrong side of the tree, because the tree itself was turned about in the Change, and has not grown new moss yet. Your person took bearings from the side the moss was on, and for whatever reason did not recognize this is a Changecircle." She spotted something else ... something that was very much not good ... and groaned. "I am so sorry," Sherra said.

:Why? What?:

Sherra held up a torn bit of yellow-dyed cloth, only as long as one of her own fingers. She flicked out her forked tongue, which vibrated up and down at the very tips. "There is blood in this mud. The taste of it is faint but there. Whoever your Chosen is, they're losing blood and I can't sense any of the protective oils like we have. Or rather, wait—not much of it. There was some, once." Sherra frowned and searched a little more, blinking her nictating lids against a persistent cloud of midges. "These little scraps of cloth seem to be discarded bandages."

There was a flattened patch of grasses, vines, and mud, and then a faint trail of broken greenery headed in what, by the mistaken bearings, would be what the Chosen thought was east. That meant the Chosen was headed back into the Mire.

:My Chosen's mind is feeling worry and despair, and fear. Of death. But not for herself? Himself? That way.: Vesily nodded her head twice to show Sherra the way, but Sherra already knew. The Path had changed direction, now that they'd reached that Circle, and now was a critical moment. "Vesily," Sherra began, "We should rest here where the ground's solid and—"

:I know,: Vesily stated. *:But I can't. I know I should rest but I feel like I'm killing my Chosen if I wait.:*

"You could kill your Chosen *and* yourself if you don't wait. There is a saying among guides and scouts— 'sometimes you must be slow to be fast.' Being too bold means you get stuck or hurt, and spend your time extricating yourself instead of making miles." Sherra reached up to pat Vesily's foreleg. "You have done everything you could, and you were smart when you could have been reckless. Don't do something stupid now."

:My Chosen is in there!: Vesily cried in Sherra's mind, and the Companion stamped her hooves. *:What if we rest a candlemark here and find my Chosen a candlemark too late? What about your guide-wisdom then?:*

"And what if we do not rest, rush in, and get delayed *two* candlemarks because we were too tired to see a mudpit? Believe me to my last breath, Spirit Horse, that is *far* more likely. You don't know *how* lucky we've been *this* far. But I am concerned by this too. I say that we rest now, as best we can, and then we let our emotions push us when we need it the most."

Vesily stood, watching the middle distance, in the direction of her Chosen. She didn't chase after her Chosen, at that moment, and Sherra took it as the victory for wisdom that it was and wasted no time getting fresh water and food. Sherra had an uneasy feeling that she hoped Vesily couldn't pick up on—that this was no longer a guide trip and more of a salvage and rescue journey. She didn't ration her food as if she'd need it for a return leg. Something told her she'd only restock at the Vale, this time, because she couldn't get home. She found herself examining her weapons and triple-checking their thumb releases when she "heard" Vesily's Mindspeech.

:She's insane," the Companion said softly. *:She's— everywhere she turns is the right direction, she thinks. She crawls and then rests, wants food and cold water. But it's so incoherent. She falls down, holds her belly, thinks of— everything. Randomly. I know her direction, Sherra, but I don't know her.:*

Sherra tugged on Vesily's tail. "Come here. Lie down and sleep. Look, your kind believe in destiny, yes? That spirits guide you to where you need to be? Our kind, we know these things to be true. Our spirits are agents of change long after the beings they were are dead. So lie down, here, and listen to me. Would the spirits that guide your people lead you through this, only to have you fall short?"

:Your logic is flawed,: Vesily retorted petulantly, *:Because why would your agents of change allow my Chosen into the swamp again?:*

Sherra frowned again. "I don't know. Maybe they couldn't reach her for some reason having to do with the Mire, or the Changecircles, or how her mind is." Wait. What was that the Companion had just said? "What do you mean, *my* agents of change and your Chosen?" She blinked, thinking fast. "You mean that your Chosen is Tayledras?"

:She isn't Valdemaran. She keeps thinking of places and people I don't recognize, and there are images of birds of prey and magic. Big stones that glow. A lot of bathing, a lot of food. A shadow of a gryphon, maybe. But no places in Valdemar that I have ever heard of.:

"There is a chance things are not as bad as they seem. Many Tayledras can survive in the wild." Sherra didn't mention that probably three-quarters of the Hawk-brothers never left a Vale more than once a year. It might help Vesily's morale if she went right on thinking that *all* Hawkbrothers were scouts.

The overcast sky darkened as they set off again and soon drops of rain made rippling rings in the swamp-water. Thunder boomed from their left, then right. The drizzle picked up, and by the time they were again deeply into the swamp, it was a downpour.

This had its advantages; the rain was clean to drink, and it kept many of the dangers of the Mire hunkered down. But it was absolute misery to trek through.

Finally Vesily stopped. *:This is ridiculous. I can go faster with you on my back, and you weigh almost nothing. Take to my saddle.:*

Sherra hesitated, looking up at the Companion through the pouring rain. "Ah . . . I cannot ride, Lady," she admitted.

Vesily snorted. *:Neither can most of the Chosen when we Choose them. Take to my saddle.:*

Sherra didn't argue; she simply crawled up onto the saddle and let the Companion pick through the deeper parts of the swamp. Vesily seemed to take the direction straight from her mind now; certainly she was going exactly the way that Sherra sensed they should.

The storm picked up. About three hundred horse lengths away was deep swamp. Again, mixed blessings; it would shelter them from the storm, but be slower to traverse. Out here they were exposed, and dusk was already here. Gods forfend, they might even be struck by lightning out here. There certainly was a lot of lightning around to be struck by. One particular cloud-to-cloud lightning flash lasted so long that it illuminated the entire Mire as clearly as bright daylight.

It lit up a particular *something* at the edge of the deep swamp.

Sherra leaped onto a vine-twisted snag for a better look, hanging on to Vesily's saddle for stability. Visibility was poor, thanks to the rain, even for her sharp eyes, but she was sure she caught a patch of yellow, like the bandage fragments in the Changecircle, amidst the orange glow of what she hoped was not webbing. It was at the base of a huge tree, of the kind that only the Pelagirs could produce. Sherra knew of only six other of this kind, and this was half again bigger than those she had known before. Its form was twisted and massive, and its trunks split into scores of branches, and each of them in turn into dozens more, all weighed down with vines by the thousands, each as big as Sherra's arm. It did not obscure the canopy; it *was* the canopy, reaching far beyond what Sherra had ever seen from anything in the Mire. It filled the horizon so that the lightning seemed to come from inside it. In more than one of the gaps between the trunks, an orderly latticework could be seen, but it emitted light of its own, rather than shining silver in lightning. The larger sections glowed a mottled deep orange, and the thinner parts were a brighter orange, all about the brightness of an oil lamp. As they moved closer, Sherra hoped they were human- or *hertasi*-made, but with a sinking heart, she recognized them as being more akin to spiderwebs than ironwork. Her Pathfinding told her *there*, that is where they must go. "I see something," she began to say, but her heart rate surged when she saw, despite the rain, that there was something in the water. Moving. A serpentine distortion in the rainsplashed surface, sending a wake behind it, angled towards the patch of yellow, and it was—it was bigger than the Spirit Horse, by far. Her other Gift almost physically hit her, and she spoke without thinking. "We need to move, Vesily, we need to get over *there* now, right now!"

It was a bad thing to say to a Companion that was wound up too tight already about her Chosen, and Sherra regretted it right away, because Vesily lurched up from the muck and took Sherra with her. Sherra's "Wauuuugh!" would probably not be mistaken by anyone as a war cry, but Vesily seemed spurred on by it. The *hertasi* managed to hang on as the Companion plunged desperately for the tree, but right now she couldn't tell which direction was even *up* for what felt like a day of being pounded by water, mud, debris and reeds on one side, and Companion on the other. It was less than a minute, it turned out, and Sherra regained her senses when Vesily finally slowed alongside the patch of yellow she'd spotted.

The patch of yellow was a woman, in Hawkbrother clothing, or rather, it had once been. Face down, on the arched, forked root of an ancient tree, the woman appeared to be on her knees with her belly between the fork, though the waterline obscured anything below the waist. Every spot of exposed flesh was ravaged by insects, her clothing torn away and used as makeshift bandages. Sherra jumped off of Vesily's side onto the tree itself, then scrambled down to where the woman was. Sherra braced for the worst, but discovered the woman was alive. Carefully, Sherra lifted her head up from the moss and found the woman's eyes opening, and turning towards Vesily.

In her mind, Sherra heard the words, :*I Choose*—: and then got a profound sense of confusion from Vesily. :*Wait*.: Sherra got a mental impression akin to a case of mistaken identity.

"Chosen or not, we need to get her out of here," Sherra snapped, and pulled up on the woman's shoulders. Sherra's footing slipped, and she tried again, and finally backed off to rig a rescue noose with her waxed rope. Sherra became aware of a taste in the air, something like the bleach the Tayledras used on cloth and cookware but with a tinge of copper. It was a little anesthetic, in fact, numbing the hertasi's tongue the longer she was near the latticework. She blinked, realizing that she was standing on some of this glowing latticework, and looked up, following the lattice from one joint, to another, to another. They made a platform, three horse-lengths wide, that was in turn caged in by many smaller strands. Every part that glowed was warm, like a living thing.

Sherra couldn't stop herself from looking. She *had* to see what was in the cage of strands, even while her intellect screamed at her that she didn't really *want* to know.

She pulled herself up on the strange resinous links of the platformed cage, finding that the stuff wasn't like spiderwebs; it didn't flex in the slightest. The stuff was as hard as any wood she'd ever felt—even when it was as thin as an arrowshaft it might as well have been a roofing beam. Sherra's claws held firm and she pulled herself up to peer into the cage. Inside she saw, lit in that mysterious orange glow, a single egg as large as Sherra. It was so ornate in design that it was more like an *artwork* of an egg than it was like any egg she'd seen before. Whorls and pits and bands of color repeated around its circumference, and it was on a nest of sorts made up of smooth riverstones. It sat, as if it was a display, in the center of a dished platform of tiny resin rods woven so tightly Sherra probably couldn't have wedged a finger between them.

In the distance, just after a roll of thunder, the roar from the Mire sounded again. Sherra's danger-sensing Gift nudged her, and she climbed down quickly to rejoin Vesily and the stricken woman. The Companion was resting her head against the woman's forehead, as if trying to push strength into her. "We'll get her up into saddle. It will just take time." And again, she spotted movement in the water. If it had just been a dark shape, she wouldn't have the sense of terror with it— no, this shape displaced so much water that the surface swelled upward, and the *hertasi* had a dreadful feeling of what was coming. Stepping back up on the root, Sherra dug out the vial of repellant oil and slung the liquid in a wide arc, on woman, Companion, water, and tree alike. "That will buy us some time," she snapped, and looped the rope on Vesily's pommel. "Step in, yes, there. There," Sherra directed, until Vesily was in position, and then the *hertasi* pulled, hoisting the barely conscious woman up. She was heavy. In a few more tugs they understood why.

She was very much pregnant.

:*My Chosen*—: Vesily said in astonishment.

There was no time left to say more before the water around them opened up.

What had been an ominous swell finally broke the surface, and it was a snake beyond the measure of *any* that Sherra had seen before. To Vesily's eyes it was an image of death itself. Lighting cracked all around them, further reinforcing the snake's demonic appearance. Translucent fins and frills, some bitten through, cut, or marred by unknown decades of combat for Mire supremacy, were backlit by a roll of lightning that all but blinded Sherra. It projected not just a sense of fear, but also of great age, and tremendous weight. Sherra sensed, as it reared up farther into the rain-streaked air, that a hundred Companions couldn't match the sheer mass of even the part of the great snake that was exposed outside the water. Its eyes weren't even discernable, among the complex of scars, scales and plates of its head, and that somehow made its visage even worse. Its head was wider than Vesily was tall, and Sherra wouldn't even be a snack to it.

No rescue was going to come for them. No gryphons from the sky, no Hawkbrothers from the ground—here there was only terrain that wanted to kill them, storm that wanted to blind them, and this implacable, ancient creature that wanted to eat them. There was no escaping any of it, and they knew it.

The three of them could only stand there, paralyzed. Sherra's danger-sensing Gift went quiet. Her Pathfinding Gift took over. And it told her—*stay here.*

The snake opened its mouth. It gaped upward at the rain, as if gathering the downpour to drink, and extended its tongue. Its tongue was easily as wide as Sherra's entire body, and ended in flexible, spike-like points half a horse length long. As the titanic monster lowered its head again, it closed its mouth, leaving the tongue extended to whip up and down, taking in the air. Thunder boomed closer than ever before, and the snake weaved its head side to side. Sherra pulled on the rope, getting the pregnant woman onto Vesily's back, but the whole time the *hertasi* watched the demon snake. Her limbs just worked on their own. Vesily was rooted in place, and Sherra could sense Mindspeech screaming, but not directed toward her. She wrenched her attention away from the snake and looped her rope here and there in Vesily's tack, cinching the woman to the saddle. It was as well, because Sherra could see what was left of the woman's legs. It was best that there was little light here. The bandages the woman had made covered only a few of the gouges in her lower legs, and Sherra could—

—could not taste or smell the wounds at all. In fact, she could not taste or smell *anything* at all.

If it had been possible for Gifts to be independent of her and exude an aura of smugness, they would have. They had led her here, to the Chosen and safety, as one.

"This tree," Sherra whispered to Vesily. "Get in closer to this tree. Climb up if you can, but be careful. Look down. Look away from the snake, Vesily. Listen to me. Look away and get in closer to the tree." Vesily turned her head and looked dazed in the orange glow. She took a few sidesteps in and the snake swung its head and stopped when Vesily did. It was clearly tracking the movement.

:*Something about this tree or this—stuff—is dulling the snake's senses. The lightning blinds it. The heat from this lattice hides us. The vapors from the tree numbs its ability to taste us. The rain and thunder deafens it,:* Sherra projected hard to Vesily.

At that moment, the roar of the unknown beast of the Mire sounded over the thunder, and it was close. Closer than Sherra had ever heard before. The giant snake unfurled every spike and fan it bore, in its most threatening display, first in one direction, then another. The display slackened and then the snake scanned its head up high around the stormy swamp, then low, and then gathered itself. It knew there was prey here. Somewhere.

Another roar came from the deep swamp, closer still. Despite the rain, despite the splashes and ground cover, it actually echoed.

That was enough for the snake. Its body tensed into a rigid S-shape and then it uncoiled and headed to the southwest. Its body seemed to never end, pushing wave after wave against the tree roots where Sherra, Vesily, and the Chosen hid. Sherra followed the fleeing snake with her eyes as long as she could, and then Vesily and Sherra both Mind spoke to each other, simultaneously.

:We're leaving. Now.:

The Path broke upon Sherra's mind, as welcome as a ray of sunshine would have been. She led the way, as sure as if she had been in her own little house. And somehow it was a Path free of obstacles, of mudholes, of sinks and snakes and crocodiles and perils. The rain did not let up, but didn't get any worse either, until they were out of the Mire. When they arrived at a clearing, lit by a sliver of moon, Vesily stopped suddenly and a streak of gray went through the air past them, and looped back. A Tayledras bondbird owl looped over them twice, then vanished into the distance. A candlemark later, a *dyheli* stag crashed out of the forest, and accompanied them until they crossed a cartpath leading to the Vale. The *dyheli* vanished into the forest and by morning, in the haze of pain and fatigue, the three travelers felt warm hands helping them along, lifting them, and tending to their aches and travel wounds.

By noon, in the embrace of the Vale, the three became four.

The Tayledras woman, with the help of the Vale's Healers, gave birth to a son.

:*My Chosen,*: Vesily Mindspoke to the baby, and nuzzled at him with her warm, soft nose. Vesily's blue eyes shone in the thousand lights of the Vale, and she looked to Sherra, who was wrapped in blankets nursing a bowl of soup.

"A little young for a Herald, isn't he?" Sherra asked.

Vesily's eyes showed mirth and she whickered, and then returned to nuzzling the child. :*Yes. Yes. But it is all right. You have showed me the wisdom of patience. The moment to leave will come in its own time and there is no use in rushing forward to exhaust us both to no purpose. I will wait.*:

In Burning Zones We Build Against the Sun

Rosemary Edghill and Denise McCune

At the coronation of Queen Alliana, an envoy of Karse had told her that if she and all her people renounced their heathen ways and banished the white horse-demons from their land, Vikandis Sunlord would welcome them as His worshipers. And that King Nabeth of Karse would surely consent to her marriage to his eldest son, Prince Salaran. Of course she had refused both offers, saying Valdemar was pleased with things as they were, and any who wished to worship Vikandis in Valdemar were free to do so, so long as nothing they did violated Crown Law. The coronation festivities ended, and the Karsite envoy departed, and everyone was sure that was the end of things.

Less than a year later, Alliana was forced to summon her armies to defend her borders. Hardorn remained neutral, but that did not mean she would obstruct the Karsite armies traveling across her frontiers to strike at Valdemar from the east.

It soon became clear she did not dare, for the red-robed priests of Vikandis Sunlord conjured demons to wage their war, and the Sunsguard carried with it captives to slake the demons' blood-hunger until the moment they would be loosed against the foe.

Hedion could hear the sound of the screaming from the foot of the hill. The voice had gone thin and hoarse with a sound, not of fear or pain, but of a fathomless unslakeable rage. He paused a moment to collect his strength for the climb up the path to the guard tower. Two years ago—five—the hike would have been nothing. These days, weariness burdened his shoulders and made his very bones ache. He looked upward toward his goal, wincing when the sunlight threatened to rekindle his headache. South of the Old Quarry Road—though not even the Collegium's Bards could say what had been quarried here, or when—the air was sharp and cold even in summer, and the sun was mountain bright. Here in Yvendan they were only a few miles from the invisible line where the Terilee River changed its name to the Sunserpent River.

From the border that separated Valdemar from Karse.

He pulled the hood of his cloak forward in a futile attempt to shade his eyes, and sighed as he began his ascent. Every Healing took its toll these days, awakening savage headaches that never quite went away. He knew his old mentors would tell him to rest, to take care of himself, that a Healer's health and stamina were his greatest tool and he should husband them always.

He couldn't do that.

Every day of rest was a day someone who needed him suffered. Died, if he didn't reach them in time. Nor was that the worst. The worst was what they might do to others.

He wrenched his mind determinedly from the well of memory and quickened his pace up the hill.

*   *   *

"Healer, thank goodness you've come!"

"I came as soon as your message reached me," He-dion answered. "You're Captain Dallivant?"

The garrison commander hung back, looking wary. The man who had greeted Hedion was a captain, to judge by his uniform. His face bore the characteristic bruises of one whose helm had deflected a sword-blow. The bruises were faint now. Perhaps a sennight old. Karse had tried the border here around that time.

"Yes, sir. Is it true what they say, you can—"

"You don't have to call him 'sir,' Dallivant, he isn't in the army." The new speaker was the garrison com-mander. A veteran, from his scars. A good man, but a hard one. "You're Healer Hedion? The Mindhealer?"

"Yes." Hedion waited. He couldn't do his work if people meant to get in his way. There was a trick—simple but effective—that usually gained him the coop-eration he sought. He listened intently. Yes. There. "Tell me, Commander Felmar—did Brion hurt anyone before you captured him?"

Felmar grimaced, refusing to acknowledge—aloud at least—that Hedion had impressed him. "Had to put down three of the horses after he got at them. Broke Maret's arm before we got him down. Don't know why I bothered letting Dallivant talk me into waiting on you, except I thought he might like to say a few words before we hanged him."

"Sir! You can't!" Dallivant burst out. "Brion would never—"

Hedion held up his hand for silence. He'd had this conversation, or a variant of it, more times than he could remember. But it was necessary every time.

"You don't strike me as the sort who'd hang an in-nocent man, Commander."

"Innocent!" Felmar snorted. "He had blood all over him—and Maret saw him!"

"Maret saw a Karsite weapon. A demon," Hedion answered.

"Pull the other one, Healer. Demons can't come over the border," Felmar said.

"No," Hedion agreed. "But the damage they do *can*."

At least he had Felmar's grudging attention now. Behind them, from the closed door of whatever storeroom was being used as a makeshift cell, the screaming continued, as regular and monotonous as if it were a mechanical sound from an unliving source.

"We all know demons can't enter Valdemar. No magic can," Hedion began, his voice taking on the gentle, distant, lecturing quality of one who seeks to instruct, not confront. "We also know the Karsite priests can summon demons, and do. That's why the war's gone on as long as it has—we don't dare chase the Karsites across the border and finish them once and for all."

Felmar growled, faintly, deep in his throat, as if he wanted to disagree, and couldn't.

"Of course, we *do* cross the border," Hedion continued. "With a Herald or two in the vanguard, you usually have enough warning the Red Robes are bringing up one of their creatures in time to retreat. But sometimes you'll just send out a scouting party—volunteers, they know the risks—and sometimes the demons can't be seen." He stopped, pushing the hood of his robe back to rub his aching eyes. "When their horses spook, though, your men know it's time to run for it. The thing is—" He stopped, taking a deep breath. "Sometimes running isn't good enough. Sometimes the demons get them anyway. Only it isn't an injury you can see. It's here," he tapped his forehead. "Inside. And there's nothing they can do.

It's like a poisoned wound. When it gets bad enough ... things happen."

"It wasn't Brion's fault, sir, I told you it wasn't!" Captain Dallivant said, his words tumbling over each other with his haste to speak them. "He'd never hurt a horse, never, not in a thousand years, sir, Brion comes from horse country, and—"

Felmar made a curt gesture, demanding silence. "And you can Heal this 'demon curse,' Healer Hedion?"

"If it were a curse, I'd tell you to have your company priest pray over him," Hedion snapped. "It's an injury to his mind. And *that* I can Heal. Now show me where he is—and tell me you won't just hang him when I'm finished. Otherwise, this is a waste of my time."

Commander Felmar looked a bit taken aback by such plain speaking. "I—If it was a demon, I guess he'll tell me, won't he?"

"Yes," Hedion answered. He shouldn't be this tired before starting a Healing, but it wasn't just an innocent man's life at stake. Felmar meant to hang young Brion. You weren't manacled when you were hanged. Your hands were bound with rope. Brion would be able to break those bonds—easily—and he'd do far worse than just slaughter a few soldiers if he did. He'd escape. And a Karsite demon would be loose in the Jaysong Hills—one no Gift could sense nor Wards could ban.

He turned to Dallivant. "And when I'm finished, tell his friends to keep a close watch on him and tell him everything I've said. I don't care what he thinks or what he wants to believe. Nothing he did after he was demon-touched was his fault, and I won't have someone I've Healed slitting his own throat out of stupidity."

The silence stretched until Felmar cleared his throat.

"Well, I think we're finished, Healer. Kailes, take the Healer to the prisoner."

"Yes, Commander." A young woman armored—incongruously—as if she were expecting immediate battle rose gracefully from her seat at the desk at the back of the hall. "If you'll come with me, Healer?"

The message that had reached Hedion was less than a sennight old, but young Brion-from-horse-country looked as if he had aged a moonturn in that time. He was nearly naked, long red gouges in his skin showing that he'd ripped off his own clothes everywhere he could reach. His knuckles were red and puffy from constant battering at the stone, and his wrists were raw and scabbed—not because of any mistreatment, or because the shackles were too tight, but from his constant attempts to drag his hands through them. His lips were puffy, bitten and bleeding, and the cell, cold as it was, stank of human waste.

"We've tried to feed him, and, and give him blankets, Healer," Kailes said. Hedion could sense guilt and shame radiating from her like heat from a stove. "It doesn't matter what we do. He throws the food and rips up the blankets. And he won't stop—"

"It will be over soon, Kailes. Now go and leave us alone, please."

"You—you won't hurt him, will you, Healer?" she asked uncertainly, her cheeks flaming with embarrassment at asking.

"I'm sorry," Hedion answered. "I probably will. But I'll save his life."

The door closed behind him, and Hedion took a moment to remove a shim of soft wood from his belt-pouch and jam it into the crack between the door and the frame, wedging it in tightly. Few cells locked on the inside, and he didn't want his Healing interrupted. He removed his cloak and belt, piling them carefully in a corner, then added his overtunic. It was cold in the cell, but it was also filthy: as Kailes had said, Brion had flung all the food brought to him as far away as he could manage, and hadn't bothered with the chamber pot. There were two trays—obviously dinner and breakfast—sitting on the floor far outside his reach. Hedion didn't really blame whoever it had been for not wanting to get too close. He bent down and picked up a tankard. Sniffed at it. Water. Good.

The screaming had stopped when he entered the cell. Now the damaged, demon-imprinted creature was staring at him silently, bloodshot eyes startlingly blue in a face as pale and glistening as a rock-grub.

"You're thirsty, I know," Hedion said soothingly. "I've brought you water. See? Here it is."

The manacles that shackled Brion were connected by a three-foot length of chain threaded through an iron ring. Madness if you wanted to try to control a prisoner, humane if you were chaining someone to a wall. Hedion approached Brion deliberately, noting the rusty streaks of blood on the stone floor where the boy had scoured his heels raw. The streaks gave him some idea of Brion's reach.

"Water," he said again, in the same low soothing voice. "Here it is. I won't take it away."

He held the mug out to the boy, but just far enough away so that Brion had to strain toward it, pulling himself to his knees and hanging the whole weight of his body from the manacles that circled his wrists. In that position, there was little he could do to harm anyone.

Hedion held the mug of water to Brion's lips, and as Brion slurped greedily at it, Hedion reached out and placed his other hand on the crown of Brion's head.

There was always a moment of panic when you began a Mindhealing. The spirit, his teachers had told him, yearned to protect itself, and feared the touch of another mind as a weak swimmer feared deep water. To give in to such panic was dangerous, a thing that could cause the Mindhealer to lose himself and the one he sought to save. Hedion was an Adept; he conquered the panic with an indrawn breath and sank into the depths of Brion's mind.

There were a thousand metaphors for what Healers did—all ways to clothe in homely ordinary words a thing that could not be expressed in words at all. For Hedion it was as if he unknotted the tangled strands of a spoiled weaving until they could be rewoven and made smooth. Or as if he tilled and seeded a garden, freeing the earth of weeds and stones so the young plants could grow strong and tall. Or cleaned a cow-byre that had grown filthy and poisonous through years of neglect, so that it became a safe haven once more. Or walked through a darkened wilderness, seeking a lost and frightened child.

Or all of these at once.

Inside his mind, Brion was frozen in the terrified moment when the demon had touched him, the power of it enough to force his wounded spirit to attempt to remake itself in the demon's image. *When you become the thing you fear, you no longer fear it. But see, Brion, I am here, and the demon is not. Look at me, Brion. Look to me . . .*

Over and over he fought the same battle: defeating the conjured demon-image inside Brion's mind, calling to that mind to see itself as whole and well and free. Brion's screams rang off the stone walls of the prison—Hedion could hear them, though they seemed far away and irrelevant—since each time he defeated Brion's inward demon, it carried Brion with it into its death-agonies.

But it also grew weaker. Each time it died Hedion could sense more of Brion behind it.

"Help me! Oh please, please—can't someone help me?" Brion cried at last.

Hedion did not allow the relief he felt to pass from his mind to Brion's. Fear—doubt—mistrust—could undo all his work in an eyeblink.

I'm right here, Brion. Take my hand. Look at me.

A whole and healthy mind does not need Mindhealing. That was the first lesson Hedion had learned. To use his power to force himself into a healthy mind, to shape it according to his will and not its owners', would be an utter betrayal of his Gift. And so the second lesson he had learned—so deeply ingrained that by now it was reflex—was to surrender—instantly—to the push of a Healed consciousness trying to regain the isolation and solitude of normalcy by banishing the intruder from itself.

Hedion did not remember what it was like to be isolated and solitary in his own mind. If he ever had been, it had been a very long time ago.

As he surrendered himself to the thrust of Brion's mind, his awareness of his surroundings sharpened. His knees hurt; he was kneeling on the stone. The cell stank. He could hear Brion's hoarse breathing, shading into tears. Hedion drew a deep breath, and clenched his teeth as the first hammerblow of the headache struck him behind the eyes. He would not cry out. He wouldn't.

"Ypon— Ypon—" Brion gasped. "What have I done?"

"Nothing," Hedion answered. "You have done nothing."

"Ypon" was a goddess who took the form of a white mare; well, Dallivant had said Brion came from horse country. Hedion pushed himself to his feet, and this time he *did* groan as the change of position made his headache flare into brighter agony.

"Wait here," he said, as if Brion could do anything else. "I'll get someone to unchain you."

On unsteady feet, Hedion walked to the door. He had to force himself to bend down to pick up his belt so he could use his knife to unjam the door, and the effort left him feeling sick and exhausted.

But he'd won.

One more time.

Afterward they always wanted to celebrate. Hedion just wanted to sleep. He got his way more easily these days— probably because Healings left him looking like a man in desperate need of a Healer himself. Brion had been taken away to the infirmary—Dallivant had gone with him—and Commander Felmar had just offered Hedion the use of his own quarters when Hedion got to his feet and sighed.

"I'm afraid that won't be possible, Commander. But thank you for the thought." He swayed, and reached for the back of the chair to steady himself, when a young woman, mud-spattered and wild-eyed, burst in to the room.

"Commander—" she said, sketching a salute sloppy from weariness. "The Mindhealer—has he left yet? I missed him at Chapel Hill and Semolding—he's got to come—have you—"

"I'm right here," Hedion said. Forcing his voice above a whisper was an effort, but he managed.

The messenger's name was Esclinet and she'd been chasing after him for three days. There'd been an outbreak of madness at Stone Tower—not one person, or three, but dozens. Hedion knew all that in an instant. Esclinet was so terrified—her father had been one of the first afflicted—and so exhausted that her mind shouted out the message she was terrified of forgetting. It struck Hedion with the force of a blow, and he tightened his grip on the back of the chair. To show her how weak he was would only frighten her more. For the same reason, he let her gabble out her message, interspersed with directions and advice he didn't need.

"I'm on my way." It would have been nice if Yvendan could use the signal mirrors to let Stone Tower know he was coming, but no one was quite sure whether or not the Karsites had broken their signal codes. It wasn't worth the risk.

"I'll—" Esclinet began.

"You'll stay here and rest," Hedion said. His weariness gave his voice a rasp that sounded like anger. "Follow when you've recovered. I know the way."

Every step his horse took was agony. The aftermath of a Healing should be treated in the same way as woundshock: blankets and hot sweet tea and rest. The thought even of a cup of wine made Hedion's stomach roil with nausea, and there was no time to rest. Stone Tower was three days away—and only if he didn't have to detour to avoid Karsite raiding parties. At least the Nightstalkers—those elite Sunsguard regiments that traveled with red-robed Sunpriests and their demons— never crossed the border. Small mercies.

He reached the bottom of the ridge and the eastward road that would lead him to Stone Tower. Hedion knew he presented a pitiful sight: hunched over, eyes squinted nearly shut, alternately gripping at his temples and clutching the pommel of the saddle. At least if he was set upon by bandits, he didn't have anything of value worth stealing. Everything he valued had been taken from him long ago.

The pain in his head pulsed implacably in time with the beating of his heart. He should stop soon and force himself to drink a little wine before going on. He had to go on. They needed him at Stone Tower.

:Wake up. You need to wake up now. You can't stay here.:

"—can—" Hedion mumbled. The sound of his own voice propelled him further toward wakefulness. He rolled onto his back, and the sudden realization that he was supposed to be on his horse—that the last thing he remembered was being on his horse—jolted him the rest of the way awake. He sat up quickly, and the sudden jolt of pain and nausea caused him to curl forward, clutching at his head and groaning.

:You can't stay here.: someone repeated.

Hedion forced his eyes open. The Companion stared back. It wore no harness—not the blue with silver bells that marked a Herald riding Circuit, nor the slightly more circumspect and bell-less harness the Companions wore when their Herald meant to cross over the Border into Karse. For one utterly horrified moment Hedion thought the Companion was here because he'd been Chosen, but it shook its head, much as a horse would, and radiated negation. He'd always been able to Hear the Companions, just as he could Hear human minds.

:My name is Rhoses. I am here for you, Hedion, but not in that way.: Rhoses' mental "voice" held both amusement and anxiety. *:You fell from your horse. I found you.*

You can't stay here. Come. Get up. You can hold on to me.:

He didn't think Rhoses would ask him to get up if it wasn't important, and Hedion was pretty sure Rhoses wouldn't go away until he did what he asked. Besides, he really couldn't stay here. He was lying on the side of a hill, and it was getting on toward sunset.

He forced himself to his feet—gasping with weakness and pain—and clutched at Rhoses' mane as Rhoses wanted him to. He clenched his fingers tightly in the silky strands and let Rhoses drag him back up the hillside.

"My horse . . . ?" he croaked, when they reached the top. Tallese was a good animal, and if he'd fallen from his back, as he obviously had, should have stayed nearby.

:Come.: Rhoses repeated, and Hedion tightened his grip on the white mane and stumbled along beside the Companion.

Hedion allowed himself to drift as he stumbled along beside Rhoses. In the last several years, he'd learned the art of sleeping anywhere at any time, and he knew he desperately needed rest. He opened his eyes to the smell of wood smoke. He'd expected Rhoses to lead him to Tallese, not to a camp.

There was a man sitting beside a small fire. The sight of him surprised Hedion; he'd heard no one's thoughts. The man was burly and unkempt, his skin lined and weathered in the way of one who has spent most of his life outdoors. His hair was streaked with gray, and had bits of twig in it. He looked up at Rhoses' approach, and his face transformed into fury.

"You! Go away!" He picked up a clod of earth and

threw it, but his target wasn't Hedion, Hedion realized as he reflexively ducked.

It was Rhoses.

"Go away, damn you!" the man shouted. "Why won't you leave me alone?" Hedion covered his ears and moaned.

More missiles followed the first: clods of earth, tufts of grass. Most of them struck their target. Rhoses bounded forward and took the front of the man's ragged tunic in his teeth, shaking him until he dropped his handful of earth. *:Stop it, Garaune! Stop it! Oh, I wish you could hear me, foolish headblind Herald! Hedion needs help! Garaune! Garaune!:*

Rhoses might as well have been shoving an icepick into Hedion's temple by shouting in Mindspeech, and Gaurane's roaring was like being kicked on the side of the head he wasn't being stabbed on. Hedion felt a rush of hot bile in his throat, and the jarring impact of the earth against his knees . . .

And then he felt nothing.

It was a very long time before Hedion awoke again. He opened his eyes warily. His head always hurt these days; the only difference was between the bright shattering pain that immediately followed the use of his Gift and the bruised sort of tenderness he felt after he'd gotten a little rest. This pain was the bruised sort, and he realized he was staring up at a little shelter made of sticks and string and a blanket, constructed to shield his face from the sun.

The sun.

It was morning, and Hedion sat up so quickly he brought the entire fragile structure down. He flailed at it for a few seconds before Gaurane pulled it off.

"Thought you were going to sleep forever," Gaurane grunted.

He moved away before Hedion could form a coherent reply, only to return a moment later to push a cup into Hedion's hands.

"Drink this. You look like a man whose head hurts."

"My head always hurts," Hedion muttered. He sipped. Willowbark tea, its bitterness disguised by a stunning amount of honey and a generous splash of brandy.

"You should see a Healer," Gaurane said blandly. "I'm Gaurane. You?"

"Hedion," Hedion answered. "And I am a Healer."

Gaurane gave a bark of laughter. "If that's true, the world's in worse shape than I ever suspected." He took Hedion's cup and got to his feet. A moment later he was back. This time the cup smelled of meat and herbs, and Gaurane held a cup of his own. "Thanks for the wine, by the way," he said unapologetically. "I was almost out of brandy."

"You went through my pack," Hedion said slowly. He looked around. Tallese was there, unsaddled, his halter-rope tied to a log, and so was Rhoses. The Companion gazed at him worriedly. Hedion frowned, remembering how he'd come to the campsite, and what had happened here. Why hadn't Rhoses told Gaurane who he was? Was Gaurane a new Chosen? It was possible ...

"Had to find out if you were a Karsite spy. Vicious bastards, Karsites," Gaurane said without heat. He tipped back his mug, drinking deeply.

:Tell him he has to come with me. Tell him we should go back to Haven: Rhoses said pleadingly.

Hedion winced reflexively at the Mindspeech, but it didn't seem to hurt as much as it had before. He glanced at Gaurane. He acted as if he hadn't heard anything. Automatically Hedion reached out to listen, to see why Gaurane would ignore his Chosen—

—and heard nothing.

"I'm a Healer," he heard himself say, desperation and fear in his voice. "A Mindhealer. I hear . . . "

"I don't," Gaurane said bluntly. "Not any more. Look, why don't you have some wine? It helps."

"Rhoses says you should go back to Haven," Hedion said.

Gaurane froze in the act of getting to his feet again. "You can Hear him?"

"I can Hear everyone," Hedion said, setting the half-full cup aside to rub his aching eyes. He cringed inwardly at the misery in his voice, but it had been a very long time since he'd thought of his Gifts as a blessing. "Everyone but you."

"Ah, well, you can thank Vikandis for that. And as for you, you can go back to Haven—without me—and find someone who actually gives a damn."

This last was obviously addressed to Rhoses. *:You are my Chosen, Herald Gaurane. I will not leave you.:* Rhoses looked at Hedion, obviously expecting him to convey the message.

"He says no," Hedion said.

Gaurane made a grumbling sound and threw a stone at Rhoses. The Companion calmly took a step to the side, letting the stone fly by. "I'm not drunk enough. My aim's off," he said, getting to his feet.

Hedion rubbed his temples. Time to get up. Time to go. They needed him in Stone Tower. He flung back the blankets—it was his own bedroll; he spent enough time in the hills and following the army that he couldn't always be certain of finding an inn or a bed—and started to get to his feet.

"Hold—hold—hold—" Gaurane said, rushing back and thrusting his full cup into Hedion's hands even as he eased him back down to the blankets. "A man who's lain like the dead these three days can't just leap up and go running off."

"*Three days?*" Hedion said in horror. He should have been there already—he should be riding up to the keep right now, offering them encouragement and hope. He slitted his eyes against sun that had suddenly grown intolerably bright and clenched his fists. His palms were wet and his hands were shaking, and he could feel the chill trembling all through his body that was the forerunner of a spectacularly bad headache.

"Drink this." Gaurane took several deep swallows from his mug and then held it to Hedion's lips.

Hedion drank—his mouth felt dry and tasted metallic—and ran a hand through his hair. "I have to go. They need me at Stone Tower."

"Yes, yes, yes, of course they do. And I'm sure you'd get a good two miles down the road before you fell off your horse again."

"*I have to go.*" Something like panic tightened his chest. "I'm a Mindhealer—they—they'll kill innocent men—it looks like demon-possession, but it isn't—"

"Couldn't be, this side of the border." Gaurane was calmly unimpressed. "And you won't make it, and if you do, you'll be in no shape to Heal anyone."

Hedion sank back to his bedroll with a moan. The ground seemed to be rocking beneath him, and he shuddered with chills. Healing took a toll. The Healer had to pay back to his own body what it spent to Heal others.

He hadn't done that for a long time. He'd thought he could go on stealing from himself for longer.

"Please," he whispered. "Please. They know I'm coming. Please. Send word. Tell them I'll be there as soon as . . . Please." Tears leaked from the corners of his eyes. Hedion no longer knew whether they came from pain or weakness or the knowledge of his own failure.

Gaurane patted his shoulder. "I'll write them a letter and tie it all up with a pretty blue ribbon. That jumped-up circus pony has to be good for something—if he shows up with a message they'll have to take it seriously."

:Do not fear.: Rhoses said. *:I will carry your message to Stone Tower.:*

"Thank you," Hedion mumbled.

It was as if a hidden part of his mind, realizing it had found help and allies, surrendered utterly. Hedion slept. Each time he woke, Gaurane was there with a cup. Sometimes it held willowbark tea. Sometimes it held broth. Sometimes it held watered brandy.

"You should sleep," Hedion muttered.

It was night, but he had no idea of *what* night. Normally that information would have been available to him from the thoughts of those around him, but though Gaurane was there, it was as if Hedion were utterly alone.

"If you had my dreams, you wouldn't say that," Gaurane answered. "Go back to sleep."

"I think I might be finished sleeping, at least for a while," Hedion said, surprising himself.

"Well, if you can stand up without falling over, there's a creek that way—" Gaurane jerked his thumb over his shoulder, indicating the direction. "Go wash up, then come and sit. There's some roast rabbit."

*   *   *

"Can't expect the pony back for another two days, minimum," Garaune said, when Hedion came back. "Unfortunately, he always comes back." He took a long drink.

Hedion wasn't sure he'd ever seen Gaurane without a mug in his hand. "I'm going to run out of wine soon," he said, just for something to say.

"You did that yesterday," Gaurane said. "Let's hope you're well enough to ride by the time I run out of brandy. I can get supplies at Stone Tower."

"I, uh, I never thanked you for saving my life," Hedion said awkwardly.

Gaurane fixed him with a piercing look. The firelight turned his brown eyes amber. "Don't be insulting. I know the sort of man who'd spit in someone's eye if they saved his life," he said.

"Are you one?" Hedion asked boldly. It was odd to only have surface things to judge someone by—face and voice and the movement of the hands. But he had been trained by those who had to rely upon only those things. Mindhealing was the rarest of the Healing Gifts, and the only other Mindhealer Hedion had ever met was of Journeyman rank, and would never go higher. There'd been no one who could truly explain him to himself.

"If I meant to be dead, I could have cut my throat a hundred times over," Gaurane said. "You know damned well what happens to the surviving half of a Bonding. No, I'll just suffer," he added, with a crooked smile.

Hedion found himself smiling back. "I don't understand. Rhoses called you 'Herald Gaurane.' He's your Companion. But you can't Hear him, can you? And I can't Hear you."

"Eat your dinner," Gaurane said.

There was half a rabbit set out on a tin plate, along

with several ash-roasted tubers and a mug of hard cider. Hedion discovered he was hungry and began to eat. He didn't think he was going to get an answer to any of his questions, but after the silence had stretched for a while, Gaurane began to talk.

"I keep hoping he'll go off and find himself some bright-eyed young Herald, you know? They have to have some way to ... to un-Choose someone. I'm not the Herald type. I knew—*he* knew—when he found me, Chose me, it was for one thing. And we did that. We did that," Gaurane repeated, as if to himself. Then he fixed Hedion with that knowing gaze once more.

"I was a drunk. I'm still a drunk, but, well, in those days I was living in the gutters of Haven. Happy to be there. Don't know how I got there. Don't know how I got to Valdemar, actually. I'm from the Hardorn side of the Kleimars. Good farming land. Good life."

The silence stretched, and Hedion knew better than to break it.

"My brother, his wife, my wife. Our children. A little farm. One day a Karsite supply party came through. I don't know what happened. I was mending a fence when I smelled the smoke." Gaurane looked down at his hands. Strong and blunt-fingered. Farmer's hands. "You studied at the Collegium. I guess they told you about how it is with Gifts. They show up when you're a kid, just like you cutting your second teeth. Or you can go your whole life not knowing you have them. Unless something rips you open."

"You felt them die," Hedion said softly.

"I wish I had. I *heard* them die," Gaurane corrected sharply. "Heard them hope, heard Liodain lie to the babies and say it would be all right. Heard them beg the Karsites for help. Heard them realize they were all going to die. Heard. Them. Die."

The fire crackled and popped. The silence was absolute.

"The next thing I'm sure of, Rhoses was telling me Valdemar needed me." Gaurane sighed. "What do you know about the priests of Vikandis Sunlord?"

"Too much," Hedion said, and Gaurane raised his cup in an ironic salute.

"The black-robes just kill people and chant. The red-robes kill people, chant, and call demons. Lord Brondrin said we needed to find out what they were doing in their Temple. Queen Alliana agreed. They knew something big was coming up. They knew they couldn't get a spy in and out. Rhoses went to find me—or someone like me, I don't know—he told me I had a thing called Mind-Hearing, and it was strong, strong enough to do what Queen Alliana needed. Of course I said yes."

"What happened?" Hedion said quietly.

Gaurane shrugged. "I don't know. I was there—and then I was on Rhoses' back and he was running like hell. I kept shouting at him, but he never answered." He reached for the keg beside him, and Hedion heard it gurgle, half-empty, as he filled his mug again. "They said in Haven I'd "completed my mission," and that I might get better. They said I should stay and get proper Herald training. What good is a crazy old drunk to Valdemar? I walked out. Rhoses followed me. I never got better. He won't leave."

"He's your Companion," Hedion said. He felt helpless, unsure of what to say.

"*Heralds* have Companions," Gaurane answered. "Me, I don't even care who wins the war, not any more—no one man can take on the entire Karsite priesthood. You, on the other hand, care too damned much."

"It's better than giving up!" Hedion said hotly. "No one else can do what I can. If I don't care, people will die."

"What of it?" Gaurane said, shrugging. "Do you know how many people die each moonturn here on the Border because Karse has crossed to Valdemar or Valdemar has crossed to Karse?"

"I don't care," Hedion said through gritted teeth. Abruptly he realized he'd been sitting here as if he had all the time in the world when he could be riding toward Stone Tower. He got to his feet. "Thank you for your hospitality, Herald Gaurane. But they need me at Stone Tower. Each time Valdemar crosses to Karse, it's a chance for a Karsite demon to inflict a wound only a Mindhealer can Heal." He turned away. His tack had to be around here somewhere—unless Gaurane had thrown it in the stream.

"You'll kill yourself trying, you know," Gaurane said conversationally.

"I don't care," Hedion repeated, stepping away from the campfire's light.

"Then if you're going to help, help *smart*—or do you want to die just so you can get out of a task you know is hopeless?"

"It isn't hopeless," Hedion protested. Even to his own ears the words sounded weak and unconvincing.

Gaurane laughed; to Hedion's surprise there was no bitterness in the sound, only joy. "Never lie to a drunk, boy. *You* think it is, and you'll do anything not to see yourself fail at it—even die."

"I—" Hedion began, and stopped. Was Gaurane right?

"Oh, come back and sit down, boy," Gaurane said, gesturing expansively. "The night's young—but it isn't young enough for you to go haring off in it."

"Don't call me 'boy,'" Hedion said, because it was the only thing Gaurane had said that he felt he could safely protest.

"I won't call you 'boy' if you don't call me 'Herald,'" Gaurane agreed. "Now come, sit, have a drink, and let's figure out how you can solve all the problems of the world without killing yourself."

Elade waited in concealment, every muscle tense. In the distance, she could hear the sound of Meran's harp. The sound put her teeth on edge, but—she'd be the first to admit—she had no ear for music. Bard or not—and a day didn't pass that Meran didn't bring up his Collegium training and Collegium credentials—all that *plink-plink-plink* was just noise, and Elade wouldn't say otherwise.

Most of the time their patients had been captured before they were called in, and then all Elade had to do was guard the door so no one came in while Hedion was doing a Healing. Of course, that meant she had to listen to Meran and his damned harp, too, but both Hedion and Gaurane swore it soothed the Touched and made Hedion's work easier. And Meran was a handy man to have in a brawl. No one grew up on the streets of Haven without learning to defend themselves.

There was a flicker of movement from the trees edging the meadow. *Damn him, he's gone round the other side,* Elade thought, as the man burst out of concealment. *Naked, covered in dried blood, no ear for music— that's him,* she thought, springing forward. She wouldn't reach him before he reached Meran. She'd owe Meran a new harp. She hoped that was all—Hedion was a great Healer, but the man couldn't Heal anything useful to save his life . . .

Elade was focused on her target, her hand clenched tight on the grip of her truncheon. She carried a sword, and she was damned good with it, but it was only for use as a last resort. You couldn't Heal someone after they were dead.

Meran saw her, and she saw him realize she wouldn't reach him in time. He got to his feet, one hand going to his own truncheon, when Elade saw a flash of white.

Here comes the cavalry.

Rhoses hit the Touched hard enough to knock him from his feet. It was enough time for Meran to get the first folds of the net over him—a good strong net, the same kind the fishers up north used when the speckle-fish were running in the spring—and by then, Elade had arrived. She gave the patient a light expert tap with her truncheon—enough to stun him and let her and Meran finish rolling him into the net.

"You owe me a new harp," Meran said.

"What? He never touched you!"

"If Rhoses hadn't been here, he would've."

"All right—shall I break this one first?" Elade said. "I mean, if you're getting a new one."

Rhoses tossed his head, and Elade knew he was probably saying something. She tossed him an apologetic glance. You couldn't have a conversation with Rhoses unless Hedion was there.

"Is it safe to come out now?" Hedion came out of the woods leading his horse. Gaurane rode beside him, leading the rest of their mounts and a pack horse they could use to carry the patient. She'd always wondered why Gaurane didn't ride Rhoses, since Rhoses was his

Companion, but she'd never quite worked up the nerve to ask. Maybe next year.

"This is him," Meran said cheerfully. "I think," he added.

"Or someone else who doesn't like music," Gaurane commented.

"No," Hedion said, kneeling beside the man struggling in the net. "This is Ablion Taus."

"Who is going to have to find another line of work now that his smuggling business has taken such an unfortunate turn," Gaurane added.

"Yes," Hedion said, in tones indicating he was answering a question Elade hadn't heard. "But not for murder. Taus didn't murder any one. Karse did. There will be charges," he added, for their benefit.

She and Meran got Taus settled on the back of the pack horse before mounting their own animals. The village of Estidan was less than half an hour's ride from here, and they'd already arranged for everything they'd need: a secure place for Hedion to work. A quiet place for him to rest afterward. Or for Gaurane to sit on him, more than likely, because they'd already gotten word of another case, and Hedion would work himself into the ground if they let him.

"Hush, you," Meran said to Taus. "Healer Hedion is going to save your life."

Mindhealers were rare. Powerful Mindhealers were rarer. If you couldn't find more, or train more, you had to make better use of the ones you had.

The one you had.

Hedion had sacrificed everything to his desire to put right what the Sunpriests had spoiled. He'd had a home, a family, a wife, a child. He'd lost them all. He'd nearly lost his life, refusing to admit what he already knew: the task was too big for one man and too endless for one life.

None of them could do what Hedion could do. But they could do everything else. Elade was quick and clever, able to capture a patient if that was what they needed, able to guard Hedion during a Healing, or restrain a patient when a Healing went wrong. No one—town mayor, village elder, post commander—wanted to argue with Elade when she made up her mind.

And Meran: if a Healer couldn't be Healed by another Healer, he could be soothed to sleep by a Bard. Gaurane would never tell anyone—especially Meran—that he valued him more for that than for any skill in luring or comforting one of the demon-touched.

As for him, Gaurane had no illusions. He was mostly deadweight. A sometimes-charming distraction. Someone who could tell Hedion no and make it stick. And of course, where he went, Rhoses went. He was becoming resigned to that.

Gaurane looked sideways, and saw Rhoses watching him. The one thing he still regretted was not being able to Hear Rhoses' voice. Hedion had offered to try to Heal him, but if he did, would the memories in that black missing time in the Sunpriests' city return? Were they something he could live with?

Gaurane wasn't sure he was willing to take the risk.

Maybe someday.

Unintended Consequences
Elizabeth A. Vaughan

She heard nothing beyond the man's first words.

"Your husband, Lord Sinmonkelrath, was killed in an attack on Queen Selenay."

Ceraratha's senses failed her, as did her weak grasp of Valdemarian. Surely she had misunderstood. Sinmon, killed? Committing treason? It could not be so.

But to her dawning horror, it was. The man, the Queen's Own, spoke on, but his words were so much noise in her ears. Dryness caked her mouth, and her vision narrowed to the man and the desk and the papers in his hands. A plot to slay the queen?

She'd known something was terribly wrong when she'd heard the alarms ringing out and strident calls in the halls outside her door. Her maidservant had tried to go out to get word, but had been prevented by Guardsmen in dark blue, with stern faces.

That had been no hardship. Sinmon rarely permitted her to leave their quarters, small as they were. He preferred to forget that he was wed to a wool merchant's daughter, a woman more trained in the ways of the loom and spindle then court airs and graces.

Sinmon was the second son, and had seemed glad

enough at the time of their marriage to wed the daughter of a wealthy merchant. Her father had been more than willing to buy a small farm for them to set up their home and lives. But Sinmon had rejected that bride price in favor of a settlement of funds. Those were gone now, despite her attempts to run a frugal household.

The first time he'd taken his fist to her had been over the cost of his clothing. Thankfully, her skills were such that she could keep him clothed as he demanded. She herself retained the country styles, to save a bit of coin.

But then this most recent plan of his, to follow Karathanelan to a strange land, with strange ways, little more than a sycophant. As swept up as Sinmon had been in the visions of wealth and power, Cera had not dared to protest the move.

Since the Royal marriage, Sinmon had left her to her sitting room and embroideries and silences, with little more than her handmaiden for company.

Now she stood before the Queen's Own, his scarred executioner at his side. Palace guardsmen just behind her, their weapons at the ready. Cera tried to swallow, to concentrate on what had happened.

Treason. Sinmonkelrath, her lord and husband, had committed treason against the Crown of Valdemar.

Treason. She would be executed, her family shamed. . . .

She stood straight as an arrow, as she'd been taught, head high, hands clasped before her, paralyzed, unable to breathe.

The executioner, the one who wore dark gray, with his scarred face and cruel eyes, stood next to the seated man. His face stern, his hand on the hilt of his blade. Was her death now? Without a prayer? Without a plea?

She would have spoken, but what words could she

say? Sinmon had betrayed her, betrayed this new land, on the promise of that false prince. She knew in an instant that Prince Karathanelan's charming smile and honeyed tongue had done this.

The executioner's eyes narrowed, and he spoke softly to the Queen's Own, who looked up at her face. There was a flash of concern there, and he paused. "Lady, perhaps you should be seated."

Ceraratha stared at the man, not sure she really understood.

A hand at her elbow then. Cera turned to see Alena at her side, her face filled with worry. The executioner was shutting the door, as if he had summoned her maidservant from the hall. But—

Alena urged her back, and Cera felt a chair press against her legs. She sat, trying hard to understand what was happening. Alena was speaking in a hushed whisper, her familiar voice speaking in Rethwellan, a balm to Cera's heart.

"Sit, my lady, sit," Alena raised a cup to her lips and pressed the cool rim to them. "Drink."

Cera sipped obediently of the sweet wine, but pulled back as the liquid hit her stomach. She reached out her hand, and grasped Alena's hard. "Did you hear? Do you know?"

Alena nodded, keeping a tight grip on Cera's fingers. "Lady, yes. I heard," she whispered softly, her lips close to Cera's ear. "But hear the Queen's Own, lady. Hear his words."

"A shock," Talamir said, this time speaking in Rethwellan. "I ask your pardon, lady. This day has been a long one."

The executioner, the one known as Alberich, returned to his position, his face solemn and stern.

"Your husband was involved in a treasonous plot against the queen, Lady Ceraratha. We must ask, were you involved in—"

"No," Cera jerked back to her feet, staggering. "No, no, a thousand times I say this. Not I nor my servants would ever—"

"Lady, please," Talamir gestured for her to return to her seat. "We can verify that with a Truth Spell easily enough."

The tightness in Cera's chest eased a bit, as she sat. That was right, this strange land held no magic, but it did have that spell. They would believe then. That was well.

"There is still the matter of your future, lady," The Queen's Own said.

Cera jerked her head in a half-nod. What was to be done? To return home, after this had happened? To the shame of her parents? Or the retribution of her in-laws? For the fault would be hers, that she was certain of. Without thinking, she reached for Alena's hand.

Alberich spoke then, a soft comment meant only for the Queen's Own. Cera blinked in surprise. Had he said something about sheep?

"Queen Selenay had issued a grant of land to Lord Sinmon shortly after her marriage to the prince," Talamir said, looking down at the papers in his hands.

Cera frowned, remembering. Sinmon had said something to that effect, just in passing. Cera had asked if they would be leaving court, but had been met with a sharp rebuke and a blow. Sinmon had disparaged the gift in private, while publicly expressing his gratitude.

"Herald Alberich reminds me that it is not the most prosperous lands. Sheep country, really. On the borders of Rethwellan and Karse."

Sheep?

"The war has depleted the lands and its people, but there is enough there to make a beginning. To rebuild. You understand, this is not a rich—"

Just for a moment, Cera could hear the bleating of newborn lambs and the squalls of sheep being sheared. The sound of her mother's loom filled her head, her mother humming as she worked. "Mine?"

"Yes, lady," Talamir's look was sharp. "Both Crowns would prefer that this matter be dealt with quietly and quickly. Her Majesty is willing to confirm the lands and title in you, upon your oath of fealty and prompt departure for your lands."

"Never to return" was the implication, but that troubled Cera not one bit. Never to have to tread these halls of power and cruelty seemed more gift than punishment. But her own lands . . . her own herds . . . was it possible? A strange feeling rose in her breast. It took her a breath to recognize it for what it was.

Hope.

"We'll provide an escort, to see you safely south, and the necessary documents to claim your holdings." Talamir continued. "If such is acceptable . . . ?"

He offered land, work, her own income. Her emotions threatened to overwhelm her. She clutched Alana's hand even tighter.

"It is," Cera said firmly.

Alana was sent back to their chambers to pack what she could as fast as she could. The Heralds explained Cera would be taken directly to a carriage when her audience was over. Anything left behind would be sent to her later.

Cera found herself hustled down a long silent servants' hall by her escort. The Heralds were polite but firm, and Cera had no argument with that. She had no desire to parade through those halls, dressed in her country best, under the eyes of the nobility.

Oddly enough, she found herself emerging through doors that led to the queen's garden.

The day was fair enough, the sun shining down through the new green leaves.

The queen was seated on a bench, her bright white Companion at her side. The Companion's lovely head close to Selenay's, as if they were confiding in each other. Or offering each other comfort. It seemed somehow a private moment; Cera looked down as she and her escort advanced.

There were other Heralds all around, on guard, tense. No others, which meant no prying eyes or gossiping tongues. The gray one was there as well, with his own Companion.

Talamir appeared at Selenay's side as Cera approached. There was a cushion there before the queen, and Cera knelt, placed her palms together, and bowed her head.

"Your Majesty, this is Lady Ceraratha, wife of the late Lord Sinmonkelrath. The lady wishes to become your loyal subject and hold the lands that were gifted to her late husband. The lady has expressed her desire to swear fealty to the Crown under the Truth Spell and then to depart to her estates for a period of mourning."

"Let it be so," Selenay's voice seemed to echo out over the garden. For one so young, it sounded tired. Worn.

Hands came around hers then, young hands of a noble woman, warm against her cold fingers.

A murmur then, from one of the Heralds, probably

casting the Truth Spell. Cera felt nothing, but knew the glow would demonstrate the truth of her words.

"Repeat after me," Talamir said. "I, Lady Cerarath, do solemnly swear that . . ."

Cera dutifully repeated the words, staring at Selenay's hands. They were not as perfect as she'd thought a queen's would be. There were calluses there, both of the sword and the pen. But there was pain there too. And worry.

"That I shall hold the lands in fealty and honor, striving to serve the land and the Crown, as long as my breath shall issue from my body and the Gods see fit to preserve my life."

Cera spoke the last with fervor, her voice cracking slightly. She wanted this woman to understand, to know that she meant every word with every fiber of her being.

With the last of her words, she looked up and into the eyes of her queen.

Cera caught her breath.

In those blue eyes, it was there to see. The anguish of betrayal. The pain of the truth. The joy of release. The guilt that joy brought.

Selenay's eyes looked into hers and then widened with the shared knowledge of shared pain.

The oath was completed. Talamir was reaching out his hand to assist Cera to her feet. But in that long instant, Ceraratha and Selenay stared at one another. And each knew the bond they shared, with no need for words.

Cera pulled her hands away as the queen released them. She reached for Talamir's hand, allowing her wide cloth sleeve to fall back.

A soft hiss left the queen's lips at the sight of the fading bruises. The Companion snorted softly, its head jerking back. Cera knew then that the queen, at least, had not suffered that at the prince's hands.

Ceraratha rose to stand straight before her queen, allowing the sleeve to fall back down. She curtsied low before Selenay, then lifted her head proudly and spoke carefully in Valdemarian. "In me, your Majesty will have no more loyal and devoted subject in all your Kingdom."

Selenay studied her, then nodded. "I wish you well, lady."

Cera retreated a few steps and then turned and headed back the way they had come, her escort following a few steps behind. Head high, back straight—

And free.

The Education of Evita
Mickey Zucker Reichert

The forest seemed extraordinarily green to Evita as she danced through the shadows with Bruno, as if some mysterious woodland creature had sprinkled the branches and underbrush with crushed emeralds. She ran toward the familiar babble of the brook, snagging a fallen branch in mid-movement. Seeing it, Bruno chased after her, barking wildly.

Evita laughed. Bits of leaf and twigs tangled into her mouse-brown locks. Her lanky teenaged legs carried her swiftly along the whisper of a path whose mud revealed its origins: light, cloven-toed deer tracks and the overlapping, crosslike prints left by rabbits. Bruno crashed after her, his clumsy hound's body bouncing from copses and deadfalls, tripped up by clusters of vines. Saliva drooled from a tongue that flapped in the breeze and hung so long it seemed impossible that the wet, ropey thing ever fit inside his head.

"Eviiiiiiitaaaaa!"

Evita sighed. A clear note of irritation had entered her mother's tone. She would have to respond soon or risk her mother's wrath.

Not that that wrath consisted of anything terrible. A

raised voice, a disapproving look, a quiet air of motherly disappointment that would color everything else that evening, and an exasperated, out-loud wondering: "Why do we have to play this silly game? Why can't you just come the first time I call you?"

Evita no longer bothered to respond to that query. It didn't matter what she said; the question was wholly rhetorical and the answer downright obvious. Evita preferred the imagination-provoking wilds of the forest to the confines of the village and the thrill of discovery to the drudgery of chores.

"Come on, Bruno. Mother's getting upset." Evita turned to retrace her steps.

Bruno did not obey any better than his mistress. He snuffled curiously at a dense copse of swampweed growing on the riverbank.

Evita hopped back down the deer path, making a game out of dodging hoof marks and Bruno's massive paw prints in the mud. Within a few steps, she could no longer hear his coarse breathing or the crash of his legs through the undergrowth. She whirled back to where she had left him, seeing no sign of the hound. "Bruno?"

The dog did not respond.

Huffing in irritation, Evita headed back toward the river. "Come on, Bruno." She turned a gentle corner, just enough to take a ledge of tall marsh weeds out of her vision and bring the tiny clearing into focus. Bruno remained exactly where she had left him. Beside him stood a snowy white horse, its silver hooves planted in the muck. It held its triangular head aloft, its mane riffling in a mild breeze, its eyes enormous and cornflower blue. Evita could not recall ever having seen anything so beautiful in her life. "Companion," she whispered. Joy as pure and sparkling as gold rushed through her.

Evita ran to the horse. "You came for me. You came for me!"

Bruno had not made a sound when the Companion had appeared, but he barked at Evita as she rushed the creature.

:*I came for you, Evita,*: the Companion confirmed. :*My name is Camayo.*:

Evita could not recall clambering or jumping; but a moment later, she found herself safely on Camayo's back. She settled into a saddle that seemed custom made for her own comfort and took reins that she believed utterly unnecessary. "I've had dreams about you." Day and night, Evita had envisioned herself on a horse as white as the most perfect cloud, soaring skyward on its back, and watching the rest of the world unfurl below them. "I've had the most wonderful visions, Camayo. You can run like the wind, can't you?"

Amusement brushed Evita's mind. :*I'm fast enough, but a good squall will always get there first.*:

Evita barely listened, too engrossed in studying the animal.

:*What are you looking for?*:

Excited to the point of breathlessness, Evita answered, "Wings."

:*Sorry to disappoint you, Dear One. I'm strictly ground transportation.*:

Evita laughed. Sitting high on a Companion felt strangely normal and right, as if her life before this moment had existed only to mark time. "Let's go! Let's see the world. Let's have . . . adventures." She threw her arm fiercely into the air, expecting Camayo to take off like an arrow fired from a hunter's bow.

"Evvvvvvvvvv-iiiiiiiii-taaaaaaa!" Her mother's voice sounded worried . . . and hoarse.

The Companion did not budge. :*Don't you think you should you tell your parents where you're going so they don't worry? Shouldn't you take your dog home and pack a few things?*:

Evita dropped her arm. The mundane had fallen from her thoughts the instant she had spotted the Companion. Bruno would find his way home, but her parents would worry if she just disappeared. Her father worked late into the night, which meant that she would need to wait until morning to give him a proper goodbye and explanation. "You're right, Camayo, of course." Impatience stabbed her like a knife, but she had no real choice. "Can you take me home first?"

Camayo fell silent, mentally and physically. They headed through the forest toward Evita's home, Bruno trotting at the Companion's heels and Evita riding tall in the saddle. At least, she had a good excuse for being late.

Camayo and Evita rode out the next day with a pack of clothing and provisions secured behind the Companion's saddle. The girl could not stop talking. "I told them special things would come to me. I told them I didn't need to learn to cook and clean. I didn't need to patch and mend. There's so much more to life than sewing clothing and powdering babies. I wasn't going to be just some man's wife. I didn't have to . . . "

Camayo had not responded for a very long time, just continued walking, hour after hour in the warm spring sunlight to the sound of Evita's incessant jabbering.

Finally, Evita looked down at her Companion. "Camayo?"

:*Yes?*:

"You've been awfully quiet."

:*Yes.*:

"Don't you have anything to say?"

:*If you wish me to speak, you must give me the opportunity.*:

"The opportunity?" Evita hesitated, uncertain what Camayo meant. The Companion's "voice" came directly into her mind. "I'm sorry. You should have told me. Is my mind not open enough for you to speak to me?"

:*The problem is not the openness of your mind. It is the openness of your mouth.*:

That silenced Evita for the first time since she had discovered the Companion near the river. "That's not a very nice thing to say."

Camayo did not miss a step. :*I apologize if my phraseology displeased you. I can think of a dozen less considerate ways to have elucidated the matter, but I discarded those.*:

Evita could not help taking offense. "Indeed."

:*For example, I could have told you to shut up your endlessly spewing food hole.*:

Evita gasped. No one had ever spoken to her in that manner. Not a single harsh word had ever passed between her parents, nor had she heard them speak to others callously. At least in her presence, they always kept their tongues wholly civil and hid the occasional criticism amidst heaping amounts of praise.

:*It was only an example of what I might have said, but didn't.*:

"Yes." Evita did not know what to do or say. She shifted in the saddle. Her family owned an old pony that Evita had ridden many times, but she had never spent so many hours in one position. Though far smoother than the pony's, Camayo's gait still pounded muscles Evita did not realize she had. "I was talking an awful lot, and

I'm sorry. I haven't shown a lot of manners myself. Let's start with 'thank you for Choosing me.'"

Camayo lowered and raised his head. :*You're welcome, Dear One. You do have strong potentials in Mindspeech and Empathy. I Chose you for those, in fact. I wanted a compassionate partner with a fully developed voice. I'm afraid I don't possess the patience for vague feelings and pantomime.*:

Evita tried to make sense of the Companion's words. "You mean, I can talk into your mind like you do mine? Without . . . 'spewing words from my foodhole?'"

:*With some practice, yes.*:

Evita considered that. It certainly seemed worth trying. As the miles disappeared beneath Camayo's hooves, Evita turned her focus wholly on this new pursuit. Nudged and shaped by Camayo, the Mindspeech took form until it became nearly as easy as physical speaking. The conversation, however, remained superficial, geared toward the act itself. Sundown came upon them still on the forest pathways, and Camayo came to a sudden stop.

:*I need some rest.*:

Evita slid to the ground. She went to take a step and her legs buckled beneath her. She wobbled on them for several moments, readjusting their balance, and recognized a stiffness that had crept over her as they had traveled. Her thighs and buttocks ached. Her hips felt out of place. Her stomach rumbled painfully, and she suffered a craving for anything foodlike and solid.

Camayo stripped foliage from a nearby tree, chewing thoughtfully. The decorative reins slid along his neck, and Evita realized they attached to a bitless bridle. She had never been in control of their speed or direction, nor had she thought to worry about it. Now, she unstrapped the package from Camayo's rump and pulled

it to the ground. Opening it, she found some extra clothing and packets of food her mother had lovingly put in
place. Evita unwrapped a random packet and stuffed
the contents into her mouth. It crumbled delightfully on
her tongue; and, only after Evita had chewed for several
moments, did she recognize her mother's buttered black
bread. It could have been tree bark for all she worried
about the flavor. At the moment, only the sustenance it
provided mattered.

Camayo looked over his shoulder. :*Hungry?*:

Evita only nodded. She took several more enormous
bites before her hunger receded and she could focus
more on what she was eating. Only after she had de-
voured the entire packet did she feel a wistful stirring.
She loved her mother's black bread and the thin, watery
butter she purchased when finances allowed it. :*Halfway
starved*,: Evita finally returned after a long silence.

:*I was wondering how long it would take you to remember you don't need your mouth to converse with me*.:

Evita swallowed and smiled. :*It's still all so new*.: Only
then, she finally thought to ask. :*Where are we going, Camayo? Where are you taking me?*:

Still stripping the brush, Camayo snorted. :*To Valdemar, of course. You need to start your training*.:

Horror stole over Evita. She knew of Valdemar, of
course; everyone did, she believed. The Heralds all came
from there, trained in mind magic at their Collegium.
She knew it all, intellectually, but she had not yet inter-
nalized the full understanding of what this must mean
for her. The idea of formal schooling, with its rules and
regulations, its masters and underlings, its stodgy, stifling
confines and customs dismayed her to her core. "No!"
she shouted, so suddenly that Camayo stiffened.

Slowly, the Companion arched his neck, bringing his

head in Evita's direction without actually turning his
body. :*What happened? Are you hurt?*:

"No." Evita clarified. "I'm not hurt." She twined her
fingers anxiously. "Well, I'm a bit sore; but, otherwise,
I'm not physically hurt."

:*What's wrong?*: Camayo repeated, a hint of discomfort and suspicion leaking through with the words. :*And
use your Mindspeech, please.*:

Evita had forgotten. :*Yes, of course. It's just that . . .*:
Even using Mindspeech, she found it difficult to put her
thoughts into relatable concepts. :*I don't want to go to
Valdemar.*:

Camayo turned fully to face Evita directly. He lowered his head. :*Ever?*:

Evita shook her head, fingers still intertwined. :*No,
not . . . "not ever."*: She frowned at the double negative. Or was that a triple negative? She tried to make
her point more clearly. :*I know I have to go eventually.*:
Secretly, she hoped not. :*Right?*: She turned Camayo a
hopeful look.

Camayo did not even hint at wiggle room. :*Of course.
Do you think Heralds know what to do wholly by instinct?*:

Evita knew only that she had no intention of clipping
her newfound wings so quickly. :*Well . . . I think someone
with a reasonable amount of common sense could do a
decent job without necessarily having to take classes on
it.*:

If possible, Camayo's huge eyes seemed to grow
larger. :*Is that so?*:

Evita did not wish to sound offensive. :*I suppose a
Herald would have to learn mind magic. But, if it's anything like Mindspeaking, well, I picked that up easily
enough.*:

Camayo only stared. If he blinked, Evita did not see it.

:And, obviously, my horseback riding could stand a lot of practice, but you can give me that without some instructor droning on about balance and grip and knee position.:

Camayo's nostrils flared. He huffed out a warm breath. *:How's your weapons work?:*

"Weapons?" Evita repeated aloud with a shiver of revulsion. "Why would I want to know that?"

:So that if a basilisk attempts to consume you, you can disabuse it of the notion.: Camayo reminded, *:And, please, Dear One. Use Mindspeech.:*

Evita switched, *:I've survived this long without basilisks attempting to eat me.:*

:You've been confined to a tiny portion of the world. You requested travel and adventure, and you will get them. But you'll need to know how to defend yourself.:

Evita refused to touch a sword, but she saw no reason to argue that point with Camayo. She would save it until she faced an instructor with arms and hands.

:Do you know how to interact with royalty?:

:I know how to treat everyone with kindness and respect.: To Evita, that was enough. *:Accidents of birth should not be the sole determinant for how you behave toward a stranger.:*

:Agreed.: Camayo stamped a forehoof. *:But protocol serves a significant purpose. And you will need to learn history, diplomacy, languages . . . :*

Though safe in open forest, Evita could feel the dull walls of the Collegium closing in on her, squeezing the life from her like a massive and deranged snake. "Details. People are people, Camayo. If you're good to them, they respond in kind. All it would take to get rid of wars and weapons is for people to treat one another with the kindness and dignity they want for themselves."

:Mindspeech,: Camayo reminded. *:And your naiveté is charming, but dangerous.:*

Evita bristled at the notion. "Just because I believe there's good in everyone does not make me naïve! If everyone just gave peace a chance—"

Camayo breathed a horsey sigh and turned back to grazing.

Evita did not appreciate the brush-off. "Don't turn away from me, Camayo. You know it's true. If everyone just gave peace a chance, we would have nothing but peace."

Camayo lowered his head and hesitated before turning back to face his Herald-to-be. *:Do you think no one in the history of the world has ever "chosen" peace? Do you imagine that all humans but you slide out of the womb with a sword in hand and destruction at heart? Peace is the normal state of human existence. You see it every day, in every corner of the world.:*

Evita gritted her teeth. She could not believe anyone would dispute such obvious and inarguable points. "Of course, I know that. But in the places that do have war, if they only tried peace . . . "

:But isn't peace merely the absence of war?:

"Yes, but . . . "

:So unless an area has been in an unremitting state of war since the beginning of time, they must have 'tried peace.' One has to assume that, for some reason or another, peace proved ineffective.:

Evita did not appreciate the argument. She did finally realize that she had lost her grip on Mindspeech and attempted to regain it. *:It's just a turn of phrase, Camayo. You're not supposed to take it literally. I just mean that* *there are better ways people can work out their differences than by fighting about them. If weapons were not invented, if none of us ever learned how to use them . . . :*

Camayo interrupted, *: . . . the strongest, greediest men would take everything. Then others would band together, employing branches and rocks, to overcome them.:*

Evita rolled her eyes. *:You're a hopeless cynic, aren't you, Camayo?:*

:One of us,: Camayo said diplomatically, *:is not living in the real world.:*

Dreams of entrapment invaded Evita's sleep. She found herself running from one container, only to find herself hopelessly caught up in another. No matter how hard she tried to escape, she either wound up cornered, shut in, or closed up in dark, musty places that threatened to suffocate all reason. She awoke with a gasp, heart racing, warm against something furry. She smiled, petting what she initially took for Bruno. Then, her eyes snapped open to white hair and a form far more massive than any dog. Camayo lay against her, staring at her through one startlingly blue eye.

:Are you all right, Dear One?:

Remembrance came rushing back and, with it, excitement. "I'm fine. Just bad dreams." Evita leaned more fully against Camayo's warm body. "Do we have to go to Valdemar?"

:Of course, Dear One. And use Mindspeech.:

Dutifully, Evita switched. She wondered if she would ever get used to it. *:Can't we take a . . . longer route?:*

Camayo went utterly silent for so long, Evita worried he had fallen back to sleep. But, when she looked at him, the eye she could see remained wide open. *:How much time do you need, Dear One?:*

:Five years?: Evita tried.

Amusement trickled into Evita's mind. *:I was think-ing more like a week.:*

The panic of her dream assailed Evita. Her heart pounded, and she felt as if the trees crushed in on them. *:Two years.:*

:A month.:

Bartering, Evita understood. *:Half a year.:*

:One season.:

It was more than Evita had expected. She could make the most of a season, especially if it stayed as beautiful as the previous day. *:Deal.:*

Camayo added conditions. *:At the end of which, you go to the Collegium without complaint. And you attend every class and session with an open mind.:*

Evita took offense. *:No mind is more open than mine.:*

Camayo clearly snapped off an answering comment. Evita received nothing but a hint of cynical irritation that only upset her further.

"Are you suggesting I don't have an open mind? Because I pride myself on being the most open-minded person I know. I look at sides of situations that most people would never even consider."

Camayo drew his legs tighter to his hip-shot body. *:Your so-called wide open mind snapped shut faster than a trap when I mentioned weapons training.:*

"Well, that's just . . . wrong. Weapons are . . . "

:Evil?: Camayo suggested. *:Bad? So, let me make sure I understand this. As long as a person wholly condemns something with an unpleasant adjective, it's perfectly ac-ceptable to close her mind about it?:*

Evita knew she was treading on thin ice. *:As long as it's truly . . . bad.:*

:So, if I declare that horses sporting flaxen manes are bad, it's all right for me to hate them.:

"No!" Evita caught herself speaking again. *:Because horses with flaxen manes aren't actually bad.:*

:By whose standards?:

:What?:

:Who gets to decide what's actually bad?:

Evita wondered if she had condemned herself to a life of arguing with a horse. *:Everyone just knows. Flaxen manes have nothing to with good or bad. Weapons are . . . just bad.:*

:Weapons have saved the lives of many Heralds and Companions. I don't think you could find five other Heralds who agree with your statement, never mind this elusive 'everyone.'.:

:And I doubt you could find any Herald who believes that flaxen manes make a horse bad.:

Camayo nodded. *:Which brings me back to my original query. Whose definition of 'bad' takes precedence when determining whether or not we can close our minds to something?:*

Evita knew when she had lost an argument. *:Fine. I'll keep an open mind about the Collegium. Including . . . :* She could not help making a bitter face as she finished, *: weapons training.:*

:That's all I'm asking.: Camayo closed his eyes.

But I don't have to like it. Evita snuggled against Camayo's legs, using his side as a pillow. Within seconds, all discomfort from the argument left her. She found her mind suddenly at peace, as if she had spent all of her life searching for the missing piece of a puzzle that had come to her at last. She could not remember a finer pillow or a more comfortable bed. This, I could definitely get used to.

*   *   *

True to his word, Camayo kept the trip to Valdemar slow. They slogged mostly through woodlands, stopping to cavort on the open meadows or just sitting for hours staring at the sky. They splashed through creeks, chasing water birds into the sky, sending frogs leaping in all directions, driving fish into silver flashes of hurry beneath the water. Birds of every color and combination flitted through the trees, scolding them or regaling them with brilliant song and plumage. Woodland creatures appeared around every turn. Evita knew many of them, but as the terrain changed from the familiar broadleafed trees of home to squatter conifers and gnarled older-growth forests, she made delightful new discoveries as well.

As they rode, Evita became more comfortable with Camayo and his irascible nature, as well as Mindspeech. But as the month wore on, she found herself craving human contact and the sound of spoken words. She missed her parents and Bruno more than she expected, and she found a void she thought Camayo had completely filled. Her pack had become uncomfortably empty, even supplemented by the berries, stems, and roots she gathered. *:What do you say we ride through a town today?:*

Camayo hesitated, as if the thought had never previously entered his mind. *:Are you sure you're ready?:*

The question seemed nonsensical. *:Ready for what? Do you think I've never been around people before?:*

:Not astride a Companion.:

Evita could only see that as a bonus. She wanted people to see her sitting proud atop Camayo, one of the Chosen. *:Will that matter?:*

:Greatly.: Despite his obvious concern, Camayo did

not seem afraid. His voice came through strong, with just a hint of discomfort. *:There are still a few places where Heralds are mistrusted, even hated. Some would kill the Gifted on sight.:*

Evita suffered all the dread Camayo removed from his sending. *:Is this one of those places?:*

:No. Here, Heralds are loved and respected.:

Evita clutched her chest. As the fear drained away, outrage replaced it. *:Then why are you trying to scare me?:*

:I'm just preparing you for the variety of people that exist in Velgarth.:

:In their hearts, all people are the same.: Evita felt certain of it.

Camayo did not accept what seemed clear to Evita. *:Perhaps. But, in other vital organs, you will find that people vary to a great extent. How they treat you, and what they expect from you, will have far more to do with their own prior experiences than your current actions.:*

Evita nodded and tried to prepare herself. *:And what will they expect from me in the nearest villages?:*

:On schedule, Heralds pass through here only three times a year and do not stay long. They will expect wisdom and assistance.:

Evita liked the sound of that. She straightened to her full height and made a solemn vow. *:I will try my best to give that to them.:* She expected Camayo to appreciate her pronouncement, but he seemed more perplexed than satisfied.

:Very well,: the Companion finally said, *:but you need not forget. Not only have you not yet earned your Whites, you have not even received your Grays. You are not a Herald, Evita, not even, officially, a Herald-in-training.:*

:I know that,: Evita said, more crossly than she in-

tended. She could not help wondering why Camayo seemed duty-bound to point out her every shortcoming.

The village of Bonarme took up most of a large hill, with the poorer dwellings at the bottom giving way to finer cottages on the upward route and a manor house at the top. Garlock's Inn sat about midway, solid stone with a heavily thatched roof. Spotted well outside the village, Evita and her Companion found themselves escorted to the building without having made any formal inquiry. Surrounded by a swell of townsfolk and children, all talking at once, Evita saw no reason to even attempt speech.

Before Evita could decide whether or not to protest, they had separated her from Camayo and ushered her into the tavern. It contained a single large table in the exact center of the room and a wide-open kitchen where two men and a woman worked over a fireplace and several low tables. Surprised by the greeting, Evita barely managed to send a message to Camayo as she entered. *:Will you be all right out there?:*

:I'll be fine. The children seem determined to hand-feed me every blade of grass in the village.:

Evita could not help smiling. One of the villagers pulled out a seat for her. A moment after she took it, every other one at the table was suddenly full. As the single table could not seat everyone, others gathered in layers behind them. Evita tried to focus on one person at a time, as they all begged news of various homesteads, settlements, towns, and individuals.

One man finally took control. "Easy! Easy! She only has two ears."

Evita hoped they did not think she could use both separately and simultaneously.

Someone shouted, "Let Larram speak. He has the most pressing issue."

Murmurs suffused the crowd, some grumbling and some happy, but the general gist seemed to comprise agreement. A slender man with a sunburned face stepped directly to Evita's side. "My Lady Herald, we were hoping you'd adjudicate a problem for us."

Adjudicate? Evita swallowed hard. In her own village, she had heard that people sometimes saved difficult issues or decisions for Heralds to decide, but she had never actually witnessed one. "I'm not a Herald," she protested.

Everyone went silent at once. The expressions on their faces ranged from stunned to angry to disappointed. The man at her side, apparently Larram, pointed vaguely toward the door and Camayo. "You mean, that's not a . . ." He brought his finger back to Evita. "And you're not a . . ."

Evita amended quickly. "Oh, Camayo is a Companion. And I will be a Herald. When I complete my training. My name is Evita, by the way."

The conversations restarted softly. Excitement reappeared on the many faces. Larram said, "You're the closest thing we've got to a Herald for a long time. If the others agree, I'm willing to be bound by whatever you decide, ma'am."

Murmurs of agreement spread around the table. Their gazes mostly fell on a heavyset, filthy man in patched homespun standing on the outskirts. "All right," he said carefully.

Evita grinned. She could scarcely believe the esteem with which these villagers held the Heralds of Valdemar. She could imagine herself riding from town to town, thrilling the people not only with her presence but with her renowned and wise proclamations. Evita the Just, they would call her, the fairest judge in all of Velgarth, a champion of righteousness who had no equal. She would never need to wield a sword. If a basilisk attacked, her many followers would dispatch it and consider themselves lucky for the opportunity.

Plates of food began to appear, the first in front of Evita herself. After so many weeks of forest fare, she found the aroma of mashed roots and pulled pork impossible to resist. It took tremendous self-control to eat in a slow, mannerly fashion while Larram presented the facts of his case.

"You see, ma'am, my animals had been disappearing one by one over a period of time. At first, I thought it was some kind of beast, except it never left anything behind: not a bit of torn skin, not a patch of fur, not a bone or feather. Never found a single track that wasn't made by a boot or a cow, chicken, goose, or pig." Larram interrupted himself. "See, that's the kinds of animals I have. And my neighbors were noting the same thing about their animals. No fences seemed to be able to stop this thing. We started thinking it must be a monster. Then, last night, I caught the culprit red-handed."

All eyes returned to the heavy-set, filthy man on the outskirts who seemed to be trying to lose himself in the very crowd that fingered him.

In case Evita had not caught on to the obvious, Larram pointed. "I caught Stelkaw strangling one of my geese and stuffing it into a sack."

Every other person in the tavern stepped away from Stelkaw, leaving him fully open to Evita and her judgment.

Stelkaw stood alone, clearly frightened, and miserable. He kept his shaggy head low, dodging Evita's gaze. Sympathy welled up in Evita. He looked so utterly broken, a damaged image of a once-proud man. "Did you steal Larram's goose?"

Stelkaw's voice emerged thin and reedy, muffled by the hair hanging over his face. "My lady, my family was starving. I couldn't look at their hungry faces, their needy eyes, any longer. I had to do something."

Evita nearly choked on her dinner. She could imagine his scrawny, filthy children, their eyes as enormous as Camayo's and desperate with hunger. "Oh," she said softly.

A dense silence followed as Evita considered her words. No one should have to go hungry when food existed. No man should have to suffer his children begging for food, to helplessly watch them die. She cleared her throat. "From this day forth," she proclaimed into the hush, "if a man or woman needs sustenance for himself and his family, he must only ask."

Evita looked up to find the entire room staring at her. Every face appeared rapt, waiting. She stood, the remainder of her food forgotten. "If someone comes to you requesting food for his family, you must invite that family to your table and freely share whatever you are eating. Either that, or you must supply him with the same amount of foodstuffs, meat and vegetable, that you give your own family for a day."

Evita stepped up on her chair. "From now on, no one in Bonarme will ever go hungry again!" Having made her point, Evita sat back on her seat to finish her meal.

For a few moments, nothing happened. Then came a small smattering of applause that gradually grew to encompass the entire room. Riding on this wave of approval, Evita stuffed the last of her dinner in her mouth, walked out of the tavern, mounted Camayo, and rode off into the sunset.

Evita's second chance to play Herald came only two weeks later. She and Camayo huddled beneath a crude, wayside structure clearly built to shield travelers from the rain. Alone together, they listened to the hammer of rainfall on wood and thatch, defining rhythms and song from the chaos. Camayo worked with Evita to refine her Mindspeech, but he refused to assist in developing her Empathy skills because, he stated, he would not do so without the support of the Collegium and its many skilled teachers.

A flash of lightning rent the sky, outlining a small figure rushing toward their shelter. Evita pressed closer to Camayo to allow more room for the stranger to join them, which he did. Water dripped from the sodden hood of his cloak, and he dodged into the shelter, threw down his pack, and turned toward Evita. Safely beneath the ceiling, he tossed off his hood to reveal young, swarthy features, silky black hair in a snarl, and a broad-featured face. Despite being wet from head to toe, he smelled faintly of unfamiliar spices.

"Herald Evita," he said breathlessly. "I've been searching for you."

Camayo whickered. *:Tell him you're not a Herald.:*

Evita smiled at the newcomer. "My name is Evita, but I'm not a Herald. Not yet. I'm newly Chosen."

The man made a broad gesture. "That doesn't matter. We've heard what you've done for Bonarme. My people are greatly oppressed, and we want you to help us as well."

Evita's brows twitched upward. She turned to look at Camayo. *:They know what I did for Bonarme.:*

Camayo's response seemed wary. *:I've informed you that everything a Chosen does affects the entire world. That is why you must consider everything you do with utmost attention to detail.:*

:I want to help them, Camayo. They're oppressed:

Evita had grown accustomed to Camayo's oddities, his elegant speech, his cynicism, his unwillingness to accept the most obvious morality as definitely right.

:I've found,: the Companion said as slowly as Mindspeech allowed, *:that when one allows people to act wholly within their natures, they usually get exactly what they deserve.:*

Her Companion's words scandalized Evita. *:No one deserves oppression, Camayo. No one.:*

Camayo did not argue the point, though he did not concede it, either.

Evita turned her attention to the stranger. "What's your name?"

"Ahjaman," the young man said, huddling deeper into his cloak.

"I'll look away," Evita said. "While you change into something warm and dry. When the rain stops, we'll ride for ... for ... " Evita realized she had no idea where they were going. In fact, for all she knew, Camayo might have carried her to the moon. She recognized only that they had ridden far from her home and probably much nearer to Valdemar than she had ever been.

"It's called Firisain, ma'am."

"Firisain," Evita repeated. Only then, she wondered what one lone woman could do to help an entire village of the oppressed.

Ahjaman explained the situation as they rode. According to him, the citizens of Firisain had been at odds with their savage neighbors from Arran for as long as anyone could remember. Three decades earlier, the Arranis captured Firisain in a bloody war that saw many Firisainians killed. Since that time, the Arranis had oppressed the Firisainians by occupying their land, utterly disarming them, and greatly limiting their freedom. Unable to ply their trades, the Firisainians had descended into squalor. "If someone does not help us soon," Ahjaman told her, "our people will die."

Evita's heart went out to Ahjaman, but this seemed far beyond anything she could handle. She told him as they rode together on Camayo's back. "I feel for you and your people, I truly do. But I'm just one person. How can I possibly help?"

Ahjaman grabbed Evita's arm, pleading, his dark eyes brimming with pain. "The Arranis respect the Heralds of Valdemar. If you tell them to leave our land, they might. If you tell them not to oppress us, they will listen."

Evita could only nod her head and hope he spoke the truth.

Muddy and overcrowded, Firisain was a tent city filled with the stench of urine, vomit, and feces. Women carried enormous burdens, their backs bent, their limbs marked with burns and bruises, their faces filled with anguish. Children walked around the puddles; they did not run and squeal like those of Bonarme or her own hometown. The men huddled in a group around a roaring fire, caught up in discussion. Ahjaman dismounted and pointed westward. "You see, Evita? You see the Arrani pigs." He spat into the mud. "They treat us like animals. They stand there in their fancy uniforms with their weapons and keep us from crossing the border."

Evita looked in the indicated direction. A row of young men and women stood attentively at a border that could not have been more striking. Grass grew lush beneath their feet, and beyond them stood neat rows of cottages that might have looked welcoming if not for the grim stone walls around them.

Camayo picked his way carefully through the mud, but his white legs still bore a series of brown stripes and his silver hooves turned black with grime. Cautiously, they approached one of the Arrani guards who met them with a friendly smile. "Are you a Herald, ma'am? It's the first I've seen one dressed in normal garb."

"I'm Chosen but not yet a Herald," Evita explained for what seemed like the twentieth time. "My name's Evita. May I speak with someone in charge?"

The woman gave Evita a formal nod. "Wait right here, and I'll fetch Captain Fasson." She hurried off, leaving Evita to marvel over the drastic differences between the villages. She had never seen such a stark and sudden contrast. Even riverbanks did not form such an intense and severe division between land and water. An infant could not miss the boundary between Firisain and Arran: on one side, a thriving paradise; on the other nothing more substantial than rubbish. The obvious disparity upset Evita, so obviously and blatantly unfair.

The female soldier returned with a middle-aged man astride a chestnut mare. As she stepped back into her position, the captain took over her duties as host. "I'm Captain Fasson, and I understand you're a Herald-in-training called Evita."

:In training to be in-training,:, Camayo grumbled, but Evita saw no reason to relay that information. She had made the significant point that she had not yet earned the Herald title. "Yes, sir," Evita said simply. "I was asked to talk to you about Firisain."

"Welcome to Arran." Captain Fasson gestured past the border. "Would you like to come see it?"

Evita considered. Her stomach clamored for another village-cooked meal, and the layout of Arran did look inviting. She glanced over her shoulder. The abject ugliness of Firisain filled her vision and reminded her of her objective. Worried that the Arranis might sway her mind with comforts, she shook her head. "I'd like to speak here."

Captain Fasson merely shrugged. "Very well, my lady." He took Evita and Camayo to a small building just over the boundary. Dismounting, he opened the door and gestured Evita inside.

:Will you be all right?:

:I'm fine,: Camayo assured her. *:It's you I'm worried about.:*

The words squeezed Evita's chest like a fist. *:Do you think he might hurt me?:*

:No, I'm worried you might hurt him.:

The words made no sense, but Evita had little time to ponder them as her hesitation left the captain standing awkwardly with the door in hand. Swiftly, she climbed off of Camayo and headed through the opening.

The building consisted of a single room. Barrels of provisions lay stacked around a single long table stained with bowl-rings and splotches of soaked-in drinks. Fasson took a seat at the table and gestured for Evita to do the same. She accepted the one directly across from him and studied his features. Lines scored his brow and the area around his mouth. Dark bags settled beneath hard, hazel eyes that seemed to hold a wisdom she could not yet fathom. He gave her a promising smile. "What can we do for you, Evita?"

Evita cleared her throat, uncertain where to start. "It

has come to my attention that Arran oppresses the citizens of Firisain."

Fasson sat back wordlessly. He rolled his tongue around his mouth, as if to taste as well as reconcile Evita's accusation. "Many Firisainians live and work in Arran, as appreciated and productive citizens with the full rights of any Arrani. Only those who incite violence, those who demand that we must die, those who drag weapons into our village and use them against us are barred."

"They say you do not allow them to leave their village."

"We prevent them only from entering Arran. And only those who wish us harm."

"They say you took their village in war."

Captain Fasson nodded. "That's true, but they initiated the war by attacking Arran with the intention of wiping us out and taking our village." He smiled. "We won that war and took their village instead."

That news surprised Evita, but she still saw a great disparity that needed fixing. "Captain, you've taken everything from them. Of course they hate you. How do you expect them to live on what remains?"

The captain's expression turned cold. "They hated us long before we took their village in a war they started. Had they won, they would not have allowed us to live in any fashion whatsoever. They boldly state that they would have slaughtered even our infants and children. They would do so now if they could."

Evita found it difficult to reconcile the two sides. "It's thirty years since the war, Captain. Why must you punish the children of the combatants? Why do you make them live like this?"

"Make them?" Fasson rose. "Make them! They choose

to live as they do. They treat their women like slaves and make no attempt to better themselves. They live like animals because they fester in their own hatred, blaming us for all their weaknesses. They raise their children in foolish ignorance, teaching them only that we must all die. They wallow in their own filth. Any money that comes into their hands, they spend on weapons to raise against us. When we disarm them, they rage against our theft and cruelty. They do nothing to make their own lives better, only disparage ours."

Evita pointed out the obvious. "You are occupying their country."

Captain Fasson could not deny it. "For the sole purpose of keeping our people safe. We don't want their country; it is a burden to us. We ask nothing from them but to leave us in peace."

Evita sighed. At least now, she could see both sides. "You have everything; they have nothing. It's up to you to fix this problem."

"Fix it." Captain Fasson heaved a bitter laugh. "How would you have us fix it?"

Evita believed she had the answers. "First, you give them back their village and all title to it."

The captain cocked his head.

Encouraged that he seemed willing to listen, Evita continued. "You allow them to come and go as they please, treating them as equal humans."

Fasson remained in position, listening so intently he even seemed to have stopped breathing.

"You give them the money it takes to rebuild their village and teach them how to live as civilized people. Once you start treating them as decent beings, they will behave like decent beings."

Needing some feedback, Evita paused. The captain

seemed to be waiting for her to finish. As such, a long silence ensued, which Fasson finally broke.

"And in return? What do we get for giving up our land, our security, our money, and our resources?"

Evita had not thought of the situation in that light. "You get the satisfaction of knowing you helped out a hapless group of people."

The captain made a wordless noise. "Satisfaction doesn't keep our families safe. Do you think we like babysitting a vile village of barbarians? Don't you think we would rather keep our young men and women at home learning trades rather than serving time on the border? Surely, you realize that we wish we had kind, civilized neighbors with whom we could trade recipes and goods rather than swords and spears." He shook his head broadly. "To go along with this, we would need a guarantee of peace."

"That . . . " Evita started even as she considered her response. " . . . seems infinitely reasonable." Her heart pounded with excitement. She could truly make a difference, could actually show Camayo what could happen when two sworn enemies actually did give peace a chance.

"Bring me a leader of the Firisainians," Captain Fasson said. "We will make the concessions you ask for nothing more than a signed and sworn statement of peace. That's all we've ever wanted."

Evita rose, fairly tripping over herself to get to the door. "I'll bring one here at once, Captain." She opened the door herself and headed out into the field.

Captain Fasson's words chased her, "With the power of Valdemar behind us, we know we're safe. And if the peace is breached, you will stand behind us."

Buoyed by excitement, Evita ran toward Ahjaman.

*   *   *

For six days, Evita rode the joy of her accomplishment. The sky seemed bluer, the clouds puffier, the foliage more brilliant than an entire pile of jade. Perfumed with flowers, the air tickled her nostrils, making every breath a pleasure. She had worked past all the soreness, and riding Camayo became comfortable as well.

On the seventh day, Evita realized that she had become so engrossed in her successes that she had barely noticed Camayo's lengthening silences. Only then, she thought to ask, *:Are you angry with me?:*

Camayo shook his horsy head. *:Not angry, Dear One. Just disappointed.:*

:Disappointed?: Evita could scarcely believe it. She had worked the negotiations like a professional, getting two warring nations not only to speak, but to normalize their relationships. *:Those two have hated one another for thirty years. Thirty years. And, now, they will coexist peacefully, side by side.:*

:You have that backwards, Dear One.:

Evita could make no sense of the words. *:What do you mean, Camayo? What's backwards?:*

:For only the last thirty years, only since Arran conquered Firisain have they had peace. Prior to that time, they warred for centuries, maybe longer. It was the avowed express purpose of Firisain to slaughter every person of Arrani descent, and they attempted to do so at every opportunity.:

Evita did not see the significance of that information. *:But this time the Firisainians agreed to peace. They signed a paper—:*

:A technicality, Dear One. To get the Arranis off their land. For money, and for power, they signed a nebulous pledge for peace. So they will not lead a village-wide

offensive sanctioned by its leaders. People killed by so-called spontaneous acts of violence are just as dead.:

Evita still did not follow the logic. *:Camayo, the Ar-ranis signed as well. If they didn't think the leaders of Firisain could control their people, why did they agree?:*

Camayo had an answer for that as well. *:Because the Arranis are so desperate for peace, they would do any-thing for it. And they convinced themselves that you had the power of Valdemar behind you.:*

And I did not disabuse them of the notion. Guilt as-sailed Evita, and she found herself so struck with diz-ziness she sank to the ground. *:Camayo, are you sure?:*

:I wasn't,: the Companion sent. *:Until I saw them.:* He tipped his head suddenly toward a distant hill.

Evita craned her neck. Nevertheless, it took several moments before the scene came into view. Riding at full gallop over the rise came a dozen ghostly figures. They rode in perfect symmetry, the riders bedecked in white moving in rhythm to milky steeds. They moved with such grace and confidence, Evita could do nothing more than stare. *:Heralds.:*

:Heralds,: Camayo confirmed. *:And not due in these parts for months.:*

Real Heralds. They took Evita's breath away. She could only stare as they grew larger in the distance, so regal, so strong, so obviously in command. They moved in unison with their mounts, like human and shadow, bonded more powerfully than any human relation-ship could define. The mantle of Evita's competence fell away to reveal nothing beneath it. She felt as if she was awakening from a long, strange dream. What have I done?

Evita grabbed Camayo. *:It's my fault they're here? Isn't it?:* She moved into the shadows. If she had to face those Heralds, she would die from humiliation and embarrassment. If those did not kill her, she would take her life with her own hand.

Apparently, Camayo could Mindspeak over a bit of distance, because he came back to her with an answer he could only have learned from the Heralds or, more likely, their Companions. *:Firisainians infiltrated an Arrani birthday party. They slaughtered everyone, including twenty children. The Arranis are fighting to regain control.:*

Horror froze Evita, already sitting on the ground. The world had always seemed so simple; Evita thought she had all the answers. If people only treated one another with respect, with tolerance, they could all live in the same immense utopia. Tears streamed down Evita's face. Her body lost all of its tone, and she collapsed into a heap.

Camayo caught her against his body, cradling her head against his warm, furry side.

:I might just as well have murdered those children with my own hands.: Evita could not live with that knowledge. Had she a bit of strength left, she would have cast herself from the highest mountain.

:No, Dear One. No.: Camayo would not accept those words. *:I Chose you, and the Companions of Valdemar do not make mistakes. I saw in you great potential. I see it still. I only had to find a way to break down that wall you built with the bricks of good intentions and the mortar of ignorance.:*

Evita could only sob. She could imagine only the shining, gentle faces of those children, the potential she had stolen from them and from the world. She gritted her teeth so hard that pain shot through her cheeks, and her jaw felt as if it might snap from the pressure. *:I killed them.:*

:*No, the Firisainians killed them. And many more like them.*:

:*I flung open the door and invited murderers in.*:

:*As many optimists have done before you.*: Camayo nuzzled the back of Evita's neck. :*The fault is mine, Dear One, not yours. The blood is on my hooves. It was my job, my obligation, to bring you directly to Valdemar.*:

:*I wouldn't let you.*:

:*You could not have stopped me. Many Companions have carried their Chosen directly to Valdemar, kicking and screaming all the way.*: He huddled closer, until Evita felt almost squashed by his great love and presence. :*But I knew you needed more. A mug of ice water in the face, perhaps. A sword flat to the back of the head. A massive dose of reality before you would open your mind to the Collegium.*:

Evita could scarcely believe what she was hearing. :*So you encouraged me to . . . to murder twenty children.*:

Evita could feel Camayo cringing against her. He clearly felt as bad about the situation as she did. :*I expected the Firisainians to cause mayhem. I did not anticipate they would slaughter children.*:

A fresh round of tears stung Evita's eyes.

:*Companions make mistakes, too. And we suffer from them as well.*:

It suddenly occurred to Evita that Camayo needed her as much as she needed him. She managed to raise an arm and flop it around him. :*I want to die,*: she said. :*Take me home and Choose another. I clearly can't handle the responsibilities.*:

Concern seeped through the contact. :*Not yet. But, once you're trained, you will. Evita, you're stronger than you think. And while you need to temper your compassion with knowledge, it will serve all of us well for all the*

*many years of your life to come. You're exactly the type
of companion I needed. And, once trained, you will make
a fine Herald:*

Evita could barely contemplate the past. A moment
ago, she would not have believed she had a future. *:I
don't deserve to live, let alone be rewarded for the evil I've
done. Please, Camayo. Just let me go.:* The bare suggestion pained her nearly as much as her previous thoughts.
She had not known Camayo long, but he had already
become an integral part of her. Losing him would be
like amputating half her body and all the limbs and organs that entailed.

Camayo nudged Evita so hard, she toppled like a rag
doll. *:Suicide is not the answer, Dear One. Nor depriving
yourself or the world of a Herald. There is only one way
to atone for this.:*

Evita had to know. She could not go on much longer
with the guilt of those young lives on her conscience.
:How?:

*:To suffer it for eternity. To give all of yourself to every
class, to every situation and remember the reason why.
To become the best Herald you can and know that every
decision you make reflects not only on you, but on me, on
every Herald and Companion, on Valdemar itself. To use
this mistake, and every one you make, to better the world.:*

Evita had never loved anyone as much as Camayo at
that moment. She wondered if every situation she faced,
if everything she did, could ever come close to the value
of those twenty lives lost. Nevertheless, a new sense of
purpose filled her. She would do as Camayo said, throw
her entire being into the knowledge, the classes, the
learning, to glean every detail Collegium could furnish
and become the most devoted and competent Herald
ever to grace Valdemar.

With purpose came strength. Evita clambered to her feet and looked off toward Arran and Firisain. *:Can we help them?:*

Camayo also stood, shaking his head until his reins and bridle snapped in the wind. *:Let the trained Heralds sort them out. That will give us a head start to Valdemar.:*

Evita supposed they would need one. She had no idea how the Collegium would punish her, but she felt certain they would do so. Both she and Camayo deserved it. She also realized that they needed it. Without some disciplinary action for their crime, they would have to live with the burden of shame and responsibility forever. She would rather die than live a life running from the guilt. She suddenly understood why people sometimes turned to drink to escape something horrible they had done. Fuzzy minds did not have to deal with reality. That realization triggered something else. "Stelkaw and Larram."

Camayo looked at Evita, and she thought she saw a deep hope, bordering on excitement, in the one eye he focused directly upon her. *:What about them, Dear One?:*

Evita cringed. She had thought herself compassionate in her decision at Bonarme; and yet, she had left Stelkaw fully unpunished for his theft. In fact, she had rewarded it. *:Is it too much to hope that Larram became a more charitable man? That, overwhelmed by his neighbor's generosity, Stelkaw became a hardworking father who now shelters those less fortunate?:*

Camayo lowered his head, his fine neck sagging. *:Do you really want to know?:*

:I have to.: Evita realized it was true. She did not know where Camayo got his information, but she trusted it and him.

Camayo sighed. *:The more well-to-do in Bonarme became besieged by clamoring hordes of poorer neighbors demanding daily handouts. Soon, they had little left for themselves or those who came to them for sustenance. Since they gave their animals and crops to the likes of Stelkaw, they had no money left for the causes they had previously championed, such as the orphanage and local widows. With their charities no longer chosen from the goodness of their hearts, but forced upon them, they came to despise giving. Those who never liked work saw no reason to continue, instead getting their sustenance from those who still had money for as long as they still . . . had money.:*

Evita groaned.

:Those still willing to work became so burdened by those who saw no reason to do so when others were mandated to feed them, that they left Bonarme. Currently, no one remains but Stelkaw and the other beggars.:

Evita did not know what to say. At least, her decision had not killed anyone in Bonarme as it had in Arran. *:So . . . what can I do to fix that mistake?:*

Camayo shook his head, repeating the exact words he had used earlier. *:I've found that when one allows people to act wholly within their natures, they usually get exactly what they deserve.:*

This time, Evita allowed herself to explore Camayo's meaning. *:You're saying to leave them alone. In new places, they're no longer bound by my words. Those willing to work hard will regain their fortunes and restore their faith in charity.:* Evita thought she had it. *:While those who prefer to gripe, whine, and steal rather than try will find the same low place in society no matter how much we give them.:*

:You're learning already.:

Evita winced, not liking the direction the world seemed determined to take her. :*So there's no place for compassion? No room for assistance? Are you saying those things make no difference?*:

Camayo snorted. :*Even the most brutish don't believe that. Compassion, charity, aid. Some of the most wonderful concepts in all the world; but, like all things, knowing when and how to use them is the key.*:

:*The Collegium will teach me . . . that?*:

:*Not directly, perhaps, but you will learn it. And so much more.*:

What she once dreaded, Evita could scarcely wait to start. :*What are you waiting for, Camayo? On to Valdemar!*: She clambered onto his back.

Camayo broke into a ground-swallowing gallop. They could not possibly arrive too soon.

A Charm of Finches

Elisabeth Waters

Maia was working in the mews of the Temple of The-noth, the Lord of the Beasts. The birds were all out in the weathering yard, which gave her the chance to make some improvements to their quarters. She had been a fletcher before coming to Haven, and she had Animal Mindspeech as well, so she was familiar with birds, although she was more accustomed to wild birds than tame ones. In fact, when she had moved to the city of Haven, some of the wild crows from home had chosen to come with her and Dexter, her raccoon friend.

But even a tame bird could become incoherent if badly upset, and something had upset the owner of the new voice she suddenly heard in her head. :*No!... sharp...hard...hurt!*: Maia set down her tools and headed toward the voice, meeting the novice who had been sent to fetch her on the way.

He led her to the infirmary, where Sara, a young Healer Trainee, was attempting to hold a finch in place so she could Heal it. Maia couldn't see the full extent of its injuries from the doorway, but she could see a miniature dagger stuck in one wing. The bird, which was a combination of colors (gold, purple, red, and blue) not commonly found together in nature, thrashed about mindlessly, and the confusion was made worse by a girl of about ten who was sobbing hysterically. She was being restrained by a man who was probably her brother; the resemblance was strong, but he didn't look old enough to be her father. He also looked extremely annoyed.

"Maia!" Sara looked up in relief. "Can you get through to the bird? I can't do anything to help it if it won't hold still!"

"May I suggest that we start by clearing the room?"

The young man scowled at Maia. "I'm not leaving without my dagger."

"You'll get it back much faster if you wait for it outside," Maia said calmly. "The sooner the room is quiet, the sooner we can remove it from the bird's wing."

He promptly left, dragging his sister with him. By the hair.

Once the door had been closed and the girl's crying was at least muffled, Maia moved to stand at the shoulder of the Healer Trainee and mentally reached out to the bird. *:Be still, little one.:* The bird stopped thrashing, looked at her, and cocked its head, obviously trying to puzzle out what sort of bird Maia was. She held the link with it while Sara removed the dagger and worked her Gift on the wing. Now that the bird had stopped fighting, it didn't take long.

"All done," Sara said with relief, placing the bird gently in a cage at the side of the room. "It was a lucky hit—"

"It must have been well-nigh miraculous to hit a moving target that small!"

"No, I meant lucky from the bird's point of view. It didn't hit anything vital, nothing broke, and the wing should heal cleanly with no loss of flying ability."

"That's good news." Maia picked up the dagger and studied its jeweled hilt, frowning. "I'll return this to its owner, shall I?"

Sara sighed. "I wish I could confiscate it."

"I sympathize, but I don't think you have grounds for that," Maia pointed out. "But we can keep the bird, at least for a while, if you express enough concern for its recovery."

That got a grim nod in reply. "That, I can do."

Maia opened the door and the two of them went out into the courtyard, where the girl sat on a bench, sobbing quietly, while her brother paced impatiently.

"Here you are," she said, handing him the dagger. He took it without so much as a word of thanks. "I was wondering," Maia asked, "what do you use that for? It seems too small for any practical use."

"You're wrong," he said flatly. "It's a cloak pin."

"Oh." *That would explain why it's so sharp.*

The girl joined them then, asking anxiously, "Is Aurelia all right?"

Sara smiled gently at the child. "I believe that she will be, but she will need to need to stay here for a while until her wing heals."

"But I want to take her home now!"

"Be quiet, Lena." Her brother sounded more bored than annoyed now. "Nobody cares what you want, and it's not as though you don't have four more of the stupid things at home."

"But she'll be lonely," Lena protested.

"She's resting now," Sara said encouragingly, "and she'll heal more quickly here under the Peace of the God. We'll take very good care of her, and you can visit whenever your parents allow."

"My parents are dead," Lena said bleakly. "He's my

guardian." She indicated her brother with a slight jerk of her head.

"I'm so sorry," Sara said, then hastily added, "about your parents."

"She can visit here at any reasonable hour," her brother said, "as long as her governess accompanies her."

Sara nodded in acknowledgment, and the brother and sister left without further argument—or any word of thanks. Both girls looked after them, and Sara shivered. "He reminds me of a snake," she said with distaste.

"No," Maia shook her head. "A snake will curl up next to you in search of warmth. That man is so cold I don't think he cares about warmth."

Lena was back early the next morning; Maia found her huddled in the courtyard when she came outside. To her surprise, Dexter was curled up in the girl's lap, allowing her to pet him.

"Where is your governess?" Maia asked, hoping the child hadn't been wandering around the streets by herself. This was a fairly good neighborhood, but even so . . . She sent a mental call to a crow perched on top of the wall surrounding the temple, asking if he and his flock would be willing to keep an eye on Lena. A few crows diving in to attack could deter nearly any would-be attacker.

"She's in bed with my brother." At Maia's horrified gasp, Lena quickly added, "it's not her fault. She doesn't even like him, but if she doesn't do what Markus wants, he says he'll dismiss her without a character. And he'll do it, too. I told the cook where I was going, so somebody will tell her when they get a chance."

"I hope your brother doesn't miss you," Maia said. "I

don't think that would be good for either your or your governess."

"You're keeping Aurelia because you don't think I took good care of her, aren't you?"

"She really does need time to heal," Maia said, heading toward the infirmary. Lena fell in at her side, carrying Dexter cradled in her arms. "But the Healer and I did wonder how she came to have your brother's cloak pin stuck in her wing."

Lena looked stricken. "I wish I knew," she replied. "I wasn't in the room when it happened. It was just my brother and his friends; I went in when I heard the birds screaming. Aurelia was pinned to the wall, and the rest of them were all out of their cage and flying around near the ceiling." She shuddered. "It was horrible—and a couple of my brother's friends had daggers in their hands. I don't like his friends."

Maia decided that as soon as Lena left she was going to see if she could find out from the bird what had actually happened. Home didn't sound like a safe place for the bird—or the child either.

When Maia finally got a chance to communicate with the bird, she discovered that home was not only unsafe, it was very, very strange. She *had* thought that she'd seen the worst of big brothers—hers had been executed with the rest of his group of bandits after they attacked a Herald and her Companion—but Lena's brother was . . . well, Maia couldn't find the right words to describe him. Of course, the finch couldn't either, but it did give her a good view of what happened before its injury.

A group of young men lounged around the parlor, drinking to excess and making jokes—Maia thought they must be jokes, because the men were laughing at them, but they made no sense to her.

"To the Brotherhood of the Bereaved—long may it flourish!"

"To long, drawn-out funerals!"

"To devoted servants who attend them along with the entire family!"

Each seemingly meaningless utterance got another round of drinks to accompany it, and each one appeared to be funnier to the men making the toasts, even as the voices making them became so slurred that Maia couldn't understand what they were saying.

Two of the young men either fell asleep or passed out. Markus and the two others who were still conscious looked at them in disgust.

"We need priests who can hold their liquor," Markus remarked.

"I'm bored!" one of the others said petulantly.

"Me, too, Lars." The other one looked around the room in search of diversion. "How about a hunt?" His eyes lit on the birds, and both Maia and Aurelia shuddered as he came toward them, opened the cage, and pulled them out. He continued to reach into the cage until he had all of the birds loose, and then he walked over to where Markus's cloak lay over the back of a chair. He pulled out the cloak pin and held it up. "I'll wager ten gold pieces that I can hit one of the birds with this."

"Nah," said Lars. "It's too small, Algott. I'll bet I can hit one with my dagger before you can hit anything with that!" He pulled out a dagger and stood poised to throw it.

Algott threw the cloak pin, and it pinned Aurelia to the wall by her wing. Maia was nearly blinded by the

pain and the shock, but she was fairly certain that, with
the cloak pin out of play, Algott pulled his dagger. She
thought he said something about another wager, but
the rest of the birds were screaming, and then Lena
was there and she was screaming too, and there was a
woman who detached Aurelia from the wall with gentle
hands and put her into a box . . .

Maia pulled her mind free from Aurelia's memories.
"We'll keep you here as long as we can," she promised
the bird.

Between them, Sara and Maia managed to keep the bird
for three weeks. Lena came to visit every day, accompanied by her governess. Her brother did not return, for
which Maia privately thanked every god she had ever
heard of. She also prayed that Thenoth would keep
Markus far away from His temple.

Meanwhile, the crows that Maia had asked to watch
out for Lena had exceeded both her instructions and
her expectations. They seemed to like Lena, but, in addition to watching her, they also watched Markus. Not
because they liked him—but because they disliked and
distrusted him. By the time Aurelia was healed enough
to return home, Maia knew what the toasts the bird had
heard the day she was injured were about.

In an extremely successful endeavor to supplement
his inheritance, Markus had started his own religion and
recruited a few of his friends to be "priests"—in return
for a share of the income, of course.

The Brotherhood of the Bereaved took "offerings"
in return for promises to say prayers for the deceased.
The reason they were fond of long funerals attended by
servants as well as family was that it gave them a chance
to search the house while everyone was out. They didn't

steal anything—usually—but they looked for evidence of how much money the mourners had so that they could suggest the maximum possible amount for the "offerings."

The other thing they looked for was blackmail material, and one of the few exceptions to their "don't take anything that will be missed" policy came when Markus stole the diary of a young woman who was now, thanks to the deaths of the remainder of her family, a considerable heiress. The diary told, in unfortunate detail, of her feelings for a young man she shared math classes with at the Collegium. Both of them were Blues—students who were not future Heralds, Healers, or Bards. She had been taking classes because her family lived in Haven and was in attendance at Court year-round, while he was studying to be an artisan. Markus, of course, ignored what this said about the young man's intelligence and determination and concentrated on the fact that he was not of noble birth.

By the time Markus had spent a few weeks paying "condolence" visits, the poor girl was convinced that the artisan didn't love her, was in love with someone else, and would find her feelings for him hilarious and would ridicule her to all their classmates. Having completed step one, Markus moved on to step two, and now he was betrothed to a girl who would make him three times as rich as he already was. He was also pushing for an early wedding, while the girl desperately tried to stall on the grounds that she was in mourning.

Maia was sufficiently dismayed by the situation that she spoke to her first friend from Haven. Although Clyton was not, as Maia had first thought when she saw him, a horse, her Gift of Animal Mindspeech worked with him. Both of them had strong "voices" and were located near each other—the Temple of Thenoth being in the next circle of the city down from the Palace and the Collegium—so she didn't have to leave the temple to talk to him. Given the fact that he was both male and not susceptible to blackmail, he wasn't as sympathetic to the girl's plight as Maia was, but he must have spoken with his Chosen, because the next day Samira came to visit the temple.

She didn't look like a Herald; instead of her Whites, she was dressed in the sort of clothing a moderately prosperous storekeeper might wear, and she carried a kitten in a basket.

"If anyone asks you," she told Maia, once they were sitting together in a corner of the courtyard, "I brought the kitten because he hurt his paw."

"How?" Maia asked.

"He's not really hurt," Samira said, as if Maia were missing the point.

"I know he's not hurt," Maia replied, "but we should keep our stories straight. Did he get it caught in a door?"

"That will do," Samira nodded. "Clyton says that you're upset about something, but he doesn't seem to understand why."

Maia poured out the whole story, from the bird injured by drunken idiots to the made-up religion to the theft and the blackmail. "There's got to be something we can do!" she finished indignantly. "It's just *wrong*!"

"We can't do anything about the blackmail unless the girl is willing to file a complaint. Do you think she's up to that?"

Maia shook her head emphatically. "She's just lost her entire family, and I suspect that she was the scared-of-her-own-shadow type even before that."

"Unfortunately, it doesn't matter if they made up

their religion to make money for themselves," Samira said. "Remember, 'there is no one way'—people in Valdemar are free to worship as they choose."

"But it's not a real religion," Maia protested. "If they believed in *any* sort of god, they wouldn't dare make such a mockery of faith! Not to mention their total lack of concern for people's feelings—how would their patrons feel if they found out they're not saying prayers for their deceased loved ones?"

Samira's gaze was suddenly intent. "Say that again."

"That they don't care about anyone's feelings?" Maia asked in confusion.

"No, the part about not saying the prayers they've been paid to say." Samira looked at her in triumph. "*That* we can do something about. For them to take money and fail to perform the service they took the money for is fraud—and *that's* illegal."

"We'd still have to prove it," Maia pointed out. "I could testify that they're spending all night drinking in the parlor until they pass out—assuming that a court is going to let me swear on the basis of what I'm getting from a charm of finches . . . "

"A charm of finches?" Samira laughed. "Is that really what a group of finches is called?"

"Yes, really," Maia said. "After you told me that a group of crows is either a murder of crows or a storytelling of crows, I started keeping a list of the strange things that groups of animals are called. But does a court accept witness through Animal Mindspeech?"

"We don't need it," Samira said. "If they're questioned under Truth Spell it will be obvious they're not doing the rituals. But we need someone to pay them to do the rituals, and that's hard to ask of anyone who has been recently bereaved."

:Maia could do it.: Clyton's voice sounded in both their heads.

"But I'm not bereaved—" Maia started to protest, and then remembered that, technically, she was. "Oh, that's right. My brother did die less than a half-year ago, and while I don't *feel* particularly grieved by the death of an abusive brother who ran a group of bandits, tried to kill both of you, and was executed for it, I could certainly pay for prayers for him. I can simply say that my brother died, which is true, and that I feel that he needs praying for, which is equally true." She looked down at her hands which had clasped themselves tightly in her lap. "I've been selfish," she added softly. "I've been so happy here in Haven, and my life is so much better than it was while he was alive. I should at least have prayers said for him—by a real priest. However wicked he was, he was still my brother."

"You can have all the prayers said for him that you like," Samira said. "I'll even arrange for some. My religion tells us to forgive our enemies. Besides, I gained you as a friend out of his attempt to kill me."

"There's one problem with my going to Markus and paying him to pray for my brother," Maia pointed out. "He's seen me."

"How many times?"

"Just once, I think. The day that his sister first brought her bird to the temple for healing."

"And you think he paid enough attention to you to remember what you look like?" Samira laughed. "The way you dress when you're working at the temple, I'd be surprised if he noticed you were female. He won't remember you because he probably didn't notice you in the first place. Unless he thought you would be useful to him, he wouldn't have really looked at you."

"You said 'probably'—can we really afford to risk it? Especially if I'm the only one who can do this?"

"We've got a Herald Trainee who comes from a family of Players," Samira said. "We'll dress you up, fix your hair, and he and I will teach you how to act highborn. Then we'll bring you to court and let you encounter Markus and his so-called religion."

Maia was a quick study, and Robin, the Herald Trainee, and Samira were good tutors—and Samira actually was highborn, a fact which Maia had not known before. Samira persuaded one of her cousins to sponsor Maia at Court, and two weeks later, Markus encountered her at a musical evening. She was dressed in black, complete with a light veil, and sitting on the sidelines. A lady in mourning could listen to music, but not dance. So when he asked her to dance, she politely refused on the grounds of the recent death of her brother. Markus promptly declared he would sit out the dance in her company, seated himself in the next chair, stared into her eyes—as best he could through the veil—as if he found her fascinating, and then proceeded to talk about himself.

:Typical of the type,: a disgusted voice sounded in her head.

:Clyton? Why are you listening in?: Maia was careful to keep her face blank and her eyes on Markus.

:It's just a precaution,: Clyton replied. *:Samira wouldn't like it if anything happened to you, and she can't link to you.:*

He fell silent after that, but Maia could feel his presence. She found it rather comforting, especially since further contact with Markus was bearing out her initial impression that snakes had warmer personalities.

But now he was touching on the subject that interested her. "Have you had prayers said for your brother?" he asked.

Maia lowered her head as if in shame and tried to blush, although she couldn't tell if she was successful or not. "I mean to," she said softly, "but I haven't yet. His death was so sudden and such a shock, and then I was ill for a time ..." She let her voice trail off hoping that she sounded feeble and not too bright.

"Perhaps other members of your family—or his friends—had prayers said for him."

"He and I were all that was left of our family," Maia murmured, "and his friends were— um, they died at the same time he did. I'm afraid that my brother was not a very *good* man," she added earnestly, "so he could use prayers."

Markus picked up his cue and told her all—well, all he wanted her to know—about the Brotherhood of the Bereaved.

She looked up at Markus from under her lashes. "Could you and your Brotherhood say prayers for my brother? It would be such a comfort to me."

"Of course we could," Markus said promptly. "I would be happy to comfort you." He paused and continued with feigned awkwardness. "There are expenses: candles, incense, that sort of thing."

"I would be happy to make an offering to cover the cost of supplies in return for your prayers." Maia said. "I'll send a servant with the money tomorrow. Can you pray for him tomorrow night? I feel horrible for having left it so long ...."

"Tomorrow night," Markus said in the tones of a solemn promise. "It is a dreadful thing to lose your last family member, especially when it is sudden and you have had no time to become accustomed to the idea. Was it a sudden illness? An accident?"

"No." Maia turned her head, as if something across the room had caught her attention, and spoke in an absent-minded voice. "He fell in with a group of bandits, and they were all executed."

Out of the corner of her eye, she caught his quickly hidden smile of satisfaction. *:Do you think he'll try to blackmail me with that?:* she asked Clyton.

:Does it snow in Sorrows in the winter?:

Maia had grown up at the edge of the Forest of Sorrows, where they had been snowed-in at least one each winter. Fortunately she managed to get her handkerchief in front of her face in time to make her choking appear to be sobs of grief, rather than hoots of laughter.

The next day she sent Robin, dressed as a page for the occasion, to Markus' house with the promised offering and a note, reminding Markus of his promise to say prayers for her brother than night. The note was dated, both Samira and Robin read it before Robin left, and Maia kept a copy.

One of the crows followed Robin, and when Markus went out immediately after Robin left, the crow followed Markus. Maia remained in her room watching through the crow's eyes as Markus moved about town. She noted that he was spending his time going from tavern to tavern with his friends, rather than entering any shop that might sell either candles or incense.

Of course, that's not proof, she reminded herself. *He could have a supply at home.*

But when he and his friends wove their way back to his house and continued their drinking in the drawing room, she could watch his every move along with the finches. The nearest anyone came to a prayer—before they all passed out—was "Gods, this is good brandy"—as if, she thought, they were sober enough to tell brandy from dishwater.

She saw Markus at court the next night and asked if he had said the prayers for her brother.

"Of course," he replied superciliously, as if insulted that she would even ask.

"That's not true," she said. "I may not be Gifted enough to do anything important, but I do have enough of a Gift to know that you are lying to me."

He gripped her forearms hard enough to leave bruises. "You are not going to say that to anyone," he whispered harshly, "and you are going to continue to make offerings for prayers for your brother."

"Why would I do that if you're not saying the prayers I'm giving you money for?"

"Because if you don't, I'll tell everyone that your brother was executed as a bandit."

:What a surprise.: Clyton's voice in her head was sardonic in the extreme.

:I'm shocked, simply shocked,: she replied in a similar tone.

"Do we have an understanding?" Markus snapped.

"I understand," Maia replied. *But I don't think you do.*

Pretending to be upset, she fled the room and went out into the gardens. From there it was a simple matter to disappear into the Companions' Field, where Robin and Samira were waiting with Clyton and Robin's Companion.

"One good thing about wearing mourning," Maia remarked, "it makes it fairly simple to vanish into dark shrubbery." She tossed back her veil and grinned at Samira. "Sort of the opposite of your Whites."

"Whites are useful if you want to vanish into a crowd of Heralds," Robin quipped.

"Wait until you have to try to keep them clean," Samira advised him. "Clyton told us what happened. Are you all right?"

"I'll have bruises on my forearms tomorrow," Maia said, "but other than that, I'm fine."

"Will you really?" Samira and Robin exchanged glances.

Maia shoved back her left sleeve. "See? The skin's bruising already."

"So it is," Samira said, bending her head to inspect it.

"You don't have to sound so delighted."

"It's not that you were injured," Samira said, "I'm delighted that we've got visible evidence. Of course, this means we'll have to get this on the docket for tomorrow's court."

"Can we get a case heard that quickly?" Maia asked.

"Not in the City Courts," Robin said, "and the Court of Justice would be iffy—"

"And do you think that Markus would be willing to present himself before either of them?" Samira said, mocking the snobbish tones of the worst of the highborn.

"Not unless you dragged him by the hair," Maia said. "So what do you have in mind?"

"The Royal Court," Samira said. "Markus is already appearing there tomorrow."

"He is?" Robin said.

"That's right," Maia suddenly remembered. "He needs royal consent to his betrothal. He was talking about what a stupid nuisance it was."

Samira nodded. "I'll talk to the King's Own, and make sure that you're called right before he is."

The two girls grinned at each other, and Robin said softly, "I'd pity the guy—if he didn't so thoroughly deserve this."

The next day Maia, dressed in yet another black gown supplied by someone in Samira's far-flung family, sat quietly off to the side of the audience chamber. The bruises had come up nicely overnight; she had a set of fingerprints on each arm, and the sleeves of the dress were loose enough to slide up to her elbows. Samira was there to support her, too; Maia saw her with a group of Heralds on the other side of the room.

She had sent a note by one of the crows to the priest who supervised her work at the temple, telling him that she would be gone at least one more day but that she hoped to return after today's Court. The Brethren at the Temple of Thenoth had been kind to her, and she felt bad about leaving them without her work as long as she had, so she had made it a practice to send a report every few days. She knew the crows had been delivering her messages faithfully, but she was astonished, as she looked around the room, to see the Prior standing quietly near the back, chatting with what appeared to be priests representing several of Haven's temples.

The king came in then, and the formal business of the Court began. By the time her name was called, Maia was starting to feel decidedly nervous. She walked forward reminding herself of the pain and terror visited on the charm of finches—and of Samira's advice, "just stand up straight and tell the truth."

As concisely as she could, Maia told her story: that she had paid Markus to say prayers for her dead brother, that he had claimed to have done so when he had not, and how he had threatened and injured her when she confronted him about it.

"Don't pay any attention to her," Markus snapped. "She's just a low-born liar. Her brother was executed as a bandit!"

"I am willing to repeat everything I have just said under Truth Spell," Maia said, looking at the king. "Is he?"

"Lord Markus?" the king asked.

"Why should *I* be put to such indignity?" Markus demanded indignantly. "I'm high-born; does my word of honor mean nothing?"

"Was that a no?" the king asked, in a tone that strongly suggested that it had better not have been. "I would like to hear your explanation of the bruises on her arms." He turned to the King's Own. "Truth Spell, please."

Samira had set a Truth Spell on Maia the night before so that Maia would know what to expect. She couldn't feel anything, but she could see a blue glow over Markus's head and knew that there was one over her head as well. At the king's nod Maia repeated her story.

Markus tried to bluff his way out. "Her brother was executed as a bandit," he started, and Maia could see that the blue glow remained steady. It was, after all, the truth. "Why should I bother to say prayers for him?" Markus continued. "It's not as if he deserved them!"

"Did you say prayers for him?"

"No!" The blue glow was steady. "What difference does it make, anyway? Does anyone really believe that there are gods or that they care what men do?"

Maia stared at him wide-eyed. *How can he not*

believe? she wondered. *He's been in the Temple of Thenoth—couldn't he* feel *the Peace of the God?*

"So you have taken money for prayers you have not said to gods you do not believe in," the king said. "Is that what you are telling us?"

"Really," Markus sneered. "Who cares?" Then a puzzled look came over his face, and he crumpled to the ground.

Maia stepped quickly aside as a Healer rushed forward and knelt beside Markus. After a moment he shook his head a looked up at the king. "He's dead, Your Majesty."

The king sighed and rose to his feet. "Court is dismissed for today. We will arrange for restitution to be made from his estate." He withdrew, and the room erupted into dozens of conversations as soon as the doors closed behind him.

Samira crossed to Maia. "Are you all right?"

"I think so," Maia said unsteadily. "What happened to him?"

"His heart stopped," the Healer said. "It's not the first time this has happened to a young man in his family."

"Why does he still have the blue glow?" Maia wondered aloud.

"I guess he must be *truly* dead," the King's Own said with morbid humor. "Odd. I've never heard of anyone dying while Truth Spell was on them; I would have expected the spell to end." He turned to Maia. "I'll take it off now."

The Prior of the Temple of Thenoth and several of the other priests joined them then.

"The gods are not mocked," one of the priests remarked.

The Prior was more practical. "Are you ready to come home now, Maia?"

"Oh, yes," she said fervently.

Samira came to the temple the next day to return the money that Maia had paid to Markus. "Today seems to be my day to make restitution for Markus; I've just returned the diary to its rightful owner."

"Good," Maia said. "Do you think the gods really did strike him down?"

"Only they know, but if I were you, I'd say prayers for your brother at a real temple."

Maia nodded. "The Prior is helping me arrange it." She grinned suddenly. "We just got a new Novice here. It turns out that the reason Lena was so upset when Aurelia was hurt is that she's developing Animal Mindspeech. She hid Dexter in her room while I was away at Court, and he convinced her that this was the best place to live in all of Haven."

Samira started laughing. "Did her birds come with her, too?"

"Absolutely. In addition to its storytelling of crows, the Temple of Thenoth now has a charm of finches."

Healing In White
Kristin Schwengel

Shia felt herself shrinking, trying to be small and un-noticeable on Eodan's back, the closer they got to the Collegium. Haven by itself was an overwhelming riddle of streets and crowds to one who had spent the whole of her remembered life in the small mountain town of Breyburn. But going to the place of the Heralds, going to *be* a Herald, was beyond overwhelming.

:And don't you say that I'll be fine,: she grumbled in Mindspeech.

:I wouldn't!: the Companion—*her* Companion—responded in the over-bright voice that made it clear he had been about to do exactly that. *:Although I think you're worrying too much—people are still people, in Haven and in Breyburn. Rain, on the other hand, is very different.:*

Shia almost laughed aloud at the rueful tone of his Mindvoice. Eodan had not cared for the rainy season in Breyburn, for after he had braved the violent storms to reach the village and Choose her, he had been forced to wait the last two months of the season before the roads became passable enough for him to bring her back to Haven. To the Collegium. To—Shia cut off that thought, refusing to probe again the hollowness that threatened to swell up within her at the thought of the last person from Breyburn to have made this ride on a glistening white back. Instead she looked up from her fixed view of Eodan's neck, and at once regretted it. While she had been lost in her thoughts, Eodan had brought her to the very heart of Haven—the spires of the palace he had shown her in mind-pictures now rose before her in enormous reality.

:The King's Own's Companion knows that we are near, and he will make sure a Herald or a Trainee comes to greet us and help you get settled in.: There was a subtle note of hope and excitement in his Mindvoice, and she knew that he was looking forward to their arrival.

:What will you do?: she asked. *:While I am studying? Where will you be?:* A sudden shiver of nervousness gripped her—she, who had been so alone for those years after her mother's death, and yet never felt the pain of loneliness.

Eodan tossed his head, making his harness-bells jingle loud enough to draw the attention of those around them. *:I'll be part of your training, of course. And when I'm not, I'll be in Companions' Field, ready to meet you. After having made you wait so long for me, Chosen, I'm not going to abandon you!:*

As they neared the Collegium's gates, Shia saw a Companion waiting, a figure in Whites standing beside, and with a sharp pang lancing through her, she knew.

"Teo," she whispered, and with the name, the hollow pain flooded in to overwhelm her other thoughts and worries.

Eodan was silent as she stiffened in the saddle, and she felt a wave of comfort and reassurance from him. He slowed his pace, but as they approached near enough that she could almost make out Teo's features, sudden panic gripped her.

:I—I need a moment . . . : Even her Mindvoice seemed faint. Eodan stopped, and the other Companion shifted sideways, drawing Teo's attention away from the newest Chosen. Shia took the brief opportunity to slide gratefully from Eodan's back. Her knees wobbled, but somehow it was better to have Eodan's warm bulk beside her to lean against. Reaching up to knot her fingers in his silky mane, she walked forward.

:Shield, Chosen,: Eodan reminded her, and she went through the exercise he had taught her in those rainy months in Breyburn, wrapping the calm stillness of her herb room around her as they neared the gate.

"Eodan! You're back at last—you've been gone for months! How far did you have to go to find your Chosen?" Teo twisted his head to look around the Companion's body, his eyes meeting hers at last.

"Breyburn, during the rains," Shia said with a slight smile. "We had to wait them out." She took in a slow breath, glad her voice had not quivered.

Teo stared, stunned, as the silence between them stretched. "Shia?" he managed in a strangled voice, and his Companion nudged against him and snorted.

"Trin tells me I'm being rude," he said, his words slow, as though finding and forming them was an effort. "Shia, this is Trinelan—but everyone calls her Trin."

Teo's Companion stepped daintily forward, lowering her head so that Shia could brush her soft nose. *:Welcome to Haven,:* she Mindspoke, to Shia's astonishment, then shook her head at Eodan. *:We don't often Mindspeak anyone other than our own Chosen, but if you ever need to talk sense, I will be happy to oblige. This one is not known for sense.:*

"I will bring you up to the Dean of the Collegium." Teo's voice was still a little dry, but otherwise he seemed restored to his usual sunny self. "Herald Kindo and I leave for my internship on Circuit tomorrow, so Dean Merchan will find a Trainee to show you everything you need to know."

"Kernos and the Bright Havens know we need Healers more than ever! And what happens? This mere colt, not even five years old, goes haring off and brings back a girl with a strong Healing Gift and more herbcraft than most second-year students! To be a *Herald!*" The head of the Healers' Collegium paced the floor, her gestures sharp and angry. "I'd like to give him a piece of my mind. And as for the Healer at Torhold, well, I've already sent a letter demanding an explanation. How he missed testing this girl for the Gift after she became the herbalist for the entire town of Breyburn is beyond me!"

"Sereth, please," Herald Merchan, Dean of the Collegium, was finally able to get a quiet word in edgewise. "Her Healing Gift and Empathy are not her only Gifts— her Mindspeech with her Companion is quite strong, as well. And that is not so common as some would believe." He held up a hand to forestall another outburst. "The King's Own also told me his Companion believes she has a touch of Foresight, linked with her Healing Gift."

"All the more need for her to be in Healers'! Someone who knows what injuries will happen beforehand would be a godsend!"

"I rather suspect her Gift isn't quite like that, although I can't say how it is. All we can do is trust her Companion. Companions do not Choose wrongly, Sereth, even if they *are* shockingly young. We may not understand their choice until later, but they are never wrong." Merchan watched the older woman finish her energetic round of his office. It didn't take her long, as most of the room was buried under piles of books and scrolls.

Healer Sereth rounded the corner by the door one more time and brought herself up short. "I know." She sighed. "But for a Healer to have been Chosen—it frightens me to think what that might mean for the Karsite border. Companions always Choose someone with the right combination of Gifts at the moment they are needed."

"A Herald who can Heal—yes, it does exercise the imagination. But we know that a Healer can't keep up with a Herald."

Sereth's shoulders slumped. "I didn't want to give the approval, you know I didn't. But ... "

"But Healer Kevrel was so desperate to be involved, to do *something* after the abduction of his family, and the unmatched Companion was so willing to help after the raid ... "

A long silence stretched between them, each mourning the loss of one of their own—four years had not made it any easier to think of.

Life in the Collegium soon settled into something of a routine for Shia, although because of her older age and active Gifts, she split her time between the usual classes of a first-year Trainee (history and basic schooling, riding, and combat training) and lessons in Mindspeech (which she wasn't very strong with, other than with Eodan and a few Heralds). And, of course, every day she spent a long period of time in the Healers' Collegium, learning to use her Healing Gift and expanding her herb craft. This was where she shone, for her knowledge of the mountain herbs was more extensive than any of her teachers expected, and her experiments in Breyburn with growing herbs indoors over the winter season impressed Revyn, the Herbalist-Healer. She spent many extra hours in the Collegium sunhouses, tending the vast array of plants. Any time left over was spent down in Companions' Field with Eodan.

In fact, the first part of Shia's training passed in a busy daze, until the day she felt a strange hollow feeling in the bottom of her stomach. In Breyburn, before Eodan had come through the massive winter rains to Choose her, she had several times felt that same sinking sensation—and in each instance there was a simultaneous attack by the mercenary bandit that had plagued the village that year.

This feeling had started one morning just as winter began to ease its grip on Haven. It developed as a slight twinge, unlike the sharp throbbing she had felt before. Eodan felt the same unease, but none of the other Companions, not even Domar, the King's Own's Companion, shared it.

:Domar said that if something were wrong that would affect Valdemar, the Heralds, or the Companions, we would all know or feel it.:

Shia leaned her head against Eodan's flank. Her afternoon classes were over, and she had seized the few minutes before she started her kitchen duties to run to Companions' Field. *:But it's stronger each day. And it seems, I don't know, somehow to the east.:* Eodan nodded in agreement.

:Maybe Domar is wrong. Maybe . . . : Shia's body trembled and she grabbed Eodan's mane for support as the feeling of wrongness sharpened and blossomed into something hard and certain.

"Teo," she whispered. "Something's wrong with Teo.

I have to find out . . . " She was gone before she even finished the sentence, racing from Companions' Field to the Collegium, while Eodan galloped toward the stables.

"If something were wrong, Herald Trainee, we would know already. Herald Kindo is a powerful Farspeaker—that's why he and Herald Teo were assigned to that part of the Iftel Circuit." Dean Merchan frowned down at her.

"But what if he were sick himself, in fever-dreams?" At this point, Shia didn't care if her persistence annoyed him—she had to make him understand.

The Dean's door was flung open, and Healer Sereth burst into the room. "I was *trying* to cross over to Bardic to test this boy they think has Songhealing, and a Companion positively *herded* me over to Herald's. Yours, I assume?" Sereth glowered at Shia. "What is the meaning of this?"

Merchan opened his mouth to answer, but stopped before he could form a word. His face took on the listening expression that came over most Heralds when their Companions Mindspoke to them.

"I'm sorry," Shia said, "but I have to go. You have to let me go—something's wrong in the east."

"What on earth are you talking about?" Sereth glanced over at Merchan, but he was still listening to his Companion, his eyes widening.

"Teo—Herald Teo—something's gone wrong and he needs me."

"How do you know *that*?" Sereth demanded, but Shia couldn't find words to describe the bone-deep certainty within her.

The Dean cleared his throat. "I don't know how,

Healer Sereth, but something does seem to be wrong on the Iftel border. The King's Own's Companion just received a call for help from the intern's Companion. There is a plague or contagion of some sort in Norflank, and they've quarantined themselves. The senior Herald is very ill, the town's Healer has succumbed, and Iftel's borders are closed, even to those who might otherwise pass through them." The Dean scrutinized Shia. "Perhaps this is that strange Foresight of hers."

In an instant, Sereth's mood changed from infuriated to determined, like a general planning for combat. "A plague, a contagion? Did the Companion tell what form it took?" She didn't even wait for the Dean to respond before she began pacing the room. "Local Healer gone, no knowing where the nearest Healer is or how Gifted. There are other border towns, but usually only one strong Healer works with several. Bright Lady, why do these things always happen on the borders, where it will be weeks before we can get enough Healers out there? Even if we send a few riding ahead, we'll need to pack carts, we need the abbreviated copies of the tomes of Healing, all the medicinal stores we can spare . . . "

"I have to go," Shia repeated. "I need to go now."

"No!" The Dean and the head of the Healers' Collegium spoke in resounding unison.

"You're barely a Herald Trainee, much less a Herald. You cannot just up and leave and . . . " Merchan was drowned out by Sereth.

"You've just started Healer's training. What makes you think you could succeed where a full Healer failed?"

"This." Shia reached into her belt-pouch and held up a spray of leaves that she didn't remember plucking when she was in the house that morning. "I'm not saying that I could succeed, but with this, I may slow it down.

It might be enough to give Norflank more time. To give *you* more time."

Sereth reached out and brushed her fingers over the leaves. "What is that? It looks like mountain pirimora, but the color is wrong."

"Healer-Herbalist Revyn has encouraged me to experiment with mixing plants. This is a cross of mountain pirimora and the desert anejja that we traded for with the Shin'a'in. Both are good at stalling infections, and I hope this will be stronger than either. My first plants have just reached maturity."

"Then we send a full Healer with it."

"But a Healer can't travel as fast as a Companion," Shia argued. She was unprepared for the stunned expressions the two turned on her before looking at each other.

"Kevrel," Sereth murmured, in almost the same breath that Merchan whispered, "Dameo."

"But this isn't the same at all! This isn't a dangerous rescue, and Healer Kevrel was not bonded with the Companion who volunteered to carry him."

"How do you know about it? Few outside the Palace and the Collegium knew about that ill-fated attempt," Merchan asked.

"Eodan told me. I think he meant it as a lesson—although I'm still not sure whether it was a lesson in doing something bold or not doing so." Shia's lips curved in a wry smile. "Either way, this is a very different situation—and I believe I'm the best one for it."

The Dean and Sereth studied her for a long, reflective moment.

"I think she might be right," Merchan said, tapping a finger on his chin. "She is, after all, several years older than the usual first-year."

"And she's got solid herbcraft, even if her Healing Gift is mostly untrained."

:Is that agreement, then? It took them long enough. Our gear will be ready at first light tomorrow morning, Chosen—that should be enough time for you to prepare what you need from the sunhouses.:

The East Trade Road flew by under Eodan's heels, although it was still days of hard riding before they even turned onto the road toward the border with the shadowy land of Iftel. Now that she was *doing* something, the warning sensation had abated to a faint throb of wrongness, and all of Shia's attention was given to staying in the saddle—especially when Eodan started to leave the road to shorten the journey, cutting through areas impassable for any but a Companion and Herald. He even showed her mind-pictures of how to sit to balance her weight for him as he zigzagged down snow-covered slopes, and sometimes she knew as soon as he did when the footing was uncertain and how she should shift to help him stay upright. Up in the hills, winter still clung stubbornly, and Shia was glad of the well-stocked Waystations when they stopped each night. As the days wore on, the two of them started to share less and less Mindspeech, as every bit of energy was focused on maintaining the brutal pace.

:Chosen, I can Mindspeak Trin.: Just after dawn that morning, after more than a week of long days of travel, the two had raced past a tiny hamlet between Hunterston and Norflank, astonishing a few early risers. *:She says we'll be there within a candlemark. Herald Kindo is very ill, but Herald Teo is not as bad. Most of Norflank has been sick to some degree, and it seems at least one person has died each day since the Healer succumbed.*

She said it starts on the skin, but then spreads through the body, with great boils and fever. Once it gets into the lungs, they start coughing and it isn't long before the end. Some few have recovered from the skin infection without it spreading.:

:Can you Mindspeak Domar, so he can relay the information to the Companion traveling behind us with the rest of the Healers?: Shia built a little wall in her mind around the fear that had sprung up at the confirmation of Teo's illness. Dwelling on it would not help him or the people of Norflank.

:I can't reach him alone. Mindspeech isn't always reliable this close to Iftel. That's why Herald Kindo was on this circuit, because his Gift is so much stronger than most. When we reach Norflank, Trin and I should be strong enough together.:

Eodan put forth an extra burst of effort as they rounded the last curve of the road and saw the town walls nestled in the valley ahead of them. He galloped to the main gate and pulled up before the guardhouse, his flanks heaving, sweat dulling his coat.

:Why is no one posted, Chosen?:

Shia slid off Eodan's back, her knees wobbling from strain, and knocked at the guardhouse door.

After several long minutes, a window on the second floor opened a crack. "No one gets in or out, order of the town council," a raspy, weak voice called down.

"I'm here on Herald's business," Shia cried back. The window creaked closed, and there was silence.

Her hands clenched into fists, Shia pounded at the gate. "Let me in! I'm here to help!"

To her relief, her answer was a trumpeting neigh and the sound of hooves approaching the other side of the gate, followed by wood scraping on wood.

:Step aside, Chosen,: Eodan warned, then shouldered past her to throw all of his weight against one edge of the gate. It parted a crack, and he moved back and pushed again, until he had widened the opening enough that he and Shia could slip through to meet the other two Companions.

"Trin, help me. Where are the town Healer's records and stores?"

The older Companion gave her an affronted look, and from the tossing of Eodan's head, there were clearly words being exchanged.

:Mount up,: Trin replied, ignoring the other two. *:I'll take you.:*

Grasping a double-handful of mane, Shia pulled her groaning body onto Trin's bare back. Trin waited only until she was settled before loping down the deserted main street of Norflank.

:They're using the town hall as an infirmary,: she Mindspoke, nodding at the large building on the left. *:That's where most of the sick folk are. The remaining healthy and the least ill, like the guardsman, are trying to stay apart. The worst are up at the Healer's buildings— that's where—:*

"Where Herald Kindo is. And Teo?" Shia no longer bothered to hide the strain and fear in her voice.

:No. It hasn't spread to his lungs yet.: The Companion's own pain and worry shaded her Mindvoice. She pulled up before the door of a small building. *:This was where the Healer lived. The larger building behind is the regular infirmary. The smaller is his herbroom, but I don't think that much is left there.:*

Shia slid off Trin's back, her muscles protesting, and, testing the door, swung it open. "I promise you, Trin, I will do everything I can to save him. To save both of them, if I can. Herald Kindo's Companion must be . . . "

:Sjien is almost as exhausted as Eodan—since he became fevered, she has been spending all her energy Shielding him and blocking his Gift so he doesn't broadcast half-insane Mindspeech from here to Haven. I could barely tear her away long enough to help me reach Domar, when Teo and I couldn't get through the Iftel border—and Teo started to show the boils.: Even as she spoke, the other two Companions trotted up behind her, and Shia could see the older Companion looked distracted and somehow wan. Ignoring Shia, she moved out of sight around the back of the house, to the larger infirmary building.

Going to Eodan, Shia removed his tack, tucking each piece inside the door of the Healer's house, her herb-packs to one side. "Is there stabling for you two, someone to groom out Eodan?" Trin tossed her head in a nod, and Shia sighed with relief.

"I'm sorry to leave you to someone else, Eodan, but you two need to get as much information to Domar as possible while I find this Healer's notes, and see what I can learn." When Trin led Eodan back down the road toward the town hall, Shia closed the door and faced the room. Digging a tinder out of her packs, she lit a lamp in the fading daylight and started to explore.

A candlemark later, having found the Healer's notes, she visited the two infirmaries. Things were not quite as bad as she had feared, although the progression of the illness was serious enough. The town had a midwife and two others who had assisted the Healer as they could. The midwife and one of the assistants were ill now themselves, but Curana had been a lucky survivor of the boils, and it was she who now had the care of the remaining patients, dosing them with the last of the Healer's sleep-tea and feverdraw. Her relief on seeing Shia was clear, although she eyed Shia's Grays with surprise. Most of the sick, including Teo, were asleep, some tossing in fevered dreams. Herald Kindo was one of the worst—his breathing was faint and ragged; the boils had spread to cover his chest and neck; and despite being unconscious, his pain was obvious. He had been placed in a makeshift room at the back door to the infirmary, so his Companion could nose in and out at will. Now she lay on the floor beside his low cot, her head resting on a pillow to brush against his arm. Even in his delirium, his fingers were woven into her mane.

Somehow certain that no one was likely to perish that night, Shia returned to the Healer's rooms to study his notes—and begin adding her own.

The next day dawned bright, with spring warmth, and Shia took that as a good sign. She had spent much of the night reading through the Healer's notes, concentrating on his descriptions of the symptoms and what his Healing Sight had shown him as he had attempted to treat them. She hoped the Healers who were following her would understand his speculations on the source of the illness, for much of it was beyond her. She had also set some of her dried leaves to steep overnight, hoping that a longer preparation time would increase their potency. With the dawn, she drained them off into two clean-boiled flasks, carefully saving the leaves for reuse, if necessary.

The first visit was to the infirmary behind the Healer's house, to the most ill. There were eleven in all, with only two or three who seemed to be farther along the progression of the illness than Herald Kindo, but among the eleven there was little to differentiate degrees of sickness. All had boils spread over large portions of their skin, fevers, and ragged, raspy breathing. Washing her hands carefully, Shia centered herself and, thinking of the peace of her herb room in Breyburn, wrapped her Shield of calm stillness around her Gift.

Entering the first small sickroom, she released a tiny portion of her Gift to swirl around her right hand. Holding that hand just above the young man's head, she sent a silver tendril of her essence into his body, questing through flesh and bone, seeking out anything that had gone wrong within him. The boils were first to her awareness, a seemingly simple infection that appeared as dark spots to her Healing Sight. She resisted the temptation to use her Gift to draw the boy's waning strength together to push them out, instead sinking her focus deeper. His lungs were also darkly spotted, and she saw a swelling like water in the lungs—but then her Sight noted something else. In his blood, tiny spots rode throughout his body.

This was not in the notes that the Healer of Norflank had left. Had they been missed, these tiny shadows among the larger? Looking at the rest of the young man's organs, Shia found more spots of infection, but none that surprised her in size or location. Visiting each sickroom in turn, she repeated her search.

At the end of the building, in the makeshift room for Herald Eodan, she finished under Sjien's watchful eye. She had seen the same thing in each patient, varying only in the size and thickness of distribution of the spots. Drawing her Gift back into herself, Shia sat back on her heels, racking her brain for everything she knew about illnesses of the blood. It was so little, and fear clawed at her, her will faltering at the thought of facing so many, so ill, alone.

:Not alone, Chosen. Never again alone.: A wave of strength rippled through her from Eodan, and she smiled despite her apprehension.

:You and Trin have to tell Domar that it's in their blood. I won't know if it starts there until I see those who are less sick. But those who are most ill, it's in the blood, not just the skin and the lungs.:

By now, Curana had come to the infirmary, and she helped Shia dose the eleven with her newly steeped herbs and more sleeptea. With her Healing Sight, Shia had noted three of the sick, along with Herald Kindo, whose lungs and organs were nearly covered with the spots of infections, and to their draughts she added one of the strongest herbs for pain that she had brought with her.

:I do not know that I can do anything more than ease their pain,: she Mindspoke to Eodan.

:Then you will have given them more than they have had this last week or more, Chosen,: he replied, his Mindvoice unusually somber. *:Domar assures me that your information is relayed to the Healers that follow us.:*

Taking the larger flask of her decoction and an herbpack, Shia stepped out the door of the shadowy infirmary into the brilliant sun. Closing her eyes, she tipped her face up to feel the warmth soak into her skin and bones, savoring the strength of it. Eodan brushed up behind her, and she leaned against him for a moment, seizing a brief enjoyment of the day before going to the rest of the sick.

Although every fiber within her cried out to tend Teo first, Shia worked her way around the makeshift infirmary, using her silvery Healing Sight to assess the progress of the illness within each patient. Even so, she could not help but be aware of where he was, and how many more she had to care for before she would approach him.

Teo was lost in fever when she came to the side of his pallet, but he lay still and a faint hint of a smile flickered across his face. Kneeling beside him, before she even extended her Healing Sight beneath his skin, relief swept through her, for she somehow *knew* that his blood would be clear. She studied his lungs and blood with the same thoroughness, however, and her own breathing relaxed at last when she saw no spots of infection other than the boils themselves.

:Trin?: Shia Mindspoke softly, confident that his Companion would be nearby and listening for her.

:Yes?: came the anxious reply.

:He will be well. His blood shows no signs of it, and I will not let him fail now.:

A burst of gratitude was Trin's response, and Shia smiled as she continued around the great hall. When she had completed her circle of the building, she stepped outside to where Eodan stood waiting for her. Leaning against him, feeling him sharing his strength to restore her, she closed her eyes with relief. Of all of the patients here, none had shown signs of the spots in their blood. Although many of the townsfolk stayed away from the sick, she was glad to see that some came with broth and porridge for those who were awake and had appetite. And nearly all who had survived the boils either remained to help Curana, or came each day to see if anything was needed.

"What now, Herald-Healer?" Curana had followed Shia, and she waited, wiping her hands on the small towel she had tucked through her belt.

"I am neither Herald nor Healer yet, Curana," Shia

said with a faint smile. "But now we wait to see how the sick respond to the new herbs." *And we wait for the real Healers to come*, she finished in her head.

:Had your training begun in the time it could have, you would be nearly both.: Eodan's Mindvoice held a strange note of regret.

:Then I would not have been your *Chosen, and I would not wish for that.:*

Eodan was silent, but he rubbed his head against her shoulder until she scratched behind his ears, each of them lost for a moment in other thoughts.

For several days, she continued to minister to the sick in much the same manner, steeping her herbs each night and dosing them out, with other medicines drawn from her dwindling stores. More of the people began to recover from the boils, although she was not sure if it was her herbs or their own natural resistance to sickness. At the very least, the infections did not seem to be spreading through the blood and the lungs of those in the town hall, although many, including Teo, stayed fevered. And more people got sick, but with her herbs she seemed to be able to keep the new cases of illness at the boil stage, where the patients had the best chance of recovering on their own.

On the fifth afternoon, one of the sickest patients at the Healer's infirmary, the one who had shown the most spots over her lungs and inner organs, succumbed to the illness. Standing by the shallow grave as the acolyte of Kernos gave a blessing on the woman's soul was the longest respite Shia had taken from monitoring the sick since she had come to Norflank.

I pray to Kernos the Healers get here soon, she thought. *Eodan can Mindspeak the Companion with them, so they're not too far, but we went off the road so much, he can't tell how close they are. Even one more death is too great, for this town has lost so many.* She joined the rest of the villagers in throwing a handful of earth over the wrapped body, then returned to the Healer's infirmary to check the remaining ten serious patients.

Most, the ones with fewer spots in their blood, were no worse than they had been when she had first examined them nearly a week ago, but no better, either. Herald Kindo and two others, a young girl and a man of middle years, who had been nearly as infection-filled as the woman just buried, now had more signs of the dark spotting throughout their bodies. With a sinking certainty, Shia knew that she would have to use her barely trained Gift for more than just Seeing the illness within them.

Carefully Shielding herself in calm stillness, she knelt beside the first of the three, the young girl, and this time sent a green tendril of her Gift into the child's body, connecting herself with the girl's energy, first feeling the girl's heartbeat as well as her own, then, more faintly, the girl's faltering natural ability to heal. Instead of just observing the spots in the child's blood, she wrapped her Gift around them, trying to trap them and draw them together, then channeled the girl's natural healing strength at them until the dark spots faded, dwindled and disappeared. With slow care, Shia unknit her Gift from the girl's energy, step by step releasing the strands that connected the two of them, until all of her Gift was once again behind her Shields. She swayed, touching her hand to the floor to steady herself, glad that she was already on her knees.

:Have a care or you will lose yourself, Chosen,: Eodan warned from his favorite post outside the walls of the infirmary.

:*Don't they always say that the first one is the hardest?*: she responded, her Mindvoice faint in her own head. :*I hope that for once they're right.*: She gathered a silver tendril of her Gift and sent it back through the girl's body, searching out the spots of infection. Although her skin and lungs still showed heavy darkness, her blood now looked clear, and she even seemed to be more comfortable on her cot.

Shia brought the tiny bit of her Gift back into herself and, reaching for her herbs, gave the child two doses— one of her herb concoction, and another of the purple-flowered plant that seemed to strengthen the body's own natural healing. Then, she repeated the process in the next chamber before moving to Herald Kindo's sickroom.

As usual, Sjien lay beside him, although now at least Shia had insisted that straw be brought in for her comfort, dust in the air be damned. The Companion maintained her constant watch, although her Herald had grown so weak Shia doubted he could even use his Gift, much less spread chaos far and wide with it.

"He's getting worse, Companion Sjien, so I ask your permission to use my Gift for him."

The Companion rose and looked Shia up and down, then finally nodded her head and shifted to stand away from the Herald's cot.

"Thank you," Shia said, sinking to her knees and breaking a tiny opening in her Shields, extending the green tendril of her Gift down into the older Herald's form.

After days of concentrated use of her Gift, even just her Healing Sight, weariness had sunk into Shia's mind, and this time it was more difficult for her to mesh her Gift with the Herald's energy. The pulse of his healing ability was so weak, it took greater effort for her to find it and twine her Gift with it. When at last she succeeded and turned her attention to the spots of infection in his blood, their number and size dismayed her, but her own words rang in her head. *I will do everything I can to save him. To save both of them.*

Slowly, much more slowly than before, she sent her Gift through the Herald's blood, trying to wrap her power around the myriad spots and channel the Herald's energy toward them. Time and again, she made the attempt, but always some spots slipped away from the grasp of her Gift, and each time her weariness dragged at her, sapping her focus.

"You shall not have him," she muttered, not even aware that she had spoken aloud until she felt a flood of strength washing through her. It was like what Eodan had given her over these last days, but different, and Shia realized that Sjien had pressed her nose against her back and was sharing her own energy.

"Thank you," she murmured, and with renewed determination returned her attention to the ailing Herald. This time, with his Companion connected to her, she was able to capture the last of the spots in his blood, but she knew that the Herald's natural healing ability was too weakened to fight out all of the infection elsewhere in his body. Fueled by his Companion's power, she recklessly spent her own Gift to destroy the remaining spots, and when she was sure his blood and lungs were clear, she released the connection between them. His Companion continued to support her as she gave the Herald more of her herbs, until Eodan nosed his way into the now-crowded room and passed some of his own strength into her, helping her to stand.

"I don't know if it will be enough," she said to Sjien,

"but it's everything I can do for him." Wavering more than a little, she left the infirmary, clinging to Eodan's mane for support.

Ignoring Eodan's protests that she needed to rest, she started to walk down the road to the town hall. She wasn't even aware of taking steps, of moving; she only knew that she needed to be there.

Reaching the makeshift infirmary, she brushed past a startled Curana into the room, while Eodan craned his neck through the door to watch her. Sinking to the ground beside Teo's pallet, she reached out a quivering hand and placed it gently on his shoulder, closing her eyes and taking her first deep breath since leaving Herald Kindo's side.

"Shia?" Teo's voice was weak, and Shia's eyes flew open to meet his. He smiled faintly, his brown eyes clear of fever. "I *thought* I sensed—how is it you are here?"

Shia opened her mouth to answer, but sudden exhaustion caught her before she could form a word and she swayed. She would have collapsed atop him, had not strong hands grasped her and guided her to the empty pallet beside his.

"You need to rest—you know that is the first lesson of Healing. You will do no one any good if you overextend your Gift like that again," Healer Sereth's crisp voice broke through the exhausted haze fogging Shia's mind, and she forced her eyes open.

"How did you . . . ?" she whispered.

"I rode ahead. The others will be here in a few days. Your Eodan has relayed enough through Herald Fionna's Companion that I can start working." The older woman gave her a smile. "You succeeded, Shia. You gave us time. Now," she said, holding up her hand to forestall any other questions, "it is time for *you* to rest, if I have to dose you with sleeptea myself." When it was obvious that Shia would not disobey, Sereth whirled and left the town hall, gesturing to Curana to follow her.

Shia closed her mouth, and her eyes followed a moment later as she fell into dreamless sleep.

In the open doorway, the two Companions nudged next to each other, curving their necks together as they looked into the room. Teo shifted onto his side to look at Shia, a wondering expression drifting across his face, reaching out to interlace his fingers with hers, and she smiled as she slept.

Songs of a Certain Sort
Brenda Cooper

Two flame-haired women created colorful moving points against frost-dusted hills and a nearly frozen tree. They wore red and green, the red a bit of a clash with Rhiannon's hair, and the green a perfect complement to Dionne's green eyes. The only other movement in the scene was the stamping and shifting of two bay horses' feet and the flash of two yellow-breasted warblers flitting through swelling buds on bare branches.

Dionne stretched her arms up above her head, hands clasped, stretching. "I hope those birds mean spring's finally going to show up."

Rhiannon glanced up from the thin ropes she was using to tie her gittern—securely tucked in a lined case—onto the back of her horse, Chocolate. "At least we'll be going downhill today, and likely we'll find more cover tonight.

"And firewood. Maybe that'll put you in a better mood."

Rhiannon stopped part way through a knot and turned to face her twin. "Once more, I am not in a bad mood." The gittern case slipped. She glared and muttered, "Except I'll have to start this all over."

"See?"

Rhiannon sighed and didn't say anything at all for the next few moments.

Part way down the second hill, they came to a spot wide enough to ride side by side. Dionne spoke up again. "Give over. You've been a grump ever since we stopped at Mile Creek, and that was a nice stay in a good inn for two days. You even got to listen to someone else sing. So I don't get it."

Rhiannon shook her head. "You wouldn't get it."

"Try me."

"It's selfish. I don't want to talk about it."

Dionne let out a disgusted sigh. "It's selfish to be in this mood and not share."

"I'm sorry."

"Didn't you like the music?"

"They sang two of Crystal's songs."

Dionne was silent for a moment. "Oh. I thought you'd stopped letting that worry you. You've only been out of Bardic three years. Besides, we've not been in Haven for a year. Maybe they're singing your songs in taverns all over town."

"Fat chance."

"I bet it's true."

Rhiannon shook her head and adjusted her scarf to let a little more of her face free even in the cold. "Look. Healers don't need to prove anything to the world. But me? I'll never be a Master Bard if I don't get some songs into the common lexicon."

"I know, you want a 'certain sort' of song. Relax. I hear they come when you don't expect them."

"Soon would be good."

"Given I can't help you with that today, what would cheer you up?"

Rhiannon looked around at the winter-struck grass that lined the path, only occasionally punctuated with the tiniest bit of bright green. "A few flowers would do it." She pulled Chocolate to a stop, and pointed down. "Is that a footprint?"

Dionne looked around carefully, checking for unexpected humans. "I can't imagine people on foot out here in the cold." She urged her horse, Lily, forward and examined another track, this one a clear imprint of a boot in a muddy spot beside the trail. "It's almost two days' ride to Lookingfall."

Rhiannon smiled mischievously. "They're small tracks. Looks like women's boots. Let's follow them."

"We might be late to meet Paula and her new Trainee."

"Lookingfall won't mind Heralds for an extra day."

The trail proved fairly easy to follow even when the boot tracks diverged from the main trail and headed up. From the top of a small hill, they looked down into a pocket valley hugged by rising hills in all directions. A waterfall spilled into the valley on the right and became a slow-moving stream lined with trees.

Stream and trees alike were cut by a home made rock and wood and mud barrier complete with a walkway around the top. From this height, they could see inside the walls. There were at least five houses, a few corrals, some horses and smaller stock. The air smelled of cook-fires and dung.

"This isn't on the map," Dionne observed.

"No kidding. But we can put it on the map. Let's go."

"Maybe we should turn around. It looks peaceful enough, but they've not invited us and they're not on our regular circuit."

Rhiannon snorted. "Every town likes a Healer, if just to take the cold from old joints for a day."

"That's a lot of wall."

"I say we go." Rhiannon tightened her thighs and urged Chocolate to start picking his way down, humming loudly.

Dionne muttered a series of mild curses under her breath, but she followed Rhiannon easily enough. It was a good thing one of them pushed them to risks, or they'd have missed a lot of opportunities. Still, she eyed the fence with trepidation.

By the time they were halfway down the hill, Dionne spotted a man climbing up to meet them. "At least they have some security," she said. "They don't expect Heralds and Bards to come save them from ill."

The man carried a stave he might be hoping they'd mistake for a walking stick. He stopped so that he blocked the path at a spot with rocks on one side and a drop on the other. He looked about sixteen, with dark hair and a strong build, and seemed to be working overtime to appear threatening.

He waited until they pulled up in front of him, forced single file by the narrow width of the trail. That left Dionne behind Rhiannon, able to hear but not able to get a good look around Chocolate's ample hindquarters. "What brings you here?" he asked.

"We're riding circuit," Rhiannon said, matching his controlled tone. "We'll stay a day. Maybe sing. Help any sick or injured, then move on."

"We take care of our own," he said. "You can just go on."

"We'd like to ride on down and see for ourselves," Rhiannon replied, the look on her face betraying her surprise at the lack of welcome.

"We'd appreciate it if you'd turn around."

Dionne was pretty sure that was a great idea, but Rhiannon had got a bit in her teeth and wasn't letting go. She was probably right, too. No town or hold or home should refuse a Healer or a Bard. Rhiannon's back had gone stiff, and she poured a bit of authority into her voice. "We have an interest."

"Oh, let them come."

Dionne turned toward the speaker, an older man with a broad back and sturdy shoulders and dark hair as clean-cut as the scout's. He sounded and looked friendly, except that his eyes didn't land on her or even on Rhiannon. His gaze seemed to slide sideways, as if he were lost in thought.

She swallowed, a slight chill running up her spine. "Maybe we will go on if you don't need us."

"Oh, no, I'm pleased to be able to offer hospitality to two of Haven's own." He held his hand out to her. "I'm James, and the cretin who stopped you is one of my sons, Louden."

They finished the introductions and Louden stepped aside to clear the path. They wound through an open gate and into a small, neat compound. The corrals at the edge of the town were sturdy and in good repair, and the animals looked healthy. James led them to a neat little cottage with its own small corral attached, and bade them put up the horses. "I'll bring you lunch soon," he said. "We've no need of healing, but I won't have you going hungry."

The cabin looked neat enough to be part of Haven itself or at least one of the larger towns. Gaps in the logs that made up the walls were packed carefully with dried moss, and wood had been stacked by the fireplace.

"You'd think they expected guests," Rhiannon remarked as they set their stuff inside the door. "It almost looks like someone swept this morning.

"So why weren't they more welcoming? That was an act."

Rhiannon shrugged. "They probably don't see many strangers. We'd have ridden right by if I hadn't noticed the track."

"Something doesn't feel right."

"You worry too much." Rhiannon started out to strip Chocolate's tack. After they finished carefully setting bits and bridles across the sturdy fence, they slipped halters onto the horses and led them to the stream for water. "But then again," Rhiannon said as they stood on the bank, "where are all of the people?"

"Good question." Dionne looked up and down the stream. Two wooden bridges spanned it, built wide enough to handle the rush of spring water. The only person she saw was Louden moving between two cabins. "I've seen no women."

A thin, childlike voice spoke up from the reeds across the stream. "We're here. They just told us to stay away."

Dionne blinked and tried to look busy with her horse, Lily, as she replied without looking in the direction of the voice. "Do you need help?"

"No."

"They why are you hiding?"

"So you don't steal us."

"So why tell us you're here if you think we'll steal you?" Dionne asked.

"I don't think you will. You're a Healer and a Bard, and they don't steal."

"That's true." Dionne saw no sign of a person to go with the voice.

"He's coming."

The voice silenced, and sure enough, James stepped around the corner bearing a plate of fresh bread and some thick slices of cheese. "This is the best we've got right now. I hope it will please you. I already ate, so I hope you won't mind that I didn't bring any for myself."

Rhiannon nodded. They took the horses and followed him back to the cabin. The three of them sat down at the small hand-hewn kitchen table. "It's plenty for a midday meal. Thank you."

Dionne took her plate. "What do you call the town?"

James narrowed his eyes for a second, and then laughed. "We didn't name it. We're just a family that got permission to settle here 'bout ten years ago. There's a few families now, and we've started building for the next generation." He waved his hand around at the inside of the cabin. "Louden will need a place to live soon, and there're two others his age who'll start families in a year or two."

"So can we call it Jamestown?"

"No." He furrowed his brow. "You can call it Paradise."

The cheese was good, but Dionne couldn't really do any more than nibble after hearing the voice outside. Paradise indeed. "It's good you're planning ahead," she told James. "Your wall is strong. Have you had trouble with predators or bandits out here?"

"Bandits thought to take our livestock a coupla years back. Got one sheep, but that was all." A hint of pride had crept into his voice. "We took care of them."

Dionne decided not to ask him how. "Is there anything I can do for you or yours before we head on our way?"

"We're all fine at the moment."

She wanted to be on the horses and gone, but how could they leave before they learned more about the waif by the water? "No scrapes? No older people who could use some relief from stiff bones?"

James shook his head. "We're all fine."

"How about song? Surely your little ones would like to hear some songs. We've also got news from Haven."

"Pah. Haven's never helped me." He looked like he wanted to spit, but he swallowed instead and went on, glancing at Rhiannon with a look that seemed half suspicion and half appreciation. "But maybe you can sing later if you stay for supper." He stood up. "If you ladies will excuse me, there's work waiting. Feel free to rest up, and I'll come get you for supper."

Once he was gone, Dionne caught Rhiannon's eye and whispered, "We shouldn't have come here."

"But that girl."

"I know. We should go back to the water."

"We need to wash up anyway," Rhiannon commented. "Finish up your food."

"I'm not hungry."

"I am." Rhiannon plucked Dionne's bread from her plate and slapped the piece of cheese she hadn't started yet onto it. "All this sleuthing in small towns makes me hungry."

Dionne paced the small cabin, her footsteps quick and worried.

After a few minutes Rhiannon stood. "That's better." She stacked the plates by the sink and held the door open. "He didn't tell us we can't look around for ourselves. We're representatives of Haven."

"But we're not Heralds."

"I know."

As cold as it had been this morning, midday was almost shirtsleeve weather. Dionne felt brave and nervous as they retraced their steps, returning to the place they'd heard the voice, talking softly. She reached down to rinse her hands in the cold spring-melt water.

No one spoke to them.

"Let's sit a minute," Dionne said.

A patch of grass beside the stream had lost its frost to the pale sun and showed the thinnest fuzz of light green where new shoots were just coming up. Rhiannon sat, and then leaned back, straightening her long legs in front of her. In moments, she started to snore softly.

"Rhi," Dionne shook her.

Rhiannon didn't move.

Dionne shook harder. "Rhi!"

Then again. "Rhi"

"He's poisoned her."

The waif! The same high voice, thin and reedy.

"I knew he'd do something like that. Look. You've got to go. Now, get out the gate. Save yourself."

"I don't care about myself." She cared about Rhi. She shouldn't have followed her down here, should have listened to the part of herself that was scared of this place.

No one knew where they were.

She shook Rhi again, then stood and splashed some of the cold stream water on her sister's face. Rhi flinched, but didn't open her eyes.

She'd followed Rhi blindly, maybe because Rhi's escapades always ended up being something they could handle. Her heart pounded so hard her blood raced and her fingers throbbed. "What did he poison her with?"

"Something Henny makes up. She'll sleep for hours."

"Do you know what she puts in it?"

"Plants from around here is all I know for sure. Maybe there's more."

"Great." She ran her hands across Rhi's forehead. It was cool, and a little clammy. "Why?"

"He's scared of you. Scared you'll tell people where we are."

"Looks like we should." Maybe he had underestimated them, though. Dionne changed positions so she sat at Rhi's head, cradling it in her lap. She closed her eyes, preparing to ground.

"You've got to go!"

"Not without my sister. Come out where I can see you or go away." Dionne didn't wait to see what the girl did, but reached for the grounding force of the Earth. When she found it, she pulled energy into her body, a line of power she felt even though it was invisible to her. It filled muscles and blood, strengthened her heart. It even took some of her fear, leaving only a little gibbering around the edges about how she couldn't live without Rhiannon.

She bent over Rhi, one hand on her forehead, the other over her heart, her red hair mingling with her sister's hair like two flames.

The poison felt deep and slow. Rhiannon had eaten the part meant for Dionne as well as the portion she'd been served.

Her life force felt thin, like fog, like mist above water. She might die.

Dionne shook herself almost like a wet dog. Rhi couldn't die. Not here, not in this place. Not while Dionne was alive. Dionne reached inside her twin, trying to fill Rhiannon with her love, her need, with their bond.

Rhi's breathing grew even shallower, and Dionne's hand barely moved up and down on her chest. Dionne burrowed deeper. Chasing after Rhiannon's essence felt like running after a deer, the distance between them growing and shrinking but never closing.

She'd never tried anything so hard.

A voice spoke above her, the girl. "Don't bleed out all your power."

Good advice, the right advice. Dionne emptied her lungs and when she filled them, slowly, she pulled again on the earth, drawing on every place it touched her: buttocks and thighs, ankles, the sides of her splayed out feet.

She refocused, paying attention to the poison itself, drawing the dark tendrils away from Rhiannon's heart and blood. She set the hand that was on Rhi's forehead on the ground, building a link. She poured the poison slowly out of her sister into the earth.

Rhi twitched under her hand and breathed a raspy, shuddering breath. She rolled onto her side and coughed, retching up the rest of the cheese and bread.

Bushes rustled and soft footsteps moved, still out of sight.

Rhi opened her eyes. "What happened?"

Dionne told her.

Rhi sat up, squinting around the little clearing. She finally said, "Thank you, whoever you are."

"You're welcome. You should leave now."

"Can we please see you?" Dionne could barely keep her eyes open. She tried to draw on the earth again, but as usual when she wanted energy for herself, she might as well have been trying to fly. "Can you come out? Please?"

A thin girl with pale skin and pale green eyes and lips the color of sunset clouds separated from behind a tree, standing with one hand on the trunk. "I'm Emma. Emma Sue Emily for all three names."

"I'm Dionne, and this is my sister, Rhi."

"You look like you should lie down," Emma Sue Emily said, her voice quite serious.

"You are one very bright child."

Dionne squinted at the girl. "Your face is bruised."

"I know."

"Who hit you?"

"I get hit sometimes. It's hard around here. But I'm still alive."

Wow. Which implied others weren't. They did need to leave and report this. Now. "Will you go with us to get help?"

Emma Sue Emily shook her head. "My mom is here. So are my two brothers. I look out for them."

Dionne felt like her heart was splitting. She covered her sadness by turning to her sister. "Are you okay, Rhi?"

"I think a horse just kicked me and I need something good to eat. So yeah."

It seemed too much. Her sister almost dying and the girl, Emma, and not being wanted. Then Dionne realized what she felt—the harder a healing, the more scattered she felt for hours afterward. Or days. This had been hard. A yawn forced her mouth open against her will. "I think I need to nap."

"You two best go now," the girl said, her voice carrying a surprising authority given her frail body.

Even though the girl was right, Dionne couldn't make her legs tuck under so she could stand. It had been too much.

The world blacked around her.

Rhiannon worked quickly, pulling on bridles and bits and tightening the cinches for saddles. She had to stop from time to time and take in deep painful breaths, letting them out slowly. Dionne had healed her past immediate danger, but a month of sleep would help. It felt like forever before she led Chocolate and Lily back to the river where Dionne napped. Rhiannon smiled as she came up beside the two women. Emma Sue Emily sang to Dionne, a high voice, almost like wind in trees or the first breath of spring on a mountain pass.

Dionne did not appear to have moved, or to hear the song. Rhi knelt beside her and shook her shoulder. "Come on. We need to go."

Dionne mumbled a soft curse word and rolled over on her side.

"Now."

"I know. I can't." Her eyelids twitched but didn't open. "Maybe you should. Go."

"Right. And leave you?" She reached a hand out but Dionne didn't take it. Truth was, Dionne's face looked like birch bark, and she held her stomach like she might retch any moment.

Rhi waited. Not tapping her foot was hard. She should throw Dionne onto Lily's broad back so they could put this place behind them.

A sharp intake of breath from Emma was all the warning Rhi had before she heard James ask, "Leaving so soon?"

Rhiannon turned to find him standing only a few feet away from her, a rope in one hand and a dangerous look in his eyes.

Before she could say anything, he continued, his voice soft but hard as rock. "It would be a shame for you to miss our hospitality."

At her feet, Dionne rasped out a single word. "Go."

"No."

"Now."

James reached out with his free hand and grabbed Rhiannon's arm, and before he could clamp down hard he grunted and seemed to lose balance.

"Now," Emma hissed.

Rhiannon swung up on Chocolate. She sent him toward the gate, praying it was open and that James had no way to signal it closed.

Every instinct screamed that she couldn't—shouldn't—be leaving Dionne behind.

The ride claimed her focus, the trail thin and unfamiliar, lined with buildings that could hold men or women with arrows. Chocolate reared up once as they rounded a corner and surprised a man with two goats. Rhi threw herself forward, tangling her fingers in Chocolate's mane, and managed—just—to stay in the saddle. Chocolate came down hard on his forefeet, then leaped forward, almost unseating her again.

The next corner revealed a closed gate.

She started to pull back on the reins, but then a woman's voice cried out, "This way," and she turned to the right and found a thinner path. "Follow," the voice said, and she did, praying to all the goddesses she knew to keep her and Dionne and Emma safe.

Rhiannon wanted to race back for her sister so badly she could taste it, but that way was surely madness.

"Now stop."

She pulled Chocolate to a halt and peered around.

A woman dressed in no more than a nightshift stepped out between buildings. She had dark hair and eyes and darker bruises. Her cheeks and her thighs and one wrist had all been marked by rough treatment.

"Off," the woman said, as if the one word was all she could manage.

Rhiannon swung her far leg over the back of the saddle and came to a trembling stand next to Chocolate. The woman's voice was laced with fear. "Hurry."

She led Rhiannon and Chocolate through a thin gate clearly meant more for human than horse. To his credit, Chocolate managed it without doing any worse than scraping his saddle. He pulled sideways on the far side and stared back at the narrow opening to register his disapproval.

Rhiannon turned to thank the woman who had helped her escape, but there was no sign of her except a small rattle in the gate, now closed behind them. She whispered a prayer for the woman's safety as she climbed up on Chocolate's back and leaned forward as he scrambled up the hill. She didn't look behind her until they reached the crest where she stopped to let Chocolate blow.

She didn't see anyone following. Gods. She had left Dionne. But it was more than they could handle, and they'd almost both been captured. "Stay safe," she whispered at the fortified little town below her. "Stay alive, Dionne. I'll be back." She stared for a long time while Chocolate's sides slowly stopped heaving. When he picked his head up and scented down-valley, she turned him and started off at a steady jog.

When they arrived where she'd first spotted the footprints, she hesitated for moment.

She didn't know the path to Lookingfall. It would be mostly down, which was in some ways harder for a horse, especially in the dark. But behind her was higher, and ice would be bad footing, too.

She gave a deep sigh and turned down for Lookingfall. At least there would be a Herald there.

She and Chocolate were swaying down a steep section of the hill when the sun went down behind them and darkness leached most of the light from the sky. Eventually the moon threw a long shadow of horse and woman as tall as mountain down the path in front of her. From time to time she whispered softly to Chocolate, promising him grain and hay and a long sleep when they made it to town.

They went down and down, up again, and then down again.

She tried to feel Dionne, but there was nothing. Asleep. She must be asleep. Surely Rhi would know if Dionne were dead.

After another candlemark or so, Rhi pulled Chocolate to a stop in a small, flat place and dismounted. She felt so saddle-stiff and cold it was hard to move and equally tough to dig out a small ration of grain and water for Chocolate. She patted the horse's velvety nose as he nipped around her fingers, looking for more. "No. You'll get sick."

He sidled away from her when she tried to mount, pulling her down so she twisted her ankle.

She hopped and fell and then forced herself back to standing, gritting her teeth, almost in tears.

She still held onto the lead line. She crooned to Cholcoate. "I know you're tired, baby. Me too. But Dionne might be getting raped or killed or . . . " she heaved and a tear ran down her cheek. "We have to." She came close enough to stand in a burst of sharp pain on the hurt ankle and get the other foot into the stirrup. She grit her teeth, pulling up, throbbing in her swollen ankle as she swung into the saddle. "Come on, boy. Now you've got to do it. I can't walk."

The path turned and steepened. Moonlight no longer helped much. She murmured a prayer for safety over and over, worried that Chocolate would trip and they'd have to wait for light. Her ankle throbbed. Her teeth chattered.

She took her last sip of water. When they crossed a stream much later, she let Chocolate have a long pull of water, but she didn't try dismounting again. She was worried she wouldn't have enough strength to climb back on.

The sun had just started to strike a faint line of gray-blue behind her when she made out the chimney smoke and tall barn roofs of Lookingfall below them. She stopped to study it a moment as the light touched the top of the hills on the other side of the town. Lookingfall wasn't terribly big, although it had a main street and what looked like an inn. There was a wall, but even with a wall and gates, it looked far less fortified than the town behind her did.

Friendly. That's what it looked.

She shivered, suddenly afraid. Her legs closed so tight on Chocolate he lifted his head in spite of his exhaustion and twisted his ears back at her. Not here though, not her. It was Dionne she was feeling. She could never *make* it happen, but it happened when it needed to. The twin bond. The thing that had kept them together always. Dionne was scared.

Chocolate was too exhausted to pick up his pace, but they eventually made it to the gate, where a startled young woman gasped and opened it right way.

Rhi opened her mouth to warn her how horrible that was for security, and remind her that anyone could pretend to be a bard. But instead, she fell off Chocolate and landed on her butt, wincing as her ankle hit the ground.

The girl called a passing boy. "Steven! Take this horse and feed him."

The boy complied, looking enchanted with the big horse.

"Only a little," Rhi called. "Water him slowly, too."

The boy turned and looked at her with disdain, as if she was telling him the sun had risen. Good. Chocolate would be okay.

She turned back to the girl who squatted beside her, staring in horror at her swollen ankle. "We don't have a healer—"

Rhi interrupted her. "Herald. Need Herald."

When the girl shook her head, Rhi felt herself deflate. "Town. Leader."

The girl, wide eyed, pulled her water flask off her shoulder and handed it to Rhiannon. Then she raced away, leaving Rhi on the ground.

She drank a few heavenly mouthfuls of the cool water, letting it open her breath and dampen her mouth. Groaning, she rolled onto her stomach and pushed up onto her good foot, standing unsteadily.

Three men came hurrying up to her. "Sylvie said she had a dying bard here. That's you?"

She shook her head. "Just a sprain. But I need help." As she told her story the men began nodding. One spoke up. "My sister disappeared three years ago. Maybe that's what happened."

Another one asked her, "How many women did you see?"

"Only two. I saw one young one and one my age. The older one had been beaten, maybe raped. Both sounded scared." She took another swallow of water. "But they were brave."

The man who seemed to be the leader looked so aghast Rhi immediately liked him.

"We've got to go," she said.

"No," he said. "We've got to prepare and you've got to sleep."

"Is Herald Paula here? Has she been here?"

"No."

"I want to go back."

The man held his hand out to her. "I'm Hunter. You're in no shape to go, and we need to gather up our men and find you a horse. The one you rode in on is worn out."

"We need to go today. I'm sure she's not dead yet— I'd know. But she's scared."

"Three candlemarks."

Only then did she let Hunter lead her to his house and lay her on a bed with an extra pillow to elevate her throbbing foot.

A vigorous shake of her shoulder woke her. "Mghmgh-hhhhh." Her eyes snapped open as she felt another stab of fear, blurry and indistinct but very, very real. Dionne!

"Fifteen minutes, miss," a small voice said. "I brought you food."

She sat up, jarring her ankle so hard she almost screamed. "What time is it?"

Sylvie pushed a bowl of soup into her hands. "When we said. Paula wants to know if you can ride."

Rhi immediately felt better. Paula had arrived. She finished off the bowl as fast as her tongue could handle the hot soup, feeling as if each bite was bringing her a tiny bit more awake. She had to lean on the girl to get out by the gate, where she found Paula, her newest Trainee (a young man named Gossy that Rhi had met once before), and at least fifteen other men on horses. They all wore leather armor and carried weapons of one kind or another. Rhi spotted longbows and swords and even two staffs sticking way up above their riders' heads while the base settled into their boots.

A sturdy little palomino mare with four white legs stood bridled and saddled, her reins grasped lightly in Paula's free hand. Paula was on her Companion, Loden. Both were big and bulky, and neither had their usual look of benign humor. "Can you lead us there?" Paula asked.

Rhi felt a grin stretch all the way across her face as she realized that not only were the Heralds going to help, but that the whole town had shown up. Almost every horse in Lookingfall must be part of the assemblage.

"It's okay," Paula said. "We'll save her."

They arrived at the top of the hill overlooking Paradise just a mark or so before sundown, the shadows already long on the hills. Rhi felt despair more than fear from Dionne, a soft dull ache in her breast.

There was only one way in that she could see. Straight ahead of them. They weren't going to surprise anyone, anyway. Rhi asked Paula, "No need for quiet, right?"

The Herald shook her head. "No need."

Even though she was tired and bruised and her ankle screamed bloody murder at her, Rhiannon drew in a deep breath and started singing. She chose a simple song of Valdemar, one they taught the new students at Bardic in their first year and which people requested in inns throughout the kingdom.

As she sang, Paula and Gossy and the men of Lookingfall passed her and the little bay mare. She joined up at the end, singing them down the mountain so loud her biggest hope was that Dionne would hear it.

When they came to the closed gates, five men walked the broad top of the wall, waving bows and arrows. James stood among them, in the center, directing and encouraging and glaring down at the arriving riders.

Rhi leaned in close to Paula and whispered in her ear. Paula nodded, and Rhi extracted Hunter carefully from the group threatening the gate. He gestured for one more man to follow him. As they faded back, Paula and the others raced toward the gate, engaging the attention of the defenders. Rhi led her small party through the trees by the stream until she found the gate she'd come through.

Sure enough, it had been left open.

As soon as the men left to take the gate ambushers from behind, Emma Sue Emily appeared at her side, moving as silently as a bit of fog. She pointed, and then went ahead. Rhi followed her to a small outbuilding on a main cabin.

Inside, they found ten women, one of them Dionne, all of them tied up.

At least he hadn't poisoned them. Dionne had a bruise on her cheek and a cut above one eyebrow.

Rhiannon raced to her sister, holding her close, whispering in her ear. Emma freed the other women.

Within twenty minutes, Paula and her Trainee were letting themselves in the door, and a man and his long-lost sister were embracing.

A few months later, the twins were in the town of Ice Landing when they heard a Master Bard singing a song called "Rhiannon's Ride."

After it was over, they sat dumbstruck for a few moments, ignoring the bowls of bread pudding the cook had set before them.

Dionne leaned over to Rhiannon. "Is that the kind of song you've been pining for?"

She shook her head. "No. I want to write one that other people sing."

"Still, a song about you isn't so bad."

"It should be about the women of Paradise. About Emma Sue Emily."

"Without you, those women would still be there."

Rhi's face was nearly as red as her hair. "It's still not the sort of song I meant."

Dionne laughed. "I like it."

The conversation ended there, because the next thing that happened was the Master Bard called Rhiannon up to sing. Dionne got ready to dance.

Otherwise Engaged

Stephanie Shaver

Lelia was gazing thoughtfully at her hands when she heard a plate shatter and a child's voice shriek, "*I don't like apples!*"

The whole of the Great Hall fell into stunned silence. Heads turned toward the dais where the royal brat dined beside her royal mother. Back straight and jaw tight, Queen Selenay gazed silently at her daughter. Elspeth glared back.

A moment later, Elspeth's nursemaid rushed in and swept the child up. The nursemaid threw a helpless look over her shoulder at the queen before hurrying out, taking the howling heir-presumptive with her.

Subdued conversation resumed. Not long after, Queen's Own Talamir and Selenay departed together.

"Well," Lelia said in a low voice.

"Well," the man next to her said, looking down at his plate of baked honeyed apples.

"You have to say one thing about the heir-presumptive, Grier," Lelia said, craning her neck to look at the place on the wall where a smear of porcelain, honey, and fruit marked the tantrum. "She's got a hell of an arm."

Grier nearly choked. "Lelia. That's no way to speak of our future monarch."

"Horsefeathers. Your *brother's* more likely to earn that right before Elspeth."

Grier didn't answer, focusing on his dessert. Lelia watched his jaw work as he chewed, her own sweet forgotten. She touched his shoulder.

Suddenly, Grier stuffed an obscene amount of baked apple pastry in his mouth, looked her square in the eye, and said through a mass of dessert, "Marry me?"

It startled her into laughter. She punched his shoulder, and Grier smiled, but she didn't answer him.

"Lady Chantil hates me," Lelia said sweetly as Grier escorted her away from the dining table.

Grier rolled his eyes.

"No, really," she insisted. "Did you see that look of cool disdain she shot me? I just *know* it's hiding a seething cauldron of boiling hatred."

He kissed her cheek. "Stop being silly."

Lelia bit back a retort. She didn't *feel* silly. Grier's disregard for her comment only made her want to slug him again.

They parted ways, Grier wandering back in to circulate and chat with what remained of the courtiers. This was how they closed nearly any night they had dinner with the Court. She left to go practice, and he stayed a candlemark or so to chat. It was their preferred arrangement. They both treasured their freedom.

She strolled the long way back to the suite, taking the time to turn this latest display of the brat's temper over in her head. What new gossip would it spread?

Good thing Selenay's Bards love her, Lelia mused, *else word of this would be more broadly known. Then again, a scathing satire might be what she needs. It could provoke her to* do *something.*

She opened the door to Grier's apartments. *Like, say, building the first dungeon in Valdemar's history and throwing me in it.*

Lelia took her favorite perch on the windowseat. Grier's maidservant had already kindled the hearth and set out a pitcher full of minted water. The Bard poured a glass and took up her gittern, Bloom.

Tonight she worked on pieces in progress. She kept two notebooks: one for her latest completed songs (though she'd yet to meet a Bard who thought any of her works "complete"), and one for songs still rough-hewn, waiting to be teased from the misty grayness of her creative well.

Then she surrendered to music itself, letting her hands wander, lover-like, over the gittern, her eyes lightly closed. Her Gift unfurled, the firelight flickering against her lids. She pressed deeper, her music her only companion on the journey down into the underworld of her thoughts, and the deeper she settled, the closer she came to—

There.

She couldn't explain the shift in her Bardic Gift, but now she *felt* things, pulses of life. She *felt* the servant pass by the door to the suite. She *felt* one of the Palace cats creep past, on the prowl for gently born mice. They pulsed like heartbeats within the range of her Gift, beating a steady rhythm even through the stone walls.

Like any born with the Bardic Gift, she had always been able to overwhelm people with her music. Even more so, she could use her voice to command—she'd stopped murderers in their tracks with a single word.

But being able to sense lives without actually *seeing* them? Was that Bardic or . . . what else *could* it be?

She didn't have an answer, so she played, until her wrists ached and her fingertips went numb, until she felt Grier come in.

She looped her Gift around him, drawing him close. When she opened her eyes he stood before her, mesmerized.

She stilled the strings and met his gaze. Her Gift snapped shut, and with it went the other-sensing.

"Lord—" He swore. "Do you have colddrake blood in your veins?"

"I should hope not." She set Bloom aside. "Besides, they need eye contact to work."

"You'd know."

She smiled wryly, looking out over the gardens, searching for a lone figure wandering among the half-dead rose hedges.

"The Queen's Own does love his wine," she said when she finally spied him. He usually appeared around this time, and he had not failed her tonight. He strolled the moonlit gardens alone, goblet in hand.

"How do you know he's drinking wine?"

"If I were him it would be."

Grier leaned over to watch with her, smelling of soap and green herbs, his long, raival-gold hair tickling her cheek.

"You have an unnatural fascination with that man," he said, turning and walking into the bedchamber. He left a garment trail, the velvet and leather clothes sighing as they fell.

"He is a fascinatingly unnatural man." Lelia retrieved her gittern and toyed with a complicated arpeggio. "Jealous?"

Grier laughed. "Heavens, no. Bemused, more like. So—guess what my cousin asked me for tonight?"

Lelia accepted the abrupt change of subject gracefully. "Oh, I don't know. Could it be . . . money, a favor, or a place to stay?"

He poked his head into the room. "Right on the third!"

"Did you tell her you're entertaining a Master Bard with an unnatural fascination for the Queen's Own?"

"Next time, definitely. This time, though, I told her it's not *her* family's suite, and to stop being a leech."

Lelia gasped in mock surprise. "You *didn't*!"

Grier stepped out and struck a heroic pose; all the more comical because the only thing hiding his nakedness was his waist-length hair. "I did!"

"Kemoc will be upset." Lelia walked over and twined her arms around his neck, running her hands through all that hair. Grier was neither pudgy nor scrawny, but no one would mistake his frame for anything other than what he was: a gently born Healer more experienced with poultices and patients than swords and soldiers.

"Kemoc's . . . kindhearted." Grier waved his hand in a dismissive gesture. "Someone's got to stand up to the cousins, or they'll stomp all over him when—"

Abruptly, he deflated. "Gods damn it," he muttered. "I don't *want* him to be king."

"I'm sure it'll all work out."

"Do you really think so?" Grier met her gaze. "Do you think Elspeth will . . . get better?"

"I don't know what in the hells is going on with Selenay and her child, Grier," Lelia said honestly.

He rested his chin on top of her head. His arms wrapped around her and his shoulders relaxed.

"So are you going to answer my question?" he asked.

She blinked into his chest, trying to connect this with

that, finally making the connection to the question he'd asked with a mouth full of apples.

She tilted her head up to look at him. "No."

"Ah, well." He kissed her. "Once again, I shall have to endeavor to persuade you otherwise."

She chuckled as he covered her face with kisses and carried her into the bedchamber.

Lelia flopped onto Maresa's couch. "I'm perishing."

Her friend raised a brow.

"Of boredom," Lelia added.

Maresa snorted. "Your Death Bell Darling's not keeping you sufficiently entertained?" "Death Bell Darling" was Maresa's name for Grier, based on the circumstances he'd met Lelia by.

Both coming out to the Field to try to find who the Death Bell cried for this time, Lelia thought, remembering. They'd both admitted to feeling a mixture of guilt and relief that it wasn't *their* loved one the Companions mourned. Then Grier had suggested a drink, which had led to more drinks, which had led to—

"Is he still asking you to marry him?" Maresa asked.

"Nightly."

"Lelia, you need to let him *go*."

Lelia shrugged. "We've an agreement."

"Regardless. He's in love with you."

Lelia shrugged again.

"And what if Wil—"

"Maresa," Lelia said, an edge to her voice.

"What?"

Lelia sighed, draping an arm across her forehead to block out the late morning sunlight and her friend's disapproving look.

Ah, Wil, Lelia thought. *You're better off belonging to Valdemar and your Companion than to a ridiculous Bard. And I'm better off not thinking about you.*

"Well," Maresa said into the uncomfortable silence, "if you're so bored—what about a performance?"

Lelia uncovered her eyes, grateful for both the suggestion and the change in subject. "Go on."

"You know that new tavern, the Fancy Dancer?"

"Mmm-hmm."

"That's pretty much the story," Maresa said, her eyes twinkling. "They asked me for a Master Bard. I thought I would offer you the chance before I reached out to other contacts."

Lelia sat up, thinking. "When?"

"Oh, a week from whenever you return the contracts," Maresa said.

"Brilliant. I'm in."

"Any idea on a set?"

"Mm." Lelia's strumming hand moved unconsciously. "Have you heard of the Ostrum Cycle?"

"No. Wait. *Yes.*" Maresa squinted at her. "As your handler, I strongly advise against you playing the whole thing. Or half of it. Or one-*tenth* of it."

"Pah," Lelia said. "Even Ostrum never expected anyone to play it from start to finish. Only pretentious third-years ever try." *And I was a* very *pretentious third-year,* she thought.

"So . . . you'd be doing the Ostrum Selections?"

Lelia cocked her head. "Sure. I like that name." Keeping her tone light, she said, "I'll do two sets. One candlemark each, and a candlemark break between. Can you wangle that?"

"Should be easy." Maresa tilted her head, a faint worryline between her brows. "Why the extended break?"

Lelia was saved from having to answer, as Maresa's two-year-old chose that moment to burst into the study and climb up on his mother's lap. Topher's brown-gold hair came from his father, Mayhiu, but he had his mother's green, green eyes, sparkling like emeralds. He would slay the ladies someday, the more so if he wound up with his mother's Bardic Gift.

Topher turned around to stare at Lelia, sucking on his thumb solemnly.

"I think your son is telling me to go," Lelia said, rising.

"Trust me, if he wanted you out he'd say so," Maresa replied. "What's your favorite word, Topher?"

The thumb popped out of the child's mouth. "*No!*" he announced loudly, with a volume and sharpness any Bard could envy—and wince at.

Lelia smiled. "You have my sympathies."

"No!"

"Thank you." Maresa stroked her son's hair.

"No!"

Lelia bent down and kissed his forehead. "See you later, Tophy-apple."

"Luloo!" He exaggerated a wave. "Bye bye!"

She waved back and left, heading to the Palace, and certain boredom.

Dinner was the same as always: five courses complete with meat, bread, cheese, and gossip.

Lelia listened more than she contributed. The chatter was nothing new (the queen, the Borders, whether Elspeth would ever be the heir-in-right), but a few new threads were sneaking in, and both were centered on Talamir.

Lelia had to admit that Talamir didn't look well—his skin was more translucent than usual and dark smudges lurked under his eyes. Everyone at Court picked up on it. And talked about it.

Discreetly, of course.

The other topic was sheer speculation: Talamir's "plans" for getting Elspeth under control. Would he pack her off to Evendim to live among the fisherfolk? Foster her with the Holderkin? Spirit her away to the Dhorisha Plains? Lelia thought there might be a germ of truth to the idea of removing the child from Haven, but little substance behind the actual location.

The air in the hall was more stifling than usual, and mid-meal she went out to get a breath of air. Grier didn't accompany her—*he* was locked in conversation with the Chief Councilor, debating tariffs and trade routes.

She wandered into the gardens, letting the looming darkness of the rose hedges swallow her. *Maybe that's why Talamir comes here,* she thought. *It's quiet.*

No sooner had she thought it than someone spoiled it.

" . . . an antiquated practice."

Lelia stopped within the shadows of two thorny giants. The man's voice was one row over, practically next to her, but she couldn't see him—not in this darkness, not through the thick vegetation.

"I agree *completely*," a woman answered. "Did it make sense back in old King Valdemar's time? Of course! But Selenay has to see how disruptive it is, forcing us to go without an heir. Why, the infighting and jockeying has already begun."

"And it'll only get worse! I say make Elspeth the heir-in-right and damn the pretty horses."

Lelia stood, mildly stunned. *Are these people even aware of what they're suggesting? Do they have* any *grasp of history?*

"The Heralds are just *so* . . . ." The woman searched for words. "Elitist."

Lelia clenched her fists, her short nails digging into her palms. *This coming from someone whose wardrobe probably costs more than most folk earn in a lifetime!*

"I think it'd be a nice change," the man said, "*not* having a Herald on the throne for once."

The woman agreed, as the voices wandered off.

Lelia went back to the table to find Grier's conversation with the councilor ended. She leaned over and whispered in his ear, "Going."

Grier leapt from his seat, looping an arm around her waist.

"I heard something interesting," Lelia murmured.

"Oh?"

She filled him in as they strolled to the exit, keeping her voice low.

Grier frowned. "Did you happen to see *who* was saying it?"

"No. But if I ever hear them *here*, I'll point them out to you."

"You could do that? Just from hearing—oh, wait." He blushed. "Bard. Right."

Lelia smiled grimly. "Honestly? Those featherheads should be whipped for treason." Hastily, she added, "Not that Valdemar has any precedent for doing such to its traitors. Though there was that thing King Theran did to—"

She stopped. Grier's face had assumed a schooled, patient expression she knew too well.

"I'm boring you," she said.

"We can't all be Bards, darling." Grier kissed her cheek. "I'll be by later."

"I'll be practicing," she replied, giving him a preemptive punch in the shoulder before he could pose any questions.

"Ow!" he exclaimed. "How do you manage to always hit the *exact same spot?*"

She winked. "Just like plucking a gittern."

Back at the suite, Lelia opened the window, collected her gittern, and sat down to play.

Her mind settled and her Gift expanded. It grew easier each time; she barely had to concentrate any more. Not that she felt anyone tonight, except for the sleeping guildsman temporarily lodged in the suite next door.

Songs spun out, one by one. Too soon, her wrists began to throb, intruding on her meditation. She set down Bloom and rubbed her arms, trying to massage the fire out of them. She guessed that it had been merely a candlemark since she'd started practice.

No matter. It gave her a chance to try something.

Hands back in her lap, Lelia closed her eyes and settled once more, humming "Meetings" under her breath.

To her surprise, it worked.

A couple strolled by, and she felt the pulse of their activity. Guards made their rounds. The guildsman slept on. Out in the garden beneath her window—

Her eyes flew open in surprise.

Talamir didn't see her, or if he did he didn't acknowledge her. He sipped from his glass and gazed up at the frosty stars. Then he wandered away again, winding back toward the center, soft as a ghost.

She'd felt his life in those moments, though. Her stomach twisted like a rag being wrung dry, and tears slipped down her cheeks.

"Lelia?"

She hadn't heard Grier come in. She started badly, swinging around to find him standing behind her.

"What's wrong?" he asked, sitting down next to her and taking her hands. "You're freezing!"

"I, ah, the windows. It was too warm." She closed one with fumbling fingers. This new facet of her Gift was but one of many things she'd never explained to Grier. Truth be told—she hadn't tried to explain it to anyone, and she wasn't sure she *could* articulate what she'd felt when she'd brushed against Talamir. His pulse had blazed like a beacon being burned too quickly.

"Why are you crying?" Grier asked.

Lelia took a deep breath and smiled. "Talamir wandered close to the window and I saw his face. He looks . . . sad."

"Ah." Grier kissed her cheek. "Well, you know what might cheer him up?"

"No, what?"

"If you married me."

She bumped her head against his chest like a cat and stood, taking his hand.

"It would cheer *me* up," Grier added.

She shook her head and led him into the bedchamber.

Lelia spent the morning in the archives, hunting down the first ten volumes of Ostrum's Cycle and transcribing what she could before her hands started to cramp.

Back at the apartment, two things waited for her: Maresa's contract and a brief note from Grier stating he would be late at the House of Healing. Lelia entrusted the signed contract to a page, then sat down with her new works spread out about her and let them speak to her.

By dusk, she had the beginnings of an opening set. She lit the fires and the lamps, then sat by the window and practiced her selections. She made it through two candlemarks before the gnawing in her wrists became unbearable.

Afterward, she sat by the window, pondering arrangement and inflection as she waited for the Queen's Own's appearance. She watched until her eyes grew heavy, then went to bed without having seen Talamir or Grier.

It felt like she'd only just fallen asleep when something roused her. Lelia sat up in bed, heart thundering.

Gong. Gong. Gong.

The Death Bell.

She jumped from the empty bed and sprinted for the door. Clothes were an afterthought; she pulled on a tunic and breeches, dashing barefoot into the gardens and angling toward the Grove.

A figure rushed to intercept her.

"Lelia!" Grier called.

She staggered to a stop. He still wore his working robes. He looked exhausted, but he *knew*. She saw it in his eyes.

"Who?" she asked, hands curled into tight fists.

Grier hesitated, then said the name softly. "Talamir."

She stood agape, words failing.

Over in the Palace and the Heralds Wing, fires and lamps were being kindled, windows filling with golden illumination. Grier put his arms around her as she shivered in the cold, and the Bell's somber lament tolled on.

There was no Court dinner that night.

Lelia spent the day in the archives again, removing herself from the bleak atmosphere of the Palace. She sifted through the last of Ostrum's Cycle, taking transcriptions and writing notes until her hands burned.

Dusk crept across the horizon when she returned to the empty suite. She ate alone, working her way through a bottle of wine and a pile of firewood, shuffling and weighing the pages with a growing sense of melancholy. She'd promised Maresa something lighthearted, but it felt all wrong right now.

As if the Queen didn't have enough trouble, Lelia thought. *As if Talamir isn't needed* right now.

She randomly chose a song—one of the last from the Cycle—and began to sing, picking out progressions as she found them appropriate.

> *Who are we?*
> *What are we?*
> *In the end, lost causes*
> *Death holds to no promises*
> *And Life does not love me*
> *As much as I love her*

She heard Grier coming this time. When he spoke, it didn't surprise her.

"That's . . . cheerful," he said, sitting down in a chair.

After a moment, she cleared her throat and said, "Ostrum was a Master Bard, oh, during your great-grandfather's rule. He wrote a song a day, starting after his fifth year graduation. After three years without missing a day, he turned in the material and made Master Bard. But he didn't stop."

Grier said nothing. If she bored him, she couldn't tell; the shifting shadows of the fire made a mask of his face. She stirred the sheets of vellum with one finger. "He wrote over two thousand songs. Some were ridiculous." She smiled, thinking of the four-line ditty she'd found in honor of summer's first sprays of Maiden's Hope ("Oh pure white blooms / The perfume of hope! / Pray you aren't / Eaten by goats").

"Some were profound. He fell head over heels in love with another Bard, and there are at least three months where he writes about nothing but her. He set their vows to music." He'd done the same with the proposal, too, but she didn't mention it; she didn't want to give Grier any ideas.

"Five years into the project, he writes about a passing fever. Then a passing ache. Then he realized neither were passing." She swallowed hard, imagining how Ostrum must have felt. The slowly dawning realization. The comprehension of mortality and how little time he had left. "It was insidious, you see. Took years to manifest, and more to kill him. The Healers told him there was nothing to be done, that whatever he had was a wasting ailment, and incurable.

"His body betrayed him, but his mind stayed sharp. His wife, Lirian, started transcribing for him. Right up to the last."

Grier cleared his throat. "Is that what you were playing? The last one?"

She shook her head. "He wrote that when he . . . knew. He thought he was disappointing Lirian by dying." Her lips quirked. "No, his last song is . . . quite peaceful."

A pause. Then Grier said, "Show me?"

She didn't need to find the page.

> *How shall I haunt you*
> *So you do not know?*
> *After I am gone,*
> *I pray you move on*
> *Depart from my fond shadow*
>
> *And show me, love,*
> *Show me that you live*

Grier said nothing. Taking a deep breath, Lelia finally spoke.

"I do love you, Grier. But not enough."

"I know," he said automatically.

"You'll go back to your estates," she said. "I'll miss you, and you'll miss me. You'll inherit, and you'll be expected to have a wife who runs your home and has your children." She tapped her chest, over her heart. "I am not her."

He said nothing.

She crossed to him and kissed his cheek. "We both know that if you don't fill the role, one of your cousins will." He shuddered at the notion. "I'd never ask you to give it up for me. I—"

He put a hand to her lips, stilling her. "Let's enjoy what's left of spring," he said softly. "Let's pretend for a little longer that Valdemar doesn't expect anything from me. Let's pretend I'll still be here after Midsummer."

Lelia closed her eyes. Whispering, she said, "I just spoke to Valdemar."

"Oh?" He wound his arms around her neck. "What does Valdemar say?"

"Duty, sacrifice, no one true way. The usual."

He chuckled.

"But she agrees. It's okay for us to do this a little longer. Not much longer, though." Lelia opened her eyes. "Okay?"

He gave her a firm kiss in answer.

The Fancy Dancer smelled like fresh paint and new thatch. So much so that Lelia had to go out the back door for fresh air during her break.

She stood alone in a corner of the outer courtyard, rubbing her wrists and drinking her way through a cup of icy-cold wine. The tavern was a blessed reprieve from the unhappy Court dinners of the last few days. Meals there had become solemn affairs, with courtiers in mourning attire and the queen scarcely seen. Grier had gone without her tonight, mostly out of a sense of duty to his family's place at Court. He'd promised to come by and catch the last of her show once dinner wound down.

Lelia gauged her break nearly over and headed back in. The front door had a direct line of sight to the stage, but she decided to circle the tavern first, finishing off the wine as she went. She even poked her head into the kitchen, where the cook was trying not to burn some sort of sweet bubbling away at the hearth. Like most of the staff, the young cook seemed as fresh as the paint.

She smiled fondly at the owner, Corgan, strolling over to where he was drawing drinks.

"Welcome back, milady Bard!" he boomed. "Shall we continue?"

"Oh, that depends," she replied. "I'm just not sure they're ready for me yet."

The crowd gave a weak cheer.

Lelia yawned and leaned against a cask, putting a hand out. Corgan promptly filled it with a mug of something chilly. "Yes, definitely not ready yet."

A more vigorous cheer followed that.

"Hmm?" Lelia walked toward the tavern's raised stage, mug in hand. "Did someone say something?"

Now she had *all* eyes on her, and the cheers made her teeth rattle. Grinning, she took her seat and Bloom, launching into one of Ostrum's bawdier compositions: "Ode to the Innkeeper's Daughter (and Her Twin Sister)."

The crowd loved it. *She* loved them. They sang along

when they could, made noise with feet and hands when they couldn't, and when the music grew soft they respected the delicate, somber melodies. Despite the pain in her hands, the rush of being on a stage and being surrounded by such sheer delight buoyed her and let her fight the growing agony in her wrists. Her Gift twined through the crowd, enthralling them. She played and sang and felt them all, lively pulses of light in her mind's eye, enraptured by the songs she wove.

She didn't notice the tavern was on fire until the flames were climbing up the walls.

The shriek of the cook jolted her back to awareness. He screamed a single word: *"Fire!"*

For a dazed moment Lelia thought, *Ah, he's gone and burned dessert.*

A beam crashed to the ground, and a wall of fire leaped up to her right. People turned into indistinct, shrieking figures in the heat and smoke. Screams and crackling wood became the tavern's new song.

Gripping her gittern, Lelia launched off the stage, knowing the exit lay directly before her. Tears streamed from her eyes as fire clawed at the ceiling. She staggered to the door and into the courtyard. Voices hollered for the fire brigade, for Guards, for water.

Lelia collapsed, gasping at the stars.

Pulse.

Horror rose in her throat. In all that pandemonium, her strange Gift had not shut down. Lives pulsed around her—the ones in the courtyard, and the ones still trapped *inside the tavern.*

Her own words haunted her. *Duty, sacrifice . . .*

She hauled herself to her feet again, thinking, *Why couldn't I have been born in Rethwellan?* The thought drew a hysterical laugh from her lips as she stumbled up to the front door of the inferno, closed her eyes, and did what only she could do.

"Come here!" She reached out with more than her voice; no one would have heard her over the fire and screaming and moaning. But the Bardic Gift went deeper, and they "heard" that just fine. She touched the pulses within with precision, giving them a sense of where to go and how to escape. "This way! *Come here!*"

Figures blundered through the smoke and the fire. Burning forms surged past her, rolling on stones of the cool courtyard. She kept on screaming and tugging at what she felt inside the tavern, even as hands closed on her shoulders and tried to drag her away. She struggled against them, bellowing her Gift at the trapped people until a combination of lack of air and exhaustion overtook her, and she wheeled out into the darkness, smelling the terrible smell of burning things, and wishing it were fresh paint instead.

Lelia opened her eyes again to a pale green room. Sunlight streamed through a window and onto her bed.

She felt like she'd been smashed into a wall, soaked in oil, and set on fire. Looking down at her arms, she saw pink, tender skin.

She bobbed on the surface of awareness for an indeterminable amount of time. The door opened, drawing her fully to consciousness.

She turned to greet the Healer with a croaked, "Heyla."

Grier crouched beside her, looking scruffy and worn. "I was nearly to the tavern when I saw the fire," he said. "Your hair and clothes were smoking when they dragged you away. You inhaled massive amounts of smoke. What were you *doing*?"

It hurt to smile. *I should be happy I still have lips,* she thought.

"History," she said, lungs aching with the effort. "A Bard ... saved a house full of people. Used his Gift. Called them to ... the door. He, um, died, though ...."

She wanted to say more, wanted to tell him about the change in her Gift. The explanation hovered on her lips.

But Grier was studying her with an intensity of concern that silenced her.

Oh, hellfires, she thought, heart sinking. *He knows.*

"I aided Healing you," he said, "I ... looked you over."

Yes, he definitely knows.

"Is there something you want to tell me?" he asked quietly.

"Can't pretend ... you didn't 'look me over'?" she said hopefully. "Pretend I'm okay ... except for burns? Pretend you don't know?"

"No."

She sighed. "No fair. I did ... for you."

He touched what remained of her hair. "I'm told it's called 'Ostrum's Sickness'. You're just starting to show symptoms." He paused. "And you *knew*."

She closed her eyes. "Since before Sovvan. Before ... we met."

"Why didn't you tell me?" She thought he'd be angry, but she heard only sorrow in his voice.

"Can't ... be helped," she said, opening her eyes. "Still got ... years ... ahead of me. Why worry?"

He shook his head, standing. Her heart contracted as he turned his back on her and walked out.

Well, she thought, lashes suddenly damp, *what did you expect, you mooncalf? Shared his bed three months, and never once mentioned your life-threatening illness to him.*

The door opened again, and Grier came back, toting a chair and a book. He leveled a somber look at her as he sat down.

"Let it be noted," he said, "that I am reading history because of *you*."

She laughed, though it hurt. When she finally stopped he started to read her the tale of Herald Berden.

She fell asleep to his sonorous voice, thinking that as good as Berden's historical story was, she liked the Bard's version better.

Recovery took a long, boring month. Her skin healed quickly, but the internal bits took longer.

Occasional visits from Maresa alleviated the tedium, and one delightful one from Lyle—who rode halfway across the country to see her—caused Lelia to burst into tears for more reason than one.

She begged Grier not to tell *anyone* her secret. He promised, but not before giving her several reasons why she should. She listened patiently, letting him talk himself dry.

When Lyle left a week later, he remained cheerfully oblivious of her condition.

"Promise me," he said before he left, "that you'll leave the heroics up to *me* from now on."

She had received notes and visits from some of the people she'd "rescued," and found this flavor of attention not to her liking.

"I promise," she told her twin. *Not to mention I'd likely die of embarrassment if I made a career of this.*

Grier personally saw to her Healing, making sure she recovered from at least one of the things that threatened her life. She suspected (but could never prove) that he flavored the famously vile Healer tonics to taste even worse than usual. Somehow.

But he never asked her to marry him again. And that both saddened and relieved her.

Then Midsummer came, and with it the last Court dinner with Grier. The summons had come two weeks before. Valdemar called.

At least it was one of the grander meals, with the Great Hall decked with Maiden's Hope and ribbons. The dishes were fresh, talk lively. Gossip at Court had shifted in Lelia's absence, leaning toward the recently Chosen Queen's Own and her arrival in Haven.

"Holderkin!" sniffed an ancient baroness seated across from Lelia. "I'm not even sure they eat at *tables* down there on the Border!"

Lelia gave Grier a sidelong glance, but he paid the old woman no mind.

"Seems to me," Lelia said boldly, catching the biddy's eye, "that a couple months ago we were all wondering if Elspeth would be shipped off to a place like Sensholding." She smiled brightly and speared a slice of meat with her knife. "Looks like Rolan brought Sensholding to us, instead."

That drew a few chuckles. Grier smiled.

As they finished, he leaned over and murmured, "I have a confession to make."

She eyed him warily.

He stood and took her hand, leading her from the Great Hall and down corridors into a part of the Palace she hadn't visited often. They wound up in a study with leather chairs and an enormous number of books. Two people sat reading by the lamplight.

One was Selenay.

Lelia tried not to gape. Her queen sipped tea beside Kyril, the Seneschal's Herald. Grier took a seat and motioned Lelia to a chair.

"So," Selenay said. "This is your last night, Lord Grier?"

"Aye, Majesty."

Selenay fixed her gaze on Lelia. "Grier hasn't told you, I take it?"

"Told me . . . ?"

"I'd come here when you were practicing," Grier said.

Lelia shot Grier a startled look. The smile he returned was oddly . . . smug.

"There are certain courtiers," Kyril explained, "that we keep in confidence. Court lips tend to be . . . looser around people who don't wear White."

"We like to know what's been said and who's been saying it," Selenay said. "Most nights I entrust the debriefing to Kyril and the Queen's Own. But sometimes I attend."

"Of course," Grier said, touching Lelia's hand, "finding someone trustworthy to do the job is difficult." His eyes sparkled. "You need just the right person. Usually someone with rank and a Herald for a sibling."

"My—rank?" Lelia blurted when she realized he meant *her*.

"You're the Master Bard of my family's house." Grier removed a slip of paper from within his doublet and passed it to her. "You'll receive a monthly stipend, and since I won't be in residence any more, I think we'll bestow unto you my suite here at the Palace and the family's seat at Court dinner."

"Nice way to control the cousins," Kyril murmured.

Lelia stared, stunned, at the paper. Before she knew it, Grier knelt before her, squeezing her hand gently.

"Lelia," he said. "Will you . . . be my family's Bard?"

She held his gaze, tears making him waver before her, and said, "Yes."

Then she punched him in the shoulder.

He swore. "Every time! Same—damn—*spot*!"

"Serves you right," she said. "Keeping secrets from me."

He rolled his eyes. "Oh, like you can talk."

Lelia turned to Selenay and sketched a seated bow. "Majesty. I accept this duty and promise to keep it in strictest confidence. What would you like to know?"

Selenay regarded the Healer and the Bard a moment. Then she chuckled and shook her head.

"Well, first off," Valdemar's monarch said, "what have you heard about my Queen's Own?"

Heart's Choice

Kate Paulk

Ree felt a twinge of foreboding long before he knew why
the people of Three Rivers had sent for him. The whole
village waited in the square—an open area between the
two rows of houses built on burn-scarred foundations.
Worse, the villagers wore the somber faces that usually
meant either a funeral or the loss of crops. But this must
be something else—something to do with him—or there
wouldn't be that scent of fear. Distrust slanted eyelids
downward, and unease pinched their lips tight.

Ree walked through the space they'd made, his boots
crunching on the uneven packed dirt and gravel, tension
growing. He knew he was different from humans: his
rat tail tucked in his pants, his cat eyes lowered and his
claws retracted didn't make the villagers forget it. How
could they forget when he couldn't?

He was doubly an outsider: a stranger and a hobgoblin. Born and raised a street urchin in Jacona—too
far for any of the Three Rivers villagers to know of it—
much less to have been there. Caught in the Changes,
he'd become magically entangled with a rat and a cat.

If he were normally tolerated, almost welcomed, it
was because he'd saved the villagers from a raid a year

ago. But it was a tolerance edged about with fear. He
hunched his shoulders, looking at his boots and not at
the people around him. He didn't need to look up to
know their tolerance was on the edge of breaking.

He didn't even want to know why. But then, no one
ever seemed to care what he wanted. The middle-aged
mayor who'd summoned him led him past the silent
people into the rough square where two corpses lay.

Ree made an inarticulate sound. He should prove his
humanity by speaking, but revulsion and shock silenced
him.

He stared down at two dead hobgoblins. They were
unclothed, but they'd died holding hands. That didn't
make this easier. Nor did it help that, of all the hobgoblins they could have been, these two seemed to be cat-
with-human and looked not unlike Ree himself. One
was brown-furred with a tabby pattern and the other
ginger, where Ree's fur was rat-brown, but they had
claws and tails. It was close enough.

He walked around the corpses, looking down, trying
to keep his face perfectly impassive, as an interior voice
whispered, *This could have been you.* In many ways, this
should have been him. Except for Jem. He hadn't known
when he'd rescued Jem from worse than death on the
streets of Jacona that he'd been rescuing his own humanity, his own ability to care for another human being.

Yet Jem was the other way in which Ree didn't fit
with the village. Young men married young women.
Young women married young men. If anyone felt an
inclination otherwise, he or she kept it close and hidden. In this hardscrabble country you needed a family
to help you farm, children to look after you when you
grew old and feeble.

He'd managed to convince himself—just—that Jem

didn't want to take a human wife and breed a passel of brats in his image. Just. But that didn't make it the ideal situation. Certainly not in the village's eyes. Or in the eyes of Jem's father Lenar.

Just as well Jem wasn't here. It was only Ree—and the unwelcome reminder of what he might have become without Jem to keep him human.

He looked at the hobgoblins' hands, clasped together. The claws were broken, and one of the wom–the female's claws had been torn right out. They looked callused and rough too. He wondered if they'd forgotten and run on four feet at times. He'd seen other hobgoblins do that, though he never did.

Thanking the gods for the face fur that hid his expression, he scratched at his nose. He tried to compose himself before speaking. He couldn't ask what they were guilty of—they weren't human. They were hobgoblins, and hobgoblins were killed on sight. As Ree would have been, had he not come into the area with Jem, and had they not taken refuge with Jem's grandfather at an outlying farm.

Ree's throat felt constricted. "Was anyone injured in bringing them down?"

He was only willing to look as high as the mayor's hands, twisting his broad-brimmed felt work hat—once black and now a faded gray. It seemed as though the man feared Ree's response.

"Begging your pardon," he said, and cleared his throat. "Begging your pardon, it's not as if—" He stopped himself short of saying what it was as if, and fell back into the dialect of the region. "It was the cows, them as were in the field pasturing. We heard a cow lowing fit to break your heart, and of course the boys ran to help."

Ree looked up to see that the man was pale, the lines

on his face deeper, his hazel eyes reflecting a mixture of nervousness and confusion. He was a wealthy farmer, at least as wealth was reckoned around here, which wasn't much. His clothes were patched but clean, his face tanned a deep leathery brown by work done outside, his hands callused from plows, shovels, axes and pikes—the brutal work of keeping alive in Three Rivers.

He wasn't like the old mayor who'd been educated and almost gentry. But that one had been killed when soldiers raided the village for slaves and burned it. The only reason anyone was here at all was because Ree had saved them. They seemed to remember that, with their removed hats, their meek words. But heaven only knew what was going on in their heads. "And?" he asked.

The mayor shrugged. "Young Anders got there first. They was eating one of his heifers. They clawed him and run when he started shouting."

Young Anders was the mayor's nephew, if Ree remembered right. No wonder the man looked worried and upset. "Is he—"

"He's all right," the mayor said, too quickly for it to be true. "We sent to the manor for the Healer, and the Healer says as he'll be all right."

So why did you call me? Ree wanted to ask. *To show me what might happen if I go bad?* He tamped down the thought. They wouldn't do that. They were just worried for Anders, more than they wanted to admit. He wished he could believe it, believe that if hobgoblins so like him wounded—maybe badly enough to kill, no matter what the mayor said—one of the villagers they wouldn't turn on him. At least he knew they wouldn't turn on Jem. *He* was all human.

Besides, the Manor Lord was Jem's father, Lenar. He'd come back to the region last winter with his guards.

He'd retired from the Imperial army with enough gold to buy himself a manor house and be a lord. With all the big farms burned out and abandoned, Lenar built a manor house instead. The rest of his gold brought a Healer and a Mage to the valley to work for him. Nothing formal ever happened, but everyone treated Lenar like the lord of this valley. Except, when anything was really bad, they came to the farm up by the forest and asked for Jem or Ree.

Right on cue, Jem's voice boomed behind him. "What's going on here? Ree?" Jem had grown tall and broad shouldered, and fought a losing battle against the blond beard that he shaved off every morning. As always, the sight made Ree's heart lurch in his chest: he remembered the frail child he'd found in a Jacona alley and nursed to health. This young giant—a full head taller than Ree—surprised him every time.

"They killed two hobgoblins," Ree rushed to explain, before Jem blurted things no one should mention, like, *But they're like you.* "They hurt young Anders."

"And killed a cow," the mayor said. "It took four of the young men to bring them down," he said. "There was . . . Young Tam got clawed too, but he don't need the healer. He'll do all right with a poultice. But he said they fought like devils, clawing and spitting, like . . . like cats."

Jem squatted by the corpses, looked at them, then turned his head to talk to Ree, "Strange we didn't find them before," he said. His voice, which had grown deep, sounded businesslike. Ree and Jem patrolled the forest regularly—warning off the smarter hobgoblins, and killing those that were truly dangerous. "Odd for them to come out of nowhere and right into the village's pastures. They don't do that till winter."

"That's what we was thinking." The mayor said.

"Then the farrier ups and says the queen was nursing, and there must be cubs hereabouts."

It took Ree a moment to realize he didn't mean royalty, and merely used the name for a mother cat, which he supposed fit.

Ree swallowed. Both hobgoblins were painfully thin, so thin you could see the ribs through the skin and the fur. But the female's breasts were huge and heavy and unnaturally rounded. *Damn.* Unaccountably, he felt his eyes fill with tears, and was grateful when Jem stood and laid a reassuring hand on his shoulder.

The mayor blinked up at Jem, then glanced at Ree and ducked his head. "You see," he said. "It's that we don't know if there might not be a whole litter of them. And we don't know how old or big, either. Who knows how these things grow? And if they start hunting ... Well ... no dogs or children will be safe. No," he shook his head. "Mayhap no cows neither."

Ree bit back the response that came to his tongue— that no one could possibly nurse something large enough to bring down a cow. Perhaps it wasn't true. There were strange things in the woods that grew quite large while still nursing.

He felt his tail twitch in his pants. He tried to control it, but it was hard when he was this nervous. It tensed and whipped against his right leg, where he had it confined. He pretended he didn't notice, and hoped no one else would either. "I'll take a look," he said. "Later."

"*We'll* take a look," Jem corrected. No one argued. The mayor's hands stopped twisting his hat. He looked at Ree half in awe and half in fear, then bobbed his head at Jem.

"As soon as we can," Jem said, turning responsibility and focus away from Ree. Ree felt a surge of gratitude.

At the same time he would have laughed if it weren't so serious. It wasn't as though Jem could turn attention away from Ree completely.

Those are my kind, Ree thought. *They're like me. Not as though the village won't notice.*

Halfway home, in the shadowed lane where they walked side by side, Jem touched his shoulder cautiously. "Ree, don't worry. No one is going to think you are ... " He paused for a moment and frowned, and his lips twitched. "Unless of course, you start eating a live cow. Mind you, you're bad enough with the milking, that ... " He trailed off as though realizing his attempted joke would fall flat. "Ree. They weren't like you. Did you see their knuckles, all callused? They'd been running on those paws of theirs."

"They died holding hands."

Jem shrugged. "Ree. Animals do things that ... "

Ree turned his head away. "Which part of me is animal and which human? What makes me human but them animals?"

The laugh like a thunderclap startled him. Jem looked as surprised at his own laugh as Ree felt. "Sorry," Jem said, sheepishly. "But why is that different from the rest of us? We're all a little human and a little animal, no? It's all in how you use it."

"But you don't just kill humans for acting like animals!" Ree said.

"I bet you if a human had eaten half a living cow and attacked Anders bad enough to need the Manor's Healer, he'd have been killed too. It's self defense, Ree."

"Yeah," Ree tried to tell himself that Jem was right. Villagers hadn't killed the couple for being hobgoblins. They'd killed the couple for attacking a human. But they'd been so painfully thin. And if the female were nursing . . . They couldn't have come to the village begging for food. They couldn't have asked for help for their litter.

He found Jem's gaze trained on him, grave, but all too understanding. Understanding far more than Ree intended him to, Ree realized. Jem said, in the tone of voice that reminded Ree of Jem's grandfather, "And don't go getting your head all tied in knots when you think of their plight out there. Yeah, I saw how thin they were. And yeah, I remember what that winter was like that we spent living off the land. But Ree, when you thought I was dying of hunger and cold, you didn't try to kill a cow and bring me the chunks. Hells, Ree, you didn't try to kill Grandad when you stumbled into the farm, even though he couldn't walk, and you could have killed him and taken everything."

"But he was hurt and scared," Ree protested, unnerved at the thought that he might have killed Garrad, who had provided them with shelter and warmth and protection for years. "And he's . . . Grandad."

Jem grinned, as if he'd won a game. "Exactly. And that means that you thought of him as a human. Like us. I don't think they did, Ree. I think they were dangerous. Just because they had some human in them . . .

"Some human in animals makes animals worse. Grandad says so. Like all those things in the forest. The most dangerous ones have a bit of human. Look . . . I'm not going to say I wouldn't have liked it better if the changes hadn't been made. For one I'm sure you'd have liked it better and found it easier to be all human. But for me, you're as human as anyone else. You're just Ree."

"Papa! Da!" The shout made them both jump. It came from around the turn in the road, and approached at speed. Amelie stopped when she saw them, and made an

attempt at looking like a proper young lady. At eight, she
was starting to grow past the little-girl phase. Lately Jem
had insisted that she learn decorum. Ree would have
been puzzled by that if he didn't know all too well why
Jem did it. Lenar had just married Loylla, a well-bred
and wealthy young woman from Karelshill, the nearest
city. *She* insisted it was unnatural for "two bachelors to
be bringing up *that poor child.*" That they weren't bachelors, or that Amelie—whom they'd rescued from the
ruins of her former home after raiders had killed her
family—started crying whenever anyone talked of finding her a nice family with a mommy didn't help.

To Ree she looked just fine—a little girl just starting
to get a feeling she would someday be a woman—with
her fine blond hair, escaped from its ponytail, making a
tendriled frame for her pretty oval face and rosy cheeks.
Her pinafore had grown too short over the summer.
New winter clothes had been ordered but the seam-
stress hadn't finished them yet. So the little skirt left
a lot of suddenly long legs exposed. To compensate in
the cooling autumn air, she wore leggings that Garrad,
Jem's grandfather, had improvised by cutting the legs
from last year's pants.

Ree supposed—or rather, he didn't have to suppose, because he'd heard Lenar expound on it—that
she looked like a village urchin and would be laughed
at in the better circles of even the small cities. But Ree
knew nothing about the better circles of anywhere. Nor
did Jem. Lenar could fulminate all he wanted that it was
unnatural, and that she couldn't call them "Papa" and
"Da," but everyone in the valley treated Amelie as Ree
and Jem's daughter.

She brushed back her hair and pulled at her pinafore
skirt, trying to make it longer than it could possibly be.

Jem asked, laughter in his voice showing he was amused at these efforts, "What is it, Smidge? You need us?"

"Yes. I heard your voices, and I came . . . " She frowned. "It's Damn Young Cat."

That had been another fight. Lenar objected to Amelie calling the cats "damn." But that was what Garrad called the first stray tom who came cadging for meals around the farm. That Damn Cat brought home Another Damn Cat and they got busy making litter after litter of Damn Kittens—who grew up to be Damn Young Cats, who in turn had more Damn Kittens. It seemed every time they turned around there was a litter in the kitchen by the wood stove, and another litter playing on the kitchen floor. They'd have been overrun, except that people hereabouts, even from farms as far as a day's walk away, thought the Damn Cats were special.

The villagers said Ree trained the Damn Cats— talked to them and made them smarter than any other cat could be. Which was nonsense. Oh, Ree understood them, but any other person might. He could hear their meows in a range beyond humans. He could smell them more—so he knew when they were sick or distressed. But other than that, it was just paying attention. As for training them—it was all he could do not to burst into laughter when he heard that one. Grown men talking of anyone training cats!

But Damn Young Cat—he didn't need to ask which one—did seem slightly more intelligent than the others. It was an intelligence which the gray and white cat used to get into ten times as much trouble as any other Damn Cat. "What has Damn Young Cat done now?" Ree extended his hand to be grasped in Amelie's pink, sweaty one, and Amelie gazed up at him, anxiously.

"Don't know," she said. "I thought he was hurt, but

Granddad says he's not. But he keeps walking up to the edge of the forest, with his legs all stiff. And crying, you know, like he did when the snow bear got Other Damn Cat? Grandad says he's gone crazy or has the rabs, but he doesn't look sick. And I don't know what the rabs is. And Damn Young Cat won't let us get anything done."

"I think Grandad means rabies, and that's not right for rabies," Jem said, frowning. He picked up Amelie and carried her, with her clinging to his neck. "Well, show us."

She showed them. Or rather Damn Young Cat did. Before they entered the farm gates that Amelie had left ajar, he came running out of them and jumped in a single leap onto Ree's shoulder. It was this habit that had caused Ree to sew leather on the shoulders of all his shirts and pads underneath. He looked like a falconer, only no falconer had ever been subjected to the dubious pleasures of having a four pawed creature perch uneasily on his shoulder while yelling indignantly in his ear. Damn Young Cat didn't smell wounded. Or frightened. He smelled . . . distressed.

Another bleat-meow of complaint almost deafened Ree. He sighed, reached for Damn Young Cat and scratched under its chin. "All right, all right, but we don't know what's wrong. You have to show us."

It wasn't so much that he had trained the cats. It was that Damn Young Cat had trained Ree. He knew if there was something that needed Ree's attention, Ree would follow him.

He jumped down onto the path, raced away from the gate in the wall that enclosed the main parts of the farm: the barn, the house proper, the chicken house and the stable for the cows and goats. The other way lay fields and pastures—part of the farm though they only had rough fences around them.

"I'd better go with him," Ree said with a sigh.

"Not alone, you don't," Jem said, setting the little girl down. "You go to Grandad, Melie."

It was only as Damn Young Cat led them into the forest—stopping every few feet to stare over his shoulder at Ree, to make sure he was following—that Jem asked, "Should we have brought weapons?"

But Damn Young Cat yowled his displeasure, and Ree said, "No. We'll probably be all right. The snow bears can't hide in fall. It's only in winter they're invisible or close to it."

Nonetheless, he grabbed a large piece of a tree branch and Jem did the same, as they followed Damn Young Cat. The woods had been dangerous ever since the magic storms. You never knew what you might find.

What they found Ree smelled before he heard, and heard long before he saw. The smell was the musk of a young and frightened animal. The sound was a thin, high wail, the sort of cry a young creature in distress might make. And the look . . .

It was the cub of the couple in the village. It couldn't be anything else. The way it was nestled—in the crook of a tree, far enough off the ground to be inaccessible to anything but the most agile of the climbing animals—spoke of them having retained some of their original human intelligence.

The cub was covered too—wrapped in an uncured fur which smelled a bit, but would protect a young creature from the cold mornings and bitter nights. Another sign its parents had been intelligent. The face above the improvised blanket was thin and pinched, dark greeny-hazel eyes filled with tears. Snot and drool were dried around the mouth, as it would be with any baby that had cried for a long time. Its swollen, reddened face was obvious even under fur more sparse than that of its parents.

Seeing Ree, it shrieked once, louder than before, then seemed to go mute with terror, its arms flailing and legs kicking at the blanket. Ree reached for the all-work knife at his belt. He kept it sharp to kill rabbits that had been caught in traps, so they wouldn't suffer for longer than needed. He set a not-unkind hand on the back of the cub's head, intending to pull it back and expose the neck—only he couldn't make himself draw the knife, not fully. Not with those eyes looking at him and seeming to understand exactly what he should do. What he couldn't do.

Jem's voice startled him from his frozen indecision. "Ree? What are you doing?"

"The villagers—" Ree started to say, then realized that wasn't right. Or maybe it was and he wanted to protect himself from the villagers thinking he was like the hobgoblins they'd killed. "What if it grows up and it—" Ree said, but he looked down at the cub, whose scalp was warm and rounded against his hand, who stared up at him with something that might even have been trust. "Oh, hells." How could he convince Jem that the cub should be killed—*put down*—when he couldn't convince himself?

"It's just a baby." Jem picked the cub up and matter-of-factly pulled back the stinking blanket, revealing that it was healthy, male, and reeking for more reasons than one. "No idea how old," he said. "But just a baby."

"Yeah, but we should . . . I mean the hobgoblins—"

"He won't go bad," Jem said. His voice had that strangely affectionate-gruff tone that he got when he talked to or about Amelie. "He just won't. We'll teach him better." Jem rocked the boy in his arms as he spoke. "Won't we? We'll teach you better."

Ree knew he'd lost the argument before it started. Not that Jem wasn't capable of an argument. Oh, he was. He could out-stubborn Garrad and Lenar both, and when those three got to yelling, Ree was fairly sure the mountain peaks all around rang with their outrage. This, though—this wasn't something Ree was going to argue about. What was the point? He couldn't kill the little one, not when he knew its parents were intelligent. The question was, what kind of a creature was it? Was it really a baby? Or a dangerous wild cub?

The way he screamed and kicked and flailed in Jem's arms, all the way to the farm, Ree couldn't help thinking dangerous, and Garrad who came running at the sound of the yells looked like he was leaning to dangerous beast as well. He didn't look comforted by their explanation, either.

Garrad walked ahead of them—catch him following someone, even with the stick he had to use to help him walk—to the spacious kitchen warmed by the fancy iron stove they'd installed over the summer with the proceeds of the furs from last year's hunting. Amelie was adding cut vegetables to the soup simmering on the back burner. That was another point of contention for Lenar. He said she was too young to work, and should be in school.

That might be true for the children of minor lordlings, but it wasn't true of village children. Little girls younger than Amelie got apprenticed to the big houses down in Karelshill as scullery maids, and ended up working much harder than Amelie did. Besides, Amelie learned her letters too, before dinner, sitting at the table and writing them painfully on a slate tablet. She didn't like it much, but she learned.

Jem swept aside the slate tablet and the chalk, and set the cub right on the table—ignoring Garrad's protest about vermin and filth—and unwrapped him. Jem didn't answer when Garrad said something about catching fleas, although it was nearly too cold for that.

Here, in the cozy warmth of the kitchen, with the familiar light of the lantern above, the cub looked more like a human baby and more out of place. He really had very little fur—tabby like his mother's—and his tail was only a little stump about the size of his thumb. Looking closer, Ree thought he could see marks as if rats had eaten the rest. Which they might have: they did eat the tails off barn kittens, sometimes. And there were marks aplenty from flea bites and stings on the scrawny little body, easy to see even when he started pumping arms and legs full force again.

"The question is," Garrad said, "what is he?"

"He's a baby," Amelie said, in puzzled disdain, as though wondering how they'd failed to spot it. She'd come around the table, wooden spoon still in hand after stirring the soup pot, and looked at the baby with a fascinated, wondering expression. "He's like a baby Papa," she said, and dimpled suddenly. "Aw." She put her free hand forward, till it was just in reach of the little—clawed—fist.

"Amelie, no!" Ree said. But before the words were out of his mouth, the baby grabbed Amelie's hand and stopped crying. He hadn't clawed her or attacked her, just grabbed onto her index finger and held. He was looking at her with the curiously confident look of babies everywhere.

"Well!" Garrad said, with an explosive sound.

Jem shook his head and said. "I'd best put some water to boil. That's a right mess in that fur—besides, he has fleas."

"We ought to burn that damn fur," Garrad said turning away from the table. "I'll go grab some rags for diapering, shall I?"

They filled the big tin bath and set it right next to the stove, so the baby wouldn't take a chill. He held Amelie's wrist tight while they bathed him, and sucked on his other thumb something fierce.

"We'll have to get some food in him," Garrad said. "The poor thing is hungry. I don't suppose any of the women in the village will nurse him neither. It will have to be goat's milk." He disappeared for a while and came back with a weird contraption, shaped like a plain-glazed old-fashioned oil lamp covered in dust. He set about washing it while Jem took a towel and wrapped the baby as Ree pulled him out of the water.

"I think we'll call him Meren," Amelie said, as they lay the baby on the table, still in the towel. "Like ... My dad." Her voice trembled only a little. She'd seen her family massacred through the keyhole of the cellar where they'd locked her for her own safety. Ree didn't know what she'd seen. Neither he nor Jem had ever thought it would do any good to ask. But these days she mentioned her dead parents with less pain, as if they were part of a beautiful dream now gone. He supposed she was young enough that eventually she'd heal altogether and perhaps even forget.

"Meren is a right good name," Garrad said softly. "And it's not like we can keep calling him baby. Bound to get confusing if we call him Damn Baby too. Could get him mixed up with Damn Cats. Besides, Lenar will yell at us again on account of using bad language." He'd finished washing the clay thing and was drying it on a clean rag, as he spoke.

"What's that, Grandad?" Ree asked.

"Oh, this? One of the extra teats for my boys."

Ree blinked. He didn't think you were supposed to call them teats if they were on humans, and how did anyone have an extra one?

"Boys get extra teats?" Amelie asked.

Jem just looked helpless. Some questions you really didn't want to answer.

Garrad winked at Ree and smiled at Amelie. "Turns out we still had one. My wife, your grandmother, Jem, often went to sell cheese on Fair Days. She left me with your father and his brothers, and I had to feed them. She'd leave milk in these here jugs in the cooling room for the baby, and they all suckled from them a treat. Now what we do is we scald a cup of milk, fill this and let it cool till it feels just warm on the skin. Then we see if Damn Baby will suckle."

"I thought we weren't going to call him Damn Baby," Jem said.

"Oh, right," Garrad set milk in a small pot on the stove. "Damn Meren."

Amelie giggled behind her hand, and Jem smiled, but Ree was thinking that maybe it would be better for everyone if Damn Baby refused to suckle. Though he couldn't quite face the thought of watching the poor thing wasting away to nothing before his eyes. It wasn't as if he would have the courage to put an end to the little thing's existence. He'd already failed once.

At any rate, there wasn't any point thinking about it. They got the baby diapered and dressed in an old shirt of Amelie's—which Garrad said would have to be replaced with manly clothes, or Lenar would yell about

that too. When they put the clay . . . well, nipple was the
only word Ree could think of . . . to his lips, it had taken
Meren only a few seconds to start suckling.

"I wouldn't give him more than two teats full," Garad
said, as Ree looked at the empty-again jug in some wonder. "Bound to make him sick."

"But he's still hungry," Jem said, as Meren started
a thin, complaining wail. Which, quite fortunately, was
stopped by a sudden—startlingly loud—burp, making
Amelie stifle a giggle. A little spit-up of milk came out
with the burp, making Meren look surprised, but after
they'd wiped that down with a clean rag, he'd put his
thumb in his mouth and looked even more surprised
when his eyes started to close.

In no time at all, he was fully asleep, a warm, con-
tented bundle in Ree's arms. Which was when someone
pounded at the door.

When Garrad opened it, Ree could see past him to
the worried, cold-looking face of the mayor. "Young
Anders died," he said. "Not all that the Healer could do
would save him. We were wondering if you'd found—"
He stopped, staring at Ree and the baby in his arms.
Even from that distance it would be impossible to miss
that the baby had fur.

"You can't mean to keep the little beast," the mayor
said. "You were supposed to kill it!"

Garrad made a sound in his throat and started to say,
"There now, what has . . . "

"It's the get of those monsters as killed my nephew!"
the mayor yelled.

Ree wanted to hide. He wanted to stay quiet. He
wanted to take the baby a long way away and never
come back. Just the two of them, monsters, and no one
to judge them. But instead, and much to his own shock,

he found he was on his feet, holding Meren so tight that he woke up and let out a thin, surprised cry.

"My mother," Ree shouted, hearing the words come out of his mouth, and not quite believing them, "Was a prostitute on the streets of Jacona. Does that make me a prostitute? My father was likely a mercenary, does that make me a mercenary? Does it mean the families of people my father killed get to kill me?" Meren's thin wail made a counterpoint to Ree's shouting but couldn't overshadow it.

"Now, there, son," Garrad said in calming tones. He was the only one who spoke. Both Jem and the mayor looked shocked that Ree would actually yell—since Ree had kept himself quiet ever since Garrad took them in, hoping no one would hurt him. For all the good it did. "There's no need—"

"No, Grandad," Ree said. "Not this time. This little one's parents died for their crimes. He's not them, no more than I'm my parents, or I'm his parents for that matter. What are you scared of? He hasn't even got milk teeth yet. If you catch him gumming a cow to death, you can kill him, but not before."

Carried forward by his sudden fury he slammed the door shut in the mayor's face. He half expected that the man would pound on it again, but he didn't.

As they heard the crunch of his steps on the gravel, walking away, Jem said, "I wonder if he's going to summon a party with pitchforks . . . "

"What, and risk Ree tearing him apart?" Garrad said. "Not damn likely."

Amelie giggled, as if she thought the idea of Ree tearing someone apart was funny, but Ree had scared ßhimself.

He didn't want to tear anyone apart. "Meren's just young," Ree said. "And . . . and defenseless."

"That he is, son," Garrad said, looking at Ree, who instinctively had started rocking the baby back to sleep. "You know, if he grows up . . . that is . . . if he turns out not to be fit for human company . . . "

"I'll do what I have to," Ree said, wishing he were sure he wasn't lying. He knew his duty. He hoped he could do it.

"I think we still have the old crib," Garrad said. "Jem, come with me to get it from the attic." There might have been just a hint of mischief in the old man's voice as he added. "It will have to go in your room."

Ree and Jem exchanged a look of sudden shock at the idea of that pair of greeny-hazel eyes watching their every move.

"What's a pros-titute?" Amelie asked, looking up from her slate and chalk.

"A word you shouldn't say," Garrad said. "Unless you want Grandad Lenar at us about your manners again."

"Oh." Amelie turned back to her slate as Jem and Garrad walked away bickering, and the baby stopped crying.

And then the little hand grabbed onto Ree's finger and held it tight.

Heart's Own

Sarah A. Hoyt

This being the first warm week in six months, Ree sat milking the goats in the farmyard. Meren, the hobgoblin baby he and Jem had rescued almost a year and a half ago, was past being fed with a nurser, but he still liked goat milk. Besides, Ree had heard goat cheeses were selling well to the itinerant traders—now that peace was returning to the region.

The flock of six nanny goats pressed close, bleating softly. It was Ree's considered opinion they were doing their best to jostle him and the goat being milked at that moment, so that they could all scamper away without being milked.

But just as they had learned not to be scared of Ree—a human who had acquired cat eyes and rat fur and tail in the magic storms—he had learned not to fall for their tricks. He kept a firm hand on the nanny being milked. "You're almost finished now," he said. "Stop fussing."

The goat turned an evil yellow eye upon him and tried to head butt him in a not-unfriendly way.

A piercing scream made Ree jump. He let go of the goat. The animal, free to do as she wished, managed to head butt him on the knee, while either she, or one of her fellows, kicked over the full bucket of milk onto the flagstones of the yard. Ree fell, clutching his knee, biting his lip not to let his opinion of goats come out of his mouth. The wail was Meren's, a rising and falling scream of a young thing in deep distress. He could see Meren being dragged by the hand by Amelie—the human orphan that Jem and Ree had rescued and adopted.

Nearing ten, Amelie was trusted to go sell their daily collection of eggs in the village. Which was why she was wearing her best—and brand new—dress of multicolored striped stuff, her blouse with the lace slightly askew on the collar, on account of being her own handiwork, and her best apron with the ruffles around the edge and the pockets. She contrasted oddly with Meren, whom she had in a vise-grip around the wrist.

Meren looked more human than Ree. He looked almost fully human, save for cat eyes, a light covering of curly tabby fur, cat ears, tiny whiskers and the sharp little teeth in his wide-open mouth as he let out his scream of distress. He also looked like he'd been in a fight. His shirt and coveralls, fresh and clean just this morning were torn, muddied and bloody. His fur being light, it was quite easy to see both his eyes were bruised and would soon be black. A cut on his forehead bled profusely. He was trying to pull his hand out of Amelie's grasp, tilting his rounded toddler body backwards.

Ree jumped up, rubbing at his knee, and wondering if his tail had broken in his pants. He limped over to them, grasped Meren by both shoulders to hold him still. "Melie, what—Meren, stop wailing. You're safe. No, you can't go back there," in reply to Meren's pulling in the direction of the gate. "Now, stop crying. Stop this minute." His voice sharpened as it rarely did. Meren stopped crying and subsided into sniffles of discontent. Ree looked at Amelie, who was twisting her apron, a sign of distress. "Melie," he said, softly. Melie had seen her whole family massacred through the keyhole of the cellar where they'd hidden her. These days she rarely had nightmares, and could be quite forceful when required, but she would still startle at a harsh word. "Tell me what happened."

Melie sniffled. Now that she didn't have to restrain Meren, tears dewed her eyes and she was making sounds as though only just preventing herself from bursting into lament. Ree examined Meren and his clothes. The shirt was torn and the pants Amelie had mended, with her in-expert, hasty stitches, were ripped in a dozen new places. There were a lot of cuts on his scalp that seemed to be more than village boys would have been able to do, with their human non-clawed fingers. And there were big bruises on his shoulders, just under his clothes. As for the cut on his forehead, it was long and vicious, looking almost as though it had been made by a dagger.

"It wasn't Meren's fault," Amelie said. "Really, Papa, it wasn't."

"I believe you," he said. Amelie didn't lie, not even to defend the one she considered a baby brother. "Tell me."

"When I came out of the mayor's house, from deliv-ering the eggs—" Melie's hands twisted at the apron. "I saw Meren walking down the street. I . . . I think he was looking for me. And there were boys and they—" Sniffle. "Threw rocks at him." Louder sniffle. "And I called him, but then they jumped him and he . . . he fought them . . . So I yelled at them all, and I dragged him away . . . " Sob. "He didn't want to come, but I thought, if he bit anyone, like last time . . . "

"Right," Ree said. "You did very well, Amelie." Superbly well, considering she'd managed to get a fighting little boy out of the mud of the street without getting more than a light spattering on her skirt. Knowing that Amelie, like himself, did better when she was looking after others, he said. "Go and set the big pan of water to boil. We need to wash Meren and bandage his cuts."

He had the clothes set aside for washing, Meren scrubbed but not dressed, and was finishing bandaging the forehead, with a strip of cloth tied at a rakish angle around the mess of tabby fur and white-blond all-too-human curls starting to come in all over Meren's scalp, when Jem came running from the fields where he'd been supervising hired hands. With money from the furs of animals they hunted, they could hire day laborers—who were willing to come now there was no danger of being attacked by strange beasts or pressed into a renegade lord's service—and plow the fields that had lain fallow too long. Jem talked of putting two acres to wheat and setting five acres to corn or some such thing. Ree normally let the talk wash over him like water.

Jem was human, a blond giant of a man, and if the villagers frowned at his living in domestic bliss with a male—and a hobgoblin at that—no one would say it to his face. Besides the size and the temper that seemed to run in Jem's family, Jem was the son of the local lord, a veteran of the Imperial army who was as likely to get cross at anyone complaining of his son's way of life as he was to yell at his son for what he himself viewed as a transgression of decorum. So Jem could go out to the fields and supervise the hired hands, while Ree stayed close to home, planted a vegetable garden just past the farmyard, and looked after the animals.

Jem washed his hands and face in the used bath water and turned around, frowning as he wiped them on a towel. "What happened?" he asked, as Ree started to dress Meren in another shirt and coveralls. "The women bringing men their lunch told wild stories. That the damn boy has gone rabid and is biting all the village boys and tearing their arms out and what not."

Ree shook his head, finished buttoning the coveralls. "Melie says the boys stoned him, Jem. And that she got him from the middle of a pack of them. If he bit anyone . . . "

Jem snorted. "If he bit anyone, we'll have my father on us before we're much older. Which is why I thought I'd best come home and face His Rageness when he comes in."

"You left the field hands alone?"

"Nah. Grandad is with them. He's spent most of the morning telling them what they were doing wrong, anyway, and how much better it was in his day. He's amusing himself greatly."

Which was likely true, since by finding fault, Garrad, Jem's grandad, could prove that he was still the grown-up and the owner of his own farm, despite Jem's great stature and booming voice.

Jem squeezed Ree's shoulder reassuringly. "If you want to tidy up, mayhap we might have a few bites of food in before my lord and father comes to yell at us."

Ree emptied the tin bath and put it away, and with Melie's help set out the vegetable stew and fresh bread. Jem played with Meren, throwing the giggling boy upward and catching him again when he fell, and pretending to subdue him when he tried to climb up Jem's arm, claws extended. Ree shook his head at the matching laughter—man and boy—and was both grateful that

Jem would make Meren too tired to get into any more trouble, and worried about . . . a slip of the hand, a swipe of claws, anything that could hurt one of them. Because if Meren hurt Jem, everyone would say he was a dangerous wild animal. And if Jem hurt Meren . . . If Jem hurt Meren, Ree's heart might break clean in two.

It was impossible to raise anything from a cub—human, animal or in between—and not get attached to them. This was why this farm didn't keep rabbits and pigs, and why their chickens were all layers save for the one inevitable rooster. They bought their meat elsewhere with the money from eggs and milk.

Watching Meren soar ceilingward, thrown by Jem, and landing, little claws involuntarily extended and flailing just short of Jem's eyes, Ree wished he were more sure that there was a greater difference between this creature they called their little boy and the farm animals or the damn cats. He looked into Meren's greeny-hazel eyes as they turned adoringly to Jem, and wondered if there was a human mind there.

Amelie returned, having changed into her everyday dress. They sat at the table.

"The problem is that the damn boy won't talk," Jem said, as he tore into the crusty brown bread with an appetite. "If Melie hadn't happened to see—"

"No," Ree said, as he gave Meren another slice of bread and got for his pains a loose, sloppy smile with little needle sharp teeth showing just beneath. "The problem is that Meren wasn't supposed to go to the village again. I told him not to." He knew he looked worried. "I'm not sure he understands what I tell him at all."

"Oh, come," Jem said. He chuckled easily. "I'm sure he understands you just fine. But he's a little boy. The farm is boring. He wanted to go see where Amelie had got to!"

Which might very well be true, but it wasn't the first time Meren had got beaten up in the village and one would think he'd have learned to stay away. Ree hoped with all his heart that he at least understood the many times he'd been told not to bite or claw anyone.

But he said nothing because Lenar arrived. The first thing that alarmed Ree was that Lenar didn't start by screaming. Instead, he stood in the doorway, watching the family finish their food and saying nothing till Jem said, "Would you have some food, Father?"

"Don't mind if I do," Lenar said, striding in, pulling the one free chair normally occupied by Garrad and making it groan with his bulk as he sat on it. He looked like a larger and older version of Jem, his body hardened and muscled by years in combat. He wore rich clothes, but practical—his shirt might be silk, but the jacket over it was leather, and his breeches were fine suede. A lord he might be now, by virtue of his gold in reward for good service to the new emperor, but in fact he still spent most of his day in the saddle, tracking down rumors of bandits or any hint of preying mercenary bands. He was what made this corner of the world so peaceful.

What alarmed Ree was that Lenar had taken their invitation to eat, something he'd never done before.

Out of some protective instinct, Ree rose and picked up Meren, who was drooping to sleep in his chair, as he usually did after the midday meal. "Ree—" Jem started, but Ree didn't want to know what Jem wanted or if he wanted him to stay or was merely censuring him for his cowardice.

"Have to put Meren in his bed," Ree said. "Otherwise he'll wake up in a moment and then be fussy because he won't be able to sleep again."

He held the baby to his chest, the blond/tabby head

bobbing against his shoulder as he moved, the whiskers tickling his neck. He carried Meren all the way up
the ladder to the attic, still stocked with last year's hay,
smelling warm and dusty as it usually did in this season.
They'd built permanent walls up there to make a bedroom for Amelie, and for the last three months Meren
had shared the room with Amelie. The ladder presented
no problems for him. He liked climbing things. Ree had
thought he'd never recover from seeing Meren chase
the rooster atop the barn, but then he'd started climbing the uneven wall around the vegetable garden and
chasing a butterfly along the top. Ree had almost killed
himself rescuing him.

Though Ree relished having his room for himself and
Jem, part of him felt guilty for having Meren up here.
The little crib looked so odd at the foot of Amelie's little
bed, covered in the lace coverlet that Lenar—in a be-
nevolent mood—had given her. But when Ree had said
they should keep Meren longer in the bedroom, Jem
had said he'd be damned if he was going to have the
damn boy there till the damn boy was talking. Which
just went to show that Jem lived in another world. Ree
wished that Meren would talk.

He lay the warm, heavy little body on the quilt in the
crib, then covered him with an edge of it. Not too much,
because the attic was warm. He pulled down the side of
the crib too, because there was no point making Meren
climb over that when he got out.

Over summer Ree would have to talk to Jem about
taking a day or two and a couple of the hired hands and
helping build another little room up here for Meren.
Amelie would soon be of an age where sharing a room
with a little brother wouldn't be proper.

As Ree went down the stairs, his worry returned.

What if Meren never spoke? What if he became violent as he grew up? Oh, he was sweet and affectionate, and would sometimes put his arms around Ree, and would play and laugh with Jem, but so did kittens. And young tigers. What part of Meren was child? Which kitten? And would the kitten show himself feral?

"Look, what I'm saying, son," Lenar's voice boomed to Ree's ears as he reached the bottom floor, but he wasn't yelling. Only being his forceful self. "Is that you should put him in a muzzle."

"A muzzle, Father?" Jem said. The yelling would start at any moment.

"Oh, come, son. It's not like I'm saying he should be put down. Our Amelie says, and I trust her, that he had enough provocation, and everyone knows that a dog taunted will bite back, no matter how tame. Especially an untrained puppy."

"Meren is not an untrained puppy."

"No, of course not. Untrained kitten more like, though why your damn young man can't train that kitten when he trains the others—"

"Meren is a little boy," Jem said in the tone that meant he had gone past anger and was now very calm and also very dangerous. Ree had only ever seen him get like this in defense of himself or Amelie. "Jem! What little boy walks a mile and a half of country roads on his own?"

"An . . . adventurous one?" Jem asked, but sounded unsure for the first time.

"Look, I don't like telling you this. I wouldn't like hearing it if it were a cub I was raising. I'm just saying he's not quite human."

"He's like Ree."

"No, son. Ree grew up as a human among humans. The . . . the change happened afterward and it's not very deep, perhaps. But this . . . cub was born of people who were changed. I can tell you, Jem," in a suddenly firm voice, "that no normal human child can walk at six months the way that . . . that . . . little Meren could. And no human child can climb before a year."

Jem sighed. When he spoke he sounded tired, as if feeling defeated. "We don't know how old he is, Father. It's hard to tell. He might have been six months when we found him. Or more."

"Which would make him over two now, and yet he's not said a word."

"So? Grandad says you never said a word until you were past three, and then it was straight to normal talking."

Lenar made a dismissive sound. "That's different, son. I'm sorry it's come to this, and I'm not telling you you should put him down or that it's his fault in any way, but I don't think he is a little boy. I think he's an animal. A nice pet, I warrant you, but you'll have to muzzle him. And chain him to keep him from running out."

"Chain him!" The outrage was back in Jem's voice. The idea of little Meren chained up made Ree cringe and feel slightly sick.

"It is the only thing to—"

"No, you listen, Father," Jem said, this time sounding incensed. "You haven't been around this family enough to know Meren. If you spent more time with him, you'd know he was human. Why don't you and your lady come to dinner tonight? Simple fare, but good."

"Well, I—"

"I know that we farm folk are far beneath your new wife's dignity, but—"

"Now, Jem, I never said that," Lenar said, still calm, though Jem was now yelling.

"You as good as said it. And it's not as if she ever visits, even when you do."

"She's not used to farms. She was raised—"

"Far above our station, yes, I know, but you can't claim that Meren is an animal when you've spent less time with him than you have with the Damn Young Cat."

"The one that follows Ree around? I don't think I've spent any time with him at all."

"Exactly. You haven't!" Jem was now fair and far away and yelling loud enough the farmhands probably could hear him in the field. "If you come to dinner and bring your lady and afterward think Meren is an animal, we'll talk of having him muzzled."

"And chained?"

"Restrained, at any rate," Jem said sullenly.

Ree came into the room, trying to pretend he hadn't heard anything. Amelie was washing dishes, stonefaced. Lenar left soon afterward, as did Jem to go back to the field. It wasn't until both of them had gone that Amelie looked at Ree and said, with a narrowing of her eyes, "Grandad Lenar is even more scary when he doesn't yell."

"Yes," Ree said. "But look you, if Lenar is bringing his wife over for dinner, we need to get ready. Whatever your Da says, the place isn't fit for a lady of quality just now. Garrad has some tablecloths and things from the old days when they used to hold banquets for harvest festival."

They spent the rest of the afternoon finding the linen tablecloths and the better dishes, which were glazed and painted with red flowers instead of rough-fired. After Garrad came home, just before sunset, he opened a trap door to the cellar and brought up a massive pewter serving plate and two candlesticks. "Hid them behind the false wall down there," he said. "We ain't got no silver, but that properly shined up should make her ladyship feel more at home."

It fell to Ree to polish them, while Garrad and Amelie roasted a haunch of venison that Jem had sent one of the hired hands to get from Three Rivers.

The table, once set, looked very pretty indeed, and then Jem came in, dripping wet and bare chested, having washed himself under the water pump in the yard.

"I didn't want to give trouble," he protested, as Ree yelped in outrage, as he ran to him with a towel.

"Don't drip on the tablecloth," Ree said. "It's ironed. And watch your feet on the floor."

He hectored Jem all the way into their bedroom, where he found him clean pants and shirt and a jacket not so different from the ones that Lenar wore.

Before Jem had time to say, "Perhaps I should shave," Ree had got him warm water for the washbasin in the bedroom and his razor and soaping mug and brush.

While Jem was shaving—a ritual that baffled Ree, who didn't shave, because if he started he would have to continue over his scalp, down his neck, and over his whole body except the tail—Ree checked on the preparations for dinner.

When he came back to the bedroom Jem, who was drying his face, said, "You should dress Meren nicely, Ree. And comb his hair a little. Maybe he no longer needs that bandage around his head?"

Ree realized he hadn't seen Meren all afternoon. Perhaps he was still asleep, but if so, that alone would be a cause for worry, because the child didn't normally sleep more than a couple of hours in the afternoon.

He almost ran out of the bedroom and up the ladder to the attic. The crib was empty and felt cold. Ree felt as though he'd swallowed a lump of ice. If Meren had walked to the village again . . . Lenar wasn't requesting that he be put down, because he hadn't actually injured anyone. If someone threatened him or scared him, and Meren bit him badly . . . Ree and Jem had told Meren over and over not to bite anyone, but did Meren understand them? And what if anything hapened to Meren? He was only two, at most two and a half, though Ree doubted it was that much. He might be fast on his feet and easy of balance, but he couldn't defend himself. Worse, half the villagers would be out for him. His biological parents had killed the mayor's nephew. People had long memories.

The icy feeling in his stomach spread as he struggled down the ladder, half blind with worry. He'd get Amelie: she could usually figure out which way Meren had gone, by what seemed like magic but was more likely just that she spent a lot of time watching her little brother. Ree crossed the great, echoing room, and ran into the kitchen, where Garrad was busy around the big woodstove, while a freshly shaven Jem was lighting the candles on the pewter candlesticks. Something in Ree's face—if not his hurried exit from their bedroom—made Jem look up and blench. "What's wrong?"

Ree wanted to tell him that Meren was gone, but then again didn't want to tell him, and what came out in an odd, strangled voice was, "Where's Amelie?"

"Melie went to the garden," Jem said. "Why, Ree, what's wrong?"

He was so worried he couldn't think, much less speak. The garden on the side of the house, such as it was, was Melie's domain. She'd planted daisies and bulbs, and in spring and summer, she would cut flowers for the table. But at this time of year there were no flowers yet. "Garden?"

"Vegetable garden. You know, some of those peas you planted that you bought off that peddler? The one that said they'd be the first after the snow? Well, they're full up and tender and sweet and we thought they'd make a nice dish for the din— Ree, where are you going?"

Ree plunged out the door, running full tilt to the vegetable garden. Evening had descended and the barn, the animal pens, the big tree in the yard, all cast blueish-black shadows.

The shadows were longer past the gate in the little fence—designed to keep the goats out, not an active little boy in—that encircled the vegetable garden, except for the outer part, which was encircled in a tall stone wall. The pea plants, frail and gangly, were the only conspicuously green thing. The other plants were only starting to pierce the ground.

For a moment, he thought that Amelie had Meren with her, because he heard her voice, from behind the screen of pea stalks and poles. But then he realized she was singing softly to herself. He opened his mouth to call "Amelie," but before he could he saw Meren.

The little boy crouched on the top of the wall, making faces. In the failing light he looked like a displeased cat or a creature out of the forest. He was on all fours.

His real parents had calluses on their hands, Ree thought, dismayed. As he watched, Meren arched his back up, lowered his shoulders, opened his mouth and hissed in threat. At that moment, despite his little overalls and shirt, he looked utterly feral.

A wild beast. He's a wild beast. He was never my little boy.

While Ree stood frozen, Meren let out a yowl that could have been any of the male Damn Cats challenging a rival and jumped from the wall. Straight down into the space between two rows of pea plants—hidden from Ree's view by the screen of green tendrils and tall poles.

He's going to hurt himself, Ree thought. And then Amelie screamed, the sound tangling with a loud snarl, a sound that couldn't come from any human throat.

Ree's thoughts were all a jumble. *Melie!* And then, *He's attacking Melie. He's jealous of her. She's human. She won't let him fight. Like cats that hate the family baby.*

He ran before he knew he was. His knife was not in the sheath at his waist, where he normally kept it. He'd taken it out to cut something and forgot to put it back.

I promised Garrad I'd do what it took if this day came.

He grabbed a large, heavy rock from the side of the path and plunged forward, fear and concern for Amelie propelling him, even as he was not sure what he could do, if anything.

Amelie was still screaming "Meren, Meren!" and the snarling went on. There seemed to be a high snarling and a lower one, which made no sense. That is, until Ree rounded the screen of plants and—

For a moment, he just stared, unable to understand. There were Meren and Amelie, but Meren was not attacking Amelie, as Ree expected. Meren was . . . There was a gaunt, half-starved dire wolf, and Meren was clinging to it or it had him. Amelie was standing beside the dire wolf, obscuring Meren while she pounded the wolf with the little basket she used to collect vegetables, all while screaming, "Meren, Meren!"

There was blood on her dress, blood on her hair, and when she turned and said, "Papa, Papa. Meren!" Ree saw a long streak of a scratch across her rosy cheek.

The rock fell from Ree's hand when he realized that Meren wasn't holding the creature's muzzle, but caught between its long teeth, still struggling and scratching and biting, but trapped and bleeding. One sudden crunch of those powerful jaws and Meren would be gone forever. It was only Amelie beating it with her basket that had kept death at bay. Barely.

Ree jumped, his own claws out, reaching for the creature's neck, digging in. The thing would open its mouth to breathe. Everything did when being strangled. If only it didn't crunch down first in surprise.

He squeezed hard and suddenly, and the wolf opened its jaws, and Ree yelled "Meren!" and hoped Amelie understood and got the little boy out of the way. He didn't dare look to see if she had: the animal was starving, desperate, and he had to stop it. The hand that wasn't clutching the wolf's throat flailed for the rock he'd dropped, for anything he could use as a weapon. Then the rock was in his hand, and he was beating at the dire wolf's head, beating, beating, beating.

"Ree. Ree, stop!" He came to, as though out of a nightmare, to Jem's hand on his arm. The dire wolf was dead. In fact, there was blood and brains of dire wolf over quite an area, including Ree's suit, face, fur and the nearest plants and ground.

"Meren?" he said.

"Amelie and Garrad have taken him to the house."

"Is he—"

"It doesn't look good," Jem said. "He'll need a Healer. Amelie said she was attacked and he jumped down to defend her."

"Yeah," Ree said. "Yeah." He ran his hand over his face, trying to remove the blood and gore but only succeeded in smearing it further. He stood on legs that felt so nerveless they could barely carry him.

"You go ahead," he told Jem. "See if you can bring the Healer. I'll . . . I'll come."

Jem gave him a concerned look, but ran. Only fear for Ree could have kept him here. Ree had to hold onto plants, and stakes, and the fence, and then the side of the animal pen. He walked as though in a dream. *Meren saved Amelie. And I thought . . . He saved Amelie. Cat. Human. What does it matter? He loves. He's loved. He's intelligent enough to protect those he loves.* He struggled to the water pump and pumped out water. Cold, it felt good on his face and head, his arms and hands—even over the clothes.

Lots of humans couldn't talk. They were born with defects of mind or body that made it impossible. But they weren't animals: they were people. And Meren was at least as much people as those unfortunates.

Please let him be well, he asked the distant sky with its indifferent, cold stars. *Let me have my little boy again. I'll never complain if he doesn't talk or if he runs along the damn wall chasing the damn butterflies.*

Outside the kitchen, in the yard, Lenar's carriage with the shield on the door—showing a sword entwined with a ham and proving his lordship had a sense of humor—stood, but one of the horses was missing from its traces, and the driver in his shiny red livery was milling around, aimlessly, looking displeased with his surroundings.

The kitchen was very silent. At the still-set table, with the good wax candles burning on the burnished candlesticks, Lenar's wife sat. She was very young and bland-looking, and her eyes widened and her mouth opened a little when she saw Ree, but she said nothing.

It was Garrad, who was standing by the door to the interior of the house, who said, "Son. You need to wash."

"Meren, he—"

But before Ree could say any more there was the sound of hooves in the yard, and then Lenar's shouting voice, and a middle aged man whose face was a curious shade of pale green came hurrying through the door. "The child?" he asked Garrad. "Lord Lenar, he—"

"Meren is upstairs," Garrad said. "With his father and his sister. Just you go on up. Jem will tell you what happened."

The Healer stumbled past them, and Lenar came in. "Damned Healer. Didn't want to ride double on the horse with me, but I knew if I let him have his own horse, he'd dawdle and not get here till the child was dead. Says I made him sick to his stomach! Pah. All brain and no courage!" He frowned at Ree, then turned to Garrad. "How is he? The boy?"

"Mortal bad," Garrad said. "Let's hope your fancy Healer can bring him back."

Ree tried to walk past him, not quite sure where he was going, but wishing to go up the ladder and see his son. Garrad put an arm out. "No, Ree. You can't do anything, and Jem is enough of a nuisance up there, as worried as he is. Come. We'll get you washed and get clean clothes on you."

And Ree—nerveless, exhausted—let Garrad escort him to his room. Someone brought water. He thought it was Lenar, though the mind boggled at the thought. At least, the two men were there, helping him wash and getting him in clean clothes. Of course, no one could expect her ladyship to do it, but all the same, Ree wouldn't have expected Lenar either.

All the while, Ree kept listening for sounds from above. He heard nothing. That had to be good, right? If Meren were dead, he'd hear some sounds? At least Amelie crying?

But perhaps Amelie was sedated and Jem too stunned to speak?

"Ree?" Jem stood at the door to their room, just as Ree was fully dressed in clean clothes. He cast a quick puzzled look at Garrad and Lenar, then looked at Ree full on, his expression so grave that Ree's heart seemed to shrink into itself. "Meren," he said. "Is he . . . ?"

"He asked for you," Jem said, stretching out a hand.

"He what?"

"He asked for you. He spoke, all in sentences, like Grandad said my Da did. Will you come?"

Up the stairs, like a dream, to the little room that Meren shared with Amelie. Amelie sported bandages across her forehead and neck and arm. Ree had no idea so much of the blood on her clothes was her own.

The Healer was packing away his things, looking smug and pleased. "He'll be fine now," he said, as Jem and Ree came in. "Only try to keep him quiet and don't allow him to go running about."

Ree was about to ask if they should also ensure that the goats flew, but he had no time for sarcasm, because he caught sight of Meren, lying in his crib. He had a fresh bandage across his forehead, and a bandage around his round little toddler belly. But his eyes were open, and, at the sight of Ree, they opened further, and the little mouth opened in a sleepy smile.

"I gave him some draughts to take away the pain," the Healer was telling Jem. "They should make him sleepy."

But Ree only half heard the words. His world had contracted to that crib and the little boy in it.

"Papa," the little boy said, sleepily. He extended his little hand and Ree met it halfway, in a desperate clutch. "Papa. Mewen so 'fwaid. But Mewen bwave!"

"Meren is very brave," Ree said, his voice choked with tears. "Meren is my brave little boy. My heart's son."

The Time We Have

Tanya Huff

:Smoke!: Gervais lifted his head, ears pricked forward. *:Thatch!:*

They had to be close to the most eastern of the cattle-holds that fanned out a day's travel from Devin. And no one purposely burned thatch so early in the spring with no straw available to replace it.

"Go!" Jors bent low in the saddle, eyes narrowed to protect them from flying ends of mane as Gervais lengthened his stride.

They crested the ridge, saw the cattlehold laid out beneath them, saw smoke rising from one of the barns, saw three riders race away to the northwest.

Even with the lead they had, Gervais could have caught them—no horse outran a Companion—but just then the first flash of flame showed on the edge of the barn and a horse screamed.

:Chosen?: Gervais had turned toward the cattlehold but Jors had turned body and reins toward the riders.

The rider closest to them twisted in the saddle—a woman with a long dark braid and matching dark eyes, and a smile that faltered when she saw Jors watching. He shouldn't have been able to see her expression at this distance, but she looked surprised. She raised a hand covered in a black, high-cuffed glove and, almost without him willing it, Jors raised a hand in answer.

Another horse screamed. Then a child.

:Chosen!:

He wanted to follow her. Follow them. To bring them in. Teeth clenched, he shifted his weight to match Gervais' movements, fought to shift his attention to what was clearly the area of greater need.

They crossed the compound, pounded past a young man down with a bleeding forehead, past a shrieking child barely being held back, and on in through the big double doors in the end of the barn.

Terrified horses kicked at their stalls as Jors swung down out of the saddle. Ducking low under the smoke, sucking shallow breaths in through his teeth, eyes and nose streaming, he started unbolting the doors.

Reassured by the presence of the Companion, the horses charged out of the stalls into the center aisle, Gervais chivvying them around toward the exit, nipping and shoving until they moved in the right direction.

"Is that it?" Jors yelled, fighting for breath as the heavy shoulder of a panicked horse slammed him into the rear wall.

:That is all the horses, Chosen, but. . . .:

Jors boots kicked into something soft. Yielding.

"Think I found it!" He dropped to his knees, groped along a well muscled body, felt the chest rise and fall. "Found *him*. Gervais! He's too big to lift!"

The Companion was suddenly a warm weight at his side, legs folded to bring the saddle as close as possible to the floor. *:Hurry!:*

Half dragging, half rolling, Jors got the young man to Gervais' side and heaved the unconscious body up and over. Somehow he held him in place as Gervais rose to his feet, then clutched at the stirrup as they raced the fire out of the barn.

The compound was a seething mass of horses and people. Two bucket brigades threw water at the fire but only seemed to add to the smoke. The child was still screaming. Jors just barely made out her words over the sound of his own coughing.

"Kitties! Kitties!"

"Where?" he asked, staggering toward her.

The girl holding the child's arms looked up, lashes clumped into triangle points around blue eyes still swimming with tears. "First stall," she hiccuped. "To the left. Under the manger. There's three . . . "

Jors pulled off his scarf, dipped it in a passing bucket, wrapped it around his mouth and ran back inside.

:Chosen!:

:Don't worry. I'm not going far.:

The stall wasn't hard to find but he had to search all three sides for the manger only to find it diagonally across a back corner. He crouched, grateful for the clearer air, and groped under a board polished smooth by a rubbing horse. One. Two. He tucked the kittens inside his jacket. From the way they were squirming, he thought they were all right. The third kitten . . .

:Chosen! The roof is about to fall!:

Tiny claws hooked into the side of his hand. Jors closed his fingers around a ball of fluff, took a deep breath, and, with his other hand against the wall so as not to lose his way in the smoke, ran for the stall door. Turned right. Figured the double doors were too big to miss and, left arm cradling the two in his jacket, right hand tucking the other up under the scarf, he raced toward safety.

It wasn't that far.

It couldn't be that far.

The fire roared as the roof collapsed.

Jors stumbled, almost fell, then hands grabbed at his clothing and yanked him clear.

He twisted in the air, hit the ground on his back, and tried, unsuccessfully, not to shriek as tiny teeth sank into his chin.

"I swear to you, I took more damage from the kittens than from the fire."

Gervais didn't seem convinced. Now that the horses had been confined in a corral of half-frozen mud, the other buildings in the compound were safe, and the barn was a smoldering heap of massive beams and steaming thatch, he insisted on checking for himself.

:You went back in!: Jors stumbled back a step as Gervais butted him in the chest. *:You are bleeding!:*

"Kitten scratches, that's all." He glanced over at the little girl on the porch with the three kittens, the mother cat in her lap.

:You went back in!:

"Heartbrother ... " His back against the wall, Jors ran his hands in under the silken fall of mane and stroked the warm arc of neck. "It's okay. I came back out."

:The roof fell.:

"I know." He let his head fall to rest against Gervais' and stopped speaking out loud. *:I'm sorry I frightened you, but I couldn't leave them.:*

:A life saved is a life saved and you saved three but ... :

:Don't do it again?: He felt the Companion's soft chuff of breath. They both knew that, under the same circumstances, he'd do exactly the same thing. *:Can I get*

dressed now? It's still a little too close to winter to run around half naked.:

Gervais chuffed again, then backed up far enough to let Jors get to his clothes. When Jors' head emerged from his shirt, he found himself still under inspection.

"What?"

:When we saw the riders, you hesitated.:

Cheeks suddenly burning, Jors busied himself with laces. "I just . . . I thought we had a chance to catch them."

:Three of them?:

. . . a long, dark braid, and matching dark eyes, and a smile that faltered when she saw Jors watching. "Yeah."

:What would we have done when we caught them?:

"They're just . . . I mean . . . " He paused. Took a deep breath. "Okay, maybe I hadn't entirely thought things through."

Gervais tossed his head. *:That was obvious, Chosen. These three are dangerous. Raya says it is very likely they are part of a gang of bandits Lord Harnin's men have been hunting for some time.:*

"Raya says?" Jors stepped out away from the building so he could look out at the track leading into the compound. If Gervais had been speaking to another Companion, that Companion had to be close. Neither he nor Gervais had been gifted with distance when it came to Mindspeaking.

:Cross country.: Gervais nudged him around. *:From the west.:*

He squinted into the setting sun, and realized that what he had first thought was a patch of lingering snow was, in fact, a Herald moving quickly toward them.

:I have told Raya everything that has happened here,:

Gervais said as they watched the mare close the distance. *:And she has told Herald Erika and that will save time.:*

"For what?" Jors asked.

:For judgments before you leave.:

Jors had planned on staying as long as any judgments required. Clearly, that was no longer an option.

"Kittens?" Erika asked as Raya danced to a stop no more than an arm's length away.

"There were three of them," Jors pointed out.

"And three riders. Gervais said they headed northwest." She twisted in the saddle, frowning up at the deep sapphire sky that preceded true darkness. "We've lost the light and the temperature's dropping. We won't be able to track them until morning." Erika had learned some creative profanity from her two older brothers in the Guard, although she'd barely gotten started when Raya reminded her they had a gathering audience. Standing far enough away to give the Heralds a semblance of privacy, but close enough to hear.

"I take it *you* have a plan for when we catch up?" Jors asked as his yearmate swung out of the saddle. He bowed a greeting to Raya, who touched his cheek with the velvet pad of her nose.

"It's a long story."

"Supper first, then. And judgments, if the fire hasn't rendered them moot."

"There's fifteen or sixteen of them at least," Erika said as they settled for the night on a pile of clean straw in the milking barn's loft. Unlike the various residences, the barns were communal, thus free of any hint of favoritism, and a lot more private. Warmer, too: the six milk cows kept for the family's use threw off a lot of heat.

"That's why I followed those three. If we could capture one, and put them to the Truth Spell, we might be able to take the rest without more loss of life."

"Capture one," Jors repeated, wondering if the girl's eyes were as dark up close as they were from a distance. "And the other two?"

"Capture them as well, if possible. If not . . ." Erika's voice trailed grimly off.

The bandits had been wreaking havoc along the North Trade Road between Heraldston and Berrybay for almost a year. They were fast, they were smart, and they were vicious; there'd been no witnesses left behind. Lord Harin and his people had finally gotten close enough to take arrow fire, leaving three dead. That was when he'd sent to Haven for help.

"They've been holed up somewhere for the winter and I expect your three were bored."

"My three?" Jors snorted. Down in the large box stall he shared with Raya, Gervais snorted as well, and Jors caught a faint feeling of unease from his Companion's mind. *:What's wrong?:*

:They are not your *three.:*

:That's what I said.:

:No, you said they are not your three.*:*

"They've come a fair distance from their regular stomping grounds," Erika continued, unaware of the silent conversation, "and they're just the sort to think burning down a barn is funny. I wouldn't be surprised to find they used the distraction to cut a steer from the herd and slaughter it. They'll leave most of the meat behind too, the cocky bastards."

"If it helps, they were steer-free when I saw them."

Erika reached out and patted his arm. "It helps that you saw them. The biggest problem until now is that they could be anyone. I could have sat next to one in a tavern completely unaware. I had to Truth Spell all of Lord Harin's people to make sure none of them were involved."

"Sounds like fun."

"Yeah, well, you can do it next time. It's not like I could Truth Spell everyone who uses the road, so all we really knew was that the people actively chasing them weren't also helping them."

"That's something."

"Damned little. But now, now we know what three of them look like."

... a long, dark braid, and matching dark eyes, and a smile that faltered when she saw Jors watching.

"From the back, riding away," Jors reminded her.

"More than we had," Erika said, yawning. "More than we had."

Jors still had Circuit to ride, but these bandits had killed a dozen, probably more, and would have killed the young man he'd pulled from the barn. Gervais was strangely hard to convince that breaking away to help Erika track and capture one of the three was more than justified, but he finally gave in. Dawn found the four of them heading out of the compound.

Cut deep in the mud then frozen overnight, the tracks were easy to follow until, in the lee of a copse of trees, they suddenly disappeared under the hoofmarks of a herd of cattle. Probably the same rough-coated cattle spread out along beside the tracks, enjoying the weak spring sunshine. The closest few looked up when the Heralds approached, and ran a short ways before rocking to a stop and setting off another bunch, the ripple of movement running through the sizable herd.

"We're never going to follow their tracks out of this," Erika muttered as Jors dismounted to get a closer look at the ground. "They could have turned. They could have headed off in any direction. We'll have to circle the entire herd. And hopefully the herd won't spook and run exactly the way we don't want them to."

:Cows don't listen.: Gervais sounded insulted.

"Yeah, Raya says the same thing," Erika laughed when Jors repeated his Companion's observation. "Any luck?"

Crouched low, Jors pulled off his glove and ran his fingers through the impressions of cloven hooves, searching for the unbroken arc of a horse's print. Unfortunately, cows could cut a dry trail to shreds; a wet trail, with added thrown mud, they obliterated. A detail the three fleeing bandits had obviously known.

He straightened, scanned the horizon, and took an involuntary step. Then another. "This way."

"How . . . " Erika stopped, head cocked, clearly listening to Raya. After a moment, she closed her eyes and sighed. When she opened them, she shifted her weight and Raya began to move forward along the line Jors had indicated. "All right, then. Let's go."

Not long after, they found the place the bandits had spent the night.

A fox stared up at them from one end of the slaughtered steer, two crows from the other, all three wary but unwilling to leave such a prize.

"They couldn't have set the fire as a distraction," Jors noted as the Companions began to pick up speed, the trail clear again. "Not this far out."

"Destruction for the sake of destruction," Erika snarled. "Mayhem for the sheer bloody pleasure they take in it. And the more they get away with, the more things will escalate."

"Then we make sure they don't get away with it."

"So we'd better catch them before they get into those hills." Erika tossed her head toward the layered ridges on the horizon, still covered in snow. "Those things are crossed with canyons and gullies and some very nasty ground. They get in there, we'll never find them."

"Do you smell . . . ?"

"Beef." Jors scanned the sky for smoke but saw nothing rising against the low-lying gray clouds. "They're close." He pulled Gervais to a stop, pulled his bow free, and slid to the ground, dropping low as he reached the top of the rise. There, in a hollow, backs to a clump of leafless willow, the three bandits sat around a small, smokeless fire roasting hunks of meat on the points of their knives.

Jors figured they'd probably stopped here at the edge of the plain before they'd head into the canyon he could see as a black line in the first rise of hills.

"We move along that bank of snow . . . " Erika's low voice washed warmly against his ear. " . . . and they'll never see us until it's too late."

"We should ride . . . "

"No, they'll have loaded crossbows ready."

Now she'd mentioned it, Jors saw the butt of one bow lying close to hand.

"They've shot as many horses as people. Maybe more. Raya and Gevais can distract them, make some noise over that way where they won't be big white targets . . . " She pointed past the opposite side of the hollow. " . . . just before we move in."

The girl threw back her head and laughed, punching the man next to her in the shoulder with the side of her fist when he reached out to pull her braid. *Brother*, Jors realized, and tried not to wonder about the wave of relief.

"Jors? Can you do this?"

He twisted to see Erika staring at him, her expression so neutral she had to be hiding something. "What? Why . . . ?" He twisted a little farther to see both Companions staring at him as well. *:Gervais?:*

:The girl. . .:

:Is as guilty as the rest.: She was. Erika had tracked them to the cattle holding. They'd tracked them together this far. The girl was one of the bandits and the bandits were thieves and murderers. If she hadn't thrown the torch herself, she allowed it to be thrown, knowing that horses would die and not caring if people did.

:If you are sure.:

The girl threw back her head and laughed . . .

"Jors?"

"Of course I'm sure."

Erika glanced over at the Companions and shrugged., a quick rise and fall of her shoulders that said, *Let's get on with this* as clearly as if she'd spoken aloud. It was Erika's call. She wasn't senior but Jors had joined her hunt. Pulling her sword, she nodded toward the fire. "All right. Go."

It worked exactly as planned.

Heads started to turn as Erika rose out of her crouch, then jerked back the other way as the two Companions managed to sound like a charging cavalry unit. Jors got two shots off, confident enough in his ability to shoot past the other Herald. The first arrow pinned one male bandit to the ground through the trailing end of his jacket, and the second went into the shoulder of the sec-

ond male, causing the throwing knife he held to slide
from spasming fingers. The third . . .

The third . . .

Her eyes were as dark up close. There was grease
on her chin and a perfect line of white teeth showed
between slightly parted lips. She had a mole on one
cheek, the flat dark kind Jors had heard girls refer to as
beauty marks. Fitting. She was beautiful. Not very tall.
But strong. Her gloves on the ground by the fire, she
wrapped one bare hand around the saddle horn and
swung up onto the moving horse, feet not touching the
stirrups until she'd been in the saddle for half a dozen
strides. She bent low, tucked behind the cantle, further
hidden behind a sudden scud of blowing snow. He didn't
have a shot.

The ring of steel on steel spun him around. Erika was
fighting the bandit he'd pinned. The man—visibly older
than the bandit girl—had shrugged free of his jacket,
but the delay had given Erika time to seize the advan-
tage and she clearly had no intention of giving it back.
One blow, two, and he went down . . .

. . . as the bandit with the arrow in his shoulder rose
up to his knees, his knife in his other hand, leaning in to
slash at Erika's hamstrings.

Jors charged forward and kicked the knife clear, then
pivoted and kicked the bandit in the head.

The girl was gone, the pounding of her horses hooves
growing fainter.

"She'll be nearly to those canyons by now," Erika
growled.

"If you can handle these two, I'll go after her."

"Those canyons are a maze; you'll never . . . "

"I'm a better tracker than you are, you know I am.
And she hasn't got that much of a lead."

Erika wanted to say no. He didn't know why, but he could see it on her face. Thing was, she wanted to bring these people in more, and he could see that too. Finally, she nodded.

Gervais ran past and Jors swung up much the way the bandit girl had, bow in his free hand. As they cleared the hollow, he saw the girl reach the line of black and disappear.

By the time they reached the canyon it was snowing hard enough Jors appreciated the cover the cliffs provided. He'd left his heavy winter leathers behind in Devin. The lighter clothing he wore wasn't made for extended cold weather, but, hopefully, he wouldn't be out in it long enough for it to be a problem. *:She can't have gone far.:*

She hadn't.

Nor was she trying particularly hard to hide her trail, Jors realized as they headed up a slope steep enough he felt himself sliding back in the saddle. She probably assumed her familiarity with the canyons would help her to get away. Only that familiarity would allow her to move so fast over such treacherous trails.

If Gervais had been a horse, it might have worked.

:There!:

:I see her!:

When she realized he was close, she put her heels to her horse so that bandit and Herald ended up galloping single file along a narrow ledge. To the left, sheer rock rose over Jors' head. To the right was a drop of maybe twice his height, down to what looked like a dry riverbed. Dangerous but not deadly.

The next time he looked, the riverbed had fallen away down a tumbled hill of rock to flatten out a considerable distance below.

The girl was a brilliant rider, he'd give her that.

Jors could almost reach out and grab the blowing ends of a dark tail when the horse screamed, hooves striking wildly at the rock as it tipped to the right and fell.

She twisted around, met Jors' eyes ...

Jors clutched at the saddle as Gervais threw himself back, front feet flailing at the crumbling rock until finally he stood, sides heaving, nose out over a section of the ledge that no longer existed.

:Heartbrother? Are you all right?:

Gervais didn't answer for a moment. *:That was too close.:*

:Not arguing. If you back up about fifteen feet, there's a place that's wide enough I can dismount.:

He felt Gervais draw in a deep breath and let it out slowly. One foot at a time, raising it carefully and lowering it more carefully still, Gervais backed up until a cavity in the left wall gave Jors enough room to swing down to the ledge beside him and slide past.

When he got back to the break, the blowing snow and the angle of the rock kept him from seeing the riverbed until he dropped to his knees.

The horse was dead.

The rider ...

He couldn't see her on the riverbed. If she'd been thrown ...

There!

She lay on her back about halfway down the cliff on a triangle of ledge about six feet long and no more than two feet wide at the narrow end. One of her arms dangled; the other was flung out as though she'd been grabbing at handholds as she fell.

:Is she dead?:

:I don't know.: With her head turned away from the cliff, Jors couldn't see her face.

Then her outstretched arm moved. Pale fingers flexed.

Jors crawled a little farther forward. *:I can get to her. The rock's crumbled all the way to the ledge.:* But when he went to move again, a hoof caught the edge of his breeches, holding him in place. He twisted to stare up at Gervais. *:What? I can't leave her there to die!:*

:Raya says Herald Erika cannot leave the bandit men without shelter. Particularly not the one who is injured. She must get them to the cattleholding before she can return. She is . . . : He paused and his ears flicked forward. *:She is not happy.:*

Jors had no idea if it was Raya or Erika who was unhappy, nor did it particularly matter. Heralds made hard choices. It was part of the job. The good new was, if Gervais could still reach Raya, they hadn't gone far.

:Gervais, you need to catch up to Erika. Have her tie the bandit horses to your saddle so Raya can make a run for the cattleholding while you follow at the speed of the horses. Erika needs to grab a stretcher if they have one, boards if they don't, so we can secure . . . : He didn't know the bandit girl's name so he gestured down the cliff instead. *:. . . her in such a way we can lift her out without injuring her further. Have Erika send out a rider to meet you and take the horses,:* he continued hurriedly, feeling Gervais readying a protest, *:so that you can join her as she heads back here.:*

Reluctantly, Gervais lifted his foot. *:I will go after you reach the ledge safely. If the girl is not badly injured, you and I will pull her out.:*

Jors took another look over the edge. *:That's not likely.:*

:And yet, it is possible. Tie the rope to my saddle.:

:I can't risk pulling you over with me if I fall.:

Gervais snorted. *:I know exactly how heavy you are, Chosen. I can hold you.:*

They lowered Jors' gear first, just in case. Then, gloves tucked into his belt, as little weight on the doubled rope as possible, Jors started picking his way carefully down the path of broken rock. Most of the loose stone had been swept clear when the bandit girl went over, but the route was treacherous enough still that more than once only the rope kept him from following her horse to the riverbed. The last few feet to the ledge became a barely controlled fall.

A little surprised he'd made it, uninjured but for a bleeding scrape on his cheek, Jors knelt beside the bandit girl.

Her heart was beating.

Legs and arms were unbroken.

Bubbles of blood stained her lips and teeth with every labored breath.

:Broken ribs. Probably a punctured lung. We can't move her without a board.: He jerked the rope and ducked the loops as it slithered around the saddle horn and fell. *:Go.:*

:Be careful.:

:It's okay.: Jors forced a smile he wasn't wearing onto his mental voice. *:I think I can take her.:*

:That is not . . . : He felt Gervais sigh. *:I will be back as quickly as I can. Herald Erika says you must stay warm.:*

Staying warm would be the trick. Between the blowing snow and the setting sun, Jors could barely see Gervais up on the ledge, a white blur moving backward along the narrow path more quickly than looked safe.

He'd left a lot of his gear in Devin with his leathers

and the mule—the cattleholdings were barely a day apart and he'd intended to spend a day in each and end up back in Devin—but heading out with Erika, he'd packed against sleeping rough. A sheepskin for insulation against frozen ground and two felted wool blankets to keep out the cold.

First, he looped the rope half a dozen times and carefully worked it under the bandit girl's body, tucking her one arm up to her side, securing it against her ribs, then threading the end of the rope through the loops and pulling it snug. He had to slide her onto the sheepskin or she'd freeze, but he wanted her ribs to shift as little as possible while he did it.

Tenting one blanket around them almost sent him over the edge when he leaned out to anchor it with arrows jammed into cracks in the rock face. In spite of the best efforts of the wind to blow everything off the ledge, he finally had her safely inside a triangle of felt, his pack keeping the blanket up off their faces, one corner flipped back just enough to keep the air fresh and allow a beam of weak gray light. He pushed the second blanket between his body and the cliff, then wrapped it around them both. The bandit girl wasn't exactly in his arms, but Jors couldn't have fit a horsehair between them given the width of the ledge.

"I knew you'd come for me." Her voice was weak, thready, but their faces were barely a handspan apart. She licked at the blood on her lips and nearly smiled. "I'm your prisoner, then."

Jors wanted to say no, knew the answer was yes, and said instead, "Are you in much pain?"

"My heart hurts. And if yours does not, then you lie in spite of your pretty clothes."

"I don't know what you mean."

Her eyes met his. "I've thought of nothing but you since I first saw you."

He shrugged as much as their position allowed. "I'm a Herald and you are . . . "

"Yes." When she laughed, she choked a little and he slid his arm behind her head to help her breathe. "I am paid for my wicked ways," she said at last. "But I wonder what you've done, Herald, that the Goddess treats you so badly."

"She sent me to save you."

"From this?"

"From this as well."

"As well?" Dark brows rose. "You're late, Herald. Years and a great deal of wickedness late."

"I'm sorry."

When she sighed a trickle of blood ran down to mat in her hair, a dark line against the curve of her cheek. Jors caught it on his thumb. "I wasn't."

"You weren't what?"

"Sorry. Not for anything I've done. It was . . . " She paused long enough Jors thought she might have drifted into unconsciousness again. Then she swallowed and continued. " . . . an exciting life. Just after the ledge drops down to the riverbank, there's a cleft."

It took him a moment to follow the change.

"It opens into a box canyon," she continued slowly. "We have a base there. My cousins . . . You could take me to them."

He actually considered it. Discarded it. "No. I couldn't."

"No, you couldn't. You'll choose your pretty clothes over me."

Jors wiped the blood away again. "I couldn't move you safely the rest of the way down the cliff, and I have no way to get you to the cleft or into the canyon or to your cousins without making your injuries worse."

She stared at him for a long moment. "Ah," she said at last. "So you don't have to choose your pretty clothes over me."

"It's not the clothes . . ."

Her free arm rose and punched him weakly in the arm. "Idiot. I know."

She sounded so exasperated with him that he laughed and bent his head to touch his face to her hair, breathing in her scent. "You said you weren't sorry," he whispered against her hair.

"What?"

"Weren't."

She made a soft chuff of sound that might have been a laugh. "You caught that? I may be a little sorry now." Her fingers closed loosely around his wrist. "Tell me about you. Tell me all the things I don't have time . . . to find out."

"You should rest."

"I can rest and listen. I don't want . . ." Her fingers tightened. "I want to be with you for as long we have."

"We'll have . . ."

"Herald!"

"Jors."

"Jors." She said his name like she was telling him something she'd always known. "Please. Tell me . . ."

So he talked. Told her about growing up in the forest. About the day he'd looked into sapphire eyes and known the forest was no longer his life. About getting his Whites. About the Demon's Den. About the charcoal burner's child. He talked and he looked into her eyes and he cataloged every expression, storing them safely away.

Finally, when it had gotten so dark he could barely
see her, she lifted her hand to his cheek and he paused.

"Mirgayne," she said.

"What . . . ?"

"My name, you idiot." He could hear the smile he
couldn't see. "You never asked." Her fingertips were
cold against his skin. "Seems I'll be punished for my
wicked ways." When he started to speak, she moved her
fingers across his mouth. "Will you wait for me?"

He swallowed, nodded, and said softly. "I'll wait."

"Good." Her fingers slipped down to lie on her chest.

:Chosen?:

"A little sorry," she said, and closed her eyes.

It was very, very dark on the ledge.

:Heartbrother!:

Jors felt almost beside himself as he climbed up off the
ledge, as he helped Erika bring Mirgayne's body up, as
they rode back to the cattleholding. He told the other
Herald about the box canyon and the bandits' base and
had nothing else to say. He knew Erika watched him all
the long way back but she let him ride in silence. Gervais
was a constant presence in his mind; Jors kept his eyes
locked on the gleam of white that was his Companion's
head so he couldn't see the darkness all around.

They laid the body out in a corner of one of the barns.

"This is the beginning of the end for them," Erika
said quietly. "Even if Truth Spelling the others gives us
little else, we can take their base in the canyon. It'll be
a wedge driven in to weaken them enough we can clear
them off the road. It'll save a lot of lives."

Jors pulled Mirgayn's braid out from under her back,
laid it gently along her arm, then pulled the blanket up

over her face. When he stood, Erika closed a hand over his shoulder.

"Are you all right? When something like . . . like this happens . . ."

No one had said the words *life-bond*. No one ever would.

Jors shook his head, shook himself out from under Erika's hold, and moved blindly out of the barn until his hands touched familiar warmth and his arms wrapped around a familiar neck.

:Chosen?:

"My heart hurts," he said.

And he wept.

A Bard by Any Other Name

Fiona Patton

Oh! Roses sweet upon this wall,
Where p'haps your rapturous gaze might fall,
And to my pining breast give cause,
to live for love's first kiss to pause.

A crisp autumn breeze whispered along the capital's quiet thoroughfares as Sergeant Hektor Dann of the Haven City Watch read the words splashed across the mill wall in as neutral a tone as possible. Nevertheless, the mill owner who'd reported the "vandalism" to the Iron Street Watchhouse first thing that morning softened his customary scowl just long enough to squint up at the brightly painted green letters with an expectant expression.

"Pause fer what?" he demanded.

Hektor just shrugged. "I dunno, sir. A longer kiss, maybe?"

"Humph. Maybe." The mill owner crossed his arms over his chest. "This be, what, the fifth time The Poet's struck in as many days?" he asked, content now to discuss the situation once he'd had his curiosity about the poem's meaning satisfied.

Hektor nodded with a resigned expression. There was no point in trying to pretend that the rash of verses appearing on walls all over Haven in the last week wasn't the talk in every shop, tavern, and private parlor across Valdemar's capital city. The citizens had dubbed the mysterious author "The Poet," and there was wild speculation about his identity and purpose. Less wild was the speculation on how long it would take the city's watchmen to find him. Hektor's youngest brother, eleven-year-old Padreic, himself a Runner with the Iron Street Watch, and a depository of all news and gossip since being promoted two months ago, had reported that local betting stood at three to one against them finding him at all.

"And you lot still have no idea who he is, I suppose?" the mill owner sniffed.

Hektor sighed inwardly. "We're making inquiries, sir."

"Don't seem to be getting too far with 'em, it seems to me."

"They're coming along, sir."

"Well, just you come along a little faster or I'll be sending you the bill to get this cleaned off."

"You'll be removing it soon, then, sir?" Hektor asked, eyeing the crowd of people that had begun to gather around The Poet's latest work.

The mill owner's expression softened. "Well," he allowed. "Soon enough I suppose." His lips moved a little as he reread the words scrawled across his property. "He's not too good, is he?" he noted after a moment's reflection.

Hektor just shrugged. "I couldn't say, sir."

"Cause there's not too many roses bloomin' at this time o' year. An' them vines be ivy, not roses." He sighed. "Still, it makes you think about things for all that,

I suppose. You know, love and the like. It's been some years since Haven had a really good poet to boast of." He rubbed at his bearded cheek with a thoughtful expression, then shook himself brusquely. "And I reckon it'll still be a few more years 'til we do," he decided.

"Yes, sir."

"Pining breast, eh? They're not getting any better, are they?"

Corporal Aiden Dann was waiting in Hektor's office when he returned to the Watchhouse. Not at all surprised that The Poet's latest work had beaten him back there, Hektor threw himself into his chair, upsetting a pile of reports sitting precariously on the edge of his desk.

"No," he answered glumly as he bent to retrieve them.

"Kinda reminds me of some of those scribblings of yours I found under the mattress when you were thirteen. Remember when you were first courting Ismy Smith? And here you are showing interest again. An' here's The Poet spoutin' off about rapturous gazes." Aiden fixed his younger brother with a penetrating stare. "Can anyone vouch for your whereabouts last night, Hektor Dann?" he demanded sternly.

"Shut up, Aiden."

"You're right. Your poems were far worse. It couldn't have been you."

"Don't you have a beat to walk, *Corporal*?" Hektor hazarded, trying to sound more in command of his older brother than he ever had been.

Aiden just showed his teeth at him. "No, I don't, *Sergeant*. The Captain's set me to help you. Apparently he's got a bet on with the Breakneedle Street Watch Captain that we'll find The Poet before they do. So . . . " He made himself comfortable on the edge of Hektor's desk, upsetting the pile of reports once again. "What do you figure? Think he might be a Bard? Some of them are pretty ... " Aiden scratched thoughtfully under the collar of his gray and blue watchman's uniform, searching for a word that wouldn't be too insulting. " ... flowery."

Hektor glanced down at the scattered reports, then just let them lie there. "They're all denying it," he answered. "An' they're better'n this. An' they don't write on walls," he added.

"He's used up a lot of ink by now. Maybe we should go talk to an inkmonger. See if anyone's bought up a big supply lately."

Hektor shook his head. "He's writing in paint, not ink," he corrected. "An' paint's not sold, it's mixed special as needed by the artists themselves."

"So you figure The Poet's an artist then?"

"Probably a muralist by the looks of it."

"We don't know any muralists," Aiden pointed out.

"No, but we do know an artificer. Maybe he knows a muralist." He stood. "Why don't you go check out the studios near where the first poem was found? I'll go talk to Daedrus."

Aiden gave an amused snort. "So, I'll be telling' Ma that you'll be late for dinner then?" he noted.

Hektor sighed. "Yeah, you might better," he answered.

"My dear boy, what a lovely surprise! Come in, come in!" The retired artificer waved Hektor inside his brightly lit but very narrow hallway with a beaming smile. "Now, now, Pebbles, don't go growling at the Watch, it's rude. My niece's dog," he explained. Hektor cast a concerned eye at the heavyset white bulldog glaring suspiciously at him from under a long side table covered in clocks and timepieces. "She's a Fledgling Healer. My niece, not the

dog, of course. Pebbles stays with me for an afternoon
or two each week as my niece can't always take a dog
along on rounds. But enough of my days; I couldn't possibly make them sound interesting to a young man of
the Watch, could I? So, come in and tell me to what do I
owe the pleasure of your visit.

"My children, look who it is!"

An explosion of singing from a dozen ornate bird
cages greeted Hektor as he followed Daedrus deeper
into the house. The old man's front room was even more
cluttered than it had been the last time he'd visited. He
negotiated the piles of books, scrolls, drawings, blue-
prints, maps, lanterns, candles, tools, and odd pieces of
metal and wooden machinery with care until he was
pulled up short by the sight of two well-dressed people,
one a young woman in pale green Healer's robes, the
other a tall, older man garbed in scarlet, seated together
on Daedrus' overstuffed settee.

"Forgive me, sir, I didn't realize you had guests," he
stammered.

"Nonsense, my boy," the old man waved a dismissive hand at him. "This is my niece, great-niece actually,
Adele, who I've just told you of, and our cousin, Master
Musician Hiron of the Bardic Collegium. Adele, Hiron,
may I present Sergeant Hektor Dann of the Iron Street
Watch, a particular young friend of mine. Now, we are
all known to each other and we shall take tea and young
Sergeant Dann can regale us with his adventures keeping the mean streets of Haven safe and sound."

He gave a broad wink to show that he was teasing,
and before Hektor could protest that he would return at
a more convenient time, the old man had maneuvered
him farther into the room with a well-placed elbow that
belied his age and had bustled away into the kitchen,

all the while chattering happily amidst the trilling and chirping of his many little finches and yellow-birds.

Moments later, Hektor found himself sitting opposite Daedrus' other guests with a far too delicate china tea cup clutched in one hand and a jam tart in the other. When pressed by the old man, he sketched out the reason for his visit in as few words as possible, recited The Poet's latest creation, then fell into an uncomfortable silence.

Sipping at his own cup, Daedrus leaned forward, his rheumy blue eyes twinkling. "I must confess that I have been following The Poet's exploits with a great deal of interest. The first verses were scribbled on a stone bridge span, were they not?" he asked. When Hektor answered in the affirmative, he nodded happily. "And then on a granary wall. Something to do with braided locks of hair and unrequited passion, as I remember. It reminded me of the works of the great Bard Valens. Don't you think so, Hiron?"

The Bard gave an eloquent shrug. "His earliest works perhaps," he allowed in a polite, well-modulated tone. "His poetry settled down and became somewhat less melodramatic once he'd entered into his twenties."

"Yes, well, not so much *unrequited* passion to report of, I would imagine," Daedrus said with a chuckle. "By all accounts he was a powerfully attractive man in his youth."

"He was said to have been the most beautiful man in all of Valdemar," Adele agreed. "And that his voice could charm the very trees to bursting into leaf in winter when he sang of spring."

"Indeed it could. I had the pleasure of hearing him sing towards the end of his days," Daedrus said with a faraway smile. "And it was exactly as you say. I was very young at the time and most of my attention was given over to the science of construction, but I do remember feeling as if the whole of the world should be in love at that very moment." He sighed happily. "A singular experience and one that I shall never forget."

"Yes, but he was the most famous for his love poetry," Hiron explained. "His gift of Projective Empathy was so strong that you could feel it through the words themselves. There was a time when no Bard in Haven would dare venture out without at least a dozen examples of his work well memorized. Even the patrons of the most lowly drinking establishments in the farthest reaches of Valdemar were demanding his poems. They were collected in several volumes in his lifetime and again just after his death. I'm afraid that would be the only way to become acquainted with his work today," he said with real regret. "Poetry's fallen rather out of fashion in these last few years."

"Although thanks to this new poet, it seems to be making a resurgence," Adele noted. "You can hear snatches of poetry from one end of the Collegium to the other."

"I think I must have book of his about somewhere," Daedrus said thoughtfully. "Yes, I'm sure I do."

"So you think The Poet to be well educated, then, sir?" Hektor asked before Daedrus could begin searching his very extensive library.

"I do," Hiron replied. "His work is both derivative and antiquated. It's unlikely that he would write in such a manner without having become both familiar and enamored of Valens' style."

Hektor glanced at him briefly, then plunged ahead before he could reconsider his question. "Could a Bard do it, sir?" he asked.

Hiron raised one fine eyebrow at him. "A Bard could do it, Sergeant," he allowed, "but a Bard would not do it. Not in such a manner as this."

Daedrus smiled. "The Bardic Collegium frowns on graffiti as a medium for creative expression," he said with a chuckle. "Besides, Haven's Bards have plenty of other stages on which to express their art. No, my dear boy, I believe your poet is someone for whom a proper stage is unavailable."

Hektor nodded. "We had thought maybe an artist, sir. The letters are all well formed, almost stylized, and the paint's of good quality and well mixed such as a practiced artist might create."

Daedrus drummed his fingers against his lips in thought. "It could be an artist," he allowed. "But I don't know of any artist of my acquaintance that fancies himself a poet or for that matter a muralist-poet. Adele? Hiron?"

When the others answered in the negative, he nodded to himself thoughtfully. "Were there any other objects painted besides the words, Sergeant? Any flowers or birds or such like?"

"No, sir."

"Well, then, I shouldn't think it was an artist. They're too enamored of depicting physical objects. No, no, you may rely on it, you're definitely looking for a poet, to be sure, but one with access to an artist's materials, I shouldn't wonder. There are a number of studios and private drawing schools north of Breakneedle Street." His rheumy blue eyes suddenly lit up. "Would you like me to make a few inquiries for you?"

Hektor breathed an inaudible sigh of relief. He'd been wondering how he was going to trespass on the territory of the Breakneedle Watch House without incurring their wrath. "That would be a great help, thank you sir."

"Don't mention it, dear boy, it's my pleasure."

Using this as an excuse to take his leave, Hektor set his cup down very carefully, but as he rose to go, Hiron caught his eye.

"Another thing to consider," he said. "I believe you'll discover that your poet is young. Very young."

"Sir?"

"To live for love's first kiss? Think about it, Sergeant."

"Yes, sir."

Later that evening, as eleven people sat down to eat in the crowded Dann family kitchen, Hektor laid out the interview for Aiden as he accepted a bowl of fish stew from their mother.

"Valens, huh?" his older brother said around a steaming spoonful of his own. "Never heard of him."

"I ain't surprised," their grandfather snorted as he helped himself to a large piece of bread and butter from the towering plateful in the center of the table. "He died afore you were born. Believe it or not, I used to read bits of his poetry to yer gran when I was courting her. Powerful words they were. To this day I credit 'em with her saying yes to me."

"Nonsense, Thomar," their mother said with a laugh, "Leila told me that you were the most handsome man ever to wear a watchman's uniform. That is, until my five boys came along," she added, smiling around the table. Both Hektor and Aiden looked embarrassed, but their twin brothers Raik and Jakon beamed back at her.

"So what have we got so far?" Jakon, the slightly taller of the two, said, leaning back in his chair. Aiden's eight-month old daughter, Leila, was balanced on one knee. "Someone well-educated who can get hold of books an' paint an' who fancies himself a poet, but isn't old enough to write in his own voice yet."

Eleven-year-old Padreic bridled at his words and Jakon waved a dismissive hand at him.

"Fine, hasn't got enough experience yet," he allowed. "Happy?"

Their only sister, thirteen-year-old Kasiath, glanced up from the small messenger bird she was tending in her lap. "No," she replied somberly. "I don't see what experience has got to do with it. You can know your own feelings enough to express them at any age. I do."

Hektor rolled his eyes at her. "Don't tell me that our serious, hard-working Kassie has fallen under The Poet's romantic spell too?" he teased. "Half the citizens of Haven are wandering about with moonstruck expression on their faces."

"And they keep knocking into each other," Aiden added. "I've never sorted out so many fistfights."

"It's calmed the night beats down, though," Raik observed. "The taverns are a lot quieter an' some of 'em are even having poetry singing."

"You're kidding," Aiden snorted.

"Nope. That young Bard, what's-her-name, Lexi, had 'em spellbound at The Broken Arms last night. They all sat there as still as mice until she finished."

"Maybe The Poet's not doin' such a bad thing, then," Padreic said quietly.

The entire family turned surprised eyes on him.

"Maybe not," Hektor allowed. "But it's still vandalism and it needs to stop before it spawns a whole crowd of lovestruck copiers across the city. The Poet can put pen to paper like anyone else. You don't know who he is, do you, Paddy?"

"Course not. I'm a watchman first, Hek." Padreic glared at his older brother. "It's just . . . well . . . "

"Rosie from downstairs likes The Poet's works, doesn't she, Paddy?" Aiden's wife, Sulia, said, not unkindly. "Not like that, my little man! Where are your manners?" She caught three-year-old Egan's fingers in hers just as he was about to snatch his great-grandfather's bread right off his plate. "I thought you were watching him, Aiden," she admonished.

Aiden accepted his unrepentant son into his arms with a look of mock contrition.

"Rosie's worried about what'll happen when The Poet's caught," Sulia continued, handing Aiden a smaller piece of bread to feed to Egan.

"Yeah, maybe." Padreic shrugged.

"Well, tell her not to fret," Hektor told him. "It's not like he's killed anyone. He'll probably just be made to clean the verses off."

"I'm surprised no one's come forward to lay claim to 'em, frankly," Aiden noted. "With the effect they're having on everybody. Here, here, the bread, boy, not the fingers. Honestly."

"I'm surprised no one's answered them," Hektor replied. "Half the city thinks The Poet's speaking to them."

"So, someone young," their mother prompted, setting the teapot and a tray of mugs onto the table. "But someone already in love."

The gathered Danns now glanced up at her curiously.

"The Poet's speaking to someone, that's plain enough, but someone in particular," she explained. "Hoping she'll pass by. And what was that verse about entwining? The one you found on that vintner's wall two days ago?"

Hektor leaned back, his eyes closed to better remember the verses.

> *Wouldst that our hearts might thus entwine,*
> *So mine's be yours and yours be mine.*
> *And never part except at Death*
> *that vexing hand that . . .*

He stopped and the rest of the people around the table stirred expectantly.

"That what?" their grandfather demanded.

Hektor opened his eyes. "That's all there was. Looked like he got interrupted in mid-verse." He poured himself a mug of tea with a thoughtful expression. "Someone must have come on him," he finished.

"The Watch?" Their mother asked.

Hektor shook his head. "It were . . . "

"Was."

He sighed. "It was Toby's route and he didn't report seeing anything amiss that night."

"Amiss?" their grandfather asked, winking at Padreic. "He musta missed it."

Raik and Jakon began to snicker. "He did miss it," Jakon said.

"A clear night with a moon, an' bright green letters a full three foot high an' ten feet up, an' he never saw a thing," Raik added. "He took some grief for that come morning."

"Well, something musta interrupted The Poet at work, if it wasn't the Watch," Thomar said irritably.

"Maybe he couldn't find anything that rhymed with death," Jakon ventured.

"Not death, *Death*." Raik gave a dramatic emphasis on the last word.

"Maybe he couldn't find anything that rhymed with *Death*."

"That's because nothing does rhyme with death," Hektor pointed out.

"You should know," Aiden noted.

"Shut up."

"Breath," Kasiath said quietly.

"What?" The family turned to look at her and she blushed slightly.

"Breath," she repeated. "Breath rhymes with death."

"That vexing hand that ... ?"

"Endeth breath."

"Yeah. Sounds like The Poet, all right," Padreic allowed.

"Sounds like our Kassie has the makings of a poet as well as a birder," their grandfather teased.

"Hm." Aiden fixed their sister with a look of mock severity. "And where were you last night, Kasiath Dann," he demanded, his tone belied by the smile that kept trying to twitch at his upper lip.

She cast him a sharp glance but didn't answer.

"So, we're looking for a young person who's already in love—here, Sulia, she's wet," Jakon said, handing his niece to her mother just as she started to fuss.

Aiden snorted. "That could be anyone from Paddy to Hektor," he noted. "And half the city in between these days."

"It's a wide circle," Thomar allowed. "Better cast a wide net and soon, boys. I've a bet on with Kiel Wright's Da that you lot'll find The Poet before he does."

"Oh, we'll find him, Granther," Raik promised him. "Won't we, Hek?"

His older brother nodded thoughtfully.

Later that evening after Jakon and Raik had left for their shifts and the rest of the family had headed off to bed, Hektor joined Kasiath at the small rooftop coop where she and Thomar raised both domestic and messenger birds.

"Anything you want to tell me?" he asked gently.

Returning the bird she'd been tending to its box, Kassie shook her head.

"It's not you, though, is it?"

She smiled wistfully at him. "I'm not well-educated, Hek," she pointed out. "An' I can't get my hands on books an' paint, can I?"

"No. But I'm thinking you know someone who can."

"Maybe. I'm not sure yet."

"A friend of yours, though?" he asked leaning against the coop.

"It could be. But I shouldn't like to say anything until I was sure."

"Fair enough." He straightened. "Go be sure. But if it is a friend of yours, tell 'em to stop, all right? There're better ways to tell someone you love 'em than by scrawling it on a wall."

"I will."

"Laryn, you have to stop."

"But I can't stop, Kassie! How can I possibly stop while the love of my life remains unaware of my most true feelings for him!"

The girl Kassie was arguing with spun about, her long braids smacking against her shoulders with the motion.

Across the sunlit artist's studio, her father glanced up then, from his work, then just as quickly bent his head to it once again. For a moment Kassie felt some of the depths of Laryn's passion, then, shaking herself firmly, Kassie took the girl's elbow and drew her outside to the small, walled garden at the back of the studio.

Of an age, the two had met one afternoon three years ago when Laryn's father, one of Haven's premier sign painters, had set up shop across from the Iron Street Watchhouse. Kassie and Thomar regularly cared for the watchhouse messenger birds, and one day rather than wait on her granther, who could spend hours "visiting," Kassie had wandered across the street to where Laryn was sitting just outside the shop, trying to paint a black border on a tavern sign for her father with one hand while holding a book with the other. Kassie had taken over the brush and Laryn had read her "the True and Stirring Tale of Berden's Ride." They had become good friends after that, despite Laryn's tendency to overdramatize far too much for the more serious girl's liking.

Now Laryn clutched at her friend's arm with a shiver of desperation. "Do you think he saw them?" she asked breathlessly.

Kassie blinked rapidly to keep the other girl's emotions from overriding her own. "Who?" she asked.

"Why, Jarred Chandler, of course, haven't you been listening to me?"

Kassie frowned. "Isn't he that tall boy who's learning the gittern with you?" Laryn's father was successful enough to pay for all three of his children to attend private lessons; her friend had tried her hand at so many musical instruments in the last three years that Kassie had lost track of them all.

"Oh, yes," the other girl's expression grew dreamy

and once again Kassie had to blink rapidly to keep her own feelings in the foreground.

"He walks past each and every one of those sites on his way to lessons every day," Laryn continued. "So do you think he's seen my declarations of love?"

"I can't imagine he hasn't by now. The letters are all quite large," Kassie answered. She was rewarded by a beaming smile and basked in it for just a moment before bringing herself firmly back on topic. "But I know the Watch has seen it, Laryn, and they're calling it vandalism."

"Vandalism! How could they!" Laryn sank onto a low stone bench and Kassie felt her own eyes fill with indignant tears at the sight. "It's art expressed in its most tactile and basic form!"

"Well, yes, of course it is, but can't you express yourself just as well on paper?"

Laryn waved a hand weakly in her direction. "Paper's much too restrictive a medium to express all the emotions I feel churning about inside me. I could fill a volume ten times the size of the biggest book I've ever seen and it still wouldn't be enough. That's why I chose the walls, you see," she added brightly, sitting up straighter as she waxed to her subject. "They're large enough. Barely," she added after a moment's reflection. "And no one else seems to mind, do they?" she added in a reasonable tone. "Everyone I've heard speak of my work seems to be eagerly awaiting the next one. And besides, the Great Bard Dion used walls as a venue before being discovered and invited into the Bardic Collegium when she was not much older than I am now."

"Who?"

Laryn's expression changed to one of exasperation. "Oh, please, don't tell me you've forgotten about her already, Kasiath? I read you a whole volume's worth of her poetry just this summer? She lived some two hundred years ago?" Laryn gave a loud snort of impatience. "O! How I wouldst have your love be like the lily flower, where birds do sing for oft an hour?" she declaimed.

Kassie started guiltily. "Oh. Right. The one who wrote about birds."

"They were a metaphor, but yes, the one who wrote about birds."

"Fine, yes, I remember her, but this isn't two hundred years ago, Laryn, and you're going to get into trouble. *I'm* going to get into trouble now that I know for sure that you're The Poet. Hektor's already figured out that I know more than I'm tellin' an' he's going to expect me to tell him."

"Hektor? Isn't he the one with the tousled, black hair and the smoldering eyes?" Laryn asked, the dreamy expression back in her voice. This time, however, her tone caused Kassie to frown in confusion.

"What? Hek? Well . . . ." She struggled to see her older brother as a besotted thirteen-year-old girl might see him and then shrugged. "I suppose."

"Oh, well, that's all right then." Laryn jumped up happily. "I shall just go over to the Watchhouse directly and explain the whole thing to him and he'll understand, I'm sure he will. He has the heart of a poet, I can tell."

Laryn tripped back into the studio, kissed her father on the top of the head, then sailed outside and across the street with Kassie drawn reluctantly along in her wake.

Word of The Poet's identity spread quickly and, although some of Haven's citizens expressed both surprise and disappointment that he turned out to be a thirteen-year-old she, some of the city's more astute gamblers were seen with extra money in their pockets.

Laryn herself was kept busy not only cleaning the walls of her creative endeavors—with Kassie's grudging help—but also in answering the dozens of entreaties for love poetry and requests for private and public readings from taverns and alehouses across the city. Her father put a swift stop to those; however, he did allow her to attend one public reading at a gathering at the Compass Rose Tavern arranged by retired artificer Daedrus for his cousin, Master Hiron of the Bardic Collegium.

Meanwhile, the walls of Haven returned to their previous unadorned state. Hektor, somewhat wistfully, he had to admit, put the entire incident behind him until an irate blacksmith summoned the Watch one week later.

Hektor read the shaky blue-painted letters scrawled on the rough surface of the forge wall with some difficulty.

Away your yearning passion's cry,
And send on threads of gossamer forth,
On winds of gale or hooves of horse,
No more requited sad remorse.

He winced. "That one's the worst so far," he noted.

Beside him, Aiden nodded. "Better go talk to our budding Bard again."

"That wasn't me!"

In her father's studio, Laryn fixed Hektor with an indignant scowl. "I would have thought you of all people could see that in a trice! I don't ever leave the first line hanging! It's awkward! And besides, forth and horse don't rhyme, do they? It smacks of . . . haste!"

"Haste?"

"Haste. And besides," she added in a somewhat petulant tone, "Papa has locked up his paints and taken away all my brushes." She drew herself up. "And even if he hadn't, I promised Master Hiron that I shouldn't resort to expressing myself on the walls of Haven any longer. He's promised me a place at the Bardic Collegium. He says I have the Bardic gift of Projective Empathy, like the great Dion and the great Valens. Does this poem project any empathy for you? No," she answered for him. "So you see it couldn't have been me."

"So who do you think it might have been, then?" Hektor prompted.

"Clearly an admirer of my . . . " She stopped in midsentence, her face brightening considerably. "It might be Jarred!" she exclaimed. "Yes, it might be! He has seen my work and now that he knows it's me, he's answered it! It is *true love*! I knew it was! Oh, I must fly to him, I must! May I, Papa, say yes, won't you say yes! I shan't be more than a moment, I promise!"

She clung to her father's arm and he just nodded weakly. As she ran for the door, he glanced apologetically at Hektor. "I'm sorry, Sergeant. If it is the boy's hand, I'll pay to have it removed."

"Have him remove it himself," Hektor answered resignedly. "For that matter, have her help him. If the rest of Haven's youthful poets see them at it, it might discourage them from following in their footsteps. Besides," he added, unable to keep a faint smile from tugging at the corners of his mouth. "Who are we to stand in the way of *true love*, eh?"

Later that evening, as a crisp autumn breeze whispered along the capital's quiet thoroughfares, Hektor stood at the end of Saddler's Street, considering what he might say to Ismy Smith. Years before he'd tried his hand at impressing her with a bit of poetry of his own—as Aiden had reminded him—and although he didn't think he could manage it today, he wondered if their granther hadn't had the right idea in reading someone else's aloud.

As he made for Ismy's door, the words of Laryn's first public poem came back to him.

> *A scattering of flowers fall,*
> *Upon the paths your foot may tread,*
> *And to my love I give my all,*
> *Lest morrow find me stiff and dead.*

He paused with a faint shudder. "Maybe not," he decided.

Change of Life
Judith Tarr

The world was coming to an end again. The wedding was in three days, and the bride was barricaded in her room and refusing to come out. The groom had stalked off in a roaring snit. Both had declared, loudly and at length, that the wedding was off. *Off*, by all the gods and powers.

Marlys could hear Ronan chopping wood out behind the cow barn. From the sound of it, he was proceeding with rather more violence than efficiency. After the third sulfurous expletive and a long pause, the sounds of ax on wood slowed down, as did the cursing.

She released the breath she had been holding and went back to embroidering the hem of Ginee's wedding tabard. One more handspan of excruciatingly elaborate vinework and she was done. "And that will be that," she said with relief so deep it came out flat.

"You are a fortunate woman," her friend Brenna said from amid a billow of fine white linen that would, on the day, drape the bride's table. "I've still the two girls to go, and Karol has been making eyes at that girl from Longmeadow. I've years of bridal nightmares still ahead of me."

"And you said I was mad to marry as young as I did,"

said Marlys. "Not that you weren't perfectly right, but when I look at five girls married fair to decently and number six about to be, no matter what she might be thinking right this moment, I must admit I'm not sorry to be finished with it. Three days from now I'll settle down to a fine and pleasant life as a mother-in-law and a grandmother, and watch in unbecoming glee as my daughters suffer through all the horrors of motherhood that they visited on me."

Brenna grinned. A woman lost a tooth for every baby she had, the grandmothers liked to say, and Brenna was proof of it. But she was still a handsome woman with her thick iron-gray hair and her fine aquiline features. Marlys used to envy that profile bitterly when they were younger. Now she was content to admire it, and to reflect that while she might not have been blessed with such dramatic looks, she still had all her teeth, and her fair brown hair was barely gray yet, either.

"Somehow," said Brenna, "I don't see you as the retiring sort. Don't you still dream about having adventures?"

"Six children and a husband leaving before number six came and a dairy to run and a menagerie of animals that the children acquired and left me to take care of when they up and married? That's not an adventure?"

"You know what I mean," Brenna said.

Marlys met her friend's stare. Yes, she knew. Farm and family were just life. Adventures were kings and queens and Heralds and magic and saving the world. "Every child dreams about that," she said. "Then she grows up. I've got enough to do breaking that filly Ginee doesn't have time for now she has a household to set up, and keeping the filly's dam in work, and even with the girls taking over the dairy, you know they won't let a day go by without asking me for something desperate and urgent that no one else can know or answer or do."

"Still," said Brenna with a distinct tinge of wistfulness, "don't you sometimes wish you could walk away from it all? Pack a bag and saddle the horse Ginee foisted on you and set out to see what's over the hill?"

"I know what's over the hill," Marlys said. "More villages just like this one. A string of towns. Haven, eventually. Where the adventures are. Where they can stay. I'm happy where I am."

She believed it when she said it. Maybe Brenna did not, but she shook her head and gave it up, and went back to hemming the tablecloth.

Marlys had no business letting that conversation stick in her mind, but it had lodged in there and would not let go. It was still there that afternoon as she cleaned stalls in the horse barn, hiding out from the chaos in the house and doing something useful while she was at it.

Ginee and Ronan were speaking again, which was a good thing. The wedding was back on. The baker had sent word that one of her ovens had caught fire that morning, but the other ovens were still working and the bakery was only a little scorched. She thought she would still have the bread and pastries done in time for the wedding feast.

"She thinks," Marlys muttered to herself, catching a load of manure fresh out of the horse in her waiting pitchfork and tossing the odorous pile into the cart. "She'd better, or never mind Ginee, *I'll* pitch a shrieking fit."

Ginee's mare slanted an ear at her and snorted. She was head down in a manger of hay, lost in equine bliss. Marlys scratched the ample bay rump with the fork, which elevated the bliss to nose-quivering rapture.

Marlys laughed at her. "Silly horse," she said, tossing the fork into the cart—to the mare's visible regret—and trundling the lot down the barn aisle to the stableyard.

The manure pile was getting high. Time to set the boys to taking it apart and spreading it in the fields.

After the wedding. That was the way of Marlys' world these days. Everything was wedding, wedding, wedding. And then when it was over—what?

Peace and quiet. Back to the daily round of farm and dairy, with Marlys' little bit of adventure added in, the horses that Ginee had bequeathed her.

She had never ridden a horse before she married. She loved them, dreamed of them, admired them from afar, but horses were working stock on the farm, and the lovely light-boned saddle horses that she yearned after were far out of her family's reach. She expected to live a life of faint and bittersweet regret for that, as a woman did, while the rest of her went on to be a wife and a mother and a grandmother.

Of all her daughters, only Ginee, the youngest, had inherited her mother's love of horses. She had not inherited Marlys' acceptance of the way things were. What she wanted, she found ways to get. She made friends with the horse farmers down the road, traded milk and curds and her own attempts at cheese for riding lessons, and for a while between short skirts and her wedding to Ronan, apprenticed to the trainer.

Ginee had moved on, but her first dream was still there, like Margali's flock of finches in their cages, Kaylin's horde of barn cats, Elspeth's ancient and flatulent dog . . .

Daughters dreamed. Mothers inherited the detritus of their dreams.

"Sometimes," Marlys said to the filly in her paddock

on the other side of the manure pile, "mothers get their own dreams after all, a few decades late."

The filly, who was was some years yet from being a mother, tossed her mane and flagged her tail and danced. That was all she knew or cared about, and that was exactly as it should be.

"Gramma," said a young voice behind Marlys. Then when she did not turn quickly enough: "*Gramma!*"

Her third-eldest grandson was windblown, dusty, breathless, and hopping from foot to foot. "Gramma, come see!"

"Come see what?" asked Marlys.

He shook his head. Whatever it was was beyond words.

It was not bad, she thought, or he would be howling. His eyes were huge with wonder. "Come *see!*"

There was no time. She had a hundred things to do, and a hundred more behind those. The last thing anyone needed was for Marlys to go chasing rainbows with Kaylin's four-year-old.

She held out her hand. "Show me what's to see," she said.

Kaylin had married the innkeeper's son, and lived down the hill from the farm and over the bridge that spanned the river. On market days the inn filled early and stayed full late with people who came in from the farmsteads and the horse farms and the smaller villages within a day's wagon ride.

Today was not a market day, but there was a crowd around the inn. The crowd was thickest in the square in front, where the innkeeper set tables in fair weather. Marlys, who was not tall, had to strain to see what they were staring at.

At a table under the awning sat a man dressed all in white, with no hint of color anywhere. There would be no doubt as to what he was, not in that uniform. There was a Herald in Emmersford.

In spite of herself, she sighed. That had never been her dream, even when she was young. She had wanted to marry and settle down and be a mother. Heralds were like adventures and Haven: all perfectly well for some-one else.

And yet, seeing the Whites and thinking of the Her-alds' mysterious mounts that were not, appearances to the contrary, horses, Marlys could be just as dazzled as any half-grown girl in Valdemar. That was why she had let young Devyn take her away from her responsibili-ties. She had recognized the look in his eye.

This was his first sight of a Herald. It was, by her count, the fourth that she had had in her life. Heralds did not often ride through Emmersford.

The Herald, Marlys heard as she came near, was on his way north; naturally he did not proclaim his errand to the world. But he had taken the wrong turning near Twin Hills where the road split twice—travelers more often than not took the first fork instead of the second, and found themselves in Emmersford instead of on the straight way to the North Road.

"I suppose you get the odd bit of business from that," the Herald said to Marlys' son-in-law, who had brought him a tankard of ale.

"We do get a little now and then," said Devyn the elder. Devyn had wanted adventures before he married Kaylin; he had spent a year in Haven, helping his aunt run a tavern in a part of the city that was not, Marlys had deduced, the most savory. He never would say how he had broken his nose.

He seemed remarkably at ease with the Herald. When Devyn the younger slipped free of Marlys' grip and darted through the crowd, his father swept him deftly up before he could launch himself at the Herald. "Manners," said the elder in a warning tone, setting the younger on his feet.

"Manners," the child echoed, then grinned at the Herald. "Good afternoon," he said. "Don't you ever get dirty?"

The Herald laughed. "All the time," he said.

Marlys had only been seeing the Whites. Now she saw the man: not a young man, though far from old; not handsome, if by no means ugly either. He looked like someone she might have been at ease with if he had lived in Emmersford.

When young Devyn climbed into his lap, he waved off Devyn the elder. "It's no trouble," he said. "Is that meat pasties I smell baking?"

Young Devyn had fallen in love by then, and not only with the glamour and the dream. Marlys was rather taken with the man herself. So was everyone else she could see.

They were all ordering ale, now the Herald had his; and speaking up for pasties fresh from the oven, too, or bowls of thick savory soup, or new-baked bread with wedges of cheese thrust into the loaves, melting into deliciousness inside.

Marlys was neither hungry nor thirsty, but she was intrigued. The Herald was good for business, and she had a feeling he knew it.

The sound of bells teased her ears. How she could have heard so soft a sound through the hubbub, she could not imagine, but there was no mistaking it. It almost seemed to be calling her—though even as the thought

took shape in her mind, she dismissed it, She was looking for ways to escape wedding hysteria, that was all. A
Companion was a singularly effective distraction.

This one was a mare, and she was settled comfortably
in the stable, eating her elegant way through a manger
of hay. The stall door was open; her saddle and her bitless bridle waited for her on a stand just outside. The
bells on saddle and bridle were perfectly still, and yet
Marlys could hear them in her head.

She would have thought the Companion would attract an even larger crowd than the Herald, but there
was no one in the stable but Marlys and the white being
who was not a horse.

Truly, she was not. Marlys knew and loved horses. This
was something else altogether. But the shape it wore ...

"It's good," she said before she realized she was
speaking aloud.

Amusement washed over her, warm and ... indul-
gent? The Companion's clear blue eye was watching
her; the little lean ear slanted toward her. Marlys could
not help peering into the stall—yes; the hooves did look
like silver, even close up. But the coat felt like a horse's,
warm and satin-soft.

She jerked her hand back. "I'm sorry," she said.
"That's not at all what I—"

The Companion shook her silken mane. *:You're not
presumptuous,:* she said. The words were clear, the voice
in Marlys' mind a firm, practical woman's voice—like
Brenna's or like Marlys' own.

Marlys blinked. "I thought you could only talk to
your Herald."

:It's not could,: the Companion said. *:As a rule, it's*
would.:

Oh, she did sound like Brenna. Marlys sat on the stool

that the stableboy had left in the aisle, because her feet
were not as young as they used to be and she had been
on them enough today as it was, and smiled up at the
Companion. The Companion's face was not made for
smiling back, but Marlys felt the warmth inside, a deep,
peaceful, altogether wonderful feeling. It asked nothing
of her except that she be there; it expected nothing. It
was exactly what she needed.

The Herald left well before sundown. Marlys was long
gone by then, back to the farm, but she heard the fading
sound of bells and the distant chiming of silver hooves,
and knew a momentary pang of regret—though for
what, she could not have said. She had no ambition to
be a Herald. But to be a friend: in another world, that
might have been possible.

In this one, she was what she was. There were six crises and a handful of disasters to avert before dinner, and
Ginee's wedding tabard to finish embroidering after, because tomorrow would be full from dawn to midnight,
and if she did not do it now, it would never get done.

By the time Marlys fell into bed, she was ready to
sleep like the dead. Her dreams were full of white light
and the sound of silver bells. Even in the middle of them,
she laughed at herself for dreaming like a silly girl.

:Good morning.:

This voice was male. It was as warm as the other Companion's voice had been, and it had a beautiful timbre in
Marlys' sleep-fogged mind, soft and rich and deep. The
white light around it had a distinct golden cast, like a
memory of summer. There was, over and under it all, a
ringing of silver bells.

Marlys sat bolt upright. The wind blowing through

the open window smelled strongly of rain, and the light was ominously gray.

With any luck at all, Ginee would sleep for hours yet without the sun to wake her. That would postpone, if not, unfortunately, dispense with the eruption altogether. Today the wedding tent was to be delivered and set up in the daisy meadow, which in wet weather was also known as the swamp. Ginee would not be happy about that. Oh, no. Not at all.

:The rain will stop by evening,: said the Companion, who should have receded with the rest of her dreams. But he was still there, and she was wide awake. *:It will be a little wet still tomorrow, but not enough to make the tent impossible. You'll have a fine dry day for the wedding.:*

For a magical being, he was remarkably practical. That stood to reason, since he was a figment of Marlys' imagination. Even in flights of fancy, Marlys kept a grip on reality.

:Oh, no,: he said. *:I'm quite real. You had better get dressed. The tent is almost here.:*

"What in the name of—" Marlys sprang to the window.

He was there in the kitchen garden, grazing on the grass that insisted in springing up along the outside wall. He had been very careful not to step on the squash vines or to knock down any of the beanpoles. He was saddled, bridled, and groomed to a luminous sheen. The rain seemed powerless to penetrate the light that surrounded him.

He lifted his head. He was not particularly large; the Companion in the inn had been a good hand taller. But he was well and sturdily built, and he had a good, solid head, the kind Marlys liked best: not too small, not too dished in the face, with plenty of brain space between the ears.

:Thank you,: he said. *:Do you want the tent in the barnyard? That's where they're headed with it.:*

Marlys flung on clothes more or less at random, snatched her oiled rain cloak from the peg, and managed to get her hair braided out of her face before she had to head off the wagon. By the time she had dealt with the tent and the people who belonged to it, sent Ronan and the boys to help them, settled three lesser crises, and fed the horses, she was as ready as she was going to be to face the wrath of Ginee.

To her amazement, there was none. Her daughter was awake, dressed, and cooking breakfast, and her expression was profoundly bemused. "Did you know there's a Companion in the garden?" she asked.

The last time she had sounded that reasonable, or that much like herself, she had been walking out with Ronan but had yet to tell him they were getting married. It was so unexpected that Marlys almost forgot to answer the question. "Yes, I did notice."

"Did you happen to notice who he's here for?"

Ginee was doing her best to sound elaborately casual, but Marlys could sense the disappointment underneath. It was buried deep; she probably was barely aware of it.

But Marlys was her mother. Marlys could read her with practiced ease. "I haven't had time," she said. "Why? Has anyone said anything?"

"Not a word," Ginee said. "I don't think anybody's seen him but us. You don't think—after all—"

"Did he speak to you?" Marlys asked.

Ginee shook her head. "Really, I know it's not me. I don't want it to be me. I've got the life I want. I don't want to give it all up to be a living, breathing, mounted target."

"I guess we'll find out, then," said Marlys as Ginee filled a bowl with porridge and honey and cream and set it in front of her. She was careful not to make a great show of appreciation, because Ginee hated that, but she smiled and dipped her head in thanks, and ate her breakfast while it was hot.

Then, after certain preparations, she went to the kitchen garden, where the Companion had finished off the grass and was asleep with one back foot cocked, as much like a horse as made no difference. The rain had backed off for a bit, and he was still perfectly dry.

"All right," she said as he started awake. "If you're here to Choose somebody, do get about it, but could you make sure they stay until after the wedding? If it's somebody essential, we can't spare her, and if it's family, we'll be needing some time to get used to the idea of losing her. Or him?"

:For me it would be "her,": the Companion said. *:My name is Kellen.:*

"Marlys," she said. "If you don't mind, the stable's probably more comfortable, and it's certainly less wet."

:I would be glad of that,: he said civilly. He dipped his head as a man would, a small bow of appreciation. She had done the same for Ginee not an hour before.

Marlys could appreciate the strangeness of it all, but it felt real enough. The Companion approved of his clean and deeply bedded stall, greeted the mares politely, and was clearly relieved to be rid of his saddle and bridle. *:There are times,:* he said, *:when one misses the convenience of hands.:*

"They are useful, aren't they?" Marlys said.

She had a sense of quick humor, like the flash of a grin, before he got down and had himself a long, delicious roll in the straw. The mares watched intently, but they were not offering any opinions—which for those ladies was remarkable.

It seemed logical, once Kellen was on his feet again, to brush the straw off him. There were endless duties calling, and Marlys would go to them. But not just yet.

She was doing her best not to think a thought that kept niggling at her. That it felt ridiculously comfortable and right to be here, picking straw out of the long waving mane, while the Companion ate his way through a manger of hay.

He had not come for her, of course. She was much too old. Her daughters were all spoken for and her granddaughters were hardly more than babies. It must be one of the farmhands or a girl from the town.

Maybe it was one of Brenna's girls. Brenna would be beside herself, between grief at losing her child and heart-bursting pride at having a Chosen in the family.

That was it, Marlys thought. It was Tara or Elin. Either would make a fine Herald, as bright and bold as they were, and afraid of nothing.

Still. The Companion was in her barn, not Brenna's, eating her hay and carrying on a lazy, meandering conversation with many pauses. There was nothing deep or significant about it. Kellen knew something about dairy farming and more about weddings than one might easily expect.

:We take time to observe the world,: he said. *:Humans have so many rituals, and tie themselves in so many knots about them.:*

"Now that is the truth," Marlys said with a sigh. He was as clean as he was going to get, and she was dallying, combing his tail to rippling white silk. "I'd better get to my ritual, or it won't get done. You're comfortable?"

:Perfectly,: he said.

It was harder to leave him than she would have thought. But he was a dream, and not for her. Her reality was outside the barn, falling into chaos as things always seemed to do without Marlys there to keep them in order.

"Two more days," she said. "Just two more days."

His assent was warm inside her. As if he counted the days, too, and understood perfectly.

One would think that the whole of Emmersford would be in a flutter over the Companion in Marlys' barn, but except for Ginee, no one seemed aware of him. He made no move toward any of the eligible young women as far as Marlys could detect. He seemed content to idle in his stall, keep the mares company, and offer the occasional pithy mental comment when wedding hysteria got out of hand.

He was keeping her sane—though the family might beg to differ. She had to be careful not to break out laughing at some of his more penetrating observations.

People did notice something. "You look as happy as Ginee is supposed to," Brenna said the morning of the wedding. It had dawned with fog and damp, but before either the bride or the groom could give way to panic, the fog burned off and the sun shone bright and warm. It was a beautiful day, as lovely as any bride could ask for.

Ginee was in the bathhouse with her flock of friends, getting ready for the wedding. Everyone else was delegated to this task or that. For Marlys and Brenna, that was the weaving of the last garlands, and making sure the bride's gown and tabard were finished, ready, and spotlessly clean.

"There's been a light on you for days," Brenna said. "Are you really that glad to be getting this over with?"

"Gladder," Marlys said. Which was true, but that was not why she kept wanting to break out smiling. Kellen had wandered down to the river pasture, where he was pretending to be an ordinary gray horse and watching the last of the wedding preparations come together in and around the tent.

She could see them through his eyes. It was peculiar and a little disorienting, but entertaining, like being in two places at once. It was useful, too, she told herself: she knew exactly what people were getting up to.

"You know," said Brenna, "if I didn't know better, I'd think you'd found yourself a man."

That shocked Marlys out of her doubled reality. "Not bloody likely," she said.

"I didn't think so," said Brenna, so mildly Marlys darted a suspicious glance at her. But she did not seem unduly skeptical.

Marlys thought seriously of telling her who else was there, watching and listening through her. But that meant explanations, and probably misunderstandings, and certainly incredulity. What, after all, would a Companion want with a grandmother from Emmersford?

:You might be surprised,: Kellen said.

"Hush," she told him, turning it into a loud sniff and a sneeze before Brenna could ask what she was talking about.

After all those eons of preparation and the drama attendant on them, the wedding came and went with supernatural speed. The weather was flawless, the bride was beautiful, the groom both handsome and besotted. Some of the guests wept, though Marlys did not, and a few became so drunk afterward that they had to be hauled off in the cart that Marlys had hired for just that purpose.

It all went off as close to perfectly as anything could. Marlys allowed herself a little tightness in the throat as she saw Ginee and Ronan off to their new home, but only a little. It was not as if they were moving to Haven. She could see them every day if she had a mind.

She might. Or she might not. When it was all over, when the feast was cleared away and the guests had stumbled and staggered and rolled on home, she sat in her empty house with the last of the wine.

It was blissfully quiet. The night was warm; the air was sweet. Somewhere not too far away, a bird called, sweet and lonely.

Marlys was not lonely at all. The presence inside her head was silent, but she could never forget that he was there.

For no reason she could think of offhand, she changed out of her wedding clothes into much more practical garments, putting on the divided skirt and the sturdy boots that she wore to ride. Then she wandered down to the stable, where a silver light illuminated the sleeping horses and the Companion, who was not asleep at all.

He was saddled and bridled. Marlys had had nothing to do with that, but there he was.

She felt a pang. So: it was time. He would go to his Chosen. And she—

:Ready?: he asked her.

She had not been expecting him to say that. And yet she had. "What would I be ready for, except a good night's sleep?"

:You know,: he said.

"I'm not the one," she said. "I'm too old. I have no hankering after adventure. I look like a corpse in white."

:You do not.: He came out of the stall, his hooves ringing faintly on the packed earth of the floor. The bells on

his saddle and bridle rang more softly still, hardly more than a shiver in the air. He blew warm breath in her face, and lowered his head into her hands. *:Are you going to waste time arguing, or will you have some sense and get on my back? We can make good time on the road tonight, and be well on our way by morning.:*

"On our way where? Haven? The Collegium?" Marlys choked on the word. "What in the world would I do in a classroom full of children a third my age?"

:Study,: he said. *:Learn. Teach. Be a wonder to them as you are to the rest of us.:*

"I am not—"

:Mount,: he said. *:There's water and food in the saddlebags, and a change of clothes for you. If there's anything else you'd like to take—:*

"Take? I'm not even going." But Marlys' boot was in the stirrup, and she was swinging astride, because there was no resisting the lure of that saddle or that broad white back.

The saddle fit her as well as the one her son-in-law the saddler had made for her. The Companion fit her even more perfectly. The height and breadth of him, the swoop of his proud white neck, the way he moved with both power and grace, they were all just right. Like his voice in her head, and his presence that she could not imagine living without, even while the practical side of her counted up the many reasons why this was completely, utterly impossible.

:That's why it's worth doing,: her Companion said.

He *was* hers. Improbable as that might be. "We're both out of our minds," she said.

:It's what we are,: said Kellen. His amusement, washing over her, made her laugh.

She had never done anything like this before, even

when she married Pitar. Just mounting up and riding away—

"What about the birds? The dog and the cats? The horses? The farm? The family? I can't—"

"I can," Ginee said.

She was there in the stableyard instead of in her marriage bed where she belonged. Her hair was braided so tightly it must have hurt, and her face had the same look to it. But there was no mistaking the set to her chin. "You go on. We'll do what needs doing. There are plenty of us, and we've been piling it on you for long enough. We'll manage."

"But—" said Marlys.

"Go," her daughter said. "I'll tell everybody."

"They'll never believe you."

"Maybe not at first," said Ginee, "but they will."

If Ginee set her mind to it, they would. Marlys spread her hands. "All right, then. This is the craziest thing I ever heard of, but it seems I don't have a choice."

:You don't,: Kellen said.

She slapped his neck so hard her hand stung. He did not even flinch. "I hope you're not sorry you did this."

:I'm not now,: he said, *:nor will I ever be.:*

The truth in that rang so deep it made her bones hum. She bent down from his back to hug Ginee; there were no tears on either side, because they were not a teary family, but they both sniffed hard.

"Be good," Marlys said. "Tell Brenna."

"I will," said Ginee.

Either Marlys left now or she never would. Kellen shifted under her, gathering himself.

She could stop him. She still had that much control.

Now, she said silently. *Go.*

He launched like a shot from the sling, but so smoothly

she barely rocked in the saddle. Three long strides and
he was out of the stableyard. Three more and the road
rang beneath his hooves. It was only a country track, but
it joined soon enough with the road out of Emmersford,
and that met the road south toward Haven.

"Just when I thought I'd finally get some peace and
quiet," she said.

:You'd be bored out of your skull,: her Companion
said.

"Some people *like* to be bored."

He snorted at that and tossed his mane. As she drew
breath to curse him for an idiot, he showed her just how
fast a Companion could run.

The wind whipped her long braid straight back behind her, made her eyes stream and her cheeks sting. It
emptied her of resistance; as for regret, there never had
been any.

He bucked; she laughed. Maybe she was not so old
after all. She bent over his neck, wound her fingers in his
mane, and let him carry her away from everything she
had ever known—except one thing.

:And that is?: he asked.

"Dreams," she said.

It did not matter what he thought of that, or even if
he understood. It was enough that he knew.

The road spun away beneath his hooves. The world
wheeled from night into dawn. She turned her face to
the sky, and filled her eyes with the rising sun.

Lack of Vision

Nancy Asire

The westering sun lay warm on Perran's shoulders, the day having cooled somewhat since noon. He rolled his shoulders, loosening muscles tight from riding since morning. His horse shook its head, fending off the more persistent flies. Thoughts of return to Sunhame flitted across his mind. This final stop on his circuit would be the last required of a traveling judge, member of the justiciary, eyes, ears and power of judgment bestowed on those chosen by the Son of the Sun to provide adherence to the laws of Vkandis, the laws of Karse. It had been a long circuit this time but, fortunately, none of the cases he had presided over had proved taxing. This last, however, could turn out to be the most vexatious.

A murder case. He reviewed what he knew about the murder of a man and the capture of the culprit. On the surface, it appeared cut and dried, but Perran knew all too well murder cases seldom turned out to be that simple.

Berron's Bend lay only a league in the distance. He could see the buildings of the town, having passed through farmland and well-tended fields on the way. He rode with companions, guards who had authority to bind and return convicted criminals of the worst kind to Sunhame for ultimate justice. Most cases could be easily solved in the villages and towns he visited, but the more serious offenses needed caution.

Murder. Reasons for *that* crime were many and varied. He had a broad overview of this case, but could not decide anything until the actual trial. He hoped the evidence would make it easy to prove the charge, but knew from past experience this was often not the way things played out.

"Settle down, will you?"

Bred glared at his visitor. He turned and stalked from one end to the other of the small room he was chained in.

"Did you come here just to gloat?" he snapped. "How am I supposed to settle down? I'm imprisoned for something I didn't do. How would *you* feel if you were here, not me?"

"That's for the judge to decide," the visitor said calmly. "You know what we found in the tavern. How can you deny what we saw with our own eyes?"

"I deny it and I'll deny it until my last breath!" Bred replied. "I had nothing to do with it! Nothing, you hear me?"

"So you say. We'll see how the judge decides. Tomorrow's trial will come soon enough."

Bred snorted and turned away from his visitor. It took all his self control not to lash out at the well-dressed man who stood in the doorway. *You're the one who accused me of something I didn't do,* he thought, *and now you tell me to settle down? To the Fires with you! I'm innocent!*

The visitor muttered something and closed the door. Bred heard the lock slide in place and lowered his head.

Now he could let anxiety show on his face, allow his hands to tremble. Tomorrow. He voiced a small prayer to Vkandis that the god's justice would avert an all too real fate he saw looming in his future.

Perran finished the last of his dinner. The tavern had filled with customers, the hum of their voices rising and falling. A nondescript man sat across his table, one who would easily be ignored in a crowd—a man Perran had sent ahead in the guise of a traveler to gather information about the case he would judge the following morning. What he'd learned from his informant raised questions concerning the murder. Citizens of Berron's Bend were outraged by the incident, though few actually thought the prisoner guilty.

"So, Levron," Perran said, leaning forward. "This Bred . . . you say people seem to think him innocent. Even when presented with the evidence?"

"Aye," the man replied, finishing his tankard of ale. "Most of them can't imagine him guilty. He works for the town blacksmith and has never been in trouble of any kind. They say he's generally soft-spoken and courteous to everyone."

"Too much drinking can bring out the worst in anyone," Perran commented. "And he was found in this very tavern with the murder weapon on his table."

"True. But he claims he was sleeping when the murder was committed."

"Were the any witnesses?"

Levron shook his head. "Not unless you count the blind man who lives in a small room at the back of the tavern. He was in the common room at the time."

Perran frowned. This wasn't going to be a pleasant trial. The man who accused Bred of murder was one of the more important citizens of Berron's Bend, a merchant who had profited greatly from the trade that passed through the region. He had a wife and daughter . . . a girl who was, by all reports, a beauty.

Perran leaned back in his chair, stared at the ceiling, and thought longingly of his return to Sunhame. Complications arose wherever his circuit led, but this trial wasn't going to be easy. Not easy at all.

Bred kept his head up as he was led into the large meeting room that had been set aside for the trial. The chains that bound his wrists and ankles rattled as he walked. The judge, clad in somber robes, the chain of his office glinting in the sunlight, sat at a large table at the far end of the room. On either side of him stood two burly men, fully armed. Bred's accuser, Tolber, sat to one side of the table, with onlookers crowding the back of the room. As usual, nothing happened in Berron's Bend without an audience.

Nothing, save the murder he was accused of.

During the days he had been held, chained in the darkened storeroom, he'd reviewed what had happened the night of the murder. None of it made any sense. And now, he would be judged for a crime he knew he had not committed. With the trial under way, he barely controlled a shiver of apprehension.

One of the guards pulled out a chair facing the judge and motioned Bred to sit. He complied and met the judge's eyes.

"This court of judgment is now called to order. Let me remind everyone present that what you say is given under oath to Vkandis. Now, let us proceed. State your name," the judge said, looking at Bred.

Bred stood and briefly bowed his head. "Bred, your lordship."

"Bred, you've been accused of the murder of Wylden, who was found stabbed to death in the tavern. You were found with the murder weapon on your table. How say you? Innocent or guilty?"

"Innocent, your lordship," Bred replied, squaring his shoulders. He wanted to say more, to protest the entire proceeding, but had decided he would try to answer only direct questions. The less he said, the less chance of being misunderstood.

The judge glanced over at Tolber. "As accuser, you may make your statement first. Your name?"

Tolber stood. "Tolber, your lordship."

"Your profession?"

"Merchant, your lordship."

"Tell me what you saw."

Tolber grimaced. "It was horrible, your lordship. I'd gone to the tavern to meet an associate of mine, a fellow merchant. It was late, but he'd arrived after dark and I wanted to confer with him about goods he carried."

"How late?"

"Quite late. Most folk had retired for the night."

"Was the tavern keeper awake?"

"Not that I could tell. He lives behind the common room. There's a bell on the door that, when the door is opened, alerts of latecomers."

"I see. Continue."

"When I entered the tavern, the man I was to meet had already gone to his room, no doubt weary after his travels. It was then I saw the body." He licked his lips, drew a deep breath and continued. "Wylden was lying in a pool of blood. The prisoner was passed out on the table he was sitting at. I saw the knife beside him on the table."

"And what did you do?" the judge asked.

"I immediately went to the authorities here in Berron's Bend and took them back to the tavern. They shook the prisoner awake, bound him and imprisoned him."

Bred stared at Tolber, rage beginning to cloud his vision. He couldn't lose his temper now, of all times. How could he have possibly murdered someone and have absolutely no memory of it?

The judge nodded at Tolber and motioned the merchant back to his chair. Bred stiffened slightly at the judge looked in his direction.

"And you, Bred. The evidence seems overwhelming here. What is your version of the events that took place that night?"

Bred kept his shoulders squared and his back straight. "Only this, your lordship. I'm innocent of this crime. I'd worked a long day at the smithy. A large order had come in and we had only a few days to meet it. We worked well past sundown that day. I came to the tavern for my supper and a few ales."

"A few?" the judge asked. "How many, Bred?"

"Two, your lordship."

"That's what all the drunks say," interjected Tolber.

"Enough!" snapped the judge, sending the merchant a stern look. "If you only had two ales, Bred, why were you passed out on the table where they found you?"

"I was exhausted, your lordship . . . tired and full. I knew Wylden. He was a good man." He spread his hands, chains rattling. "I've never had a quarrel with him. Never a cross word. You must believe me. I'm innocent!"

* * *

Perran leaned back in his chair, steepled his hands and glanced around the room. Bred's testimony had the ring of truth to it. He'd kept eye contact and displayed none of the nervousness Perran had seen in other murder trials. Granted, he admitted to consuming more than one tankard of ale, but likely he'd imbibed greater amounts at other times and been none the worse for it. He was a big man and probably could hold his liquor easily. Exhaustion had overcome him after a hard day of work. He'd put his head down on the table and gone to sleep.

"I would speak with the blacksmith," Perran said.

A large, bull-necked man stood at the back of the room.

"Your name?"

"Colvyn."

"All right, Colvyn. Did you work long hours the day of the murder?"

"Aye, your lordship," the blacksmith replied. "As he said, we had a large order to fill and had been working our butts off to complete it."

A ripple of laughter crossed the room.

"Thank you." Perran said, hiding a smile. The blacksmith looked relieved and sat down. Perran glanced at the townsfolk who filled the back of the room. He'd thought the evidence presented before his arrival in Berron's Bend would ensure this trial to be a quick one. But now, he wasn't so sure. "I think we'll stop the proceedings until after the midday meal. I want everyone to reconvene two hours later." He stood and made the circular sign of the Sunlord. "Vkandis support our endeavors here," he intoned.

"This doesn't look good for Bred," Perran said to the

nondescript man who sat across from him at table. "He protests his innocence, but the evidence clearly points to his involvement."

Levron shrugged. "I agree, but I think there's more to this than meets the eye. Someone isn't telling the truth. It's either the merchant or Bred. Let me wander around and listen to what people are saying. So far, I've attracted little attention. Once the townsfolk accepted me as a traveler who chose to rest here for several days before continuing my journey, they seemed to forget about me. I'll try to get back to you before you start the afternoon proceedings."

"Do so," Perran said. "I'm inclined to believe as you do. I've always considered myself as one who can read those brought before me, and Bred doesn't act like a guilty person. He's either innocent as he claims or one of the best liars I've been presented with in years. We still have more people to testify this afternoon. See what you can find for me."

Bred glanced around as he was led back into the meeting room. Once more, his neighbors and other citizens of Berron's Bend had gathered to view the trial. Tolber sat in his chair by the judge's table, and the two guards stood motionless behind the judge. Bred swallowed, lifted his head and tried to calm his beating heart. He bowed to the judge and took the chair facing him.

"Once again," the judge said, "I caution anyone present against falsehood. What is uttered here is spoken before me, chosen representative of the Son of the Sun. We shall proceed now."

Bred watched the judge's eyes scan the meeting room as if he was searching for something or someone. Then the judge turned to Tolber.

"Merchant Tolber, I have further questions of you."

Tolber stood, smoothed the wrinkles from his tunic. Bred noticed he had changed clothes during the break for the noon meal, and what he wore now appeared even more costly.

"Kindly tell me more about Wylden. You knew the man well?"

"Not all that well, your lordship."

"Yet from what I understand, he was seen numerous times in the company of your daughter. Is that correct?"

Tolber flushed slightly. "Correct, your lordship. He was one of many young men who found my daughter beautiful."

The judge nodded briefly. "Aside from his seeking your daughter's company, did you have anything more to do with him?"

"Little, your lordship. He was an aspiring merchant who liked to think he could work with me."

"And did he?"

"Every once in a while." Tolber shrugged. "I'd send him on errands, have him meet with various traders who passed through Berron's Bend."

Bred watched this exchange, puzzled by the merchant's words. A quiet murmur ran through the room. Everyone in town knew Wylden as more than an errand boy. He and Tolber had worked together for several years.

"Did you ever have cause to fault your dealings with Wylden?"

Tolber hesitated a brief moment and shook his head. "Not really, your lordship. There were times when . . . ." He spread his hands. "Sometimes he annoyed me, but nothing more than small problems that arise when people deal with each other."

"I see." The judge leaned back in his chair, appearing to review what the merchant had said.

Bred glanced at his accuser, torn between anger and a real growing fear. The whole town had been witness to Tolber's ease in speaking, had listened as he'd put forward ideas and solutions to problems that arose in the past. Silver-tongued, some called him, and today he was living up to that reputation.

"The prisoner has a temper," Tolber said, unprompted. "As you can see, your lordship, he's a big man. Strong, too. Years of working with the blacksmith has made him stronger than other men. He could easily kill someone and not show signs of it."

This time the murmur that ran through the room was louder. Bred felt his jaw tighten. A temper? Everyone had a temper. But since an early age, he'd learned to control his. Bigger, stronger than his year mates, he knew what damage he could do if provoked into unreasoning anger.

"Have you ever quarreled with the accused?"

The merchant appeared to think deeply before responding. "No, your lordship. But then I've had few interactions with him."

"You may be seated," the judge said. "I may have further questions of you."

Perran rubbed his forehead and looked at the townsfolk gathered at the back of the room. From their expressions, the people of Berron's Bend disagreed with what Tolber had said. That, in itself, was telling. He sighed quietly.

"At this time, I will take statements from anyone who knows the accused."

A stir ran through the gathered townsfolk. Then the blacksmith stood.

"I've worked with Bred for years, your lordship. He was apprenticed to me as a youth and I've never seen him lose his temper. Oh, he gets out of sorts like the rest of us, but not to the stage where he'd lose control."

The blacksmith sat and another man stood.

"My name is Abend, your lordship. I live in a house next to Bred. He's always been a good neighbor. Works long hours and hard, but he's always available if anyone is in need."

Perran leaned back in his chair. One by one, men and women stood and testified to the fact that Bred had never been in trouble, had always been reliable. Though no one said straight out they thought him innocent of the charge brought against him by Tolber, Perran grew convinced a major piece of information was missing in this case. There had to be more to it than he could see.

He glanced at Bred. The big man's face had reddened in embarrassment. He obviously had no idea he was held in such regard. Yet Tolber's accusation, along with the evidence found, weighed heavily against him and Perran was keenly aware of the fear that Bred attempted to hide.

So much for a quick trial, evidence notwithstanding. Perran sat in silence, weighing his options. He could declare the case too convoluted for him to decide. If so, he would then be obliged to take Bred to Sunhame where he would be questioned by the priests, some of whom could probe a man's mind to sort out the truth.

Yet something held him from making that decision. He sensed an undercurrent driving Tolber's charge against Bred and acknowledged his responsibility to get to the bottom of it. Even if it meant spending yet another night in Berron's Bend.

"It's late afternoon," he said into the silence. "We'll resume this trial tomorrow morning. Vkandis support our endeavors here."

The crowd in the back of the room rose and began to file out the door. Perran had turned to speak to Tolber when he noticed the last person to leave—a small, slight man, head lowered, feeling his way with a long cane. The blind man. The one who had been in the common room when the murder took place. Interestingly, he'd not joined his neighbors when asked to speak about Bred.

A sudden thought flashed through Perran's mind. He rose, motioned for the two remaining townsfolk to take Bred back to the room where they had confined him. He gave a brief nod to Tolber and left, followed by his two guards.

"Here's what I want you to do," Perran said to Levron, as the two of them sat in the guest room Perran had been granted in the tavern. "See if you can find the blind man. Bring him to me. I have questions for him that might shed more light on this case. I can't ignore the evidence Tolber presented, that was seconded by the authorities the merchant brought to the murder scene. On the other hand . . . ."

"On the other hand," Levron said, as Perran's voice trailed off, "there's something going on here beyond what we can see. And you hope this blind man might clarify things?"

Perran nodded. "And, I'll send a message to Tolber that I want his daughter to attend the trial tomorrow. See what you can find out about her. Surely someone in the household or a neighbor will talk."

*   *   *

Another night spent chained in the storeroom. Another night that held little sleep. Bred heard the approach of the men charged with taking him to the trial. He stood, smoothed his hair as best he could and waited. At least they fed him regularly, though his nerves prevented him from enjoying what he ate.

The door opened and he nodded to the two men. He knew them only in passing, but they didn't seem to harbor any hatred of him. He preceded them down the street, across the square, and into the meeting hall. Once more, the rear of the room was filled with townsfolk. The judge sat in his place behind the heavy table, the merchant again seated to his right. Only this time, Bred was amazed to see Tolber's daughter sitting in a chair beside her father.

Few people had seen her lately. Word came from Tolber's house that she had been visiting a relative and had only returned several days ago. She was, by all accounts, one of the most beautiful young women in the region and certainly looked the part this morning. Clad in a loose-fitting dress, her hair gathered behind her neck, she sat motionless, her face rather pale.

Bred bowed his head to the judge and took his chair.

"The proceedings will begin now," the judge said, his expression even more serious than the day before. To Bred's eyes, the judge looked tired, as if he had not slept well. "By now, I don't have to remind any of you of the severe penalty of being less than truthful. This trial is sanctioned by the laws of Vkandis Sunlord. Speak falsehood before me and the god if you dare."

A chill ran up Bred's spine. The atmosphere in the room had changed from the day before. A terrible thought crossed his mind. Had the decision been made?

Was he to be found guilty? He briefly closed his eyes. *Vkandis, let it not be so. You know I'm innocent! Protect me now!*

"Merchant Tolber," Perran said. "I realize this might seem odd to you, but I'd like to question your daughter today."

The merchant's face went blank. Perran had noticed Tolber seemed somewhat flustered when he'd entered the meeting room, his daughter's hand on his arm. Now, he appeared even more ill at ease.

"Of course, your lordship. May I present my daughter, Lysa."

Perran nodded at the young woman. "You may remain seated," he said, "but I have a few questions for you. How well did you know Wylden?"

"I—not all that well, your lordship," she replied.

Perran noted the quaver in her hushed voice.

"Yet he was one of the young men who sought your company, was he not?"

"He was, your lordship."

"I would imagine his death shook you hard."

"It did, your lordship."

"Let me remind you of the penalty of lying to me, Lysa. I want the truth from you. Not half-truths. Once again, let me ask you . . . how well did you know Wylden?"

The young woman glanced at her father, her eyes gone enormous. "Better than I told you before, your lordship."

"How much better?"

An anguished expression crossed Lysa's face. "He was courting me, your lordship."

"I see. And how did your father take this?"

"He wasn't pleased, your lordship."

Tolber stirred in his chair. "I don't see how this has any bearing on the murder, your lordship."

Perran fixed the merchant with what he hoped was a chilling look. "You've not been given leave to speak, Tolber. I'm questioning your daughter. She's already lied once or, at best, shaded the truth. Do you have any objections to my authority?"

The merchant's jaw tightened. "No, your lordship."

"Then I'll proceed. Lysa," Perran said, pitching his voice to a softer tone. "I have reason to believe you and Wylden had plans to marry. Is this true?"

The young woman nodded, seeming to have lost her voice.

"And your father forbade you?"

"He did, your lordship."

"Did you continue to see Wylden?"

Lysa darted a quick look at her father. "I did."

The merchant stiffened in his chair.

"Was he angry when he found the two of you continued to see each other?" Perran continued.

Now tears started in Lysa's eyes. "He was, your lordship."

"Did he ever say anything to you about seeing Wylden again? That you would be punished if you did?"

Lysa raised a hand and brushed the tears from her eyes. She glanced at her father, but he sat staring straight ahead, his own face gone pale.

"He vowed to punish me, your lordship. But I loved Wylden. I truly, truly loved him. And when he died . . . ."

"I'm sorry for your loss, Lysa, but a man's guilt or innocence will be proved today. Did your father ever say anything to you about punishing Wylden?"

"No . . . not in words."

"You mean?"

"It was the way he looked at Wylden, your lordship." Lysa now stared straight ahead, no longer making an effort to exchange glances with her father.

Tolber stood, his face gone from pale to flushed. "I must object, your lordship. This has nothing to do with the case!"

"Sit down!" Perran snapped. "Not another word from you until I give you leave to speak! Do you understand me?"

"I do." The merchant took his chair again, his lips thinned.

"Lysa," Perran said, "think back to the night of Wylden's murder. Was there anything odd going on in your house?"

She shook her head. "I wouldn't know, your lordship. I was in my room all evening."

Perran nodded. "Thank you, Lysa." He turned his attention to Bred. "I have a few questions for you."

Bred stood, chains rattling.

"Was there anyone in the common room at the tavern the night you claim you fell asleep on the table?"

The big man shook his head and then looked startled. "I almost forgot. There was, your lordship. Evin, the blind man who lives in the tavern. He's the tavern owner's brother."

"How long has Evin been blind?"

"He was born that way, your lordship. Everyone in town knows him. He's always in the tavern. I guess that's why I nearly forgot he was there. Being blind, he doesn't get around much."

Perran leaned back in his chair. Now things were falling in place. He only needed one more piece of the puzzle to make it whole.

"Will someone escort Evin forward?" he said.

The townsfolk in the rear of the room stirred. One man stood and helped the blind man make his way to a chair that had been placed next to the prisoner.

"Your name is Evin, correct?" Perran asked, once the blind man had been seated.

"It is, your lordship."

"And you've been blind since birth?"

"I have."

"Do you spend much time in the common room of the tavern?"

"I don't walk around that much, your lordship. It's comfortable there and my brother looks after me."

"Do you know many of your neighbors? Other townsfolk?"

The blind man nodded. "A lot of them frequent the tavern."

Perran glanced at Tolber who was staring, wide-eyed, at the blind man.

"Would you recognize any of them if they were near you?"

"I believe I would, your lordship."

"This is outrageous!" The merchant grasped the arms of his chair. "How can a blind man know who's near him?"

Perran allowed a small smile to touch his lips. He motioned and one of his guards stepped forward. "Another outburst from you, merchant, and you run the risk of arrest for disturbing the proceedings of this court! Do you understand?"

Tolber shrank back in his chair, now decidedly pale.

"All right, Evin. Let's you and I test your claim." He gestured to the back of the room. "I want a number of you to come forward. Do not, I repeat, do *not* give your names." Several men and women came to stand at the blind man's side. "Now, one at a time, say something to Evin."

An attractive, older woman spoke. "It's a sunny day, Evin. If you went outside, you'd feel the warmth of the sun."

Perran nodded. "Do you recognize who spoke to you, Evin?"

"I do, your lordship. It's Widow Alyn."

"Is that your name?" Perran asked.

"It is, your lordship."

"Now you," Perran said, pointing at a man who stood next to the widow.

"Evin, you really should get out more. I'd help you walk the streets if you want."

"And who is that, Evin?"

"Donton, your lordship."

Perran glanced at the man Evin had named as Donton. "Are you Donton?"

"That's my name, your lordship."

Perran gestured at the next person. Once again, Evin proved easily able to identify the speaker. And the next, and the next after that.

"You may return to the back of the room," Perran said. He waited until the townsfolk had returned to their places. The meeting room grew so hushed the sound of the birds outside seemed loud. "Now Evin. I want you to think very hard. The night of the murder, where were you?"

"Sitting in my usual corner, your lordship. I'd not been able to sleep that night, and had made my way to the common room. Sometimes, when I can't sleep, I go there. I thought if I sat quietly for a while, I'd grow drowsy enough to fall asleep."

"Tell me what happened that night."

Evin drew a deep breath. "I ask for protection," he said in a small voice. "I'm afraid what I say could get me in trouble."

"Protection? You have it. As for trouble, you understand you might be in more trouble if you withhold any evidence in this trial. Speak freely, Evin. No one will hurt you."

"As I said, your lordship, I was sitting in my usual corner. It's out of the way so people don't trip over my cane. I heard someone snoring and guessed it was a customer who'd passed out earlier. My brother doesn't throw them out, you see. He's not that sort. He just lets them sleep it off."

"And your brother was asleep?"

"He was." Evin shifted in his chair. "Well, the snoring became loud enough I knew I'd never get to sleep. A while later, I heard someone come into the common room."

"What about the bell that would alert your brother that a customer had entered his tavern?"

"It didn't ring, your lordship. For some reason, it didn't ring. I guess the cord that holds it against the door had broken."

"Did only one person enter the common room?" Perran asked. A quick glance at the merchant revealed Tolber's face gone pale as parchment.

"No, your lordship. Another came in directly after the first."

"And then what happened?"

"The two of them started arguing. They weren't loud at first, but got that way."

"Could you hear what they were saying?"

"Not all of it. One man kept saying, 'Don't!' He just kept saying, 'Don't, don't!' And then . . . ." Evin's voice trailed off. He swallowed. "I heard the sound of a scuffle. A grunt. Something heavy hit the floor. And the second man to come into the common room said, 'That's what you deserve!' And then, that man walked over to the table where the customer was sleeping, stopped and quickly left the common room."

"And would you recognize the voice of the person who left? Of the man who kept saying, 'Don't?'"

Evin squared his shoulders. "I would, your lordship."

Bred sat transfixed in his chair, hardly believing what he was hearing. For the first time in days, his heart beat faster but this time not in fear.

The judge leaned forward, his face gone perfectly still. Bred could hear the audible breathing of the merchant, who sat as if paralyzed. His daughter held her hands before her mouth, her eyes dark with emotion.

"I want you to tell me whose voices you heard. Who was it said, 'Don't, don't'?"

"Wylden, your lordship."

"And the one who said, 'That's what you deserve'?"

Bred closed his eyes, afraid of what he might hear next.

"It was the merchant, Tolber," Evin said, his voice clear and steady. "I know his voice well."

Bred quickly looked from the judge to the merchant. A hot flood of rage ran through his body.

"You!" he shouted. "You lying bastard! *You* killed Wylden and tried to lay the blame on me!"

"Silence!" The judge's voice rang out in the meeting room. He motioned the two guards forward. "Take the merchant into custody."

Before the guards could reach the merchant, Tolber

bolted from his chair. In an attempt to run to the door at the back of the room, his path took him close to Bred's chair. Bred saw his chance, stood and threw himself in Tolber's path. The merchant tripped over Bred's body, one foot kicking his head. The world spun briefly, but when Bred lurched to his feet, he saw the two guards holding Tolber in a vise-like grip.

Tolber's daughter sat as if turned into stone. Tears ran down her face and she stared at her father as if she'd never seen him before.

"Why?" she cried in a choked voice. "Why? How could you do this? How *could* you?"

"He was scum!" Tolber shouted, fighting against the grips of the guard who held him. "A nobody! Not worthy of you!"

"Silence!"

Bred cringed before the force of the judge's voice. His head hurt and he heard the roar of excited voices coming from the rear of the room. Once again, the judge commanded silence and this time received it.

"Bred, step forward."

For the first time Bred did not see the judge as his own death sentence. He took a step forward and bowed his head, wincing at the stab of growing pain.

"From the evidence gathered in this court, it's plain to see you're innocent of the charges brought against you." The judge looked at the men who had escorted Bred into the meeting room. "You may unchain Bred. He goes free."

For a brief, heady moment Bred felt he could fly. He closed his eyes, tears threatening to run down his cheeks. Unlocked, the chains fell to the floor. His hands and feet had never seemed so weightless.

"Chain the merchant," the judge said. "He will be confined in the same room where he falsely imprisoned Bred."

The merchant struggled against the guards who held him. A wild sense of satisfaction filled Bred's heart as the men who had led him to the meeting room locked the chains on Tolber's wrists and feet. He noted they were not gentle.

"Bring the merchant before me," the judge said, his voice gone very cold.

Tolber struggled again but finally gave in to the fact he couldn't escape. The two guards led him so he stood facing the judge. Bred glanced sidelong at Evin, but the blind man sat silent, his face bowed.

"Merchant Tolber, I find you guilty of the murder of Wylden. I also find you guilty of bringing a false charge to the attention of the authorities of Berron's Bend and, consequently, of the justiciary." Bred had seldom seen a face hard as the judge's. "You have lied, not only to your fellow neighbors and citizens of this town, but to me. And your lies to me bear a heavier burden. You have lied before Vkandis Sunlord. May he have mercy on your soul!" He gestured. "Take him away."

As the guards led Tolber toward the rear of the room, the merchant glanced over his shoulder at his daughter.

"Don't you understand!" he screamed. "I did it for you, Lysa! I did it for you!"

Perran stood silent as the room emptied. A woman came forward and gently led the sobbing Lysa away. The townsfolk seemed stunned by the outcome of the trial. After their initial uproar, they talked quietly to each other. He could only imagine what they were saying. He looked at Bred, who had the expression of someone who had stared death in the face and lived to tell of it. And, in a sense, he had. And Evin . . . the blind man had not risen from his chair. Perran saw Levron standing at the rear of the room and gestured him forward.

"Levron, would you kindly take Evin to wherever he wishes to go?"

Evin stood, holding his cane before him.

"Evin, you've more than done your duty here," Perran said. "You've saved Bred from a sentence of death by your ability to recognize voices. You asked for protection but I don't think you need fear reprisals now. And I imagine Bred has a few kind words for you, too."

Rubbing his wrists, the big man stepped to Evin's side. "Words? I don't have words enough. If there's ever anything I can do to repay you, let me know."

A brief smile touched Evin's lips.

"The next time you fall asleep in the tavern," he said, "try not to snore."

The Groom's Price

Michael Z. Williamson and Gail Sanders

He was miserable, absolutely miserable.

:*No, you're not.*:

:*I am too—how could I be anything else with all of these Outclans strangers staring at me?*:

:*You only think that you should be miserable; you're really having an adventure, and you feel guilty that you wanted an adventure when your Clan thought it was your duty that made you go. Besides, if you hadn't argued so persuasively, we'd still be on your plains.*:

Keth're'son shena Tale'sedrin was quiet while he thought this over. He found the gait of the Companion to be smooth and enjoyable. So enjoyable that it distracted him from his train of thought for a while.

His Companion was sneaky enough to blend into the herds being kept for youngsters to choose and train. His Companion had disguised herself using the magic that had been forbidden to the Clans until the Mage Storms had swept through the plains. His Companion was slowing her pace and moving up to a palisade partly hidden by trees. With a start, he realized that it was getting dark.

:This is Bolthaven. Tell the gate guards that you're here to see Master Quenten. If they ask you who you are, tell them. They still remember Kerowyn here.:

From a platform, a sentry demanded, "Name yourself."

"Keth're'son shena Tale'sedrin, for Master Quenten."

"Hold and wait."

He waited, nervously, but the gate was opened and another watchman gestured for him to follow. He found himself ushered and escorted through a town that seemed over-busy and overpopulated. No one paid the least bit of attention to him, other than a look of admiration for his mount. He wasn't sure if the presence of the guard was insulting; he was after all an adult by the Clan's standards. Surely he could have found the school on his own.

:The guard is both for your protection and for the protection of the townsfolk. Very few people this far out of Valdemar know just what Companions are. With the mage students here, loud noises are common; leading me along is to prevent me from running off if I get startled. I'd prefer it if very few people knew a Companion out of Valdemar was down in the Dhorisha Plains.:

Quenten jerked from his book as his mage barriers flared a warning. After the last time a Guardian Spirit gave him the collywobbles, he'd decided to set up an alarm. While he had plenty of experience thinking on his feet after his time with the Skybolts, he had reached an age where he preferred at least a little notice. After carefully putting down his book, he moved over to the window that overlooked the main gate. Sure enough, there was one of those Guardian Spirits. Perched on the spirit's back was something unexpected, a Shin'a'in youngster—the leathers were unmistakable.

"May the Blessed Trine curse that woman with children." *What does Kerowyn want now? At least last time she sent a letter ahead, even if it left out more than it told.* He had decided to meet the Shin'a'in when an apprentice knocked.

"Yes?"

"Sir, a strange child on a white horse says he's here to see you. One of the gate guards is downstairs with him."

"I know. I'll go down and meet him, Cuthbert." For some reason, using the apprentice's name seemed to make him more nervous.

The voice that spoke in his head was unexpected, but didn't scare him.

:That would be because he doesn't know how much you notice the students. Look, you've got a delicate situation here; it's going to take tact and all of your experience dealing with youngsters. This boy's considered an adult by his people, if just barely. He's got a powerful gift that needs to be trained and his people have traditionally shunned magic in general and have little experience with mind magic. I need your help to convince him to go up to Valdemar. He still thinks that I'm his horse:

:Surely being able to talk to him in his mind would have told him otherwise?: Quenten replied, shocked at holding a conversation this way. He could see why Kerowyn had complained about the Companions' highhanded attitudes in Valdemar.

:One of his gifts is Animal Mindspeech; he's used to hearing animals talk in his head. He's young enough that he hasn't learned that not everyone does. I've just got a larger vocabulary.:

Quenten moved down the stairs with an undertone of caution. He wasn't young any more, even though being a mage preserved a person. Cuthbert had taken them five at a time with the boundless energy of youth.

He emerged into twilight supplemented by the flickers of watch fires, and saw the boy leaning against the Guardian Spirit. *Companions; they're called Companions,* he reminded himself.

"Greetings to you and to your Companion. I am Master Quenten, the head of the mage school here."

"Greetings to you," the boy replied, his Rethwellan rather accented. "I am Keth're'son shena Tale'sedrin and this is Yssanda."

"I bid you come up. Cuthbert, please bring us dinner and ale after you see to Lady Yssanda. Our guest stables should be adequate to your needs, Lady, and I will have a gate to the gardens left open for you. If you will follow me?"

Cuthbert stood waiting respectfully near Yssanda. Before she turned to go, she whickered gently and nudged him towards Quenten.

:Go on, I'll be with you.: Cuthbert led her away toward the stables. Obviously setting his chin, Keth' turned to follow Master Quenten.

The meal was dispatched with the economy of the young and perpetually hungry. While the boy ate sliced meat and cheese quickly but neatly with a belt knife, Quenten mused on what the Companion Yssanda had told him about the situation. It wasn't enough to make a decision, and with a skill he had developed as head of a mage school he extracted more of the tale from the young man.

It was the tradition of his clan to prove they were ready for adulthood by choosing and training a horse out of the Clan's herds. Keth're'son had done well, especially for his age, and his pride in his skill was present in his voice. Then, when he was on his trial journey, the unexpected had happened: his horse had talked back to him. His horse had the nerve to tell him that he had been Chosen and not the other way around. Quenten could hear the bafflement and confusion creep in past the confidence. Then the horse had the nerve to say that he had mind magic and real magic. He was no Shaman. He didn't want to be a Hawkbrother, and he didn't want to leave the plains. What would a Shin'a'in do with magic anyway? He was going to train horses and trade them like his father and mother. It wasn't his fault that his mother's mother's mother had been Kethryveris shena Tal'sedrin.

The chance to tell his story paled before the attraction of more food and Keth' dug into the lentils. There was rabbit as well, with some savory spices. It warmed and renewed him. As he paused, Quenten put forth his proposal.

"I have need of your services. There is an advanced mage student wishing to study other schools. Far Valdemar has many in one town. The student is young and unfamiliar with wilderness. You, however, are an experienced traveler, and have your Companion. You'll be heading that way already, so I would ask that you act as escort."

Keth' didn't regard himself as an experienced traveler. This was his second journey on his own and he'd gone astray on his first one due to the Companion. The second comment brought him to a halt, spoon almost to his mouth.

"How did you know I would be going to Valdemar?" he asked.

He knew how, though, even as Quenten spoke.

"Keth're'son, you must develop your mind magic and your bond with your Companion. That can only be done at the Collegium in Valdemar. I thought you would know of this." The mage frowned, suddenly looking older as he did.

Keth' scowled and put down the spoon.

"It's been suggested. It's not something I'm interested in or able to do. I have plans for my life that do not include going to a strange land to be schooled as if I were still a child." He was betrothed to Nerea. His family had horses . . .

The mage looked gently at him. "Keth're'son, not everything in life is as we plan or wish, and sometimes events change our route."

:You lied to me.: If thoughts could burn with accusation his would be acid now.

:I did not. I said Quenten would have better information. It must be your choice. While you are still young, by your own people you are considered an adult. Would you leave a child to wander the plains with a lit torch? That's the potential hazard you present to your people.:

Keth' sighed and said, "Who is this student?" He was not conceding the point. He needed more information, though.

Quenten nodded slightly and flicked a bell with his index finger. The tone seemed to penetrate the very walls. A moment later, the student was ushered in. She was elaborately and impractically dressed. The sheen of the finely woven fabric moved like water. It was completely unsuitable for rough travel. The dangling sleeves and the ornately upswept hair did nothing to hide the penetrating glance she gave the young Shin'a'in. With a dismissive shrug she bowed briefly to Master Quenten.

Keth're'son looked at the girl and felt unnerved. She was pretty, yes, but it was her gaze, far more mature than it should be. She stared back, uninterested except in his potential as a guide, and clearly not impressed by what she saw. He blushed.

Still, there was good pay involved, and he was going to Valdemar, at least to deliver the Companion.

Only to deliver the Companion.

Quenten said, "This is Armaeolihn and this is Keth're'son shena Tale'sedrin." His pronunciation was quite good. Keth' was impressed.

The girl bowed slightly but politely, and he realized she was older than he'd thought. He returned the bow. He thought he should say something, but he wasn't sure what, so he turned to Quenten.

Quenten said, "You will travel together for safety. Keth're'son is bonded to a Companion. Armaeolihn, you have your pass, and I shall write one for Keth're'son. I will also give Keth're'son a letter to take to Herald Captain Kerowyn, his cousin. She'll see that he gets paid. If you choose to stay, she will ensure your learning and settle you."

"How much pay?" he asked. He understood this to be an escort duty, and Shin'a'in were well-sought for that.

Quenten named a sum, and Keth' opened his mouth to haggle, then kept it open in surprise. That was a goodly sum.

"Then I accept," he said, before realizing he should have asked for more anyway. Not that he needed to, but still, one should never take the first offer.

"Good. Rest well, and we'll prepare her horse and a pack beast. You can leave in the morning." *And be out of my hair* was unspoken, but Keth're'son heard the undertone. This mind magic was problematic. He heard whispers of things that weren't spoken, and of course, no one knew how to teach him to control it ... except in Valdemar.

Another student mage appeared and led him to a comfortable room, with a pitcher of cold, clear water, another of hot, and wine and fruit. Over his protests, his traveling clothes were whisked away, washed and the minor tears of constant travel mended, then returned. At first he was uncomfortable. It felt like an attempt to place a debt on him. Then he concluded it was just service provided to a professional.

Alone, Keth' spoke to Yssanda. :*Should I do this?*:

:*Now you want advice. Am I suddenly of worth?*:

:*You always have been,*: he protested. :*You also know these people better than I.*:

:*The journey fits my plans. You must understand that affects my advice. However, it pays you well, it gives you experience and travel, and it gets you where you must go regardless of your choice.*:

:*That's fair,*: he thought. Very fair. Yssanda hadn't actually offered advice, though, only facts.

:*Often, that is the best advice of all:*

He scowled. Why was everyone assuming he would be one of these Heralds?

He awoke at graylight, and followed the smells of breakfast downstairs to a common room. He was an outsider, but treated cordially enough. As he finished, one of the omnipresent mage students led him to the stable, where Yssanda was ready, groomed, in new harness, and Armaeolihn waited in comfortable traveling clothes with her own roan gelding and a lead to a sturdy draft pony.

"Good day," he said in Rethwellen.

She nodded politely enough, if a bit noncommittally.

He got the feeling she was unsure of his qualifications but glad to be finally going to Valdemar. It was going to be a long enough journey as it was; hopefully she wasn't going to act superior the entire way. Not that it mattered with a language barrier.

:Don't worry; for all that she's a mage she's also a young girl. She'll open up a little more as we journey. Of course, that's going to depend somewhat on you. Don't you know how to treat a girl? Or are the Shin'a'in all unlettered barbarians?:

While her tone was teasing, that was the root of this problem. He was out of his depth.

The journey through Rethwellan passed in a series of inns, where Master Quenten's letter secured them supplies and sleeping quarters, and then there were the times between the inns.

Keth' was learning Valdemaran while trying to wrap his mind around the philosophy, history, and ways of that strange land. The education did pass the time, especially when delivered with the Companion's biting sarcasm.

Once, when he laughed out loud at Yssanda's comment, he heard an exasperated sigh.

Blushing, he turned to look at his previously silent traveling companion.

Noticing his glance, she scowled at him. "What are you laughing at?"

"Something that Yssanda said." It didn't occur to him to prevaricate.

"Yssanda? Who's Yssanda?"

"You've been traveling with her." He leaned forward and patted the Companion's shoulder.

Yssanda turned her head and winked at Armaeolihn.

The crystal blue eye glinted briefly before resuming the dark brown color that Yssanda used for discretion.

Armaeolihn was silent again. Keth' hoped he hadn't annoyed her. She'd been more friendly of late.

During their lunch break at the side of the road, Lihn broke her silence.

"Is Yssanda some kind of Guardian Spirit, or are you a mage?" she started off accusingly.

"I don't know." Keth' scowled. "I'm supposed to have some kind of Gift—mind magic and true magic. But I don't want it and don't need it. Yssanda won't tell me what she is—just that she's a Companion and that they'll tell me everything in Valdemar."

"You don't want magic? How can you not want magic?" Lihn sounded absolutely shocked.

"Where I come from, only Shamans and Hawkbrothers have magic. Mages meddle where they're not supposed to and are forbidden to be on the plains. At least they used to be. Things have changed since the Mage Storms."

"So what are you doing riding a spirit horse, speaking to it using mind magic, traveling with a mage and going to Valdemar where there are many mages?"

"That's what I'd like to know."

His reply silenced her again. But this time it was a puzzled silence, rather than a hostile one.

"I would ask you the same," he said to her after they began to ride again.

"For learning."

"I was told that. What kind of learning?"

"Ah," she said, and shifted, with a breath. "I am a born mage, and have studied many disciplines. I can gather dispersed magic and build its power. Not like before the

Mage Storms, but to a level suitable for serious study. Each style has its limits, though. There are more schools, more ways, in Valdemar. I will share what I know; in exchange they will let me study more."

"I see," he said. "I wish I could unlearn mine. I have no desire to improve it."

"But you must!" she said.

"Why? I don't use it." He shrugged.

"You have been using it. You say you talk to animals. You talk to this Companion. That's why you're going for training."

He flared up again. "Everyone assumes I'm getting trained."

"Magic not controlled is magic that controls the mage. It's far better that you do. Far, far better," she said, and shuddered slightly.

"I have a life," he said. "I am happy with it."

Lihn said, "Magic changes things. You can feel this."

"Shin'a'in don't use magic."

She said nothing.

They rode on, munching rations as they traveled, resting themselves and their horses every couple of hours. It was midafternoon before she spoke again.

"Imagine a campfire, in dry grassland," she said.

Yssanda had said as much. He didn't feel that was a fair comparison, but everyone else seemed to.

:*You channel magic. That is what you must learn.*:

:*I don't have to use it and don't want to. Even this is more than I care for.*:

The trip was long. The weather was fair enough, and they were sure of supplies without hunting; the letter from Master Quenten assuring them of food, water and lodging whenever they stopped. In between, Keth' was quite comfortable on a roll under canvas. Lihn clearly wasn't, but said nothing and put up with it, though occasionally he caught what he thought was a gesture of her hands before sleeping.

One morning after rising, he felt the ground she'd lain on. It was spongy, like moss or the ground beneath evergreens. Magic.

:That is something I dislike about magic,: he said. *:It makes people soft.:*

:Only as soft as they need or want. This is why control is important.:

:I don't want to argue about that.:

:Neither do I, so let us work on language. Ten more words today. You have a good basic vocabulary now.:

He preferred the language lessons to lectures on mind magic.

He understood why he had been hired for this. Lihn was quite smart, but not skilled in wilderness. Keth' was the one who loaded the pack pony with dried fat and fruit for the ride through the mountains and White Foal Pass, with extra blankets of thick fleece and waxen fire starters. It was easier than long caravans or herding, and they made good distance each day, even in the brisk chill the mountains had even in summer.

Then they were descending into glorious greenery again, until it became humid and rich, with the scent of lush life growing in between outcroppings of stone. Shortly, grassy hills stretched on before them, not his plains but refreshing after the rocky pass.

"This is the South Trade Road," she said, showing him on the map. "We are in Valdemar. Having crossed half a continent, we have merely half a country still to travel."

"Well, good," he said.

:We shall stop before dinner: Yssanda said. *:There are now waystations and inns for us to use.:*

"I believe we're stopping soon," he said.

"Yes," she agreed. "I can tell when Yssanda talks to you."

He scowled, because it felt intrusive for her to know that and he wasn't sure how else to respond.

They soon came to a town with a guard station. Yssanda moved up to the guard and stood still. A guard came out, eyed the Companion who was no longer disguising herself, eyed Keth', and said, "Ah, a newly Chosen one, are you? We'll see you right, we will."

Keth' thanked him with what he hoped was a fair accent, dismounted and led Yssanda toward the corral, stable, lodge and watchers. He presented the letter for Lihn and she dismounted as well. The guard examined it and handed it back to Keth' along with another town chit—this one said Sweetsprings—and they were waved into the inn. The staff took charge of providing them with bathing, cleaning, food, and beds.

There were clearly apparent advantages to even association with a Companion. While he had been comfortable enough in the open air with the tarp overhead, he certainly appreciated the regular occurrence of sleeping pallets, hot meals, and sweetened travel rations. Even the waystations had been an improvement over sleeping on the ground. A Shin'a'in didn't need such things, of course, but they sweetened his traveling companion's temper—such was always to be wished as he had received the sharp edge of her wit several times.

:There are waystations from here on, so we shall have shelter each night.:

:If we must, though I may sleep outside with the tarp and enjoy the breeze.: He was even thinking in Valdemaran now, if haltingly. He was starting to grasp the lan-

guage, though the attitudes and philosophy still escaped him.

He wondered what the cities ahead would be like. This area was more populated than his Plains, and it was a remote hinterland for Valdemar, he understood. The first time a small train of goods wagons came the other way, he'd stared. There would be more, though.

:*I will teach you more of mind magic as we near, so you are better prepared.*:

:*I can accept that. I'll be sorry to turn you over to the queen's stables. You're . . . a friend.*:

:*We don't have to part ways.*:

:*Yes, we do,*: he said firmly. It would be more than a year by the time he returned home, most of it traveling, much of it with this mage girl. He went on.

:*If it were possible, I'd stay with you and let you teach me.*:

:*If it were possible, that would still not be possible. I asked for special dispensation to teach you this much. It is only to familiarize you. It could, in fact, make things worse. Normally, only Herald Trainees receive this kind of training.*:

:*How? And why did you, then?*:

:*Think of a wild youth. Unschooled, untrained, eager. Imagine that mischief, unintentional, with the force of magic. As to how, if you stay they'll teach you.*:

:*You hoped I'd learn to like it and change my mind.*:

:*Not quite. However, without familiarity, that would be impossible.*:

Three months ago, Keth' would have been furious. Now he was just bothered. He had a choice to make, and everyone was presuming to push him in the same direction. That made him stubborn, but, did they all know something he didn't? Wasn't he the best judge of himself?

Something else nudged at him and he put it aside. The training took years. It would divert his life. At the same time, there was a vibrancy to this place. It bespoke adventure and restlessness, which he shouldn't let sway him, except . . .

The nudge came again, firmer.

He quivered and said, "I think there are others nearby."

Lihn asked, "Possibly a patrol? Travelers?"

"A patrol maybe. They don't feel like travelers."

"Did you feel the previous travelers?"

He twitched at that. "Yes, actually I did, now that I think about it. Sort of a background distance noise like a camp. Something I was aware of but . . . this isn't that."

Not far ahead, a voice roared something almost intelligible, and both sides of the road erupted in men, dressed in threadbare uniform parts and twigs and leaves. In the Plains he'd have seen that deception. These plants, though, he was still learning.

There were a dozen or so, and all he had was a large knife, which he drew, and urged Yssanda forward in front of Lihn, though what good it would do with them all around he did not know.

The air shook as Lihn shouted something, and the air burst in a soft thunderclap. One man went down, and two others stopped charging to tumble sideways.

But those two were up again. Lihn couldn't fight. Yssanda had hooves. He had a knife. Here at the end of their journey, a dozen brigands were going to end it, and likely their lives.

Rage welled up, and Keth' shouted "No!" from deep inside.

*   *   *

He woke with someone slapping his cheek. "Son? Are you there? Son?"

He shook his head and garbled out, "I'm all right" in Shin'a'in, then Valdemaran when the man looked at him strangely.

He peered around to see the band of robbers in shackles, being herded by three men on horses. Another man dressed all in white was on a Companion and clearly talking to Yssanda.

"What happened?" he asked.

Lihn appeared above him.

"You did it," she said, looking down with a smirking grin.

"Did what?"

"You used the mind magic you disdain so much. I knocked down three with my Storm Blast spell, and that's all I had, my power for a day or more. You shouted and they all collapsed, clutching their heads. Then you fainted. It's been half the morning."

"I did it?"

:You did.:

"Lots of power, no control," she said. "That's why you need training."

It was hard to argue.

Two weeks later, they were near Haven. The roads carried more people than Keth' had ever seen, with wagons, carriages, horses, donkeys, packs, trucks, and carts. The roads had been graveled and marked but now they were paved in some strange material.

"That's the signpost we were told to seek," he said. Near it was a small group of people. They were set back from the road and observing the busy traffic, while being out of its way.

"Yes," Lihn said. "And that must be Master Arak. It is."

Another old man in a robe, only this one had aged with power in his physique, under the lines.

Next to him Keth' saw a woman that could only be Herald Captain Kerowyn. With her was one dressed completely in white and another that looked to be of the Plains, complete to the fringed leathers that he hadn't seen in months.

The journey was over. At least, this part of it was.

:Have you decided what you are going to do?:

:I'm going to use my Shin'a'in craft and guile,.: he replied with a grin.

Keth're'son shena Tale'sedrin squared his chin and swallowed a brief spurt of homesickness. No matter what happened, it would be many months or years before he saw his Clan, his family, his plains or Nerea again. Then he smiled. He was ready to do battle—and it would go his way, because these outlanders were no match.

:And I will help you.:

About the Authors

Nancy Asire is the author of four novels: *Twilight's Kingdoms, Tears of Time, To Fall Like Stars,* and *Wizard Spawn. Wizard Spawn* was edited by C.J. Cherryh and became part of the *Sword of Knowledge* series. She also has written short stories for the series anthologies *Heroes in Hell* and *Merovingen Nights;* a short story for Mercedes Lackey's *Flights of Fantasy;* as well as tales for the Valdemar anthologies *Sun in Glory* and *Crossroads.* She has lived in Africa and traveled the world, but now resides in Missouri with her cats and two vintage Corvairs.

Brenda Cooper has published over thirty short stories in various magazines and anthologies. Her books include *The Silver Ship and the Sea* and *Reading the Wind.* She is a technology professional, a futurist, and a writer living in the Pacific Northwest with three dogs and two other humans. She blogs and tweets and all that stuff—stop by www.brenda-cooper.com and visit.

Larry Dixon is the husband of Mercedes Lackey, and a successful artist as well as science fiction writer. He and Mercedes live in Oklahoma.

In addition to her work with Mercedes Lackey, **Rosemary Edghill** has collaborated with authors such as the late Marion Zimmer Bradley and the late Grand Master Andre Norton, and worked as an SF editor for a major New York publisher, as a freelance book designer, and as a professional book reviewer. Her hobbies include sleep, research for forthcoming projects, and her Cavalier King Charles spaniels. Her website can be found at http://www.sff.net/people/eluki.

Sarah A. Hoyt was born in Portugal, a mishap she hastened to correct as soon as she came of age. She lives in Colorado with her husband, her two sons, and a varying horde of cats. She has published a Shakespearean fantasy trilogy, Three Musketeers mystery novels, as well as any number of short stories in magazines ranging from *Isaac Asimov's Science Fiction Magazine* to *Dreams of Decadence*.

Tanya Huff lives and writes in rural Ontario with her partner Fiona Patton and nine cats—one more and they qualify as crazy cat ladies. In June of 2010, DAW released her 25th book *The Enchantment Emporium* in paperback and in September followed it with the fifth Torin Kerr space Marine book, *The Truth of Valor*, in hardcover.

Denise McCune has been writing since she was eleven—which was (coincidentally?) right around the time she fell in love with Valdemar. She has worked in the social networking industry for nearly a decade, and not having enough to do writing novels and short stories (her first short story sale was to *Jim Baen's Universe*), decided to launch Dreamwidth, an open source social networking, content management, and personal publishing platform. Denise lives in Baltimore, Maryland, where her hobbies include knitting, writing, and staying up too late writing code.

Fiona Patton was born in Calgary, Alberta, Canada, and grew up in the United States. In 1975 she returned to Canada and now lives in rural Ontario. Her beloved Chihuahua crossed the Rainbow Bridge in July 2009 and in March 2009 two lovely part Shelties came to live with her, her partner Tanya Huff, and way too many cats. She has seven books out from DAW, and is currently working on the third and final book in the Warriors of Estavia series. She has sold more than thirty short stories with Tekno Books and DAW. "A Bard by Any Other Name" is the third Valdemar story featuring Haven's Dann family.

Kate Paulk pretends to be a mild-mannered software quality analyst by day; she allows her true evil author nature through for the short time between finishing with the day job and falling over. She lives in semi-rural Pennsylvania with her husband, two bossy cats, and her imagination. The latter is the hardest to live with.

Mickey Zucker Reichert is a pediatrician, parent to multitudes (at least it seems like that many), bird wrangler, goat roper, dog trainer, cat herder, horse rider, and fish feeder who has learned (the hard way) not to let macaws remove contact lenses. Also she is the author of twenty-two novels (including the Renshai, Nightfall, Barakhai, and Bifrost series), one illustrated novella, and fifty plus short stories. Mickey's age is a mathematically guarded secret: the square root of 8649 minus the hypotenuse of an isosceles right triangle with a side length of 33.941126.

Stephanie Shaver works in the online gaming industry, where she has donned the hat of writer, game designer, programmer, level designer, and webmaster at various points in her career. Like most people who work by day and write by whenever, her free time is notoriously elusive. She can be found online at sdshaver.com and other virtual hives of scum and villainy. Offline, she is either hiking with the smirking entity she calls "The Guy," or on the couch with cats and a laptop stacked atop her, recovering from aforementioned hiking trail.

Kristin Schwengel's work has appeared in three of the previous Valdemar short story anthologies, among others. The story of Shia and Teo begins with "Waking the Baby." She and her husband live near Milwaukee, Wisconsin, with a gray-and-black tabby kitten named (what else?) Gandalf. Kristin divides her time between an administrative job, a growing career as a massage therapist, and writing and other pastimes.

Judith Tarr has written many novels and several Friends of Valdemar stories under her own name. As Caitlin Brennan she writes novels about horses—especially the Lipizzan horses she breeds and trains on her farm in Arizona.

Elizabeth A. Vaughan writes fantasy romance. Her most recent novel is *Destiny's Star*, part of the Star Series. At the present, she is owned by three incredibly spoiled cats and lives in the Northwest Territory, on the outskirts of the Black Swamp, along Mad Anthony's Trail on the banks of the Maumee River.

Elisabeth Waters sold her first short story in 1980 to

Marion Zimmer Bradley for *The Keeper's Price*, the first of the Darkover anthologies. She went on to sell short stories to a variety of other markets, including two previous Valdemar anthologies. Her first novel, a fantasy called *Changing Fate*, was awarded the 1989 Gryphon Award. She has now completed a sequel to it and is working on a third novel, in addition to her short story writing and anthology editing. She also worked as a supernumerary with the San Francisco Opera, where she appeared in *La Gioconda, Manon Lescaut, Madama Butterfly, Khovanschina, Das Rheingold, Werther,* and *Idomeneo*.

Michael Z. Williamson and **Gail Sanders** had a one night stand at an SF convention in 1991. She hasn't left yet. Both serve in the National Guard, Gail as a combat photographer and value-added paper pusher, Mike as an airbase engineer. In between active duty tours, they sell swords, costumes, photography, novels, and raise two children and various cats.

About the Editor

Mercedes Lackey is a full-time writer and has published numerous novels and works of short fiction, including the bestselling *Heralds of Valdemar* series. She is also a professional lyricist and a licensed wild bird rehabilitator. She lives in Oklahoma with her husband and collaborator, artist Larry Dixon, and their flock of parrots.